Collected Stories and Sketches: 4
Fire from a Black Opal

Etching by William Strang, 1898

R.B. Cunninghame Graham

Collected Stories and Sketches

Volume 4

Fire from a Black Opal

Edited by Alan MacGillivray, John C. McIntyre
and James N. Alison

Kennedy & Boyd
an imprint of
Zeticula
57 St Vincent Crescent
Glasgow
G3 8NQ
Scotland
http://www.kennedyandboyd.co.uk
admin@kennedyandboyd.co.uk

Charity originally published in 1912
A Hatchment originally published in 1913
Brought Forward originally published in 1916
This edition copyright © Zeticula 2011
Frontispiece from *Etchings of William Strang* by Frank Newbolt, Newnes, 1907.

Contributors:
R.B. Cunninghame Graham: The Life and The Writings
          © Alan MacGillivray 2011
Introduction to *Charity* © John C. McIntyre 2011
Introduction to *A Hatchment* © John C. McIntyre 2011
Introduction to *Brought Forward* © James N. Alison 2011
Cunninghame Graham's Treatment of American Landscapes, © John C. McIntyre 2011
Cunninghame Graham's Treatment of Scottish Landscapes, © James N. Alison 2011

Cover photograph © Craig Hannah 2011
Cover design by Felicity Wild
Book design by Catherine E. Smith

ISBN 978-1-84921-103-1

"Honour and virtue do not of necessity take with them charity; neither can base estate nor any adverse circumstance of life stifle it in the hearts of those, to whom it comes, just as the fire shines out from a black opal, almost without their ken."

Charity, Preface

Contents

Preface to the Collection

Robert Bontine Cunninghame Graham first came to public attention as a Radical Liberal Member of Parliament in the 1880s, when he was in his thirties. The apparent contradiction between his Scottish aristocratic family background and his vigorous attachment to the causes of Socialism, the Labour movement, anti-Imperialism and Scottish Home Rule ensured that he remained a controversial figure for many years right up to his death in the 1930s. Through his father's family of Cunninghame Graham, descended from King Robert II of Scotland and the Earls of Menteith, he had a strong territorial connection with the West of Scotland. On his mother's side, he had significant Hispanic ties through his Spanish grandmother and a naval grandfather who took part in the South American Wars of Liberation. His own world-wide travels, particularly in the Americas, Spain and North Africa, and his amazingly wide circle of friends and acquaintances in many countries and different walks of life gave him a cosmopolitan breadth of experience and a depth of insight into human nature and behaviour that would be the envy of any writer.

And it is as a writer that we now have primarily to remember Graham. His lasting political monuments are the Labour Party and the Scottish National Party, both of which he was deeply involved in founding. Yet he has to share that credit with others. His literary works are his alone. He wrote books of history, travel and biography which were extensively researched but very personal in tone, so that, although highly readable, they might not easily withstand the objective scrutiny of modern scholarship. Rather it is in his favoured literary forms of the short story, sketch and meditative essay, forms often tending to merge into one another, that Graham excels. Over forty years, between 1896 and 1936, he published fourteen collections of such short pieces, ranging over many subjects and lands. With such a wealth of life experience behind him, Graham did not have to dig deep for inspiration. Probably no other Scottish writer of any age brings such a knowledge and awareness of life's diversity to the endeavour of literary creation. However, the quality of his achievement has not as yet been fully assessed. One reason is not hard to find. There has never yet been a proper bringing together of Graham's separate collections into a manageable edition to provide the essential tools for critical study. Consequently literary attention has never been really focused on him, something for which the climate of twentieth-century Scottish, and British, critical fashion is partly responsible. Neither the Modernist movement nor the Scottish Renaissance seems to be an appropriate pigeonhole for Graham to inhabit. He has instead had to suffer the consequences of being too readily stereotyped. Perhaps entranced by the glamour of his apparent flamboyant persona of 'Don Roberto', the Spanish hidalgo, the Argentine gaucho, the Scottish laird, the horseman-adventurer, a succession of editors have republished incomplete collections of stories and sketches selected more to reinforce an image of Graham as larger-than-life legend rather than as the serious literary man he worked hard to be.

The purpose of this series is to make Graham's literary corpus available in a convenient format to modern readers as he originally intended it. Each collection of stories is kept intact, and they appear in chronological order with Graham's own footnotes, and retaining his personal idiosyncrasies and eccentricities of language and style. It is not the intention of the editors to make magisterial judgements of quality or to present a fully annotated critical edition of the stories. These purposes would go far beyond the bounds of this series in space and time, and must remain as tasks for future scholars. We merely hope that a new generation of general readers will discover Graham's short stories and sketches to be interesting and stimulating for their own sake and in their own right, diverse and revealing of a strong and generally sympathetic personality, a richly-stocked original mind and an ironic, realistic yet sensitive observer of the amazing variety of life in a very wide world.

Alan MacGillivray
John C. McIntyre

Robert Bontine Cunninghame Graham

The Life

Robert Bontine Cunninghame Graham belonged to the old-established family of Cunninghame Graham, which had its ancestral territory in the District of Menteith lying between Stirling and Loch Lomond. The family had at one time held the earldom of Menteith and could trace its ancestry back to King Robert II of Scotland in the fourteenth century. The title had been dormant since the seventeenth century, and the Cunninghame Grahams showed no real interest in reviving it. In fact, Graham passed his childhood officially bearing the surname of Bontine, because, during his youth, owing to a strange legal quirk relating to the entailing of estates and conditions of inheritance, the name 'Graham' could only be borne by Robert's grandfather who held the main Graham estate of Gartmore. Robert's father, William, an army officer, had to take another family surname, Bontine, until he inherited Gartmore in 1863. As a young man thereafter, Robert does not seem to have bothered which name he used, and when he in his turn inherited Gartmore, he kept Bontine as a middle name.

Graham was born in London in 1852. His half-Spanish mother preferred the social life of London, while his father had his responsibilities as a Scottish landowner. Accordingly, Graham's boyhood years were spent moving between the south of England and the family's Scottish houses at Gartmore in Menteith, Ardoch in Dunbartonshire and Finlaystone in Renfrewshire. Before going to preparatory school, he spent a lot of time with his Spanish grandmother, Doña Catalina, at her home in the Isle of Wight and accompanied her to Spain on a number of visits. This was his introduction to the Spanish way of life and the Spanish language, in which he became proficient. At the age of eleven he went to a prep school in Warwickshire, before going to Harrow public school for two years. He apparently disliked Harrow intensely and in 1866 was taken from it and sent to a Brussels private school which was much more to his taste. It was during his year there that he learned French and had instruction in fencing. After a year in Brussels, Graham's formal education ended and he spent the next two years until he was seventeen between his homes in Britain and his grandmother's family in Spain, developing along the way his passion for horses and his considerable riding skills.

Graham's adult life began when in 1870, with the support and financial encouragement of his parents, he took ship from Liverpool by way of Corunna and Lisbon for Argentina. The primary motivation was to make money by learning the business of ranching and going into partnership on a Scottish-owned *estancia*, or ranch. This was seen as a necessity, given that the Graham family had fallen into serious financial difficulties. Graham's father, Major William Bontine, had sunk into madness, the final consequence of a severe head injury in a riding accident, and had engaged in wild speculation with the family assets. Consequently, the estates were encumbered with debts and the Major's affairs had been placed under the supervision of an agent of the Court of Session. As the eldest of three sons, Robert had to find his own fortune and eventually pay off his father's debts. Much of his travelling in the following decades, both alone and later with his wife, Gabriela, had the search for profitable business openings at its heart.

Between 1870 and 1877, Graham undertook three ventures in South America. The ranching on the first visit came to nothing, although, being already an accomplished horseman and speaker of Spanish, he very quickly adapted to the life of the gauchos, or cowboys. He also observed at first hand some of the violence and anarchy of the early 1870s in Argentina and Uruguay; he contracted and recovered from typhus; and finally he undertook an overland horse-droving venture before returning to Britain in 1872. The following year he returned to South America, this time to Paraguay with a view to obtaining concessions for cultivating and selling the yerba mate plant, the source of the widely drunk mate infusion. In his search for possible plantation sites, Graham rode deep into the interior and came across the surviving traces of the original seventeenth and eighteenth century Jesuit settlements, the subject, many years later, for one of his best books. He had little success in his efforts and returned to Britain in 1874. After a couple of years travelling, mainly in Europe, but also to Iceland and down the coast of West Africa, Graham set out again, this time with a business partner, bound for Uruguay, where he contemplated ranching but actually set up in the horse trading business, buying horses in Uruguay with a view to driving them into Brazil to be sold to the Brazilian army. This (again) unsuccessful adventure was later described in the novella, "Cruz Alta"

(1900). Graham again returned to Britain and took up residence at his mother's house in London, becoming a familiar man about town and a frequenter of Mrs Bontine's literary and artistic salon, where he began to develop his wide circle of friends and acquaintances in the literary and cultural fields. It was his experiences in South America in the 1870s that formed his passion for the continent and directed so much of his later literary work. Out of this came the appellation of 'Don Roberto', which is now inescapably part of his personal and literary image.

Paris was another of Graham's favourite places, and it was there in 1878 that he met the woman whom he very rapidly made his wife, much to the apparent hostile concern of his family, particularly his mother. The mystery and (probably deliberate) uncertainty surrounding the circumstances of his marriage cry out for proper research among surviving family documents. One can only sketch in the few known facts and legends. Graham met a young woman who was known as Gabriela de la Balmondière. By one account she had been born in Chile with a father of French descent and a Spanish mother. She had been orphaned and brought up in Paris by an aunt, who may or may not have had her educated in a convent. By another account, she was making a living in Paris as an actress.

After a brief acquaintanceship, she and Graham lived together before coming to London and being married in a registry office in October, 1878, without family approval. In time everybody came to accept her as an exotic new member of the family, although there seems to have been some mutual hostility for several years between her and Graham's mother. It was not until the 1980s that the discovery of Gabriela's birth certificate showed that she was in fact English, the daughter of a Yorkshire doctor, and her real name was Caroline, or Carrie, Horsfall. Why Graham, and indeed the whole Graham family, should have gone on through the whole of his and her lives, and beyond, sustaining this myth of Gabriela's origins invites speculations of several kinds that may never be resolved.

After a few months of marriage, Robert and Gabriela set out for the New World, first to New Orleans, and then to Texas with the intention of going into the mule-breeding business. Over the next two years they earned a precarious living by various means both in Texas and Mexico, until the final disaster when a Texas ranch newly acquired by Graham and a business partner was raided and destroyed by Apaches. The Grahams finally returned to Britain in 1881 with substantial debts, and lived quietly in Spain and Hampshire. The death of Graham's father in 1883, however, meant that Robert finally inherited the main family estate of Gartmore with all its debts and problems, and had to live the life of a Scottish laird with all its local and social responsibilities.

The restrictions placed upon Graham by his new role could not confine such a restless spirit for long, and in 1885 he stood unsuccessfully for Parliament as a Liberal. The following year he was elected the MP for North-West Lanark, the beginning of an active and highly-coloured political career that continued in one form or another for the rest of his life. He spent only six years actually in Parliament, a period in which he soon revealed himself as more a Socialist than a Liberal, espousing a number of Radical causes and becoming deeply involved and influential in the early years of the Labour movement, being, along with Keir Hardie, one of the co-founders of the Labour Party. The high point of his time in Parliament was when he was arrested and committed to prison, accused of assaulting a policeman during the 'Bloody Sunday' demonstration in Trafalgar Square on 13th November, 1887. From his maiden speech onwards, he wrote and spoke out forcefully on behalf of Labour causes and finally in 1892 stood unsuccessfully for Parliament directly as a Labour candidate. Even out of Parliament Graham continued to be active politically. Although he gradually ceased to be a leading figure in the new Labour Party, his new-found talent as a polemical journalist, in great demand in the serious papers and journals of the day, enabled him to remain in the public eye with his concern about social conditions and his unfashionable anti-Imperial attitudes. He was opposed to the Boer Wars, as he was also to the new imperialism of the USA, shown during the Spanish-American War of 1898, which affronted his strong attachment to Spain and Latin America. His commitment to Scottish Home Rule led him in his later years to find a new role as a founder of the Scottish National Party.

After leaving Parliament in 1892, Graham and his wife were free to travel more frequently, sometimes together but more often pursuing their diverging interests apart, and always on the look-out for possibilities of improving their finances. Spain and Morocco were the main areas of their travel. Graham also began to diversify in his new-found interest in writing into the prolific production of travel books and collections of short stories and sketches. Yet nothing could stave off for ever the inevitable consequences of his father's irresponsibility. The debt-ridden estate of Gartmore had eventually to be sold, and the Grahams settled for financial security on the smaller family estate of Ardoch on the northern side of the Firth of Clyde. Even so, a worse blow was to befall Graham. Gabriela had never been physically strong and was prone to pleurisy (not helped by her chain-smoking habit). She died in 1906 on the way back from one of her many visits to the drier warmth of Spain. Her marriage with Robert of more than a quarter of a century had been childless, but they were a close couple and Robert missed her greatly.

As his life advanced into late middle age and old age through the new century, Graham developed his writing with more collections of short stories and works of biography centred on Mexican and South American history. His astonishingly wide circle of friends in all fields of society and his continuing political activities kept him close to the centre of society and often in the public gaze. At the outbreak of the First World War, though he had been critical of the warmongering attitudes that had marked the years from 1910 to 1914, Graham, at the age of 62, volunteered for service and was charged with two missions to South America, one in 1914-15 to Uruguay to buy horses for the Army, and the second to Colombia in 1916-17 to obtain beef supplies. The first mission enabled him to recapture some of the excitement of his early years on horseback in South America, although it made him desperately sad as a horse-lover to think of the dreadful fate awaiting the animals he bought. The second mission turned out to be unsuccessful, owing to a lack of shipping.

After the war, Graham continued to travel, now more for relaxation and for the sake of his health. He had a new close companion and friend, a wealthy widow, Mrs Elizabeth ('Toppie') Dummett, whose artistic salon in London he frequented and who travelled with him on most of his journeys. Back in Scotland, Graham continued to spend summers at Ardoch, and was well known round the Glasgow and Scottish literary scene, as well as being involved in Scottish political controversy. Among his literary friends were the poet Hugh MacDiarmid (C.M.Grieve) and the novelist and journalist, Neil Munro. Graham made a point of attending the dedication of a memorial to Munro in the summer of 1935. Graham was then eighty-three years old. A few months later, Graham set out on what he probably knew would be his last journey, back to Argentina, the scene of his first youthful adventures. In Buenos Aires, he contracted bronchitis and then pneumonia, and after a few days he died. His funeral in Buenos Aires was a large public occasion attended by the Argentine President, with two horses belonging to Graham's friend,

Aimé Tschiffely, the horseman-adventurer, accompanying the coffin as symbols of Don Roberto's attachment to the gaucho culture that had been such an influence on his life and philosophy.

Robert Bontine Cunninghame Graham is buried near his wife Gabriela in the family burial place at the Augustinian Priory on the little island of Inchmahome in the Lake of Menteith. A memorial to him is now placed near the former family mansion of Gartmore.

The Writings

It may not be too much of an exaggeration to say that the greatest blessing bestowed upon Robert Bontine Cunninghame Graham in his boyhood years was an incomplete formal education. Two years at prep school, two years at Harrow and one 'finishing' year in Brussels gave him little of the classical education deemed essential for the well-born Victorian gentleman. Instead he reached the age of eighteen with considerable fluency in Spanish and French, and an undoubted acquired love of reading gained from the books in the libraries of his family's Scottish houses and his mother's house in London. His extensive (if difficult to decipher) letters home to his mother from abroad make this latter fact clear. The proficiency in Spanish and French gave him immediate entry into two major literatures of the modern world in addition to English, a more bankable asset for the modern writer-to-be than any familiarity with the classical writings of Greece and Rome.

It is conventional to ascribe the beginnings of Graham's writing career to the period after he left Parliament and was settled back in Gartmore, in the last decade of the century. However, the habit of writing had undoubtedly been acquired by him over many years preceding, when he was writing long letters home about his experiences in the Americas, and, later on, writing speeches and articles as part of his work as a strongly involved and committed Radical Liberal Member of Parliament.

Nevertheless, we can only begin to speak of Graham as a true writer when in the years after 1890 he began to publish both fiction and non-fiction on a regular basis. Probably beginning with an essay, "The Horses of the Pampas", contributed to the monthly magazine, *Time*, in 1890, Graham went on to write extensively for the *Saturday Review* and other periodicals. There were essays, sketches and short stories, and, later, books of travel and history. Graham's confidence in himself as a writer can be seen to grow during this period, especially when he acquired the literary and critical friendship of the publisher, Edward Garnett.

What makes Graham very different in his writing from any other late Victorian upper-class traveller and man of action is his conscious awareness and absorption of the realistic spirit and literary techniques of contemporary European writers. His main subjects initially are his beloved South America and Spain, as filtered through his personal experiences as a younger man, and aspects of life in Britain, perhaps especially Scotland. Yet he describes these with, in the main, a detached unsentimental insight gained from his reading of the short stories and sketches of Guy de Maupassant and Ivan Turgenev. Equally, after reading *La Pampa*, a set of vignettes of gaucho life written in French by Alfred Ébélot, on the recommendation of his close friend, W.H. Hudson, he came to see how his memories of life among the gauchos could be structured into short tales blending close detailed observation and brief narrative. Yet it would not be true to think of Graham as always being a totally controlled and dispassionate writer. There is both fire and anger in those of his pieces that set out to confront rampant and racist imperialism, social injustice and cruelty directed against helpless human or animal targets.

There is perhaps a tentative quality about Graham's first two books. *Notes on the District of Menteith* (1895) is a highly personal short guidebook to the part of Scotland he knew at first hand surrounding the ancestral home. It almost seems to be a practice for the real thing, before going out into the territory of the big book. Similarly, *Father Archangel of Scotland, and Other Essays* (1896) is an initial attempt at the short story collection, in which Graham shares the contents with his wife, Gabriela.

Graham's first true full-length book conceived as a single narrative is his account of personal experiences in Morocco, *Mogreb-El-Acksa* (1898). The book, whose title translates as 'Morocco the Most Holy', deals in the main with Graham's time there in the later months of 1897. Paradoxically, for a man who travelled so extensively throughout his long life, it is one of the only two real travel books that Graham ever wrote. The other is *Cartagena and the Banks of the Sinú* (1920), which arose out of Graham's mission to Colombia in 1916-17. It is clear that he came to see his experiences in the wider world primarily as a fertile and energising source for fiction.

Between 1899 and 1936, Graham published thirteen collections of sketches and short stories. Generally, his approach for these collections was to bring together stories and short pieces of a rather heterogeneous nature, with settings ranging from his favourite locales of South America and Spain, and increasingly North Africa, to Scotland, London, Paris and more distant parts of the globe. Some of the stories are crafted narratives; others may be little more than detailed descriptions of life and manners with a minimum of narrative, or even personal essays on a range of diverse topics. Although his tone is mostly detached and often ironic, the persona of the writer is never far away and at times Graham's partialities emerge clearly through the text.

The first two collections, *The Ipané* (1899) and *Thirteen Stories* (1900), give the impression of being the most diverse, partly because of the throwaway nature of their titles. 'Ipané' is merely the name of an old river boat that appears in the title story of the first collection. The book has a random quality about it with no sense of a central thread behind the choices.

Thirteen Stories, as a title, suggests an equal randomness. Indeed the main story in the collection is in fact a novella, "Cruz Alta", which takes up fully a third of the length of the book on its own, the other stories being very diverse in their settings and themes. However, the collections that follow in the years before and during the First World War have titles that seem to show a more directed thinking by Graham about their central thrust or themes. *Success* (1902) and *Progress, and Other Sketches* (1905) imply an inspirational quality. *His People* follows in 1906, and *Faith* (1909), *Hope* (1910) and *Charity* (1912) seem to be linked as a group within Graham's mind. *A Hatchment* (1913) and *Brought Forward* (1916) bring to an end the first cycle of Graham's fictional output. Thereafter, there is a gap of eleven years before the final late collections, *Redeemed, and Other Sketches* (1927), *Writ in Sand* (1932) and *Mirages* (1936), the titles of which seem to suggest a disengagement from the serious business of life. And yet perhaps too much weight can be attached to the titles of these works. In all of them, the stories are equally varied and exotic in their sources, and Graham never lets himself be pinned down by a reader's or critic's desire to pigeonhole him as a fiction writer on a particular subject or theme.

It is in his historical writing that Graham does reveal himself as having a specific interest and purpose. Beginning in 1901, he published a sequence of works, mostly biographical, dealing with aspects of South American history from the time of the sixteenth-century Conquistadors right down to his own lifetime. For the writing of these books, he undertook extensive research into the original source documents, a labour in which his knowledge of Spanish proved to be invaluable. The largest group of historical biographies deals with prominent figures in the conquest of South America by the Spaniards. *Hernando de Soto* (1903), *Bernal Diaz del Castillo* (1915), *The Conquest of New Granada* (1922), *The Conquest of the River Plate* (1924), and *Pedro de Valdivia* (1926) show his interest in most areas of Latin America, not merely his own beloved Argentina. Indeed, his travel book, *Cartagena and the Banks of the Sinú* (1920), includes a sketch of the history of Colombia from the Conquest onwards. In that same year Graham also published his biography of the Brazilian religious revolutionary leader of the 1890s, Antonio Conselheiro, under the title, *A Brazilian Mystic*. Two biographies of later figures in South American history are *Jose Antonio Paez* (1929), dealing with one of the heroes of the liberation of Venezuela from Spain in the 1820s, and *Portrait of a Dictator: Francisco Solano Lopez* (1933), about the leader of Paraguay through the disastrous Triple Alliance War of the 1860s. How popular these books about a continent and culture little-known in Britain could ever be is questionable. In writing them, Graham was undoubtedly trying to counteract the contemporary craze for writings about the British Empire, an institution about which he held distinctly unfashionable views. Probably the most enduring of his historical works has turned out to be *A Vanished Arcadia; Being Some Account of the Jesuits in Paraguay, 1607 to 1767* (1901), for reasons more to do with its later cinematic connections than any historical appeal. A historical biography of more personal significance to Graham was *Doughty Deeds* (1925), an account of the life of Graham's own direct eighteenth-century ancestor and namesake, Robert Graham of Gartmore.

Graham's wife, Gabriela, had literary aspirations of her own and published a number of works, frequently infused by the deep religious feeling that developed as she grew older. Her main work was a two-volume biography of Saint Teresa, to which she devoted years of travel and research. Graham clearly played a major role in encouraging her in her writing, and helped in its publication. He had collaborated with her in *Father Archangel of Scotland, and Other Essays* (1896). After her death in 1906, he arranged for the posthumous publication of a new edition of *Santa Teresa* (1907), her poems in 1908, and a new collection of her shorter writings, *The Christ of Toro and Other Stories* (1908).

This survey has touched on all the books that Graham published in his lifetime. Selections have been made by some of his many admirers from his considerable output of short stories and sketches, usually focusing on specific subject areas of his work, such as South America, Scotland or his passion for horses. One unfortunate effect of this may have been to stereotype Graham as a particular kind of writer, an exotic breed who sits uncomfortably in a literary climate dominated by the Modernists of the earlier twentieth century. The extravagant larger-than-life image that has built up about him has perhaps skewed our perceptions of his writing, which is more European in its sensibility than British Edwardian or Georgian. Paradoxically, despite his class origins and cosmopolitan experience, Graham can also often seem to be closer in tone and outlook to twentieth-century Scottish writers like George Douglas Brown, Hugh MacDiarmid or Lewis Grassic Gibbon, writers whose work he almost certainly knew well. There is a great deal of scholarly work waiting to be done on Graham as a Scottish writer, not least the unquantifiable task of bringing into print the large body of his articles, journalism and letters that have never been properly investigated. The full canon of his work has still to be established. Until that is done, it is not possible to make any true assessment of the literary significance of Robert Bontine Cunninghame Graham.

Alan MacGillivray

Note to Volume 4

The collections in this fourth volume of Cunninghame Graham stories and sketches were published in the years immediately preceding and during the First World War. *Charity* (1912) follows on from *Faith* (1909) and *Hope* (1910). *A Hatchment* appeared in 1913, and *Brought Forward* in 1916. The latter volume is very much touched with a darker tone as Graham reflects sadly in several stories on the effects the War was having on people, even as far away as South America, where he spent some time on a British Government mission to buy horses for the Army. The stories of the volume are the creations of a man in his sixties. Although some of the stories give the impression of revisiting areas that he had explored in earlier writings, they display Graham's customary versatility and variety of subject and treatment, and his remarkable powers of recall and vivid description.

Alan MacGillivray
John C. McIntyre
James N. Alison

Charity

R. B. Cunninghame Graham

To John Lavery, A.R.A.

Introduction

Charity (1912) was Graham's ninth collection of sketches and tales in sixteen years. The first edition, by Duckworth & Co., London, had a twelve-page Preface and 239 pages. It contained seventeen sketches and tales, the average length being fourteen pages (c. 3,000 words). The collection was dedicated to John Lavery, A.R.A., Graham's close friend, portrait-painter and member of the Glasgow Boys school.

The Preface initially suggests that charity can appear in barren places; it need not be linked to honour and virtue; and a low social condition and adverse experience need not stifle its appearance. Thereafter it becomes almost a short story, with three principal characters; a beginning, middle and end; and a suggestive dénouement. In a Spanish brothel near Gibraltar, the girl Amparo falls in love with and in time 'keeps' a British customer called Scudamore. When he inherits money, he abandons the love-stricken Amparo. Though the brothel madam and Amparo demonstrate charity, Scudamore's behaviour suggests to Graham that charity is rarer than faith or hope, the titles of his two preceding collections of sketches in 1909 and 1910.

In the sketch, "Charity", a thoughtful and goodhearted British Consul in North Africa tells his listeners that charity is unreasoning and unreasonable. He tries hard to comprehend the Moors, finding them sometimes unfeeling, yet also capable of actions beyond the wit of a white man. The Consul has vaccinated locals against smallpox – in vain. When he tried to help a boy dying of plague by administering laudanum, the boy died anyway. Later, when the Consul once again tries to buy a fine brocade from a Moorish tailor, the tailor refuses to sell to a Christian, yet lends the brocade to the grieving mother, a poor widow, to cover her son's body as it is taken for burial. The Consul has glimpsed another culture's style of charity.

"Aunt Eleanor" was Graham's slightly eccentric half-Scottish, half-Yorkshire upper-class aunt. A semi-invalid from birth, Eleanor yet became an excellent horsewoman and huntswoman. She was "as upright, kind and charitable a Christian as ever I met." An example or two of this kindly tyrant's "ungracious kindness" to all her young relations might have strengthened this affectionate portrait.

Four sketches feature the Scottish landscape. In the heavily descriptive piece, "The Craw Road", Graham's early footnote explains 'craw' as a Lowland corruption of the Gaelic 'Cró', meaning cattle. 'Craw Road' therefore is a drovers' road. This desolate Craw Road winds through a fierce Scottish landscape, passing an old mansion-house where a Latin-inscribed urn reads: "A.G.S. adorned this place with far-travelled trees. 1845." The American trees planted then are now majestic. A.G.S. fought in the Peninsular War in Spain (1808-1813) and later engaged in politics and religious controversy, till his soul turned bitter. His one softness was for the planted trees. The focus is less on the long dead owner than on the neglected estate and house set in a forbidding landscape: the effect is of melancholy.

The Gaelic title, "Caisteal-na-Sithan", is immediately explained as "The Castle of the Elves." The first nine pages are almost a prose poem: dozens of adjectival formations emphasise the overwhelming melancholy of a Scottish estate. The final three pages generate a mystery resolved in a pacy climax. When the last owner, a virtual recluse, disappeared during a bitter frost, the villagers found his body frozen in pond-ice. When they cut out the block of ice, "You'd hae just thocht the laird was sleepin', if he had na been sae gash." Graham does not explain 'gash.' It can mean 'talkative; affable; wise; shrewd; witty; sharp; trim; pleasant.' None of these seems appropriate. 'Gash' can also mean 'grim, dismal, ghastly.' This second value gives impact to the ending. In spite of this oversight, Graham here is an almost perfect external narrator. His description of the decaying house and estate is well sustained. The owner is not greatly individualised, so there is no play for cheap pathos. Once 'gash' is known as 'ghastly', the closing snippet of Scots speech creates a shocking ending.

In "A Braw Day", heartbroken Scottish estate-owners have to sell up to clear debts. On the morning they leave, an estate-worker waits – as always - for his orders. Almost dumb, he finally speaks, saying: "Laird, it looks like a braw day." ('a fine day') This observation conflicts with the misery of the outgoing ex-owners and the fact that for them and for the estate-worker life may be changed for the worse. This sketch, never mentioning Graham personally, is tense and painful. Graham and Gabriela were distraught when in 1901 when in similar circumstances they had to sell Gartmore.

"A Princess" claims that beneath the hardness of life in east-coast Scotland there lies a vein of sentiment. Viewing a slab in Buckiehaven cemetery commemorating Sinakalula, Princess of Raratonga, beloved wife of Andrew Brodie, Mariner, Graham supposes that she was a South Seas damsel and that Andrew abandoned ship to stay on in her island. They married and were content – till Andrew yearned to go home. Back in Scotland, they encountered racial intolerance and she became consumptive and died. Andrew felt "vaguely, that he had murdered her whom he loved best." The real assassin is the Scottish climate. Overall, the Scottish landscape is melancholy and grim, its harshness capable of killing those from gentler climes.

Three sketches consider Scots abroad. "San Andrés" shows Scottish emigrants to Argentina, originally Gaelic speakers and Catholics expelled after Culloden in 1746 and now Spanish-speaking gauchos, clinging four generations later to Gaelic traditions. Don Alejandro's daughter Saturnina had married her first cousin, Anacleto Chisholm: they were blissfully happy. Don Alejandro had wondered how they would cope with calamity. When Saturnina died, Anacleto visited the grave constantly, till Don Alejandro explained that too much grief is a selfishness, that grieving disturbs the dead, that he – Anacleto – should grieve no more. Anacleto accepts the advice from the patriarch Don Alejandro and from the honoured Gaelic tradition. What might have been dry anthropology is made cleverly dramatic. In "A Princess", a sailor from east-coast Scotland settles in the South Seas, trades in copra and coral, becomes wealthy and is able to marry a princess.

In "Christie Christison", storm-bound in Claraz's Hotel in Buenos Aires, Christie, originally a sailor from Peterhead in Scotland and now a successful merchant, reveals to three friends two episodes from his past. The first involves shipwreck, an encounter with Patagonian Indians and the party's safe return to Buenos Aires. Christie then relates an earlier episode: marriage to Jean, his violence to her, her disappearance, their reunion in a Peterhead brothel, emigration to and prosperity in Argentina. Christie admits now his fault in hitting her. He never hit her again. As the storm peters out, he potters off home. This sketch-cum-tale has many strengths: the varied settings; the easy flow of Christie's colloquial Scots speech; and the shipwreck, the encounter with Indians and Christie's refusal to sell Jean to the Indian chief. Also impressively handled are Christie's and Jean's re-discovery of and re-dedication to each other; their hard work together in Argentina; the amiable domesticity of Jean, beshawled and knitting, and Christie's affable goodnight to his friends. Graham's touch here is very sure. Though Graham never made his own fortune abroad, his Scottish characters abroad do prosper economically.

The American landscape is seen in five sketches.

In "La Alcaldesa", the narrator Cossart describes a little Paraguayan village of the 1870s, where, with thirteen women for every man, the gentle Paraguayan women are desperate for contact with men. For Cossart this place was "a perfect Arcady." In "A Meeting", Paraguay's great forests are warmly remembered by Graham. There are glimpses of gaucho Argentina in "San Andrés": the Gaelic-speaking Scots emigrants have become Spanish speakers - with names like Alejandro, Anacleto and Saturnina fronting Chisholm - and total gauchos, riding, reciting gaucho ballads, fighting off Indians and hunting ostriches with the *boleadoras*. "Christie Christison" includes the shipwreck in Patagonia, the typical country store and the encounter with chief Yanquetruz and his band of still semi-wild but peaceable Indians. And "La Pampa" is an enthusiastic depiction of the great plains of Argentina and Uruguay and their gauchos up to the 1880s.

"La Alcaldesa" and "A Meeting" show pre-industrial native American people in a very positive light. The women in "La Alcaldesa" are kind and loving. Showing no bitterness at the loss of their menfolk in war, they share happily of themselves with passing drovers such as Cossart. Long after abandoning La Alcaldesa, Cossart recognises his loss. "A Meeting", while showing the happy encounter of the two horses, also shows the quiet simplicity and kindness that the little community dispenses to the traveller. This encounter brings "joy, at least for a short time to one of those concerned", for roan horse and possibly for the traveller Graham. Graham's American landscapes can be seen to be more welcoming than his Scottish ones.

Six sketches feature horses, four positively, two extremely negatively. "Aunt Eleanor" is a woman who utterly adores horses. In "A Meeting", Paraguayan horses surviving after the war are scarce and cherished. The Paraguayan roan, not having seen another horse for six months, romps happily with the traveller's horse. The horses' need for companionship is as great as humans'. In "Christie Christison", Graham shows southern Argentine Indians and their horses when a group of Indians calls at the country store where Christie's shipwrecked party, including his wife, has taken refuge. In Christie's words, the Indian chief's horse was "a braw black piebald wi' an eye like fire intil him... A bonny beastie..." The chief "sat his horse just like a picture." When the chief "loupit on his horse... they [the other Indians] widna mount, they didna loup, they just melted on their beasts, catching the spears out of the ground as they got up..." The unit "melted on their beasts" is perfect. In "La Pampa" the cowboys – the gauchos – are as highly skilled in handling horses as the Indians.

Much more negative is the bullfight sequence in "Aurora La Cujiñi" where horses are said to have done more service to mankind than any fifty men – which does not save them from excruciating death: "Hungry and ragged, they had trodden on their entrails, received their wounds without a groan, without a tear, without a murmur, faithful to the end; ... and, biting their poor, parched and bleeding tongues, had died just as the martyrs died at Lyons or in Rome, as dumb and brave as they."

In "Set Free", the suffering of the dying carriage horse, its leg broken by the motor omnibus, is gut-wrenching. Its death-agony, like that of the bullfight horses, is also compared to human martyrdom. And its freedom in death implies that the only freedom for humans in London's machine-governed environment is death.

Three sketches consider individuals pursuing an obsession. In "Immortality", Graham mocks the repeating urge to build a tasteless funerary monument. In Old Castile, a modernist lady's 'mushroom tomb' is seen as garish, vulgar and monstrous. Over a decade later, in an unchanged Guadalcázar Graham found the 'mushroom tomb' replaced by another, more foolish than the last. Nearby, a shepherd's appearance is unchanging and unchanged since ancient times: his monument will be only a poor wooden cross. The lady's search for a gaudy tomb for herself is tawdry when set beside the shepherd's timeless simplicity.

"An Hidalgo" is set in Spain just after 1898, when humiliating defeat by the United States cost Spain her last colonies – Cuba, Puerto Rico and the Philippines. Don Saturnino's life charts national and personal desolation. By temperament an old-fashioned minor noble, forced to work in the customs service, at age forty, he was unmarried, poorly paid and with little future. He remained excessively patriotic and Catholic, a traditionalist hostile to modernisation. To help Spain and God, he sent every tax peseta off to Madrid. The horrendous defeat shattered his traditional beliefs and he felt unable to remodel his life. Relocated to Madrid, one day a beautiful girl cast a red rose into his path. A year later, she again threw him a flower – as she drove off with her new husband. Shaken, Don Saturnino wandered aimlessly round the Retiro park and spent the night there. He then returned dutifully to work. He has proved too passive to pursue the woman and has lost perhaps his last opportunity to invest his life with meaning. His future is bureaucratic drudgery, loneliness and unremitting despair at Spain's decline.

"El Jehad" portrays a Muslim. Si-Taher-Ibu-Lezrac, once a boy shepherd in the Sahara, hated all Christians and dreamt of a rebirth of Islamic power. Seeking to understand why Christians should be richer and more powerful than Muslims, Si Taher meditated devoutly, fasted, read and smoked hemp, becoming more skeletal, ragged, terrible and ridiculous by the day. His mix of mystery, fanaticism, ferocity and a savage simpleness made the authorities suspicious. One morning Si Taher proclaimed the Jehad – Holy War against the Infidel. At the head of a huge crowd, Si Taher is confronted by a single ill-dressed French soldier who accuses him of being drunk or of having smoked hemp. Si Taher sheathes his dagger, drops the severed goat's head and meekly follows the soldier. The crowd disperses, to await the coming of the next prophet. Graham shows considerable care in building up the portrait of a traditional believer who sincerely believes it his duty to restore Islam to its former greatness. The colonial power defuses the possible rebellion with almost farcical ease.

The three obsessive personalities of these sketches seem fated not to satisfy their dreams. By contrast, two other sketches feature very striking ladies. In "Un Autre Monsieur", a chance has come into the life of the internal narrator, Elise, a high-class French prostitute in London. When a bashful young English officer falls in love with her and proposes marriage, she warns him of all that he will lose. He persists. Though taken with his shyness and innocence, she tells him that she cannot love him. She is now returning to France to recover her health. Given that this young officer is so different from the other men she has known, who knows what she might do once she recovers her health? Elise presents herself convincingly as thoughtful and wise in the ways of men and their deceits. She is also caring, having no wish to wreck the life of someone who says he loves her. She declines the young officer's offer of monetary help. This shy but sincere young officer may just possibly draw this independent lady into marriage.

In "Aurora La Cujiñi", the Sunday bullfight in May in Seville, with its African-cum-Moorish and Roman past, always generates a "mixed air of sensuousness and blood." Afterwards folk fill cafés, clubs and popular dancing-houses like the Burero. There, an older man recalls the long-dead dancer Aurora La Cujiñi. The superb dancing of an unidentified gypsy girl dressed in the style of the 1840s enthrals the audience. When she stops, she is "a very statue of impudicity and lust." She disappears, to be seen again only in an old lithograph.[1] Aurora has taken "a brief and fleeting reincarnation to breathe once more the air of Seville, heavy with perfume of spring flowers, mixed with the smell of blood." The bustle of Seville on a bullfight Sunday is well caught and the strong theme of the Sevillan admixture of sensuousness and blood is cleverly suggested and sustained.

"La Pampa" is an enthusiastic evocation of the Argentine and Uruguayan plains before 1880 - their vast extent, the endless grass and sky, the millions of wild cattle and horses and the abundance of animal, bird and insect life. When Graham arrived in the 1870s the pampa was still almost virgin. The ancient Quichua Indians named the place well, their word 'pampa' signifying 'space' - and also freedom. Graham offers no criticism of the gaucho life-style based on individualism, drinking, violence, knife-fights and reluctance to be incorporated into 'normal' or town-based society. Graham looks back romantically to "this great galloping ground" of the gauchos as it was before modern development and urbanisation.

Alternative clusterings of the stories and sketches in *Charity* might focus on: prostitutes and brothels; men who achieve; men who suffer loss; women as victims; strong women; death in myriad forms; hostility to modern life; lengthy introductions; internal narrators; or strongly-themed pieces. Published in 1912, the most 'contemporary' scenarios are in "An Hidalgo", "Set Free" and "Un Autre Monsieur". Most of these sketches look back in time, because Graham finds his inspiration and narrative magic mainly in the past.

JMcI

---

[1] See *Volume One, Photographed on the Brain, Appendix II:* "R. B. Cunninghame Graham's 'Aurora La Cujiñi' (1898): An Exploration" (by John C. McIntyre).

Charity

Contents

Preface

Hope has been said to be the quality of youth, and faith of middle age.

Therefore, it ought to follow, that the old should cling to charity as the best antidote to avarice, their chief besetting sin. If, though, they have not in their youth been hopeful, and in their middle years imbued with faith, that is both in themselves, in others, and in the world in which they live, charity is not for them in age. Hope carries in itself something that impels our admiration; faith our respect; but charity is like a mountain seedling-pine, springing up oft in barren places, rooted amongst the rocks and flourishing in the chilliest blasts of life, and in despite of fate.

Honour and virtue do not of necessity take with them charity; neither can base estate nor any adverse circumstance of life stifle it in the hearts of those, to whom it comes, just as the fire shines out from a black opal, almost without their ken.

In a dark winding lane, just underneath the shadow of the rock on which Tarik first disembarked, lived Doña Ana Alvarez. Her enormous bulk had given her the nickname of Fat Anne, which she adopted cheerfully, bearing in mind the adage "Fatness comes far before mere beauty, any day." The flesh seemed to surge up, threatening to choke her, from her breast and neck. Jet would have looked a rusty brown beside her hair, which she wore always parted down the middle and trained into two curls, called whiskers by the women of her class in Spain. No one had ever seen her dressed but in a morning wrapper, either of piqué or of muslin, a habit which she alleged she had contracted in her youth, so as to be always ready for her work. Not that she said this in an indecent way, or with a wish to raise a smile at the application of the word, but because what she thus referred to was the only kind of work that she had ever done.

Quite simply she would explain, saying: "When I was young my mother sent me to a house in Seville, where I worked with the other girls, when I was just fourteen. In summer when I used to come back to Los Barrios, for in the heat of Seville there was no one left in town, my chief delight was to wake up and find myself alone."

13

Charity

Her father was a general, which in Spain corresponds to the familiar "daughter of a clergyman," and she herself kept an establishment in a winding lane, which ran off from the main street, just opposite the church. In it she sat in an armchair, flaccid, but business-like. Although she had retired from active intervention in the duties of her trade, she still darkened her eyelids and her eyebrows, powdered her face, and upon Saints' days and on Sunday wore a bright red carnation in her hair. Report averred that her heart still was tender, and that a general in La Linea occasionally visited her, but dressed in civil clothes, and that a famous bull-fighter, when he "killed" either in Algeciras or San Roque, usually had a glass or two of Manzanilla at her establishment. This naturally gave her a position of some consideration amongst her friends, and at the same time kept up her interest in life. Needless to say, her house was the resort of all the younger officers of the British fleet, when it came into what they all called "Gib." in their bluff Saxon way.

Kind and good-humoured, after their fashion, their intimate persuasion that they were all committing an offence, made them more brutal, if more generous, towards the inmates of the house than were their fellow-sinners on board the other fleets that visited the port.

Nothing was commoner than to hear them say to one another, "What a beast one feels when one wakes up with a sore head, beside one of the girls, up at old Mother Anne's."

Most probably, no speculations of a moral kind had ever entered into the head of Ana Alvarez. She came, as she occasionally would say, in moments of expansion, when trade was bad, and when the Channel fleet delayed too long in coming, from a family who for three generations had always dealt in girls.

Her people all were old Christians, that is they had no stain either of Jewish or of Moorish blood, and in the annals of her family no thief was known, although, as she allowed, some few were smugglers, and her great-grandfather was the first man who ever trained a dog to carry on his back two little packs of fine tobacco and bring them through the lines.

Seated upon an Austrian cane chair, which she kept gently rocking with a foot, on which a satin slipper dangled from the toe, she used to pass away the time, between the siesta and the coming of the breeze, dozing, but vigilant, ready to intervene in any quarrel that arose, or put a client at his ease, as he sat waiting, smoking cigarettes, whilst the girls dressed their hair. Fat Anne was in the main a kindly potentate, all her employees liked her, for, as they said, the "mistress knows the business, has worked at it herself, and does not ask impossibilities of any of the girls."

If they got into debt, she did not press them, and never charged them interest on the debt, saying, no doubt, that the Lord God would send some gentlemen along to pay it for them, when it seemed good to Him.

To this well-ordered house, in which, as all its inmates said, they all made money, and if a girl should chance to owe two or three ounces no interest was ever charged by Doña Ana, there came one day a man.

A guest on board the flagship, his name was Scudamore. The midshipman referred to him as "Ullage," though he was smart, good-looking and well dressed. At first he had some money and used to haunt Fat Anne's, taking up with a girl known as La Jerezana, tall, active and well-built. Not too fat, not too thin, the Arabs say, and she quite came up to their standard, and for the rest, no one could better sing the Malagueña, or dance a Tango with the true movements of the hips.

At first a little flattered by the visits of the man, who she knew was on terms of intimacy with all the officers, little by little she began to love him, and at last doted upon him, with all the fierceness of affection of women of her class. Kind Doña Ana used to remonstrate, after the way a mother chides a wilful daughter, telling her that for a woman of her class nothing could be so fatal as to fall in love. "Daughter of my entrails," she would say, "love is not for us. All shall love us and waste their means to gratify our whims, but we, we shall take all, and go our way, rejoicing, till we have made enough to buy a husband, to soothe our older years."

La Jerezana owned the strength of the advice, but did not follow it, for, as she said, "Love is as obstinate as a male mule . . . and somehow . . . look, Doña Ana, you who have known the world, have you not sometimes, even with all your science, felt yourself bitten with a man?"

The matron smiled, and smoothing down her hair, said: "Yes, my daughter, for look you, the flesh is weak, and when a man talks softly, speaking of love, to one of us, whose trade it is to simulate love's rapture for a dollar . . . you know, I never kept a house where less than that was charged . . . why, it seems sweet to us, and we forget, and become just as other women are . . . or worse, for we know better than they can, what love should be. I know, of course, I know, therefore I want you to escape. See, I will change you for a girl from a friend's house, in San Fernando. You shall not lose by it, and for the ounces that you owe — three is it?" Here she drew up her skirt, disclosing underneath a pocket made of bed-ticking, hanging round her waist, and drew from it a book.

Moistening her thumb, she turned the leaves, muttering, "La Sevillana, two ounces and a half. I'll lose that money. Pepa la Malagueña . . . nothing, eh? Ah, Hueso de Cochino, La Brasileña . . . ah, here it is! Amparo Vazquez, La Jerezana, three ounces and a half, two pairs of open-work silk stockings, a fan — in all about four ounces.

"Well, that shall run on; I will not charge a centimo of interest, and at my friend's, she's a good woman, though half a gipsy, is the Chavala, you will be comfortable enough."

Amparo shook her head. "Thanks, Doña Ana," she replied. "No, I go not; this man has become all the world to me. I care not if he beats me, neglects me, or if he takes my money. He is my blood, blood of my blood. . . ." She took a pin, and having pricked her arm, drank the bright scarlet drop. Raising her fat white hands to heaven, Doña Ana said: "She loves him bestially . . . strange too when he can hardly speak a word of Christian, and has a pane of glass tied to a string, stuck in his eye, just like a figure in a pantomime."

So she stayed on, and one day Scudamore appeared a little drunk, and rather shabby, telling her that he had spent all his money, and had outstayed his welcome in the fleet.

Instantly the Jerezana borrowed two ounces more from Doña Ana, who, as she gave the money, taking it out of a knotted pocket-handkerchief, which she exhumed from beneath a loose board behind her bed, said with a sigh, "God knows that I was born for the profession that I have followed all my life; I never could say No."

In a room on the second floor of a house in a back lane, of which the Jerezana paid the rent, Scudamore soon fell into the half-shrinking, half-bullying ways of a man kept by a woman of the kind. By degrees he began to take his meals in Doña Ana's house. The other girls, who did not see him through the magnifying lens of love, all called him Tomasito, in a half-patronising, half-contemptuous way. His clothes got daily shabbier, and by degrees he drifted into keeping the accounts of the establishment. When clients came and he was seated in his shirt sleeves, either learning the guitar, or playing cards with Doña Ana, if they complained about his presence, they were told, "It is only Tomasito, the Jerezana's friend, it does not matter in the least."

She, having him to keep, for it had never come into his head to look for anything to do, had to work hard amongst the clients, to give him clothes to wear and cigarettes to smoke.

When she went, as people say in Spanish, "on the hunt," he used to pass her without a sign of recognition, saying that he must draw the line at speaking to her in the street, as after all he was a gentleman.

Months passed, until one day when he was sitting on the Alameda with the girl, watching the coast of Africa melt into shadow, and the white houses over in Algeciras turn violet in the last rays of the descending sun, the hills above Gaucin grow purple, and a red glow suffuse the limestone crags of the great fortress rock, a friend who had been at the post office put a letter in his hand.

He read and found that he had inherited some money from a far-off cousin, turned white, then red, and rising from his seat, walked towards the town, the Jerezana following at his heels, with the air of a faithful spaniel that feels its master is displeased with it.

Next day, smoking a big cigar, he paced the deck of a fast liner steaming through the Straits. His glass was in his eye, his hair well flattened to his head with vaseline, brushed back without a parting, showed he had made his toilet carefully. Bending a little to the movement of the ship, the fresh sea air just tinged his cheek with red, giving him a look as of a fine young colonist returning home after a year or two spent in the wilderness.

"Yes," he said to a kindred spirit as they walked to and fro to get an appetite, "the women, blast them, never leave a man alone. I don't know if you saw a tall, dark, Spanish girl talking to me just as we came aboard. Well, you know, don't you know, I was pretty friendly with her when I was stuck in 'Gib.,' and damn it all, there she was up on the mole with a cow-hair trunk, corded with bass rope, a goldfinch in a cage, tears running down her cheeks and bothering me to take her with me. . . . Good God, a pretty sight I should have looked travelling about, dragging a Spanish whore . . . I like her well enough; but what I say is. Charity begins at home, my boy. Ah, there's the dinner bell!"

Charitable readers, you must take my little story (or perhaps parable) in any way you choose.

Do not forget whilst reading it that charity is a shy-growing plant that often droops in what appears good soil.

At other times she rears her head, almost by stealth, after the fashion of an autumn crocus, which peers so delicately above a growth of grass that would choke hardier plants.

Charity

Hope is for fishers with a float, who as they sit, watching it bob about, may chance when they pull in their line, to find the body of a cat, or a blind puppy, in which their hook has stuck, when they had hope of fish.

Faith is the quality of prophets and of those who in its exercise fear not to slay; but charity is rarer than its two elder sisters, exceeding them in the same way that instinct outgoes reason and leaves it in the mire.

Love, kindness, toleration, whatever charity may be, or if she is compounded of them all, I know not.

All that I do know, is that she is rare, and that her emblem on a sailor's arm is always drawn between the anchor and the cross.

R. B. Cunninghame Graham.

Charity

"Charity," said the Consul, "is often quite unreasoning"; he paused and added, "but so is love, and the two things are one."

In the old Moorish house, built for hot weather, the cold was glacial, and we had drawn the dinner-table into a corner to avoid a leak, from which the water, filtering through the roof, dropped in a chalky stream. Long, milky-looking glasses swung from the ceiling in brass chains, and in them, floating upon oil, burned wicks that gave a fitful light that cast black shadows on the horseshoe arches of the *patio*. Curved flint-locks hooped with brass, with crooked stocks inlaid with ivory, hung on the walls, and Moorish daggers, shaped like scimitars, and bags with fringes, like those an Indian wears upon his moccasins. Bowls of Fez pottery stood here and there, and on the tables and the chairs were heaped up books and papers, with all the flotsam and the jetsam that a solitary man living far off from kith and kin collects and clings to, striving to fill the void in his life with something tangible.

Outside, the rain descended pitilessly, turning the narrow lanes to muddy streams, upon whose current floated orange-peel, dead rats and heads and feet of fowls.

The call to prayers boomed like a foghorn from a ship bound in fog, and seemed as if it summoned up a watch reluctant to turn out and go aloft.

The Consul, impervious to cold, after the fashion of all those accustomed to the life in a warm climate, where damp and wet are almost welcome after the summer's heat, seemed to consider that his guests shivered for fun, or as in protest against that which every reasonable man endured without a murmur as sent from God, put his feet up upon a chair and said, "Yes, charity is sometimes an unreasoning or an unreasonable thing."

The listeners drew their greatcoats round them and waited for his tale, knowing he was a man who, being thrown upon himself and having nothing else to study but the Moors, observed them as an ornithologist might study some strange bird. Cursing the people every day for their unlikeness to himself and his ideals, he had become so much accustomed to them in his long residence in the forlorn post to which the Foreign Office had condemned him that he could scarcely have existed amongst other folk, or in another place.

Raising his voice, he called out "Mokh, oh Mokh"; and when a little negro boy appeared, rubbing his eyes with sleep, he told him to bring whisky and then go off to bed. "I bought the little devil," said the Consul, and then, remembering his position, added, "I mean his mother gave him to me in the last outbreak of the smallpox when they all died like flies. I used to vaccinate 'em with some stuff I got across from 'Gib.'; but still it didn't seem to do much good, for they kept dying off so fast that we could scarcely bury 'em. Just about as much good to have done 'em with trade gin, for don't you see there was no way of keeping 'em in the least clean, and that's what does the job." We listened to his theories on therapeutics with the attention that good citizens accord to those in office, and then he wandered back again to where he had begun.

"The more I live amongst the Moors, the less I understand 'em. At times I think I have the key of the enigma, and then I seem to lose it, and find myself faced up against a wall. Sometimes they seem to have no feeling, and then just when you think they are hardly human, they'll turn right round and do something that a white man would never think of doing, that leaves you wondering at them. I'll tell you of a case."

Outside the wind still whistled, and the water running down the street, roared like a mountain burn. Lighting a cheroot, which he did at the thinner end, explaining to us that no one who had been in India ever did otherwise, he thought a little.

We huddled round the stove, on which occasionally great drops fell from the roof with a sharp hissing sound.

The Consul came back to his theme slowly, just as a ship appears to hesitate a little after she is put about, before her sails draw and she is brought up to her course.

Speaking in that constrained and as if perfunctory way in which so many cultivated Englishmen express themselves, through dread of being natural, he struck into his tale.

"During that outbreak of the smallpox, in which I bought, I mean acquired, that little devil Mokh, there was a thing I saw that stirred me up a little."

The Consul looked so hard to stir, that we involuntarily smiled. He saw it, and remarked, "Yes, it was curious. You know, the Moors often appear cruel to us, and we to them. For instance, if when I stray about the town I find a starving dog with a leg broken, my impulse is to shoot it, to put it out of pain. A Moor thinks such an act but little short of murder, for he holds that as long as there is life, hope lingers, and Allah holds the keys of life and death, and it is impious to unlock or close, but when he wishes it. Well, just at the corner of this street there lived a widow woman. She had a boy, at that time about twelve, a little ill-conditioned wretch he seemed to me, dirty and wild, and with a scabby head that turned my stomach when I looked at it. Of course, he was his mother's joy, for mothers, Christian or Moorish, are alike, just as alike as cows."

We said "Oh! oh!" although we knew that he was right, and he resumed. "Well, little Abd-er-Rahman, with his scabby head and dirty clothes, did not seem to be a treasure to the ordinary mind. Sometimes he used to hold my horse, and though I told him never to tie him by the reins, I usually found him with the reins buckled to the grating of a window, and the boy fast asleep. Naturally, when I mounted he used to hold the stirrup, and in his anxiety to put his weight upon it, he used to pull the horse's head away from me, so that it was next to impossible to mount. What he and his mother lived upon was a marvel even to me, accustomed to the Moors. Their house was bare, so I was told, for naturally I never was inside it, but clean, though I suppose not over-sanitary. In fact, a place the smallpox or any other epidemic was certain to invade. The Moors, you know, take no precautions. All is in God's hands. He will send smallpox or withhold it, as it pleases Him, for they believe in Him, just as in England we believe in doctors, and as unreasoningly.

"The widow's boy played about as usual with the other boys. One day I saw him with his friends, playing at a funeral, as boys in Spain all play at bull-fighting. One child was laid upon a board, with four to carry him. The way those little devils sang the chant the Arabs use was wonderful to hear. Born actors are the Moors; but then the funerals went down our street a dozen times a day."

The Consul lit another of his long cheroots, and added in a quiet tone of voice: "I used to go into their houses, and see the bodies. . . . No, not afraid a bit. I don't know why. It used to seem to me it was impossible to catch infection from a Moor, and then, in times like that, even their faith softens a little, and a kind word cheers them, just as it would ourselves. One day Jelali — that's my head man, you know, saddles my horse and goes to market . . . cheats me, of course, but won't allow anyone else to do it — came in and said that a poor woman wished to see me at the door. I went to see her, and she, catching me by the hand, said, 'Consul, I take refuge with you; my son has caught the plague.' Of course I went with her, taking some medicines with me, just to satisfy her. Her son lay on the floor upon a blanket, a mass of blotches, livid and horrible. He moaned a little now and then, but was already dying, as I saw at the first glance. His mother told me that a day or two ago he had come in feverish, and she, thinking it nothing, had sent him down to bathe. When he returned he had been worse, then got delirious, and before midnight was as I saw him, only a mass of sores. Merely to quiet her, I took a spoon, and opening his mouth tried to force down his throat a little laudanum."

The Consul paused, and made a movement with his hands as of involuntary disgust, as if some detail of the boy's deathbed had occurred to him, and then went on again.

"I never saw such a black, bloated little corpse as Abd-er-Rahman's when I left his mother's house just about daylight, or such a dreary-looking place as their one mud-floored room, with the boy's body lying on the ragged blankets, and his mother swaying to and fro, stupid with misery. I tell you I went home, and had a good stiff tot of whisky, not that I was afraid of the infection, but because the thing had stirred me up a little, as I told you when I began the tale. Next day there was a lot of bother in the office, an English ship had got ashore close to Martin, the port you know, and the captain came and bullied me about the want of lights and the defective charts.

"With one thing and another I forgot about the boy. You see there were so many dying in the place a fellow scarcely had the time to think, and it slipped, somehow, clean out of my head. However, one day, as I was going for a walk, I passed a tailor sitting sewing at his work. Upon his knees was spread a piece of fine brocade, that stuff the Moors in old times used to make in Fez, with gold threads running through the tissue so thickly that the thing would almost stand if you but stuck it up on edge. In the old days in Spain they called it guexi, but nowadays even the name is lost, for the Moors, as you know, care nothing for the past. When I clapped eyes upon it, I remembered that for a month or two I had bargained for it with the man, and could not bring him to my price.

"I spoke to him, and then after a word or two about the progress of the plague, the doings of the Government in Fez, and things of that kind, just to distract him from the subject, I said quite carelessly, 'Ten dollars for the piece.'

"He looked at me and smiled. 'Consul,' he said, 'this piece of guexi, as you say that it was called in Spain, is not for you, or any other Roman.' He called me Roman, not to say Nazarene, which, as you know, is a contemptuous method of address amongst Mohammedans.

"I asked him why, and he rejoined, half smiling as he spoke, 'Because you Romans have no belief in God, or His omnipotence.

" 'Consul, when little Abd-er-Rahman died, . . . may God remit the balance of your sins for what you did for him, . . . his mother came to me.

" ' "Oh, father of the awl," she said to me, "my son is dead. God willed it so, and also that I should be poor, and I have not anything in my possession fit for a winding-sheet." I too was poor, but then as now I had upon my knees this piece of old brocade.

" 'Take it, I said, and wrap it round the body of your son, as he lies on the bier, upon his journey to the cemetery. Then bring it back to me, and thus your son will journey through the streets in a befitting style.' She thanked me, snatching at my hand to kiss it, which I prevented, knowing good manners, and in due time she sent me back the winding-sheet.

" 'Consul, I trust in Allah.' " I took and shook him by the hand, and as I pass him now and then as he sits sewing at his work we look at one another, but seldom speak, except a formal 'la bas' as I pass upon my way. You see, we understand each other."

The Consul stopped, and as we rose to go he shouted loudly to his men to bring a lantern, but no one answered him, for they had slipped away to bed, leaving him all alone as usual in his bat-infested house, in the dark narrow lane. As we strolled stumbling back to the hotel the rain had stopped, and a few fleecy clouds went racing through the sky. Before the Basha's house the guards were sleeping muffled in their jelabs, and snoring lustily.

When we emerged upon the broad fidàn the moon had risen, and from a side street issued a wedding-party, dancing and firing a stray shot or two.

Their lanterns swung about, just as a ship's masthead light seems to swing, as the long rollers of the north-west trades catch her a little just abaft the beam, their bearers looking like a band of Capuchins, in their white, pointed hoods.

Charity

Aunt Eleanor

There are no aunts to-day like my Aunt Eleanor. Either the world is no more fitted for them, or else they are not fitted to the world; but none of them remain.

Scotland and Yorkshire strove together in her blood, making a compound, whimsical and strange, kind and ungracious, foolish and yet endowed with a shrewd common sense, which kept her safe, during the lengthened period of her life, from all the larger follies, whilst still permitting her to give full run to minor eccentricities, both in speech, deed and dress.

Tall, thin, and willowy, and with a skin like parchment, which gave her face, when worked upon by a slight rictus in the nose she suffered from, a look, as if a horse about to kick, she had an air, when you first saw her, almost disquieting, it was so different from anything, or anybody that you had ever met.

She never seemed to age, although no doubt time did not stop the clock for her during the thirty years she was a landmark in my life. Perhaps it was her glossy, dark brown hair, which, parted in the middle and kept in place by a thin band of velvet, never was tinged with grey, not even in extreme old age, that made her ever young.

Perhaps it was her clothes, which for those five-and-thirty years (I cannot swear it was not forty) were invariable, that made her never change.

Her uniform, for so I styled it, it was so steadfast, was, in the winter, a black silk, sprigged, as she would have said herself, with little trees, and in the summer, on fine days, a lilac poplin, which she called "laylock," surmounted by a Rampore Chudda immaculately white.

Her cap was generally adorned with cherry-coloured ribbons. Perched on her head, as if it were a crown, moral and physical, of virginity, it used to have a strange attraction for me when it trembled, now and then, making the ribbons shake, as she reproved a servant, or signified her disapproval of some necessary change. The youngest of a large family, whose members all were cleverer than she, until death set her free by taking off her sisters, she had been held a fool. Not that the imputation ever stopped her for a moment from having her own way; but only laid her open to the comments of the other members of the family, which she accepted, just as a shepherd or a sailor always accepts bad weather, without a murmur, and with a sense as of superiority to fate.

In all her sisters the Scottish strain prevailed. They spoke, not in broad Scots, but with the intonation that sounds like the whine a bagpipe gives when the player, after a pibroch, or a lament, allows the bag to empty slowly of the wind. Their mental attitude was that which their stern Scottish faith gave to its votaries. Even in Scotland it is now unknown, leaving the world the poorer by the extinction of a type of mind so much at home with the divinity, that it could venture freely to admonish him if he fell short in any of his deeds, from the full standard of perfection raised by his worshippers. So did an ancient Scottish lady on being told, during the course of a dispute on "Sabbath recreation," that the Lord walked in the fields and ate the ears of corn, not hesitate to say, "I ken that weel, and dinna think the mair of Him for that, so I'm just tellin' ye."

Aunt Eleanor was of another leaven, for in her composition the Yorkshire blood had overpowered the Scotch. Reared in the lowest section of the English Church, she used to go occasionally into a Methodist or Baptist chapel, alleging that she had no terror of dissent, although it may have been she looked on the adventure as in the light of dissipation, just as an Arab, now and then, might eat a piece of pork, being convinced his faith was steadfast, but wishing, as it were, to taste the wickedness of sin, to make it manifest.

In the same way, her caprice satisfied, Aunt Eleanor returned again to church, but always used to treat the institution as if it were a sort of appanage belonging to the county families. She used to send and ask the clergyman to tell the organist not to pull out the Vox Humana stop, which she alleged made her feel ill, and never to allow his instrument to groan at her as she came into church.

On ritual she was a bar of iron, not liking what she called "highflyers," and stating roundly that for her part she would not mind if the "man" stood up to preach in his shirt-sleeves, as long as they were clean.

These were, as far as I remember, all the religious difficulties Aunt Eleanor had to contend with, for in the practice of her creed she was as upright, kind and charitable a Christian as ever I have met. Not that her faith softened a certain harshness in her mind, that made her singularly harsh to all the failings of her sex in matters sexual.

On those of men, she looked with much more leniency, holding that women always were the tempters, and that no girl had ever gone astray except by her own fault.

Once, and once only, did she almost have the chance to put her doctrines into practice, but then the issue was confused, so that it never was cleared up, whether my aunt was better than her creed, or if she held her Scoto-Yorkshire faith in its entirety. A celebrated lady horse-breaker, of perhaps easy virtue, having come into the street in which she lived, my aunt, to the blank consternation of her friends, prepared to strike up an acquaintanceship, and when remonstrated with, observed: "She may be all you say, my dear, but what a seat she has, and hands like air; she must have learned in a good school, she rides so quietly."

As fortune willed it, the acquaintanceship was never formed, but had it been, my aunt, I fancy, would have discoursed on snaffles and on curbs, and on that symbol of all equitation, the sacred lipstrap, with as much gusto as she used to do with other of her friends. Strange as it may appear, although a semi-invalid from her birth up, a martyr as she was to violent sick headaches, which in those days were the equivalent of "nerves," she always used to ride.

She and her brother were both born horsemen, riding to hounds, and jealous to a fault. No woman, in my aunt's eyes, could ever ride, that is to say, up to her standard. Either their hands were bad, or else their seats were loose, or if both hands and seats were good, they had no nerve, or as a last resort, rode to attract attention. "You know," she used to say, "Miss Featherstone never was known to jump a fence, unless a man was looking at her. If there was but a butcher's boy she would have risked her neck, although, in that long run, the one I told you of, when we met at the Rising Sun upon Edge Hill, and finished somewhere down in Gloucestershire, she never took a fence, and then came up just as we killed, with several officers, all galloping like tailors on the road."

I hear her now, talking about her celebrated mare, "The Little Wonder," which she declared she never touched with a whip in all her life, but once, and never with the spur. This happened at a fence, at which the mare had swerved; but when she felt the whip, she put her back up and entirely refused. A Frenchman who was following my aunt, passed her, and took his hat off, saying as he passed, "Thank you for whip' your mare. I have followed you a month, but never pass you till to-day." My aunt never related this, but tears rose in her eyes: whether at her own cruelty, or at the Frenchman having passed her, I never could make out.

Horses and hunting were the chief themes of conversation with my aunt, and as she did not care the least for anyone's opinion but her own, her talk ran usually into a monologue, in which she set her theories out, as to which rein should go under which finger, and how good hands consisted in the wrist. "It is all done with a turn of the wrist, my dear, and not by butchering," a theory sound in itself and one which many would be wise to follow, if they had aunts as competent as mine to teach them the right way. Years only added to my aunt's eccentricity, and as she lived in times when gentlewomen enjoyed ill-health, no one was much astonished when one day she definitely took to a couch, laid in the drawing-room window, from which she could survey the road and watch the people going to the meet.

For years she lay there, only getting up on Sunday to go to church, which she did, either in a Bath chair, or else in Jackson's fly, for she averred that only Jackson in the whole town of Leamington could drive with decency. The other flymen started with a jerk, or sawed their horses' mouths in a way that set my aunt's nerves tingling, and used to make her open the window and expostulate in a high, quavering key. Even the trusted Jackson had to submit to adverse criticism now and then, both of his driving and of his horse's legs.

It used to be a curious sight to see the semi-invalid, leaning upon her maid, dressed in her invariable black, sprigged silk gown — she would have fainted to have heard it called a dress — a curtain bonnet on her head, a parasol ringed with small flounces and jointed in the middle, in her hand, walk down the steps of her front door and stand before the fly.

Turning towards her maid, she used to say, "Baker, lend me your arm a moment," and then advancing with the half valetudinarian, half sporting air that she affected, open the horse's mouth.

"Well, Jackson," she would say, "you have got a young one there. I think he would make a better hunter than some of those I see trotting down to the meet. They breed them far too long-backed nowadays, not like the well-ribbed-up, short-legged, well-coupled-up ones that I remember when I hunted as a girl with the Fitzwilliam hounds."

Jackson would touch his hat, and answer, "You know a 'orse, Miss, and this one, 'e is a 'orse, he ought by rights to be a gentleman's."

Then with an admonition as to not starting with a jerk, my aunt would get into the fly, Baker having first put in a coonskin cushion with the head on, made in the fashion of a pillow-case.

Into it when my aunt had put her feet, arranged her shawl and her belongings carefully about her, just as if she were going on a journey in the wilds, the fly rolled off upon its way, with my aunt looking out now and then to criticise the driver and the horse. After having lain upon her couch ten years or so, one day she suddenly got up. The ensuing week she went out hunting, dressed in her long Victorian habit, tall hat and veil, and with a boa round her neck. She hunted on, riding much harder than most members of the hunt, but in a modest and retiring way, and followed by her groom. He, a staid lad, who had been brought up with Lord Fitzwilliam as an under-strapper in the hunt stables, always used to say: "Them as rides with my lady 'as to know 'ow to ride; but then I passed my youth with Lord Fitzwilliam. They was a serious family, all rode to 'ounds, and all of 'em rode blood 'orses, from the old lord down to the little gals."

My aunt continued riding to extreme old age, and then went to the meets driven in a fly, of course, by someone she could put her trust in, though Jackson long had passed away, to drive perhaps in some particular limbo, where the shades of Captain Barclay, old Squire Osbaldiston, and Sir Tatton Sykes drove shadowy chariots, dressed in their "down the road" coats, with a coach and horses on the big pearl buttons, just as they had appeared in life, all with straws in the corners of their mouths, and with that air of supernatural knowledge of the horse which they all had on earth.

My aunt, I fancy, could she have chosen for herself, would have gone to some heaven, half stable and half country house, with just a sprinkling of Low Church divines flying about in black Geneva gowns and white lawn bands, to give an air of having been redeemed, to the select, but rather scanty, inmates of the place when they sat down to dine.

Poor lady, all her life was one long tutelage, till her last sister died. Then when she had peeped below the blinds to satisfy herself that the hearse horses all were sound, and none wore housings, a thing that she detested, saying she could not bear to see a horse in petticoats, she found herself quite free.

After the fashion of the times, she did not go herself to see her sister buried, but sat at home and read the Burial Service, although a member of the family averred on his return he caught her dozing with the Church Service closed upon her lap, and *Market Harboro'* in her hand. Years passed, and she became a kindly tyrant in her old age, making her young relations happy and terrified by her ungracious kindness to them all.

Lastly, in a Bath chair, she used to have herself dragged up and down the Holly Walk or the Parade, criticising horses and riders most relentlessly, and now and then making the chairman stop before the shops where pictures were for sale, and after looking at them most intently, usually saying, " 'Tis distance lends enchantment to the view," a piece of criticism which she thought final, as applied to art in all its branches, even to photographs.

She died as she had lived, after arranging her own funeral with the undertaker, and enjoining on him to be sure that the hearse was not started with a jerk, and all his beasts were sound.

He left her presence snorting a little in a bandanna pocket-handkerchief, remarking: "Well, I never saw such a lady in my life, a plucked one to be sure, I'll bet a suvering."

My aunt rests quietly under some elm trees in Old Milverton churchyard.

Many old Scottish ladies lie round about the grave where my aunt sleeps under a granite slab now stained a little with the weather, imparting to the churchyard a familiar air, as of the tea-parties that she once used to give, when they all sat together, just as they now lie closely in the ground, to keep each other warm. The rooks caw overhead, and when the hounds pass on a bright November morning, I hope she hears them, for heaven would be to her but a dull dwelling-place if it contained no horses and no hounds.

La Alcaldesa

"Cossart was talking to me once," said Mansel, — "you remember him? the man who was a diver and whom you gave a horse to in Mercedes, you must remember him; he was a cook."

I did, and recollected giving him the horse, a little, dark brown, with a white face, and four white feet. I gave him, as it happened, with the greater pleasure, or at least with a greater absence of responsibility, because the horse was not my own, but a stray animal who had attached himself to my *tropilla*. The brute was very hard to mount, and when at last you had got with difficulty on his back, was not worth a red cent.

"Well," Mansel said, "Cossart was talking about matrimony the other day, up at the French Cooks' Club in Sackville Street. He said that it was strange so few of us had married, for marriage, as he understood the institution, was a good thing for men, as he said, *sur le retour*; but that, for his part, he thought himself immune on account of something that had happened to him, back in the 'seventies, in Paraguay.

"Ah! here is Cossart," said my friend, and the *chef* came into the room, dressed in the long frock-coat, white waistcoat, bell-mouthed trousers, and black crêpe de Chine necktie tied in a bow, which were a sort of uniform to him, after his business hours. In one hand was his hat, curly and shiny, and in the other his thin, black stick, to which a woman's leg in ivory, figured as crutch.

He drew a large silk pocket-handkerchief from his breast-pocket, and, flourishing it, diffused a scent either of Moss Rose or of Jockey Club, throughout the room. He asked for "Gomme" and then for "Cassis," and when the waiter of the club denied all knowledge of them, called for Italian and for French Vermouth, mixed them together and added bitters and a little lemon juice and curaçoa [sic = curaçao], sowed powdered sugar on the top of all, put in a lump of ice, and said:

"This is *la boisson Cossart*, my own receipt; it tastes like nothing else on earth."

I well believed him; and he went on:

"You remember in my bar in Buenos Aires it was my chief support.

One drink, a half-Bolivian. Emilienne, you remember her, had a flat piece of marble, on which to ring them. Never a piece escaped her. Just as I almost had her trained, paf! there passes a Brazilian with the sack, and she, of course, went with him. How quick she was, how honest, I mean French honest, a harder thing by far for one in her position, than mere money proof. Clever, too, and knowing more than *père et mère*. The Brazilian! such a *macaco* as he was, *coiffé d'un Panama*; his gloves immense and *couleur sang de boeuf. Ouf* . . . a Brazilian . . . well, well, she finished, I have heard, quite nicely, and married a rich slave-owner up in Bahia. My countrywomen always finish up like that, no matter how they may have lived.

"Not that Emilienne . . . *pauvre fille*, had had a very stormy life. I got her from the house that you remember, 1, 2, 3 Cerito, where she had only been a month or two after a *malheur* that she had had at home. *Le gibier* always was my *faible*. Ha! ha! yes, I remember that print I had behind the bar, called 'Gibier d'Eau,' with two girls bathing in the sea."

Mansel cut in: " 'Tis strange Emilienne got married and not you. What was it you were telling me about something that happened to you up in Paraguay?"

Cossart lay back and let his heavy, fleshy eyelids fall like a vulture's, over his black eyes, set down *la boisson Cossart* and drummed a little with his huge and hairy hand upon the table by his side.

Over his chin, close-shaved and blue, and on his cheeks, a sort of shadow seemed to run, of greyness, as when a man looks back into his past.

He shivered slightly, and then, opening his eyes, remarked:

"Ah ! yes, that's what you call somebody walking on your grave, and what the Spaniards call *la Muerte Chiquita*, the Little Death, eh?"

Then he began to talk, at first with difficulty, as if the springs of recollection were a little rusty, and then, as they became, as it were, lubricated, more fluently.

"You know," he said, "that I have had a chequered life, diver in Buenos Aires, and in Mercedes, bass singer in the choir."

He stopped and sang a note or two that made the very windows rattle, and then remarking: "Not so bad, eh, for a restaurateur," went on: "A chapter of my life you do not know, when I was up in Paraguay. I drifted there as cook on board a river steamer, the *Iguazú*, I think. Not bad the berth, and the pay good, and when I found myself ashore without a penny in Asuncion, often regretted the snug galley where I could cook and think about the future. I was young then, and although now things go pretty well with me, I always think about the past. Well, you know Asuncion, not much to do there, at least in those days, no theatres, only one *café*, and that kept by a German. His wife was French, and pretty. I used to go and sit and look at her, not that she was the only woman in Asuncion, for you remember, there were thirteen to a man in those days, but bah! *à peine des femmes*, poor creatures, hungry and ragged, and all smoking big cigars. How it fell out, I can't recall, but by degrees we became friends . . . you need not smile, nothing but friends, upon my word; yes, *foi de Cossart*. The husband, an unreasonable man, *avec une tête de mari*, perhaps thought otherwise, and one day, seeing me talking to his wife, advised himself to call me *cochon de français* or something of the sort. I answered him in the same kind, and then, why, a *molestia*, as we used to say. The last I saw of him, he looked not very pretty, lying on the floor beside a broken chair. What heads they have, those Germans. My first shot grazed his arm. His passed my face and smashed a looking-glass. I jump for him, and fetch him with my pistol between the eyes, and then run for the door. As I passed through, the *clientèle* was mostly underneath the tables, except a few who stood holding their pistols, ready, as a man does when a *barulla de Jesú Cristo* happens to occur. I knew he was not dead, and that the thing would soon blow over, but thought it was full time to change the scenery. So, as I wandered up and down the streets between the orange gardens and past the sandy, open spaces covered with castor-oil plants, beyond that *rancho* that you must remember, which had a knot of pawpaw trees, where the road turns to Dr. Stewart's *quinta*, I met a friend of mine.

"He was an Argentine *tropero*, one Aniceto Lopez, well-doing, whom I had known in Carmen de Arreco, province of Buenos Aires, and who had drifted up to Paraguay, only the Lord knows how.

"Well, Aniceto was a good fellow, and when I told him of the trouble I had had about the German, he laughed like steam and said:

" '*Bueno*, you come with me to Corrientes and help me fetch a troop of cattle for the Brazilian troops: *Le cheval, vous savez, c'était ma passion.* After *le gibier* it is the only passion that I have found endures, for, as yet, I am not old enough to have experienced *le manie des cannes*, which is the last mania, so they say, in Paris, that a man ever has.'

"Lopez had lots of horses, and I went out and bought *bombachas*, you remember, the wide trousers, black merino, eh? a *poncho* and a saddle, and boots, of course of patent leather, with an eagle in the front stitched in red thread, and with his wings just disappearing round the leg.

"No, Mansel, not a lasso," said the storyteller, "*pas si bête*, I went, so to speak as a deck hand, for any one can help to drive a herd of cattle when it is once upon the road. When I was ready we started, going down by the trail that passes just behind Lambaré, crossing the Tebicuari somewhere near Villa Franca, right through the Estero Ñembucú and so by Paso de la Patria, across the Paraná. Oh, that Estero Ñembucú, what a place, water until you cannot rest, and still more water. Then a little mud, long grass that you hardly shove your horse through, and then more water and more mud. Mosquitoes, yes, and every living devilish bug, and hot and steamy, and you seated upon your horse, crying out, '*Tropa*,' '*Vuelta toro*,' whirling your *rebenque* round your head, and splashing through the mud. That was the kind of day I passed with Aniceto Lopez, each time we crossed the accursed Estero, driving the cattle to Asuncion. At night, if we could get to a dry patch, we had to ride for two hours each, slowly all round the herd, to keep the beasts from straying off; at daybreak, if you had had what Mansel here would call the morning watch, you changed your horse and slowly jogged along the road, dozing and swearing at the lagging beasts, till it was time to halt and take a siesta, and then jog on once more.

"You will laugh, but sometimes as I sit in the sanctum of the club, I mean the room that is reserved to me (the only artist in the place), thinking my menus out, my mind goes back to the old Estero Ñembucú.

"Why? you say, eh? Well, perhaps for the same reason that we think more often on the women who have made us suffer than upon those who have made us happy by their love.

"Well, well, my friend Aniceto Lopez used to laugh at me a good deal now and then when one of his accursed horses gave me a fall on a cold morning, and say I was a *maturango*, but I made several trips with him, and showed him how to make a tolerable stew out of jerked beef and mandioca meal. You soaked the beef in orange juice . . . and . . . anything was better than that abominable *churasco* they used to eat upon the road.

"When we had passed the Estero we used to halt a day, or sometimes two, for time was what we had the most of, to rest the horses, let the herd feed, and wash our clothes. How well I see those camps . . . eh, Daddy Mansel, do you remember them?"

Mansel, who had sat silent, plunged also deep in recollection, looked up and said:

"A dozen of them, Cossart, but I cannot somehow imagine you lying stretched out under a tree and eating jerked beef and mandioca, and sleeping in the sun."

"Necessity," rejoined the *chef*, taking the straw out of a long Italian cigar, "makes us acquainted with strange comestibles; as to bed-fellows, the stranger that they are the better, that is, when one is young."

Having enunciated this opinion with an air of having added to the world's wisdom, and to Mansel's great disgust — not that he was a hypocrite, but being English did not like men to speak their minds on such a subject — the *chef* continued:

"Ideal days we had, camped underneath the trees, the woods on every side, running like capes run out to sea into the little plain, set about here and there with groups of yatais . . . you know, those scrubby palms. An air of being out of the world, alone with Nature. *Mon Dieu*, they say a man when he grows old falls into anecdotage; but to philosophise is worse. In those days you remember that in Paraguay there were no men, that is, one man to thirteen women. Lopez, you know, was killed on the last horse in the republic, a little roan, I think.

"'*Les femmes,* yes, but they were a danger we used to fly from then, and even Aniceto's cattle men, after the first trip, would never willingly sleep in an Indian village, *c'était trop terrible*. I stood it pretty well; the French, you know, were never backward in such matters, and one has *amour propre*, but the odds were too great.

"Don Aniceto's *capataz*, a Correntino, a huge, great fellow, *un solide gaillard*, as we say, tried it and failed . . . we left him in Asuncion, in hospital.

"All the *peones* would begin, and then after a trip or two get shy and sleep out in the woods, or on the plains beside their horses, rather than face the Indian women in the towns. When I first heard about it I thought it was a joke, but one experience did me for my life. After that, I had a plan. Our road led to the south of Caapucú, luckily missing all the villages but one . . . its name I can't recall. How well I see them though, built round a square about two hundred yards across. The long, low huts ran continuously, so that they looked more like a tennis-court than houses fit for men. One broad verandah ran in front of all of them, supported on great beams of some hard wood or other, perhaps canela or some other kind of wood.

"The roofs were either thatched or roofed with old red tiles, made by the Jesuits. The walls were dazzlingly white. The pavement of the verandah either was earth beaten hard and polished, or else great blocks of wood. The church stood at the east end of the square. It too was built of wood, but wood to last all time. No storm, no rain, not even the white ants, had any *prise* upon it. The bells were good. Good water, air and bells, the proverb says. The Jesuits certainly did well in Paraguay. No, no, I am not a clerical, you need not laugh; but render unto Cæsar. What work they must have had to get these bells through the primeval woods. Faith, strong enough to move a bullock-cart out of a mud-hole, I should think. The grass that grew inside the square was green . . . greener than Ireland, more like the strip of green inside the reef on islands I have seen in the Pacific. 'Twas curious to see the inside of the church. The images made by the Indians, the gold still fresh; the gallery, in which sat the musicians. Some of their instruments were left, with the strings all broken and tied up with strips of hide. The people played on them upon church festivals, and when I came to know the place, I helped them sometimes by singing in the choir. You know, I had a voice, *basso cantante*, and singing in the choir was an old trade of mine . . . do, re, mi, fa . . . ha, not bad the *ut de poitrine*. I still can catch him, eh? How pastoral it was; so quiet, nothing but now and then a flight of parrots chattering, or a macaw sometimes sailed by and screamed. At times I used to think that I would settle down and pass my days in Santa Tecla; that was the name the village had, I think.

"I am not strong upon the Scriptures, but when the girls and women used to go down at evening to the stream to fetch the water, I used to think about Rebecca at the well, or Ruth and Boaz, *c'était si pastorale*.

"How quietly they walked, each with a water-jar upon her head, shaped like an amphora.

"Women and girls, and girls and women, all dressed in white, that is, all *en chemise*, with their hair cut square across the forehead and hanging down their backs. Only a boy or two and an old man or so, but what were those amongst so many? Women did everything, they tilled the fields, rang the church bells at eventime, for just at sunset everybody prayed, just as the Jesuits had taught their ancestors. What animals they had, the women tended. In the church they had some kind of prayers or other upon festivals. My friends, the *mise en scène* was quite ideal, a perfect Arcady. The first time that we stopped there, when we had got well camped, and I was free to look about, 1 went down to the village, leading my horse, for though my passion was the horse, I had had about enough of him, for the last week or two.

"Just as I passed the well, a woman stood there filling her water-jar. *Quelle femme!* Tall, rather stout, but not too stout, only a gracious embonpoint, fair, for a Paraguayan, that is, the skin . . . her hair, of course, was black.

"She looked at me and smiled, a natural thing to do, for I was young then, and as I said, men were so scarce, there were not any, even for a remedy, as the Spaniards say.

"So, when she smiled, I smiled, and asked her if I should help her with her water-jar. From that, we soon were friends, and as we walked back to the village, she swaying lightly with the water-jar upon her head, I touched her hand, and we began to talk. It seemed her father and her husband both were killed, her brother missing after some fight or other, and she was left alone. The other women of the village called her 'La Alcaldesa,' that is, the mayoress, and by degrees had taken to regard her as the chief woman of the place. As she talked on, telling me about this thing and of that, we came to where she lived. She asked me to come in. I followed her, just as a horse trots after a bell mare. Her house was bare of everything, and all the furniture she had was a hide *catré,* an old chair or two, and a few pictures of the saints. A hammock swung between the pillars of the verandah, with its long cotton fringes, and after having talked a little and drunk a *maté* with cold water, after the Paraguayan fashion of those days, I went and sat in it, keeping it swinging with one foot, and smoking a cigar.

"As I swung in the hammock, smoking, for La Alcaldesa never let the sacred fire of Vesta out, handing me small cigars fit for a man . . . you remember that in Paraguay the women smoked cigars as big as carrots — the night came on without a twilight . . . day and then darkness in a quarter of an hour. The fireflies flitted round the trees, the bats flew noiselessly about . . . I had to scare one from my horse's neck . . . the frogs croaked, and the moon outlined the shadows of the palm trees by the church, upon the grass. *Quoi; un vrai scène de théâtre,* but better somehow, either because you had not got to pay your entry money or because you were yourself an actor in the scene.

"You fancied that mysterious things were going on in the thick wall of forest that ringed about the town, that is, the village, the *capilla* as they called it, and when a white-robed figure crossed in the moonlight, either from house to house, or right across the square, it looked as if the opera of *Norma,* or of *Poliuto,* were going to begin."

37

He paused to light a cigarette, holding his ebony stick between his legs with its white crutch shaped like a woman's leg, which, as he said, "gave him ideas," and then, blowing a hurricane of smoke down both his nostrils, resumed.

"That evening Aniceto Lopez and the herd, the trip, and everything went quite out of my head. The Alcaldesa called a girl who took my horse to water, and then, unsaddling it, cut down some bunches of *pindó* with a machete, and tied him up outside the door. Our supper was, if I remember right, nothing but oranges and mandioca with a little chipa, that is, bread made from cassava pulp. I thought, as I sat eating, after all, it is far more artistic . . . for I too am an artist, to make no effort with your food, and eat just like the other animals, fruit and such things, than to cook badly as they do here, amongst you insularies. As we were eating, women came and looked in, and sometimes said a word or two in Guarani. Sometimes they only stared, as cannibals might stare at a young, well-fed missionary out in La Nouvelle, or the New Hebrides. Although, of course, I did not understand a word they said . . . I saw how the wind blew, either by intuition or *dans ma qualité de français, voyez-vous?* Next morning, just a little before light, the Alcaldesa got up and prepared *maté*. A girl took down my horse to water, bathed him and returned dripping herself, looking just like *une néréide* with her long, black hair upon her shoulders, and her chemise her only garment, clinging round her legs. I felt a little like a *nouvelle mariée* when women looked into the door, smiled and said something to the Alcaldesa . . . always the same thing, for I could hear the words, although I could not grasp the sense. Somehow I did not like to ask her what it was they said . . . though, *bigre*, I am not shy, but it seemed somehow as if I had arrived at l'Ile de Tulipatam or some such place where women do the love-making . . . *oui, c'était gênant tout de même*, for all those little Paraguayan girls devoured me with their eyes."

Mansel looked at him as a man looks at a five-legged sheep, and though he knew the *chef* to be a man of courage, generous and kindly to the marrow of his bones, the restless strip of sea that cuts our island off from all the world seemed to extend itself between him and his friend, not in his view of life, but in the way he spoke about the view.

The *chef*, perceiving it, said:

"*On est bel homnie, ou on ne l'est pas, mon cher*, those little Paraguayans would have eaten me if they could. Man doth not live by love alone, you say. That is so, but it makes a good *entrée*, if you have other things to eat. . . . I speak *en chef* you know, having some knowledge both of cookery and love.

"Well, well . . . a high old time . . . and during the three days we camped at Santa Tecla, my friend Don Aniceto saw but little of me. La Alcaldesa treated me *en prince*, loving me, as you remember, Mansel, the Paraguayan women loved, as if the world and love were to go on forever and a day. I often think that they were right, for after all, forever is a word that no one understands. Had it not been for her, I rather think I should have come as badly out of the three days as did some of Don Aniceto's *peones*, who struggled back to camp, with faces long as a male mule's, surrounded by a band of white-clad girls, all of whom seemed to have a sort of right of property in them in some mysterious way.

"We started on the trail — luckily there was no more Estero to go through — at daybreak. The horses were all fresh, the cattle difficult to drive, Don Aniceto in a massacring humour, and the whole country looking like a half-evaporated sea, bathed in the thin, white mist, which rises in the morning in those latitudes and hangs about the edges of the woods, like a white winding-sheet.

"When I had got my horse in hand, after his first wild plunges, I turned, and, looking back, saw the tall figure of the Alcaldesa, standing at her door, with her eyes fixed on me, just as a woman stands, looking at a disappearing ship, out at a harbour's mouth. *Mes amis, c'était dur*, I was her ship; and as I watched her, her head fell forward on her hands."

The *chef* blew his nose loudly in a Madras handkerchief, twisted his moustache, and in response to Mansel's question if he had ever seen La Alcaldesa afterwards, rejoined:

"Yes, often; in fact ours was a kind of intermittent honeymoon each time I passed by the *capilla* . . . I used to stay with her. *Une bonne, brave fille, va, donc.* . . . I often thought that I would marry her and settle down. However, it was *trop bête*, to settle down — to what? Certainly she was handsome . . . pale, with black hair, tall and well made, and with a little . . . *fossette* just above one knee . . . the left, I think, to ravish you. No, not the least idea of cookery, it was humiliating to me . . . but on the other hand, loving and kind, not the least interested, and *passionnée* . . . well, to a fault. At times, I think I hear the pounding of the Indian corn in the tall mortar and the soft whirring of the insects' wings amongst the orange trees, outside her house . . . at times . . . yes, *sacré matin,* I think

39

Charity

I will go back to Paraguay before I die and see if she still lives. . . . *Ouf!* it has cost me a good sigh to tell you this. . . . *Les femmes, les femmes, ça vous abîment un homme . . . foi de restaurateur.*"

An Hidalgo

Tall, wry-necked, and awkwardly built, with a nose like a lamprey and feet like coracles, Don Saturnino Vargas y Arispe was a type of man that you can only see in Spain, or, as he would have said, "the Spains," and perhaps apologised, then added, "but all that ended with the war." It may have ended as he said, but, none the less, even before the war, the type was never so complete in Cuba, Puerto Rico, or the Philippines, as in the mother of the Spains. In the lost colonies, perforce, men came in contact with the affairs of life, and thus became more like mankind at large, and less original. In Spain, and especially in Asturias, Don Saturnino's native land, they had become beings so much apart that it was easier by far to make a European out of a Russian, Turk, Armenian, or Jew, than of a native of the land, over which flies the blood-and-orange flag.

Timid and arrogant at the same time, and quite devoid of any kind of fear, except of being thought ridiculous, which naturally was the one thing he never could escape from, he had inherited from a long line of hungry ancestors a certain uprightness of thought, which neither training nor his false view of every side of life could quite eradicate. If fate had been more kind, he should have lived in some old house, buried in chestnut trees, deep in the hills of Sátandér. [sic = Santander] His arms and those of his illustrious ancestors, illustrious by never having done much harm to anyone, would have been sculptured in a creamy, yellowish stone in high relief above the door. The maize fields would have flowed like a great sea of green (yellow in autumn) almost up to his gate. There would have been a wild, neglected garden, in which some aloes, a bush of blue veronica, some purple irises and a few ixias strove with the weeds for life. A great magnolia would have reared its dome of flowers, just at the end of the long, glass-covered passage, which led out from the sitting-room, and the domain most likely would have had an old, grey wall, bulging and full of chinks, from which peered lizards, and with great tufts of Venus' navelwort and mullein, springing from out the stones.

A patch of oak copse and a patch of vines would have formed part of the Asturian paradise, and in the little plot of kitchen garden, great pumpkins slowly would have ripened in the sun. Outside the wall there would have been a pine wood, at the edge of which in the sparse grass, blue gromwells twinkled, and at the top, where the wood ended and the heathy plain began, a little Calvary, with its three crosses and its winding stair, would have alternately been sealed in icicles, or sweltered in the sun. Sleek, yellow oxen would have ploughed, swaying about just as a man sways walking, muffled in a cloak, whilst the rude, wooden carts with wicker sides, passed lazily along the sandy tracks, with a harsh screech as the great wooden wheels, which never had been greased, slowly and painfully revolved. Men would have trodden out the grapes in the great tank under the trellising of vines, and women washed upon the river-banks. High in the silent air a quavering song would have ascended from the fields, to be re-echoed from the wine vat or the river-bank, and haunt the mind just as the croaking of the frogs on a hot night within the tropics, once heard, dwells in the ear for life, This sort of world would have been just as suited to the Hidalgo as is a stone to an apothecary's eye, as he himself might have observed sententiously, but an untoward fate had ordered differently.

Sent to the "court" in early youth, to a small clerkship in the Custom House, by slow degrees he had risen to be chief clerk, and then had been promoted to full charge in little towns, such as Mondoñedo, Lugo, Brañuelas and Astorga, places in which he had passed a melancholy life in lodgings, eating at the hotel, but which experience gave him the opportunity to remark that he had seen a good deal of the world. This he believed most fervently, although the little towns were as much like each other as are two groups of low, black Arab tents out on the Sáhara; but he belonged to that old-fashioned, fast disappearing class of Spaniards, who never travelled during the whole course of their lives more than a mile or two beyond the place where they were born. Just as a mule's fate is to drag a cart, so the Hidalgo was one of those destined to sit upon high stools, and pass their lives in entering figures in a book, till their hair falls and all their teeth decay, at the same dreary task.

In the same way, a willing mule receives more blows than any other in the team, so does the good employee have less opportunity to rise, and the Hidalgo was no exception to the rule. At forty, after long years of faithful service, and a life passed in boarding-houses, he found himself head of the Customs in a little town upon the coast. His pay was miserable, his outlook circumscribed, and even that still more restricted by his excessive patriotism and his religious views.

Needless to say he was a Catholic, not that he troubled much about the dogmas of the Church, or his religious duties, so that, had he not been a Spaniard, he might have found a way out of the prison in which his spirit was confined. As it was, like many of his kind, to him religion was so much a part of the one country in the world (that is of course the country where he lived), that to discuss it would have been as strange as if one morning he had found himself unable to speak Christian, or heard that he was rich.

Everything new was painful to him, and though he saw at once that the electric light was better than a wick floating in a brass cup in evil-smelling oil, and that a train was far more comfortable than was the cart and its long train of mules, its tilt of straw, and hammock swinging underneath the axles, with a dog sitting in it and snarling at the passers-by, in which he first had come up from Asturias to Madrid, he did not reason on the facts. Thus he assumed, not without profit to himself in some degree, all that is most material in progress, but took good care that not an atom of the soul of the condition of affairs, out of which progress grew, should ever enter to his mind. So does an Arab pass at a jump from a long, flint-lock gun, hooped round the barrel with silver or with brass, to a repeating rifle of the most modern kind. He buys the rifle, which to him is the sum total of European culture, while steadfastly rejecting everything of our life, which is at variance with his creed. So the Hidalgo still remained as far removed from modern thought, when seated in the train, as he was in his youth, jogging along the roads upon a mule.

In some respects he was still further off, for in his youth he did not hate that which he never heard of; but now he loathed that which he felt was stronger than himself, though he would sooner far have died than have admitted it. He used to praise the writers of the "epoch of our glory," though without reading them, as when he did, their realism was a rude shock to his alambicated taste. Novels, in which the men were brave, the women virtuous, and Spain appeared set in a haze of glory, midway between the heavens and the earth, were his chief pabulum. From them he took his views of life, of art, and everything as if they were inspired. The heroes in his books all praised Murillo, calling him divine, but of Velazquez they spoke slightingly, calling him too mechanical and a mere *practicón,* that is, a man proficient in his art, but not original. The Hidalgo did the same, although it is likely that he had never seen the works of either of them, except in oleographs. Still, in the course of time, as he was not a fool, he saw that even Spain was altering, and an uneasy feeling grew on him that it was possible he was on the wrong road and going down the hill. He might have changed his point of view had not the war with the United States thrown him back on himself, bringing out in him all the best and the worst of his strange character.

Chief of the Customs in the land-locked town, with its long winding harbour, shielded by islands at the mouth, remote in the north-west of Spain, on every side were memories of the past to feed his melancholy. Memories of Spain's departed glory rose upon his view, in the grim citadel, under which the lichen-covered roofs of the old, slab-paved town nestled and straggled up the hill. In the decaying stone-faced forts upon the shore, brass cannons lay beside their carriages, around their barrels clustered serpents, cast in relief, about the touch-holes were the arms of Spain, with an imperial crown. Far up the harbour, under the heath-clad, vine-edged shores of the great inland lake, slumbered the fleet of the galleons from Cartagena, sunk by their admiral to save themselves from Drake. In the clear waters of the bay, they just were visible, after a long calm, lying like sleeping sheep out on a moor, beneath their mounds of sand. Tradition had it that their commander had perished at his post, going down, standing on the poop, waving the flag of Spain.

On holidays, mounted upon a mule, which he rode gravely, as it had been a war- horse, and shielded from the sun and wind alike in his brown cloak, he used to ride out to the spot, dismount, carefully make a cigarette, light it, drink down the smoke, expel it with a rush from both his nostrils just as the vapour issues from a *solfatára*, and reconstruct the scene. It stirred him powerfully, and as he sat, watching the vessels sink, whilst the false heretics were baffled of their prey, his sordid life was blotted out, and he felt sure that once again Spain would prevail and God be glorified. The old-world province and the decaying town, the country, with its legends of the past (did not the Tardo, that strange lubber fiend, still issue out at sundown, to fright the youths and maidens if they loitered over-much upon the roads, returning from the *romerias*?), must have done much to strengthen his beliefs, and stir his patriotism. Were-wolves and witches filled the people's talk, and as he walked under the arches of the Plaza Consistoriál, he must have almost felt he had gone back to his Asturian home. In his position, fortune was secure, had he but cared to grasp it, for from time immemorial the Custom House had been a gold mine to anyone appointed to the post.

Men sent there poor returned home rich after a few years' service, just as a Moorish Caid enters his government on a thin horse and followed by a rout of starvelings, but leaves it wealthy and a made man for life. The Hidalgo's friends all thought his luck had changed, holding quite naturally, that he would do as others did, and put his boots on, as the saying has it, in the established way. Once entered on the duties of his post, they found out their mistake. Accounts were audited, and every penny that came in had to be checked and then transmitted to Madrid. His critics were dumbfoundered, and his friends said there was a cat of some kind shut up in the bag, for none of them believed in any honesty in public life, although in private all were honourable men. Had he but pocketed the money all would have passed without much comment, and men have envied him his opportunities, rejoiced to find that after all he was as they were, and giving them the chance to shake a moralising finger and say "We told you so."

Vigo became too hot for him when it leaked out that his sole purpose was to help the Treasury with funds to carry on the war, not that the citizens were not imbued with patriotism, so far as shouting was concerned, or making speeches, but to send money to Madrid, where they knew that it would be stolen by the officials in the Treasury, appeared to them both as a madness and a rejection of that local patriotism so strong in Spaniards' minds. Some thought him mad and quoted the old saw, "Make yourself a redeemer and you will be crucified," and others thought he was a rogue who had hit upon some novel kind of fraud, and half respected him. After the truth about the miserable campaign had thoroughly leaked out, he went about dejected, in fashion of a man who has seen everything he once held in esteem, fall crumbling to the ground.

Back in Madrid, after his ill-timed sally into patriotism, he found himself still entering figures in a book, although a little better paid than in his younger days. In the long hours of idleness which are inevitable in public offices, he set about to think. Having reviewed his life, he found that to be honest he would have to change all his convictions and ideas and all his prejudices. The books he had admired he saw were rubbish, the pictures wretched, even on politics a doubt crept in and made him miserable. He saw at once the precipice on which he stood, looked down into its depths and turned away for good. Clearly he saw his view of life and faith would have to be remodelled, and felt himself unequal to the task, and all it signified.

For a brief space he plunged into what he called pecuniary love, but returned always from his excursions to the side chapels of the Paphian goddess, weary and sick at heart. Although his fortunes had improved a little, and he was recognised as an official to be depended on for work, but not of course after his escapade at Vigo to be advanced to be the head of a department, he still lived at a boarding-house, partly from lack of energy to change, partly for company. His chief delight was to sit talking with the keeper of the boarding-house — a tall and withered-looking woman from Galicia, who had been, according to herself, the daughter of a general, but had come down in life through the bad government prevailing in the land. This of course appealed to the Hidalgo, as it does usually to all his countrymen, who like to rail upon their Government just as a man will rail upon his wife, but yet endure her to the last day of a long life and suffer her caprice. Hours used to pass as they sat talking about their ungovernable land, the dearth of patriotism, and the venality of those in power and in place, in the true Spanish way. At times the Hidalgo would take up the defence of one or other minister, but the general's daughter always was able to bring forward some damning vice to shake his confidence. Not that he was a fool, or really thought that every public man throughout all Spain was venal or a rogue, but the desire to talk to somebody was strong in him, after his dreary day.

How long the Hidalgo might have gone on, attending to his work by day and in the evening listening to his landlady's conversation, is difficult to say, had he not happened on an afternoon to look up to a window, on the way from his office to his home, almost by accident.

A girl was leaning on the window-sill, and she gazed into the street. He thought her beautiful. Her hair was black and coarse, but plentiful, her forehead low, and her eyes black and jetty-looking, so dark they were unfathomable, but yet giving the look of not perhaps having much to fathom, when you had sounded them. She wore a dressing-jacket of white *piqué*, not over-clean, but open at the neck, and as she gazed into the street, biting the stalk of a red rose which she drew now and then almost up to her mouth and then let fall again till it hung resting on her chin, she smiled at the Hidalgo and, opening her lips, let the rose fall into the street. Stooping, he picked it up, holding it awkwardly, after the fashion of a man unused to love affairs. So little practised was he in such matters that he was half inclined to take it back to the fair, careless charmer, but then remembered that he had read in books that to drop flowers was a manoeuvre of the sex. So, drawing from his pocket a greasy note-case, he shoved the flower into it, just in the way he might have thrust a pair of boots into a travelling bag.

Up in the balcony, he heard a sound of stifled laughter, but when the flower was safely stowed away amongst his cards and several old envelopes, and he had the courage to look up, hoping his charmer would reward him with a smile, he found that she had gone. All the way home he walked as nearly upon air as was consistent with his temperament, and for a space forgot the ambition of his life, to make his office the most perfect in all Spain, and the most competent.

In future, as he walked to his work, he always took the street in which, for the first time in all the current of his life, a girl had given him a rose. Any other man would have found out her name, or have got someone to present him to her family, but he, whether from shyness or from some strange romantic whim, never attempted to go further in his quest, or to declare his love. Sometimes the girl appeared and smiled upon him, sometimes she fixed her eyes on space and seemed unconscious of his passage down the street, or if he were alive. Upon those days he would return with a vague feeling of uneasiness, as if in some way she had been unfaithful to him, and had betrayed his trust. Still, next day found him passing down the street as usual, eager and flushed with expectation, with his heart thumping on his ribs. Months passed, and then a year, and still he walked and gazed up on the balcony, usually empty, and without ever once again receiving even the shadow of a rose, or any recognition except a smile on rare occasions, as he passed by upon his way.

The people in the street all knew him, and the fat woman in the *estanco* who sold cigars and stamps, would remark to her neighbour who sold small coal, as he stood at the door of his dark den, "There goes the madman of the daughter of Don Paco." To which he used to answer, "Yes, a madman, yes; but the girl sits too much at the window, and paints her face too thickly for an unmarried wench. Why does she paint? you say; ah, why indeed, 'Why does the blind man's wife go well arrayed?' the proverb says," and they both smiled and winked.

The Hidalgo, quite unconscious that he had ever been remarked, still found the only pleasure of his life in his brief passage down the street, and might have gone on to extreme old age without attempting to declare his love, if it was love he really felt, had not an unkind fate cut short his dream, waking him cruelly. One day as he walked to his office gazing

47

upon the ground, but his heart turning towards the window where his *innamorata* generally sat, he stopped and rubbed his eyes. A little crowd was gathered round the door, and an unwonted air of festivity lit up the dingy street through which he had so often passed morning and evening for the last year or so. He asked with trembling at the *estanco*, foreseeing some misfortune in the air. The stout *estanco*-keeper, in her cotton dress, which left her great, unstable bust quite loose and unconfined, patted her glossy hair, arranged a side curl on her cheek, and looking at him with a smile replied, "This is the day on which Don Paco's daughter marries the captain of the Carabineers . . . her mother has good luck, for she is eight-and-twenty if a day, is getting, like myself, a little like a ham, and, as you know, has sat there in the window, like a canary in a cage, for the last seven years."

The Hidalgo thanked her, and having bought a box of matches that he did not want, walked out and stood upon the pavement to see the bride enter her carriage and drive away into the world. He had not long to wait, for leaning on the arm of a stout captain, with a waxed moustache, a sword by his side, and a thick perspiration on his forehead as he struggled with his gloves, she stepped into the street. For the first time in all his life, the poor Hidalgo found his voice, and launched a "Bless your mother," so loudly that the bride stopped for a moment in surprise. Then turning towards her husband, she smiled a little, and whispered something in his ear which seemed to tickle him. The carriage door was slammed, and as it moved away a hand in a white glove threw a flower from the wedding bouquet to the Hidalgo, as he stood stupefied. This time he understood, and, stooping, picked it up and pressed it to his lips, and it appeared to him that the white glove fluttered an instant at the window, as the bride drove away.

All day he wandered up and down the streets, and for the first time in his life his colleagues missed him during office hours and thought that he was ill. The night he spent in the Retiro, walking about the alleys, named so grandiloquently, Peru, Nueva Granada, Honduras, Mexico, and Paraguay, and after all the other great vice-royalties lost to the flag of Spain.

An October frost had turned the leaves in the Retiro a light gold, and a thin film of ice spread on the waters of the lake. The equestrian statue of the twelfth Alfonso, high on its pedestal, crowning the yet unfinished monument, had a light covering of hoar-frost on the side turned towards the north, and a chill air from Guadarrama stirred the trees, making them shiver at the coming of the dawn. Men wrapped in blankets, their mouths well covered up, began to show themselves upon the streets; then carts with a long train of horses or of mules, led by a little donkey, and with a pole tied to the wheels to act as a rough break *[sic],* jolted and rumbled on the stones. Next came men driving goats, and from the country creaked in bullock-carts, drawn by great brindled oxen such as those that the angel goaded to their work whilst the good husbandman Isidro slumbered at noonday in the shade.

Madrid woke up to talk, as other towns wake up to work, and the streets slowly filled with people, who at first sight were going nowhere, by the longest way that they could find. Daybreak still found him wandering aimlessly. Then when the sun rose fully, red and glorious, he seemed to feel the comfort of his rays, and after having smoked a cigarette pacing along the edge of the great pool, he wrapped his cloak tighter around his shoulders; and, when the gates were opened, left his Gethsemane. After a frugal breakfast at a little café he sat an hour or so, smoking contemplatively, till it was time to go. He reached his office at his accustomed hour, and taking up his pen, set himself resolutely to work, just as a horse with a wrung shoulder throws itself hard against the collar, so as not to feel the pain.

Charity

The Craw Road*

All roads are said to lead to Rome. This may be so, of course, if a man follows them right round the world. Some, though, lead you to realms in which the materialism of the City of the Seven Hills has not and never had a place.

Upon them no legionary in his *caligulæ* and with his conquering spade upon his back has ever marched. The roads he traversed led straight to some place or another, over the tops of hills, across the rivers, passing morasses, cutting the valleys, and right across the plain, just as the State that paid him made its way to fame regardless of the feelings of the world. My road was traced originally by homing crows. Men saw them fly, and thought that where they came from there must be something worth their while to see. That was before the coming of the legionaries. The world was full of interest in those days, for fairies played upon the heathery knolls, elves sat upon the toad-stools, and the white Caledonian cattle roamed the woods. The spirit of adventure was at least as strong as now, for anyone who left his home to travel, even a little way, where he had never been before, plunged into the unknown. To-day the difficulty is not, that there is not a sufficiency of roads, but that there are too many Romes. This difficulty did not beset the builders of the road I write about.

Following the flight of crows across the hills, they first of all laid a few faggots in the miry places, secured a coracle or two by streams too deep to cross, and, taking in their hands a club or a stone battle-axe, set out across the hills. Thus the road they traced in times gone by is made on other principles than those in use to-day. Twisting round obstacles and in and out between the moors, skirting the base of hills, and now and then coming back upon itself in places where the first road-makers no doubt sat down to rest, it winds upon its way.

* The name was originally the Cró Road, Cró in Gaelic meaning cattle. It was corrupted into "Craw," in the Lowland speech.

Campseyan chiefs, and then Fingalians, have passed along it in their light deerskin brogues. In places, short cuts, now long disused, still shine amongst the heath, showing stones polished by the feet of ancient forayers. Into recesses of green hills, now out again and then running along the sides of streams, it winds and penetrates. No road I know, not even that between Mendoza and San Felipe de los Andes across the stony slopes of Uspallata, where in the tempests stones roll along like leaves, is lonelier, more desolate, or looks more hostile to mankind than this wild Scottish Trail.

By rights the road should lead to nowhere in particular, but finish off in some impenetrable morass or in some corrie of the hills. That would indeed be a crows' road, and far more interesting than the majority of roads that lead to places no one has any wish to go to, except the people who are born there and cannot get away.

This is what the Craw Road should really be if it were perfect; but, as it is, it winds about the mist-filled hollows and wild hills, on which feed black-faced sheep, and passes now and then a lone farmhouse, white and four-square, with purple slates, its stack of peats at one end, cheese-stone before the door, its fank for sheep-washing, and with a woman in a short striped petticoat vigorously thumping the blankets in the burn, and crooning out a song. It leads through realms of heath and grass unchanged, save for a sheep-drain here and there, since the beginning of the world, until it reaches one of the rare, old, Scottish mansion-houses, left from an older age.

Miles from a railway station and jammed against the flank of a steep range of hills, between a melancholy little tarn, in which feed tench, and a thick wood, it stands alone and solitary. The grey peel-tower, with battlements either for defence or else to show its owner was a gentleman, stands sentinel beside a square, grey house, with steep-pitched roof and corbie steps, and with a low front door set in a roll-and-fillet moulding, opening upon the road.

The stone above the door sets forth the year of grace in which the builders rested from their task. The narrow ribbon of grey flags in front is mossed and honeycombed by time. The grass which surges up, close to the avenue, leaving a narrow space in which to turn a carriage, right before the door, has that peculiar sour and scanty look of an old pasture when only grazed by sheep. In the dank fields, which we in Scotland dignify as "parks," the trees are mostly all stag-headed, and the tall spruces on the weather side hold out bare arms, not dead, but stripped and polished by the blast like ancient ivory. Moss has spread out over the avenue, not like a carpet, but with the look of a disease, and in a corner of the grounds the ribs and trucks of an old cotton mill, built as a speculation a hundred years ago, add to the loneliness, by giving, as it were, an air of having perished in the fight with Time and destiny.

The long, dank mill-lead which once set the machinery astir is silted up, in places fallen in, and though long years have passed since it did anything but breed innumerable frogs, is still an eyesore, Nature having steadfastly refused to take it to herself and veil its ugliness.

Smoke curls unwillingly from the chimneys of the house, to be so soon absorbed in mist it leaves one doubtful whether it is smoke, or but damp floating from the trees. Squirrels and rabbits have come into their own, and look at you as on a trespasser, and from the woods even at midday roe venture forth and play. The heron's cry sounds lively, and the tinkling of the burn hidden beneath the bushes of the shrubbery almost oppressive in the deep solitude. All must look magical in the silence of the stars, when the moon ghostens in the trees, and owls float noiselessly about or pass the time of night in their long melopy *[sic= Fr. mélopée, a dirge]*, from hollybush to old Scotch fir, their cries re-echoing from the turrets of the house and sounding on the lake.

Then the tall pine trees, which throng about the little urn bearing the inscription "Hæc loca cum peregrinis pinis exornavit, A.G.S.," and the date 1845, compare their notes about the flight of time, whispering uncannily. Hemlocks and Douglasses must then vie with one another, and the Sequoias vaunt their stature, whilst trembling Deodaras shyly claim the palm of grace from all the fellowship. Long, tapering branches, looking fingerlike and human, must be agitated, waking the birds and squirrels by their movement; and if the raiser of the urn could see the trees he planted so many years ago, now grown majestic in their age, he would indeed plume himself on his Latin and his faith, in having planted them.

Martial and angular, his frosty whiskers curling round his chin, his silver snuff-box in his hand, it is not likely that the planter of the trees ever went out at night to hear them whispering, or watch the moonbeams playing on their boughs, silent and silvery; but had he done so, standing by his urn, he would have looked as much in keeping with the scene as any one of them.

Time had been impotent to bow or mellow him; so he stood still defiant, like an old ash grown on stony ground that stretches out its boughs to meet the elements. The suns of the Peninsula, in whose wars he passed his youth, the storms of politics and of religious controversy of his middle age, had but intensified his proud, unyielding soul, and made him bitter. Perhaps the one soft corner in his heart was to the trees, now grown so beautiful and so luxuriant (after he was dead), to whom, in sure and certain hope that Nature would perform her unconscious miracle, he raised his little urn. One fain would hope that when at night, released from the presence of mankind, they whisper in the breeze, his memory is cherished, and that these foreign pines, which do indeed adorn the spot on which they grow, say now and then to one another, "Do you remember that day, long ago, when we all lay together on a cart, and the stern, white-haired, eagle-eyed old man who set us in the ground?" Meanwhile they wave and whisper, tall and beautiful, their branches covering the little burn which I remember in my youth running through a grass slope on which stood some young trees, at varying intervals.

The hand that planted them is long decayed, and the old place sleeps in its corrie with something ghostly hanging over it, even in midday.

Through the rough hills, across the moors, passing the isolated white farmhouses, winds the way that leads to it; and overhead the crows caw hoarsely, and seem to say to one another when a rare traveller passes by, "There goes a man upon our road."

Set Free

A fine, persistent rain had filled the streets with mud. It lay so thickly that it seemed as if black snow had fallen, and from the pools which had collected here and there upon its surface the passing carriages were reflected, as by a mirage, distorted in the glare of the electric light. The passers-by all had a look of ghosts in the thick foggy air. Rain trickled from their hats and umbrellas, and mud and water oozed beneath their tread. The thoroughfare was blocked in places with cabs all full of people going off upon their holidays, for it was Christmas week. Bells were heard fitfully, calling the faithful to the churches to prepare to celebrate the birth of Him who died upon the Cross to bring peace to the earth.

The trees which overhang the roadway by the park dropped inky showers upon the tramps sleeping or talking on the seats. The drops splashed on the stones and on the cross-board of the rest for porters' burdens which still survives, a relic of the past, between the cast-iron lamp-posts with their bright globes of light. Here and there at the corners of the streets that lead down to the artery between the parks stood women dressed fashionably, wearing large hats with ostrich feathers. True that their numbers were diminished, for an orgasm of virtue had recently swept over those who rule, and had decreed Vice should do homage to her twin-sister Virtue, but only on the sly. Still they were there, to show how much has been achieved for women by our faith, in the last thousand years. Policemen stood about upon their beats, stout and well fed, looking with scorn if a taxpayer in a threadbare coat passed by them, and ever ready, after the fashion of the world, to aid the rich, the strong, and those who did not need their help, and spurn the miserable.

During the week the churches had been thronged with worshippers. Some went to pray, others resorted to the fane from custom, and again, some from a vague feeling that religion was a bulwark reared in defence of property in seasons of unrest, though this of course they had not reasoned out, but felt instinctively, just as a man fears danger in the night upon a lonely road. Hymns had been sung and sermons preached inculcating goodwill, peace, charity and forbearance to the weak. Yet

London was as pitiless as ever, and the strong pushed the weak down in the gutter, actually and in the moral sphere. Women were downtrodden, except they happened to be rich, though men talked chivalry whilst not refraining for an instant to take advantage of the power that law and nature placed within their reach. The animal creation seemed to have been devised by God to bring out all that was most base in man. If they were tame and looked to him as man, in theory, looks towards his God, he worked them pitilessly. Their loves, their preferences, their simple joys, attachments to the places where they had first seen the light and frisked beside their mothers in the fields, were all uncared for, even were subjects for derision and for mirth, if they were marked at all. If, on the other hand, they were of those, winged or four-footed, who had never bowed the knee or drooped the wing to man's dominion, their treatment was still worse. They had no rights, except of being killed at proper seasons, which were contrived so artfully that but a bare three months of the whole year was left unstained with blood. Woods in their thickest depths witnessed their agony. Deep in the corries of the hills, in fields, in rivers, on the land, the sea, and in the bowels of the earth they left their fellows, dumb, stricken, wretched, and died silently, wondering perhaps what crime they had committed in their lives so innocent and pure. No one commiserated them, for they were clearly sent into the world as living targets to improve man's power of shooting, or to be chased and torn to pieces in order to draw out the higher feelings of his self-esteem and give him opportunity to say, as their eyes glazed in death, There is one flesh of man, and yet another of the beasts, all glory to His name.

Through the soft rain the roar of the great city rose, though dulled and deadened, still menacing and terrible, as if the worst of human passions, as always happens in a crowd, had got the upper hand, and were astir to wreak themselves on any object ready to their hand. Machines ran to and fro, noisy and sending forth mephitic fumes, and seeming somehow as if they were the masters, and the pale men who drove them only slaves of the great forces they had brought into their lives. They swerved and skated, bearing their fill of trembling passengers, and making every living thing give them the road on pain of mutilated limbs or death as horrible as by the car of some great idol in the East. No car of Juggernaut was half so terrible, and as they took their passage through the streets men shrank into the second place and seemed but to exist on sufferance, as tenders of machines.

Still, it was Christmas week, and the glad tidings preached so long ago, so fitted for the quiet ways and pastoral existence of those who heard them first, so strangely incongruous with us of modern times, were still supposed to animate men's minds. The night wore on, and through the sordid rows of stuccoed houses the interminable file of cabs, of carriages and motor omnibuses, still took its course, and trains of market-carts drawn by small puffing engines began to pass along the street. In them, high in the air, lying upon the heaped-up vegetables or seated on the backboard clinging by one arm to the chain, boys slumbered, their heads swaying and wagging to and fro as the carts rumbled on the stones. Then the carts disappeared, and the remaining traffic increased its speed in the half-empty streets, the drivers, anxious to get home, shaving each other's wheels in haste or carelessness. Round coffee-stalls stood groups of people in the flaring light of naphtha-lamps — soldiers, a man in evening dress, a street-walker or two, and some of those strange, hardly human-looking hags who only seem to rise from the recesses of the night, and with the dawn retreat into some Malebolge of the slums. The time and place had broken down all barriers of caste and they stood laughing at obscenities, primitive and crude, such as have drawn the laughter of mankind from the beginning of the world.

In the great open space between the junction of the parks, where on one side the hospital frowns on the paltry Græco-Cockney sham triumphal arch, just underneath the monolith from which the bronze, Iron Duke looks down upon the statues of the men he qualified as "blackguards" in his life, a little crowd surrounded something lying on the ground. A covered van, battered and shabby, stood, with a broken shaft. Under the wheels the mud was stained with a dark patch already turning black, and the smashed shaft was spotted here and there with blood. A heap of broken harness lay in a pile, and near it on its side a horse with a leg broken by a motor omnibus. His coat was dank with sweat, and his lean sides were raw in places with the harness, that he would wear no more. His neck was galled with the wet collar which was thrown upon the pile of harness, its flannel lining stained with the matter of the sores which scarcely healed before work opened them again. The horse's yellow teeth, which his lips, open in his agony, disclosed, showed that he was old and that his martyrdom was not of yesterday. His breath came painfully and his thin flanks heaved like a wheezy bellows in a smithy, and now and then one of his legs contracted and was drawn up to his belly and then extended slowly till the shoe clanked upon the ground. The broken leg, limp and bedaubed in mud, looked like a sausage badly filled, and the protruding splinter of the bone showed whitely through the skin.

The little crowd stood gazing at him as he lay not without sympathy but dully, as if they too were over-driven in their lives.

Then came a policeman who, after listening to the deposition of the owner of the horse, took out a little book, and having written in it briskly with a stumpy pencil, returned it to his pocket with an air of having done his duty and passed on upon his way.

The electric lamps flared on the scene. In the deserted park the wind amongst the trees murmured a threnody, and on the road the dying horse lay as a rock sticks up, just in the tideway of a harbour, thin, dirty, overworked, castrated, underfed, familiar from his youth with blows and with ill-treatment, but now about to be set free.

Caisteal-na-Sithan

It was indeed a castle of the elves. Over all, hung an air of melancholy. From the deserted lodge, behind the high, beech hedge, which shut the place off from the lake, the avenue led through a sea of billowy mounds, on which grew trees as thickly as in the tropics, some dead and some decaying, some broken off by storms and left to die or live just as they chose.

Moss had spread like a carpet over the deeply rutted road.

Here and there by its side stood foreign shrubs, some of them growing rankly, and others which had died years ago, standing up dry and sere, inside their iron cages, as a dead body in a life-belt floats upon the sea. The bracken met the lower branches of the trees and formed a screen, through which rabbits had made their runs, like little railway tunnels.

They fed upon the mossy grass outside, retreating slowly when they were alarmed, conscious they were at home, and that a passer-by was an intruder into their domain. Where the trees fell, they lay and rotted, covered with lichens and with a growth of ferns that sprang from the dead bark.

The neglected woods seemed to have bred a strange and hostile air. Instinctively one looked around, as if some power of nature, which cultivation kills, was still unchecked, had just declared a war upon mankind, and was about to open its attack.

The passing of a roe through the deep underwood, a passage ordinarily so fairy-like and light, there, sounded ominous, and the sharp cracking of a decaying twig under its flying feet, or the soft rustling of its body through the ferns, sent a thrill through the listener, as if some monstrous creature of a dream were going to appear.

Even in summer everything seemed dank, and in the peaty soil the water oozed beneath the footsteps, making the ground seem treacherous and false.

Sometimes at sunset, when a red gleam fell on the top of oaks, turned all the bracken fiery, and lighted up the overhanging hills which peeped above the tops of the high trees, the air of menace was dispelled and a breath from the outer world brought back security. When the last gleams had vanished, and a cold, chilly air, especially before the autumn frost, crept through the brakes and stirred the frozen tufts of bulrushes in the black, awful-looking ponds, fringed with dark rhododendrons, and set about upon one side with towering spruce firs, a panic seemed to creep into the soul.

The thick, white mists that rose up from the pool hung in the trees, and seemed as if they were alive, so stealthily they crept about the branches, and twined like serpents, twisting and writhing in the air.

Owls floated like gigantic moths across the avenue, or sat and called to one another in the recesses of the woods. All was so silent and so still, you seemed to feel the waves of sound that floated from their call, just as one hears the whirring of an old eight-day clock before it strikes its bell. In the low park beyond the wood, through which the avenue led to the house, the dun or creamy Highland cattle slept on the hillocks, to shun the draughts of night. A chilly damp rose from the old bog-land, long since reclaimed, but showing black and peaty where moles had made their hills, which dotted the sour grass at intervals, and in the moonlight looked like animals asleep. A great moss ditch cut the low park in two, and in it the black, frozen water seemed like a stream of pitch. Birches and stunted oaks were set about the fields, their old, gnarled roots laid bare by winter rains, and by the stamping of the cattle in the summer, when they stood underneath the trees to shelter from the flies. Through the long, limb-like roots, rabbits had burrowed, and here and there a heavy stone was left, stuck in the crevices, looking like some lost weapon of the Stone Age, or prehistoric club.

Just where the deep moss ditch crossed underneath the road, a high, iron, double gate barred off the avenue.

Beyond it stretched a gloomy road, winding between dark trees. At night, when you rode through it, your horse snorting occasionally when rabbits ran across the path, or birds stirred in the trees, it felt as if you were a thousand miles from help. In front, the dark road wound, as it seemed, interminably, through overhanging trees. Between you and the world was the half-mile or so of the mysterious woods, and the black, sullen ponds.

At last, passing another gate, it led up to a shrubbery. A mossy burn fed a neglected duck-pond, upon whose waters floated feathers, and round whose sides grew tufts of pampas grass. Tall bushes of wygelia and syringa, dead at the sides but vigorous in the middle, with flowering currants, andromeda and rank-growing thickets of guelder rose and dogwood, concealed the house from view.

The rabbit netting, nailed to the fencing of the park, was broken here and there, and billowed like a sail. Through it the rabbits entered as they pleased, burrowing beneath the bushes, and leaving trails which led up to the lawn. Enormous beeches, and a sycamore or two, growing like cabbages, showed that at one time the neglected policies had been well cared for, and the decayed and mouldering rustic seats, set about here and there, recalled the time when children played upon the lawn, whilst nurses sat and watched them underneath the trees. The house itself, high and steep-roofed, with pepper-boxes at the angles, and a wide flight of steps, upon whose parapet two great iron eagles, that once had been all painted in the proper colours of the coat of arms of which they formed the crest, was desolate and drear. The rough-cast plaster, which at one time had covered all the walls, had fallen in patches here and there, leaving great blotches that looked like maps, upon its sides.

Right opposite the door, a roundel of rank grass, once closely shaven, but now rank and ill-tended, lay like an island in the road. Two whinstone posts, with eight-shaped irons at their sides, for hitching horses to in times gone by, just raised their heads above the turf.

The house door, left ajar, but yet made fast against the world by a confining chain, with the bolt running in a tube, gave just the touch of human interest required to accentuate the melancholy of the forlorn abode.

As one peeped through into the hall, covered with a well-worn oilcloth, and marked the absence of sticks, hats, umbrellas, and all that goes to give a hall a look of being the introduction to a comfortable home, one felt the owner was a solitary man, who in the summer evenings, when the owls hooted faintly in the recesses of the woods and swallows hawked at flies across the lawn, sat on the parapet of the tall flight of broken steps, between his iron eagles, and meditated on what might have been, had things gone differently.

Beyond the hall few ever penetrated, for an old woman, holding the door fast in her hand, used to peep out and answer, "The laird is oot," and then when the chance visitor had turned away disconsolate, flatten her nose against a window and watch him stumble down the road. The great, old Scottish stable, built round a courtyard, with the decaying clock upon its tower, one hand long lost, the other pointing eternally to twelve, stood, buried in the trees, whose branches swept the slates, showering them down upon the grass in gales, and dropping ceaselessly in rain, till a green lichen grew just underneath the drip.

Most of the doors had gone, and those that still fought on against the rain and wind were kept in place by pieces of coarse leather, roughly nailed on the jambs. Upon the wooden sheathing of the pump, hay seed had sprouted, growing a rank crop of grass, which in its turn had died, and hung all mildewed and with small drops of moisture oozing from the stems.

Such was the place, one of the last examples of the old Scotland which has sunk below the waves of Time. Perhaps, not an example to be followed, but yet to be observed, remembered, even regretted in the great drabness of prosperity which overspreads the world.

Few people ever trod the avenue, and even tramps but rarely camped in the deserted woods, though fallen trees were plentiful, and none would have been the wiser if they had stayed a week. The owner, an old sailor who had inherited the place in middle life, had by degrees become such a recluse that sometimes weeks would pass without his being seen. Shut off from all the world, he lived with an old housekeeper, as it were in a wilderness, and if by chance he met a stranger on the road would dive behind the bushes to escape, like a wild animal. Now and then far-off relations would come down to shoot, stopping at some hotel, and now and then a neighbour would drive over, always to be received by the old housekeeper with the same formula, "The laird is oot."

Occasionally he left the country and went abroad, but always to some place near the seaside, where he would pass long hours looking at ships, though without making any friends. Lübeck and Kiel, Riga or Genoa, were his favourite haunts, and those who met him at any of those ports used to report having seen him, dressed in his blue serge suit, and with the air of being the one man left in a depopulated world, in the same way that captains jot down in their log, "In such a latitude, in the first dog-watch passed a derelict."

By degrees his visits to far-off ports grew rarer, and at last he seldom passed the gates of his neglected grounds, except occasionally on Sundays, when he attended church, reserved and silent, speaking to none, but yet a little critical, after the fashion of a man who had read prayers on board his ship, and therefore should know something of the way in which a service ought to be carried on.

On these occasions he would stand a little in the churchyard, looking intently at a sort of pen, surrounded by a broken iron railing, in which his ancestors reposed.

Whether his thoughts ran on the unstability *[sic]* of life, or if he only tried to make a calculation of the probable expense he would incur if he embarked upon repairs, was never known to anyone, although some said he thought of neither, but merely leaned against the rails to pass the time until the congregation had dispersed, and left him free to set off home again.

Everyone speculated on his death, some saying that it would occur some day when he was quite alone, out in the woods, and others that he would be found dead in his chair, with the *Pacific Pilot* open in his hand. Not a bad book for an old sailor to have consulted, when just about to weigh his anchor; but as it happened he had to make his landfall, unassisted and alone.

A bitter frost, intense and black, had bound the district, congealing the dark waters of the lake into a sheet of glass. Trees groaned and cracked, and in the silent woods a shudder seemed to run through the gaunt avenues, as if they suffered from the cold. Crows winged their way, looking like notes of music on an old page of parchment, across the leaden sky.

High in the air there passed strings of wild geese, and in the stillness of the frost their melancholy cry was heard, till they were almost out of sight.

All nature seemed engaged in a stern fight for life, with some calamity which had attacked it unawares. The very streams stood still to watch the progress of the battle, fast in their bonds of ice.

Somehow or other, after the fashion that in Africa news travels always a day or two ahead of any traveller, it got about the countryside the laird was missing from his home. As, in the little inn, the constable, "the post," one or two farmers, and the innkeeper were talking of the report, the housekeeper was seen hobbling along the road. Coughing and wheezing, she averred she "couldna bide alane, up in yon awfu' house." The laird, it seemed, upon the evening of the commencement of the frost, had gone out, as was usual, just before tea-time, but never had come back. She had waited for two days, setting his meals upon the table at the stated hours, and at night putting out a lantern at the front door to guide him to the house. A day and night had broken down her courage, and given her the strength to find her way alone through the deserted avenue, for, as she said, "If she had passed anither nicht alane wi' all they bogles and they howlets, she would have gone fair gyte."

All search was useless. The woods and moors guarded their secret, and had not chance revealed it, the disappearance of the laird would have been put down as the last eccentricity of an eccentric life.

Fate was not willing that the laird's last resting-place should not be known, for as some boys were skating on one of the black ponds they saw what they took for bird's feathers, frozen in the ice. When they came home, trembling and pale, they said the feathers turned out to be the hair on a man's head, and that below the ice they had seen something that "lookit like a muckle fish, and frichted them to death."

At once the sparse inhabitants of the wild district proceeded to the place, entering the sacred grounds from which they had been debarred for years. Their lanterns, glimmering like glow-worms over the dark pond, and shedding a fantastic light on the black ice, outlining every branch upon the leafless trees, and playing on the clump of rhododendrons on the bank, gave a strange air of unreality to everything around.

One of the boys pointed out the spot, and as the ice was frozen so intensely, on the clear, windless night, they saw beneath it the laird's body, in the same way that you can see a fish which has been taken by the frost.

When they had cut it out, framed in a square of ice, he was so life-like, laid upon the bank, in the dim, quavering light of the horn lanterns, that those who saw him always used to say, "You'd hae just thocht the laird was sleepin', if he had na been sae gash."

Immortality

He stopped his oxen, with a prolonged low cry, and standing just in front of them with one hand on the yoke, the other resting on his goad, which he held like a spear, stuck upright in the ground, he said, after due compliments, as people say when they translate an Eastern letter, "I see you are looking at it."

The object that I saw was a strange building, something like a Moorish saint's tomb, but with a burnished copper roof, reflecting back the sun. It stood out, garish and vulgar, just beyond the old, brown walls of a Castilian town, built on the slopes of a gaunt sierra, at whose feet ran one of those deep, greenish rivers only seen in Spain. A mediæval palace of warm, yellow stone, the tower of the collegiate church, the strange and burnt-up country stretching almost to the walls without a suburb intervening, or a stray villa dotted here and there to break the sea of brown, rendered the building still more paltry in its meretriciousness. Lighting a cigarette slowly and painfully with a flint and steel, the bullock-driver, leaning against the yoke of his great tawny oxen, said: "Yes, what you see there we call the 'mushroom tomb.' A lady built it as you see it now, one of those modernists, who go about in motorcars, frightening the oxen and killing all our dogs. Now it is finished she does not like it, and, I hear, is going to pull it down, as she has done two others that she built. She goes on building tombs, as if one tomb was not enough to be forgotten by, as other folk build houses. Fools build a house, they say, for other men to live in, and so perhaps the Countess may build her tomb not for herself, for she may die at sea or in some foreign place."

I thanked him, and he, after accepting a cigar, which he proceeded to cut up for cigarettes, cutting it on his hand with a clasp knife a foot in length that opened with a series of clicks, gravely saluted me, stuck his goad into the near ox, in the loose skin upon its neck, and with a drawn-out *Anda-a-a* set out again towards the town. I walked towards the tomb, and saw that it was empty, unfinished, and half-plastered, and that above the door there was a monstrous coat of arms, just underneath the cross. It stood in a flat waste of gravel, which had been carted from the river, and was already disappearing in the cracked, thirsty ground. Looking more closely, I found what I had thought was copper on the roof, were tiles of orange glass, laid overlapping, like planks in a boat built clinker-wise. Half-finished stones lay here and there, with broken wheelbarrows and bent and rusty picks. The monstrous building stood upon the plain, alone, ridiculous, and yet pathetic in its ugliness, and in the evident intent of her who built it to leave some recollection of herself when she was gone.

Years passed, and I forgot the "mushroom tomb," the old Castilian town with its harsh Moorish name, the sierra, and the river, edged with willows, looking like a thin green ribbon dropped in the dusty plain. Madrid, from the mere village of my youth, with its ill-paved and tortuous streets, set here and there with convents, and broken here and there with rambling palaces roofed with brown tiles, almost by accident became a modern town. Seville went at a bound from a great, silent Moorish city, where no one but a gipsy or a beggar walked in the streets by day, to a tourist centre, with paltry little shops full of cheap fans and tambourines, on which were set forth views of the Giralda, gipsies with eyes as big as oysters, and heads of bull-fighters. Cheap castagnettes, made of unseasoned wood and warranted to crack the first time they were used, with raw-looking guitars and tinselled-handled knives all made in Birmingham or Lille, but duly lettered with inscriptions such as "Do not draw me without cause or sheathe me without honour," were hawked about the streets by turnpike bull-fighters who never faced a bull. Tramways ran through the narrow Calle de Genova that leads to the Cathedral, and bands of tourists haunted the cafés and the dancing-halls, urging the gipsy dancers to fresh indecencies, unknown to them in unsophisticated days.

Bilbao and Barcelona had become great hives of industry, the latter having developed into a Manchester or Birmingham with great tree-planted streets and a new suburb stretching out towards the hills. The walls had been demolished, and the old quays just underneath them, where once lay the fruit schooners, painted light green or white, with tapering masts and spars, and with a figurehead of Flora, or Pomona, carved and gilt, had turned to docks, from which great liners took away their droves of emigrants. Places remote as Ronda had blossomed forth in great hotels, with liveried touts standing about their doors, and speaking every language, without the smallest notion of its grammar or its form. In fact, progress had come to the more frequented parts of Spain. People in them no longer spoke of any foreigner as *El Francés*, and prices, which of course keep step with progress, had risen mightily. In fact, an air of skin-deep Europeisation *[sic]* had come upon the land, obscuring almost all the national virtues, in the favoured spots where it prevailed, and bringing out all that was worst in Spanish character.

Business or pleasure, or something of the sort, took me once more to Guadalcázar to find the scene unchanged. When the slow, rumbling train had drawn up at the little station, sweltering in the sun, two or three red and yellow omnibuses, drawn by thin mules or white, apocalyptic horses, harnessed with rope, and having nearly every one an open sore upon some part of him, described by Spanish drivers as a *flor*, waited to rattle one up the steep, stony road. Whips cracked, bells jingled, and the thin windows rattled with a noise like thunder, whilst the rough, wooden box on wheels bounded and skated on the stones. People, who must have seen it every day for years, turned out to watch it pass, in the same way they thronged the railway station every night to watch the arrival of the train from Barcelona to Madrid. Girls waved their handkerchiefs and men shouted *Adios Pepe* to the driver as if he had been setting out upon a journey of a hundred miles.

At last, battered and sore with the long twenty minutes' struggle not to be thrown against the roof, the instrument of torture stopped with a jerk outside the doorway, where sat the owner of the inn. Nothing proclaimed his status, except an air of great detachment, which seemed to indicate he was a stranger in the town. He sat, with a chair tilted up against the wall, smoking one of those oily, black cigars called *Brevas*, which only Spaniards of his class can smoke and not expire at the last puff. His spotless shirt was open at the neck, and his broad face, close shaved and blue, gave him a look as of a bullfighter, who had made money and retired. I was the only passenger, and one might have thought he would have welcomed me; but beyond a grave answer to my salutation, nothing was farther from his mind. He thought there was a room, and was just making up his mind to call to somebody to show me to it, when looking at me he said, "I think I have the honour. Were you not here ten or twelve years ago?"

A ragged boy having taken up my bag to a bare room which seemed never to have been swept since my last visit to the place, I threw the window open, and sitting down looked out upon a grassy, half-deserted square. A feeling as of having been marooned on some lone island crept on me as I watched two horses playing on the grass. No one regarded them as they chased one another up and down. At times a cat stole timidly across a street, just as a tiger steals across a forest glade, as stealthily and with an air as far detached from man. At last even the horses ceased their play and stood hanging their heads under a scanty-foliaged tree. Nothing was stirring in the town, and the hot open space was given over to the crickets, whose shrill chirp sounded so loud that one forgot a silence as of death hung over everything. Later on, as the breeze coming from the hills recalled the town to life, I strolled out on to the hot road, bordered on each side with heat-dried, ill-grown acacias, and followed it outside the town to where I now remembered that the "mushroom tomb" had stood.

Looking towards the place, I rubbed my eyes, for certainly a building occupied the place, but changed indeed, from the domed cupola, crowned with its yellow glass. Gone were the walls with their raised Moorish tracery; gone were the dazzling tiles, and in their place a Gothic structure with flying buttresses and gimcrack pinnacles stood, white and glittering, a newer and a more foolish mushroom than the last. The gravelly waste still stretched around it, and the same litter of a stone-mason's yard, the picks and shovels, wheelbarrows, and chips of stone, were strewed about the walls. Only the coat of arms, but now grown rather weather-beaten, was let into a niche above the door. The arid plain scorching and sweltering in the sun, the old embattlemented town, the river winding between its poplars, and the giant sierra, towering beyond the walls, gave the fantastic tomb a look as of a travelling circus, playing in some old, Roman amphitheatre. A shepherd stood immovable and brown, and looking like a trunk of a dead tree, as he leant on his stick, guarding a flock of brown-woolled *[sic]* sheep, who searched amongst the stones for any herbage that had escaped the drought. When they strayed out of bounds he cracked his sling, unwinding it from where he wore it, wrapped above his sash. They, knowing a shower of stones would follow if they disobeyed, put up their heads, then turned and fed towards him as he stood like a landmark on the plain. Unchanging and unchanged he stood, just as his forefathers must have looked, brown-cloaked and sun-tanned at the reconquest from the Moors.

Nothing but a poor wooden cross would mark his burial-place; a wooden cross, that in a year or two would rot and fall; nothing but a brown post he looked, standing so silently, with all his flock, now feeding quietly around him, and well within the distance of a sling's cast of a stone. His great, brown dog, with its spiked collar round its neck, slept at his feet, changing position when he moved, to keep itself within the shade its master's figure threw upon the ground. The red-roofed town. wild sierra, and the shepherd with his sling, his *angarina*, knotted quince-tree staff, his gnarled, brown hands, rough hempen sandals, his sheep-skin jacket, and his clear-cut features, shaded by a broad hat, such as was worn in Thessaly when the world was young, and men and gods so near to one another that goddesses came down and left Olympus, finding the love of men more satisfying than the serene embraces of their kind, all formed a picture of that Spain, now so fast passing.

Penelope may build her tomb, as she waits for the coming of her lord, him of the hour-glass and the scythe. Let her build on, the only lasting traces of a man's passage through the world are those that the brown, sling-girt figure that I saw standing in the middle distance, cast upon the sand.

Charity

A Meeting

It was, if I remember rightly, for it is more than thirty years ago, in the great stretch of forest between Caraguatá-Guazú and Caballero Punta, that the meeting which I think brought joy, at least for a short time to one of those concerned, took place. For miles the track ran through the woods; the trail worn deep into the red and sandy soil looked like a ribbon, dropped underneath the dark, metallic-foliaged trees.

At times a great fallen log, round which the parasitic vegetation had wrapped itself, turned the path off, just as a rock diverts the current of a stream. In places the road, opened long ago, most likely by the Jesuits, ran almost in the dark, under the intertwining ceibas and urandéys. Again, it came out on a clearing, in which a straw-thatched hut or two, with a scant patch of mandioca, an orange grove, and a thick bunch of plantains, marked a settlement. The fences were all broken, and peccaries had rooted up the crops. The oranges lay rotting underneath the trees, and as you passed along the solitary trail and came out on the clearings, flocks of green parakeets took wing from where they had been feeding in the deserted fields, and troops of monkeys howled. The four years' war had laid the country waste, and villages were left deserted, or at the best inhabited by women and by girls. In all that long, mosquito-haunted ride, that I remember, just as if I had ridden it a week ago, through the old Jesuit missions, between the Paraná and Paraguay, it was the rarest thing to meet a man, and rarer still to meet a horse. Occasionally you might come upon a family living alone amongst the woods, upon the edge of some old clearing; but if you did, they had no animals about the house but fowls.

At intervals you might chance to cross some wandering Correntino, dressed in the *poncho* and the bombachas of the Gaucho, journeying towards Asuncion; more rarely a Brazilian on his mule; but all the natives were on foot, most of the horses having been killed in the long war. The legend was that Lopez met his death on the last native Paraguayan horse, a little roan; but be that as it may, horses were rare to find, and the fierce nature of the Tropics had so reconquered all the cultivated land that there was little grass for them to eat. Fields that had once born *[sic]* mandioca were indistinguishable under a tangle of rank grass, dwarf palms and scrubby plants, whilst maize plantations had remained unsown, bearing but a few straggling plants, grown from the falling ears. Even the pathways through the woods had become impassable, through the thick growth of gnarled and knotty lianas, which, like a web of cordage, barred the way. Tigers abounded, and killed the few remaining horses, if they could catch them sleeping near the woods. Bats and mosquitoes, with enormous ticks, combined with several distempers, which the natives said had only come after the war, and when the country had begun to go back to the primeval forest, rendered a horse's life unbearable, and made him difficult to keep.

Those Paraguayans who had a horse cherished him as the apple of their eye, covering him up at night against the vampire bats, and bathing him at sunrise and at sunset to keep away ticks and mosquitoes and a thousand other crawling and flying plagues. Even with these precautions there yet remained the fear of snakes and poisonous weeds, so that a man who had a horse became a slave, and passed his time in caring for him and ministering to his welfare and his health. So as I jogged, that is, of course, walked, for the forest trails were far too deeply worn into the soil to jog with safety, I passed long strings of women, dressed in their low-cut sack-like garment, embroidered round the neck with black embroidery. Their hair, cut square across the forehead and hanging down their backs, gave them a mediæval air. All were barefooted, and all smoked thick cigars, which they kept lighted at the torch their leader carried in her hand to scare the jaguars. Upon their heads they carried baskets full of oranges, of mandioca, and of maize. Sometimes they all saluted, sometimes they only smiled and showed their teeth, and sometimes one of them would say, amidst the laughter of the rest, "We all want husbands," and added something else in Guarani that made a laugh run rippling down the line.

Occasionally a crashing in the bushes near the trail told of the passage of a tapir, through the underwood, and once as I came to a little clearing a tiger lay stretched flat upon a log, watching the fish in some dark backwater, just as a cat lies on the garden wall to watch the birds. Butterflies floated lazily about, scarce moving their broad, velvet wings, reminding one somehow of owls, flitting across a grass ride in a wood, noiseless, but startling by their very quietness.

The snakes, the humming-birds, the alligators basking in the creeks, the whir of insects and the metallic croaking of the frogs, the air of being in the grip of an all-powerful vegetation, reduced a man, travelling alone through the green solitude, to nothingness. One felt as if in all that wealth of vegetation and strange birds and beasts, one's horse were the one living thing that was of the same nature as oneself.

Had Balaam only heard his ass's voice in such a place, it would have sounded comforting to him, and might have cheered him on his way. The heat which poured down from the sun, in the few places where the track was open overhead, met the heat rising from the red, sandy soil and focussed on one's face, drying the blood that the innumerable flies had drawn, into hard, sticky flakes. After interminable hours of heat, and intervals of dozing from which one woke but just in time to save one's balance and to remember, shuddering, what would occur, if by mischance one fell and let the horse escape, alone, and miles away from any human habitation, the trail led out upon a little clearing in the sea of woods. Smoke curled from a fire under some orange trees, between whose branches hung a cotton hammock, with the fringe sweeping on the ground, as it swung to and fro, impelled by a brown foot.

To my astonishment my horse neighed shrilly, and was answered by a horse, which on first coming to the clearing I had overlooked. As I rode up, repeating as I rode, the formula, "Hail, blessed Virgin," being answered by the man who had been lying in the hammock, "Without sin conceived," I saw the horse was a red roan, fat and in good condition, and branded with the sign of Aries, set rather low upon the hip. The Paraguayan welcomed me, and bringing out two solid, wooden chairs with cowhide seats, tilted them up against the wall of his mud and straw-thatched hut, and we sat down to talk. His clothes were simple, and yet adequate enough considering the place. Upon his head he wore a home-made hat plaited from fibre of a palm leaf, and round his waist a leather apron, held in its place by two old, silver coins. With the exception of hide sandals on his feet, and a red cloak of baize hung loosely on one shoulder, he was as naked as the day on which he first drew breath upon the earth. For all that, in his bearing he was dignified enough, and after placing a long-barrelled gun which he had snatched up hastily when I approached his house, against the wall, but well within his reach, he sat down and motioning me to the other chair began to talk as a man talks who has been long alone. Where had I come from? and how was it that I was dressed like a Correntino, being as he imagined, a foreigner, perhaps a Spaniard, or some other "nation," that spoke no Guarani?

My horse, he did not know the brand, looked like a horse from the low countries down the river. I had better be careful of him, especially at night, or else the vampire bats would suck his blood. The tigers, too, were specially attracted to a white animal, but then white was such a colour for a gentleman, especially white with a black skin, suitable too for Paraguay, as a white horse is certain to swim well, and the old boat upon the Tebicuari had never been replaced, and I should have to cross in a canoe.

"Tell me," he said, "what are the 'nations' doing in Asuncion? Is there a government, and who is president? What, General Caballero? Ah, I remember him, a barefoot boy, running about till Lopez took his pretty sister to live with him. Madama Lynch was not well pleased at it . . . but then a president is just like God. What he wants, that he will have, be sure of it." It seemed his wife was dead or lost during the war, and when I pointed to some women, one pounding maize in a tall mortar, another picking oranges, and a third swinging in a white cotton hammock, he said, "Yes, women, as you see. In these times the poor things have got no husbands, and Christians have to do their best, out of pure charity."

Much did we talk about things interesting to men in Paraguay, the price of cattle and the like, the increase of tigers in the land, whether the road was open from Corrientes to Asuncion through the Estero Ñembucú, and if the Indians in the Chaco had been at what he called "their own," now that there was no law. On all these points I satisfied him as far as I was able, striving to make such news as I had gleaned upon my way, exact, but palatable.

When we had drunk a little *maté*, which after the Paraguayan country fashion was served quite cold, my host said, "By this time your horse's back must have got cool; one of the girls shall take him down to bathe."

As the girl led him past the roan, both neighed, and my host's horse reared and strove to break his rope.

When in a little the girl came back leading my horse all dripping from his bath, the roan with a wild plunge snapped his hide halter, and came galloping to meet my white, and, circling round him, at last stood with his red, wide-open nostrils close against his nose.

The horses seemed to talk, and mine plunged and would certainly have broken loose had not I run to him. My host, who had looked on with interest, told me his horse had been six months without once seeing

---

another of his kind. "Let your horse loose," he said, "to play with him. Neither is shod, and they can do no harm to one another; let him loose, then, to play." Placing some canes and brushwood to block the road, he said, "Now they are safe; they cannot get away, and horses never go into the thick woods, and if they did they cannot possibly go far."

Somewhat reluctantly I let my horse run loose, leaving his headstall with a *lazo* trailing on the ground, knowing a horse in South America, once loose, is never willing to be caught.

The Paraguayan smiled, and as my horse passed by him, caught and undid the *lazo*, saying, "I answer for him with my head, and in the galloping that they will make, the rope would be a danger to them; besides, your horse will never try to get away."

For hours the horses played, leaping about like lambs, galloping to and fro, now rearing up and now coming down with their legs across each other's shoulders on their backs. At nightfall we caught and tied them close to each other, and after feeding them with maize cut down bundles of green *pindó,* heaping it up before them for the night. When we had had our supper, which, if I remember after thirty years, was a rough stew of rice and charqui, which we ate using our long knives for spoons, we sat against the corner of the house, swinging our tilted chairs. The women brought us green cigars, and one of them, taking a cracked guitar, some of whose strings were mended up with copper wire and some with bits of hide, sang what is called a *Triste*, as the fireflies flitted through the trees.

"Don Rigoberto," said my host (for my own name was unfamiliar to him, and to pronounce it with more ease he altered it, perhaps for euphony), "look at the animals." I looked, and they had finished eating and stood with their heads resting on each other's shoulders, like the advertisement of Thorley's food for cattle, which I remember in my youth at railway stations. "Two years," he said, "I was in prison in Asuncion, in the time of Lopez, not the one that José Diabo killed at Tacurupitá but his old father Don Antonio. Days passed, and weeks and years, and all the time I never saw a man, for they let down my food and water by a string. When I got out, the first man that I met was to me as a long-lost brother. . . . I went and kissed him in the street. Therefore, Don Rigoberto, I know what my horse feels alone here in this *roza*, with not a soul of his own kind to say a word to him. This day has been a *fiesta* for him, and now let us repeat the rosary, and then to bed. . . . To-morrow is another day."

Charity

I fear the part I took in the repetition of the simple prayers was fragmentary; but at the break of day, or, to be accurate, about an hour before the dawn, I saddled up and bade my host good-bye. As I rode out into the dewy trail a thick white mist enveloped everything. It blotted out the lonely clearing in the first few yards. It dulled the shrill, high neighings of the roan, who plunged and reared upon his rope. Through the long, silent alleys of the primeval forest they sounded fainter as I rode, until at last they ceased, leaving their sadness still echoing after thirty — or is it five-and- thirty? — years, fixed in my memory.

San Andrés

Someone or other has said the dead have a being of their own, as we confess by saying such a one is dead, just as we say he is alive.

The author of the saying seems to have felt the dead had feelings and were not merely essences purified, quite separate and unapproachable by us. Few wish to see, even to think about, their dead "crowned with an aureole." We want them just as they were, just as we knew them, in their life. The rest is vanity, vanity of vanities, and all the creeds are impotent to help. At best they are an anæsthetic, such as curare, which holds the suffering animal paralysed, so that the operator may not feel the pain that it endures or get his hands scratched. So we grieve on, watching the trees turn red and yellow in the fall, blossom again in spring, and be alive with bees in summer, in winter swaying and cracking in the wind.

This is because we never feel the dead have a distinct and real being of their own. In olden times, in Scotland, people thought differently, and it was held that too much grieving for the dead, vexed them and broke their rest.

I remember once, coming long years ago to an outlying settlement in the province of Buenos Aires, where all the people came, I think, from Inverness-shire; but, anyhow, once on a time they had been Scotch. Their names were Highland, but were pronounced by those who bore them after the Spanish way, as Camerón, and McIntyré, McLeán, Fergusón, and others, which they had altered in the current of their speech, so as to be unrecognisable except to those who spoke the language and knew the names under their proper forms.

None of these Scoto-Argentines spoke English, although some knew a few words of Gaelic, which I imagine they pronounced as badly as their names.

Four generations — for most of them had left their glens after Culloden — had wrought strange changes in the type. They all were dark, tall, sinewy men, riders before the Lord, and celebrated in the district where they lived as being *muy gaucho* — that is, adroit with bolas and lasso, just as the Arabs say a man, is a right Arab, when they commend his skill in horsemanship. Having left Scotland after the Forty-Five, most of their forebears had been Catholics, and their descendants naturally belonged to the same faith, though as there was no church in all their settlement I fancy most of them believed rather in meat cooked in the hide and a good glass either of Caña or Carlón, than dogmas of their creed.

Horses stood nodding in the sun before the door of every house.

Packs of gaunt, yellow dogs slumbered, with one eye open, in the shade.

The bones of the last cow killed lay in the little plaza of the settlement, and bullock-carts, with cumbrous, high wheels and thatched like cottages, were left as islands here and there in the great sea of grass that surged up to the houses, without a garden or a cultivated field to break its billowing.

Two little stores, in which were piled up hides and sacks of wood, supplied the place with the few outside luxuries the people used, as sardines, black cigarettes, figs, raisins, bags of hard biscuits, sugar, red wine from Catalonia, and Caña from Brazil.

Climate had proved a stronger force than race, and for the most part the descendants of the Gael were almost indistinguishable in looks from all the other dwellers on the plains. They themselves did not think so, and talked about their neighbours with a fine scorn as "natives," and were paid back in kind by them with the nickname of "*Protestantes,*" a most unjust reproach to the descendants of the men who lost their all for their old kings and faith.

Protestants they certainly were not, nor for that matter very Catholic, for, as a general rule, people who dwell on plains, far from the world, have less religion than those who live in hills. Still, in the settlement of San Andrés — for the first settlers had called it after the patron saint of their old home — some of their racial traits still lingered fitfully. Born in a country where neither sweet religion nor her twin sister superstition ever had much influence upon the people (who ever saw a Gaucho either religious or the least superstitious?), in San Andrés a belief in fairies and the second sight still lingered in men's minds, with many a superstition more consonant with mountains and with mists, than the keen atmosphere and the material life of the wild southern plains.

Unlike the Gauchos and the Arabs, who bury, as it seems, in the most open place that they can find, leaving the dead, as it were, always with the living, as if they thought the pressure of a passing foot somehow brought consolation to those lying beneath the ground, these Protestants railed off their little cemetery with a high fence of ñandubay. The untrimmed posts stuck up knotty and gnarled just as they do in a corral, but all the graves had head- and foot-stones, mostly of hard and undecaying wood, giving an air as of a graveyard in Lochaber by some deserted strath.

There, "Anastasio McIntyré, killed by the Indians," rested in peace. "May God have mercy on him."

A little further on, "Cruz Camerón, assassinated by his friends," expected glory through the intermediation of the saints. "Passers-by, pray for him."

Amparo, widow of Rodrigo Chisholm, lost at sea, had reared a monument in stone, brought from the capital, on which was cut a schooner foundering, with a man praying on the poop. Her pious faith in his salvation and a due sense of local colour showed themselves in a few lines of verse in which the poet, whilst deploring the sad fate of Roderick, cut off so far away from wife and family, was confident that heaven was just as close at sea as on *la tierra firme*, and that the Lord High Admiral Christ watched over seafarers.

Such was the village, or, as the Gauchos used to say, the *pago*, for, for a league or two on every side, these Scoto-Argentines were the chief settlers upon the land. Indians occasionally harried their flocks and herds, and burned outlying ranches, but nowhere found stouter resistance than from the dwellers in San Andrés, so that, as a general rule, they used to leave the settlement alone.

The patriarchal manners which their forefathers had brought from the Highlands, joined to the curious old-fashioned customs common in those days in Buenos Aires, had formed a race apart, in which Latin materialism strove with the Celtic fervour, and neither gained the day.

A grave sententiousness marked all the older men, whose speech was an amalgam of strange proverbs, drawn from their daily lives. They used to pass their evenings playing the guitar and improvising couplets, whilst the square bottle of trade gin went round, each sipping from the same glass and passing it along. "Never go to a house to ask for a fresh horse when you see that the dogs are thin," one tall, red-bearded man would say, to which his fellow answered, "Arms are necessary, but no one can tell when." "A scabby calf lives all the winter and dies when spring comes in," and "When a poor man has a spree something is sure to turn out wrong with him," were specimens of their wit and humour, not much inferior after all, to those recorded of much greater men than them, in serious histories.

Sheep-shearings and cattle-markings were their festivities, and now and then, on their best horses, loaded down with plate, they tilted at the ring. The grassy pampa, stretching like the sea on every side of them, but broken as with islands here and there by white *estancia* houses set in their ring of peach groves, limited their horizon, just as a sailor's view is limited on board a ship, to a scant league or two.

In that horizon all of them were born, and most of them had never passed outside of it, except some few who upon rare occasions had gone to Buenos Aires with a troop of cattle, and had returned to talk about its wonders for the remainder of their lives.

Still, none of them were boors, but had the natural good manners both of the Gaucho and the Highlander. The forms of courtesy were long and ceremonious, and when friends met upon the plain, reining their horses in to show how sharply they were bitted, they used to ask minutely after each other's health and of the state in which each member of the family found himself, and then, with an inquiry after a strayed colt, touching their stiff-brimmed hats with a brown, weather-beaten finger, just slack their reins a little, and separate, each going at a slow canter through the grass, the wind blowing their *poncho*s out like sails, and making their long hair wave about like a great bunch of water-weeds moved by the current of a stream.

This was the settlement which no doubt long ago has turned into a town, with modern improvements, electric lights and drains, beggars and churches; and the few settlers of the older type most probably have all retired into the wilder districts or become millionaires by the increasing value of their lands.

There, though, the older spirit ruled, and the men who spoke Gaelic, or even those whose fathers once had spoken what they called *el Gaelico*, were looked upon as the interpreters of the spirit of the race. Of these Don Alejandro Chisholm was the chief.

Tall and grey-bearded, he had that look of shagginess which marks the Highlander. Though he knew but a few words himself, his father used to croon old Gaelic songs, and all his childhood had been passed listening to the traditions which his people treasured in their minds. Somehow they looked upon them as their chief distinction, and seemed to feel by their possession that they were in some way or another superior to the rest of those with whom they lived, the men who passed their lives caring for nothing but the present, whilst they lived in the past.

Don Alejandro used to say: "A native has very little soul. When a friend dies he never thinks of him again, and still less sees him. We, on the other hand, have glimpses now and then of those who leave us, but whose spirits hover about the places that they love."

His daughter, Saturnina, a tall, dark girl, willowy and slight, had married Anacleto, her first cousin, and thus, as her father, with true Highland pride in lineage, used to observe, had never changed her name. Her husband, Anacleto, was an amalgam of the Scot and Argentine. Speaking no word of English or of Gaelic, he yet esteemed himself as half a foreigner, although he was a Gaucho to the core. He and his wife were married in a church, a circumstance which marked them out, and people speaking of them used to say they were the couple "married in Latin," which gave them much consideration and a sort of rank. Whether because of the unusual sanctity that blessed their union, from accident or natural causes, their marriage was so happy that throughout the settlement people spoke of a happy couple as being as well mated as *el matrimonio Chisholm*, and looked on them with pride, as being somehow on a different plane from those who perhaps were married by some ambulatory priest, after their children had been born.

They had no children, and perhaps on that account were more attached to one another than are those couples whose love is, as it were, dispersed, having more objects on which to spend itself.

There seemed to grow between them that curious identity of mind which comes to all women and all men who have lived long together, but in their case was so much marked that they divined beforehand each other's thoughts, and acted on them almost without words. On the long journeys which the husband took with cattle, his wife used to declare she always knew all he was thinking of, and he, on his return, either to please her, or because she really had guessed right, always confirmed her words. The idea of death sometimes must have presented itself before their minds, but, like most happy people, probably only as a calamity, which might befall humanity in general, but could not touch themselves.

Don Alejandro, who in his long life had seen misfortunes, and was the last of all his race except his daughter, used to look sadly on them, and shaking his grey head, say with a sigh: "God grant I may not live to see the death of either of them. The children, though it is a bad comparison, Lord pardon me for likening Christians to brute beasts, remind me of two horses that I had that followed one another. One broke its neck out ostrich-hunting, and the other never seemed right, and pined in misery after its friend had died."

The inevitable came, when Anacleto was away, far on the southern frontier, out on the boleada, beyond the Napostá.

Never before had he been so long separated from his wife. Three months had passed, and now, as he drew close to San Andrés, riding a tired horse, brown, dirty, and with the oppression that the north wind often brings in Buenos Aires weighing upon his mind, the well-known objects seemed to rise out of the plain, just as an island seems to rise out of the sea, although the men on board the ship know it is there, and have been laying off their course to make it, since the beginning of their voyage. He saw the peach montés which he had known from childhood circling his neighbours' farms. He crossed the sluggish, muddy stream, bordered with dark green sarandis, hitting the pass with the unerring accuracy of the man born upon the plains. Feeling his horse's mouth, he touched him with the spur, and struck into a lope. Passing the little inequalities of ground, the swells and billows which the dwellers on the pampa know as lomas or cuchillas, and recollect as well as Scotchmen recollect their hills, though they are almost imperceptible to strangers, he saw the well-remembered old ombú tree of the settlement. Eyes just as keen as were his own had seen him too, and to his great surprise a horseman galloped out to meet him, and as he came a little nearer he recognised the well-known piebald that Don Alejandro cherished as the apple of his eye. Sitting upright in the saddle, and swaying lightly, as if he had been five-and-twenty, to every movement of his horse, Don Alejandro rapidly drew near. Just about twenty yards from where his son-in-law was labouring along on his tired horse he checked the piebald, and stopped as if turned instantly to stone. "Welcome, my son," he said. "Your horse looks tired, but he will take you home quite soon enough."

The words froze upon Anacleto's lips when he looked at the old man's countenance and saw how white and drawn he had become.

"Tell me at once!" he cried; "I see the tidings in your face of evil augury."

When they had drawn a little nearer Don Alejandro grasped his hand, and after looking at the horse his son-in-law bestrode, pointed towards the little cemetery, and said: "Let us go there, my son. . . . If we go slowly your horse can carry you."

Dismounting at the gate, they tied their horses to a post, and entering, the old man led the traveller up to a little mound.

"Underneath this our treasure lies," he murmured gravely, and with the air of one who has got done with tears after long weeks of grief.

They stood and gazed, holding each other's hands, until Don Alejandro said: "Weep, son, for God has given tears for the soul's health. . . . Laughter and tears are the two things that lift us higher than the beasts."

His son-in-law threw himself on the grave, driving his fingers into the black soil, and lay there, tired, dirty, and unkempt, like a great wounded bird.

At last he felt a hand upon his shoulder, and heard a voice, which seemed to come from a great distance, saying: "Come, let us go now, and let our horses loose. In half an hour it will be night."

When they had reached their home they both unsaddled. The piebald, with a neigh, bounded away into the night, but Anacleto's horse stood for a moment, and then lay down and rolled, and rising, shook the dust out of his coat, just as a water-dog shakes himself after a long swim.

" He will do well," Don Alejandro said. "When a horse rolls like that after a journey it is a sign that he is strong."

Over the *maté*, seated round the fire, on the low, solid, wooden benches men used to use out on the pampa, the wanderer heard of how his wife had died.

Next day he passed seated upon her grave, silent and stupefied with grief.

Then for a day or two he lounged about, going down to the cemetery at intervals and looking through the posts, like some wild animal.

Weeks passed, and he still roamed about, speaking to no one, but riding off across the plains, returning always just at sundown, to tie his horse up close to the cemetery gate and stand with his head pressed against the bars looking towards the grave. At last Don Alejandro, fearing that he was going mad, as they sat at the end of a hot day, began to speak to him, saying: "It is not well to grieve too long. It is, as we may say, a selfishness. My father, who knew the older generation, those who lost everything for their religion and their king, had listened in his youth to all the lore that they brought with them from that far region where, as they say, the mist blurs everything, My father spoke 'Gaelico'"— he said the word almost with reverence — "and those who spoke it always were versed in the traditions of our race. He used to tell me that to grieve for the dead beyond due measure disturbed them in their graves, and brought their spirits weeping back again. So I have dried my tears." As he said this he drew his hand across his eyes, and, looking at it, saw that it was dry.

"Grieve no more, Anacleto. We cannot call her back to us alive. To pain the spirit by our selfishness, that would be cowardly."

They sat till it was almost sunset, and then Don Alejandro went down to the corral to see the animals shut in, just in the way that he had gone each evening, for the last forty years.

The sun set in a glare, the hot, north wind blowing as from a furnace, making the cattle droop their heads, and bringing troops of horses, with a noise like thunder, down to the water-holes.

The teru-teros, flying low, like gulls upon the sea, almost unseen in the fast-coming darkness, called uncannily. The tame chajá screamed harshly behind the cattle-pens.

A boy, riding upon a sheepskin, drove the tame horses into the corral.

The sheep were folded, and in the dark leaves of the old ombú beside the door, the fire-flies glistened, and from the pampa rose the acrid smell that the first freshness of the evening draws from the heated ground. Coming out of the rancho Anacleto looked across the plain.

His eyes were full of tears, but with a gulp he choked them, and muttering to himself, "No, it would be cowardly to break her rest, Don Alejandro says so; he had it from his father, who spoke Gaelico," he slowly lit a cigarette, and in the last rays of the light, watched the smoke curl up in the air, blue and impalpable.

A Braw Day

Never before, in the long years that he had passed in the old place, had it appeared so much a part of his whole being, as on the day on which he signed the deed of sale.

Times had been bad for years, and a great load of debt had made the fight a foregone ending from the first. Still he felt like a murderer, as judges well may feel when they pronounce death sentences. Perhaps they feel it more than the prisoner, for things we do through fate, and by the virtue of the circumstances that hedge our lives about with chains, often affect us more than actions which we perform impelled by no one but ourselves.

The long, white Georgian house, with its two flanking wings, set in its wide expanse of gravel, which, like a sea, flowed to a grassy, rising slope, looked dignified and sad. An air, as of belonging to a family of fallen fortunes, hung about the place. The long, dark avenue of beeches, underneath one of which stood the gallows stone, looked as if no one ever used it, and on its sides the grassy edges had long ago all turned to moss, a moss so thick and velvety, you might have swept it with a broom.

The beech mast crackled underneath your feet as you passed up the natural cathedral aisle, and on the tops of the old trees the wind played dirges in the cold autumn nights, and murmured softly in the glad season "when that shaws are green."

The formal terraces were roughly mown and honeycombed by rabbits, the whinstone steps were grown with moss, and here and there were forced apart by a strong growing fern that pushed out to the light.

The seats about the garden were all blistered with the sun and rain, and the old-fashioned coach-roofed greenhouse looked like a refrigerator, with its panes frosted by the damp. Under the arch, which led into the stable yard, stood two dilapidated dog kennels, disused, but with some links of rusty chain still hanging to them, as if they waited for the return of shadowy dogs, dead years ago.

The cedars on the slope below the terraces stretched out their long and human-looking branches, as they were fingers seeking to restrain and hold those whom they knew and loved.

Charity

All was serene and beautiful, with the enthralling beauty of decay. The fences were unmended, and slagging wires in places had been dragged by cattle into the middle of the fields; most of the gates were off their hinges, and weeds had covered up the gravel of the walks.

Nettles grew rankly in the grass, and clumps of dock with woody stems and feathery heads, stood up like bulrushes about the edges of a pond. Even at noonday, a light mist still clung about the lower fields below the house, marking out clearly where old "peat hags" had been reclaimed.

Such was the place at noonday; melancholy as regards the lack of care that want of means had brought about; but bright and sunny as it lay facing to the south, sheltered by groups of secular sycamores and beech.

At night a feeling as if one had been marooned upon some island, far away from men, grew on the inmates of the house.

Owls fabulated from the tree-tops, their long, quavering call seeming to jar the air and make it quiver, so still was everything.

The roes' metallic belling sounded below the windows, and the sharp chirping of the rabbits never ceased during summer nights, as they played in the grass.

When the long shadows, in the moonlight, crept across the lawn, it seemed as if they beckoned to the shadows of the dead, in the old eerie house. Those who had gone before had set their seal so firmly upon everything, planting the trees, and adding here a wing and there a staircase, that those who now possessed the house, dwelt in it, as it were, by the permission of the dead.

One day remained to him whose ancestors had built the house; who had lived in the old ruined castle, in the grounds, and who had fought and plundered, rugged and reived after the fashion of their kind. All had been done that falls to a man's lot to do at such a time. The house stood gaunt and empty. By degrees, the familiar objects that time and sentiment make almost sacred and as if portions of ourselves, had been packed up, and on the walls, the pictures taken down, had left blank spaces that recalled each one, as perfectly as if it had been there.

Steps sounded hollow, in the emptiness and desolation on the stairs, and bits of straw and marks of hobnailed boots showed where the workmen had been busy at their task.

Here and there marks of paint and varnish on a door, showed where a heavy piece of furniture had touched in passing, as sometimes after a funeral you see the dent made by the coffin in the plaster of the passage, as it was carried to the hearse.

A desolating smell of straw was everywhere. It permeated everything, even to the food, which an old servant cooked in the great, ungarnished kitchen, just as a tramp might cook his victuals at the corner of a road.

The polished staircase, which from their childhood had been a kind of fetish to the children of the house, shielded from vulgar footsteps by a thick drugget and a protecting strip of holland, but bleached a snowy white, was now all scratched and dirtied, as if it were no better than the steps which led to the backyard.

The owner and his wife, after their years of struggle, had felt at first as if their ship had got into a port; and then as days went by, and by degrees the house which they had cared for more than their own lives, grew empty and more empty, till it was left a shell, now found their port had vanished, and they were left without an anchorage.

Still, there was one more day to pass. What then to do with it? The house was empty, the few old servants that remained, tearful and wandering to and fro, pleased to be idle and yet not knowing what to do with unaccustomed leisure, jostled each other on the stairs.

The horses had been sold, all but one little old, black pony; the dogs all sent away to friends.

Standing at the hall door, looking out on the sweep of gravel all cut up by carts, the owners stood a little while, dazed and not able to take in that twenty years had flown. It seemed but yesterday that they had driven up to the same door, young, full of expectation and of hope.

Now they were middle-aged and grey. The fight had gone against them; but still they had the recollection of the struggle, for all except the baser sort of men fight not to win, but simply for the fight.

Some call it duty, but the fight's the thing, for those who strive to win, become self- impressed, and that way lies the road to commonplace. Verily, they have their reward; but the reward soon overwhelms them, whilst the true fighters still fight on, with sinews unrelaxed.

At last, after having looked about in vain for sticks, but without finding one, for they had all been packed or given away as keepsakes, they walked out to the sundial in the great gravel sweep before the door. Though they had sat and smoked upon its steps a thousand times, watching the squirrels play at noon, the bats flit past at sundown, it yet seemed new to them, and strange. With interest they saw that it was half-past three in China, eight in the evening in New Orleans, and midnight at La Paz.

Somehow it seemed that they had never seen all this before, and that in future, time would be all the same the whole world over, or at least that it would not be marked by little brazen gnomons on a weather-beaten slab of slate. The garden, with the gardeners gone, and the gate open, seemed as strange as all the rest. The flowers that they had planted, and forgotten they had planted, in the course of time had come to be considered in the same way as the old castle just outside the garden walls, as things that had existed from the beginning of the world.

Weeds choked the gravel in the lower walk, bounded by a long hedge of laurel cut into castles at due intervals. They both agreed next week they should be hoed, and then stopped, smiled and looked away, fearing to meet each other's eyes. The sun beats on the old stone wall, ripening the magnum bonum plums, for it was in September, and both thought, they will be ripe in a few days, but feared to tell each other what they thought.

The tangled, terraced beds, where once had stood old vineries, all had been planted with herbaceous plants, which, from the want of care, had grown into a jungle; but a jungle unutterably beautiful, in which the taller plants, the coreopsis, bocconias, Japanese anemones, and larkspurs stood up starkly, as palm trees rear themselves out of a wilderness of dwarf palmettoes, and of grass.

Over the garden gate, marauding ivy had run across the stone on which the arms of the decaying family were cut in hard grey whinstone, with the date 1686 in high relief, flanked by a monogram.

Upon a bench, from which the view stretched over the great moss that marked the limits of an ancient sea, and out of which a wooded hill rose like an island, the only thing that broke the level plain between the garden and the distant hills, they sat and let the sun beat on them, for the last time, as it had often done during their years of struggle and of fight.

Descending through a gate, which slagged a little on its hinges, and grated on the stone lintel as it opened after a heavy push, they passed into the narrow strip of extra garden, taken in as it were by afterthought, in the old Scottish fashion, which never seemed to have enough of garden laid about a house. They bade good-bye to the long line of *arbor vitæ* clipped into cones which cast their shadows on the path, so clearly that you were half inclined to lift your feet in passing, they looked so firm and round.

The curious moondial, with its niches coloured blue and red; the burial-ground hidden away amongst the trees, and with a long, grass walk, mossy and damp, leading up to its old grey walls, they visited but did not see, as they were so familiar, that they had become impossible to look at, but as parts and parcels of themselves.

The day seemed never-ending, and in the afternoon, to pass the time, seeing a water conduit underneath a road choked up with leaves, the departing owner of the place set about working hard to clear it, and having done so, congratulated himself on a good piece of work. To bid good-bye to buildings and familiar scenes seemed natural, as life is but a long farewell; but to look for the last time on the trees — trees that his ancestors had planted, and by which he himself recognised the seasons, as for example by the turning yellow of the horse-chestnuts, which he saw from his bed-room windows, or the first pinkish blush upon the broken larch, whose broken top was cased in lead — that seemed a treason to them, for they had always been so faithful, putting out their leaves in spring, standing out stark and rigid in the winter and murmuring in the breeze.

The whispering amongst their branches and the melodious tinkle of a little burn that crossed the avenue, were sounds which, on that last day, pervaded all the air and filled the soul with that deep-seated feeling of amazement that looks out, hopeless and heartrending, from the eyes of dying animals.

The interminable day came to an end at last. The sun set, red and beautiful, over the low, flat moss, and disappeared behind the hills. The owls called shrilly from the trees, and the accustomed air of ghostliness, intensified a thousandfold by solitude, pervaded all the house.

The mysterious footstep which in the course of years had grown familiar, even in winter nights, as it passed up the corridor and stopped with a loud knock on the end bed-room door, again grew terrifying as it had been on the first night that they had heard it years ago.

From out the spaces where the pictures once had hung, the well-known faces seemed to peer, but unfamiliar-looking, with an air as of reproach.

The smallest footfall sounded as loud as if it were the trampling of a horse; and candles, stuck in bottles here and there, gave a dim, flickering light, casting dark shadows on the floor.

Long did the owners gaze into the night, watching the stars come out in their familiar places. The Bear hung right across the cedars, almost due north, Alphecca close to the horizon, the Square of Pegasus quite horizontal, and Fomalhaut in the south-west, athwart the corner of the Easter Hill.

A light, white frost turned all to silver, and the lake in the east middle distance lay like a sheet of burnished silver under the moon, its islands mirrored dimly and as if floating in the air. No leaf was stirring, and as they sat around a fire of logs, talking of were-wolves, fairies, and superstitions of another land, with their old Spanish friend and servant, the night wore on so rapidly that it was daylight almost as it appeared, before the sun went down.

Short preparations serve for those about to go, and when a few old servants and retainers took their leave, and a black pony slowly took their trunks down to the station, looking forlorn in the immensity of the beech avenue, they closed the door upon their house.

Quickly the trees rushed past, the pond with its tall island looking like a ship, the giant silver firs, the castle, which they beheld as in a dream, all floated by. Just at the cross-roads which led into the park, beside the gate, a man stood waiting for them.

He carried in his hand a hedgebill, and stood there waiting, as he had waited for the past twenty years, for orders for the day.

Now, he held out his hand, opened his mouth, but said nothing, and then, looking up with the air of one well learned in weather lore, said, "Laird, it looks like a braw day."

Aurora La Cujiñi

Isbilieh, as the Moors called Seville, had never looked more Moorish than on that day in spring. The scent of azahar hung in the air; from patio and from balcony floated the perfume of albahaca and almoraduz, plants brought to Seville by the Moors from Nabothea and from Irak-el-Hind. The city of the royal line of the Beni-Abbad was as if filled with a reminiscence of its past of sensuality and blood. The mountains of the Axarafe loomed in a violet haze, and seemed so near, you felt that you could touch them with your hand. The far-off sierras above Ronda looked jagged, and as if fortified to serve as ramparts against the invasion of the African from his corresponding sierra in the country of the Angera, across the narrow straits. Over the Giralda came the faint, pink tinge which evening imparts, in Seville, to all the still remaining Moorish work, making the finest specimen of the architecture of the Moors in Spain look as delicate and new as when the builder, he who built at Marákesh and Rabat, two other towers of similar design, raised it in honour of the one God, and the great camel driver who stands beside his throne. Down the great river for which the Christians never found a better name than that left by the Moorish dogs, the yellow tide ran lazily, swaying alike the feluccas with their tall, tapering yards, the white Norwegian fruit schooners, and the sea coffins from the port of London, tramps out of Glasgow, and the steam colliers from the Hartlepools or Newcastle-on-Tyne. The great cathedral in which lies Ferdinand Columbus, the most southern Gothic building in all Europe, built on the site of the chief mosque said to have been as large as that of Cordoba, rose from the Court of Oranges, silent as a vast tomb, and seemed protected from the town by its raised walk, fenced in with marble pillars and massive iron chains. The Alcázar, and The Tower of Gold, the churches, especially St. John's beside the Palm, seemed to regret their builders, as, I think, do all the Saracenic buildings throughout Spain. Though ignorant of all the plastic arts, taking their architecture chiefly from the two forms of tent and palm tree, their literature so conceived as to be almost incomprehensible to the peoples of the north, the tribes who came from the Hedjaz, the Yemen, and beyond Hadramut have left their imprint on whatever land they passed. They comprehended that life is first, the chiefest business which man has to do, and so subordinated to it all the rest. Their eyes, their feet, their verse, and their materialistic view of everything have proved indelible wherever they have camped. They and their horses have stamped themselves for ever on the world. Even to-day, their speech remains embedded, like a mosaic, in the vocabulary of Southern Spain, giving the language strength.

Notable things have passed in Seville since Ojeda, before he sailed for the new-found Indies, ran along the beam fixed at a giddy height in the Giralda and threw a tennis-ball over the weather-vane to show the Catholic kings and the assembled crowd the firmness of his head. Since San Fernando drove out the royal house of the Beni-Abbad, and Motamid, the poet king, took sanctuary in Mequinéz, as Abd-el-Wahed notes in his veracious history of the times, much has occurred and has been chronicled in blood. In the Alcázar, Pedro el Justiciero loved Maria de Padilla; in it he had made the fish-pond where the degenerate Charles the Second sat a-fishing, whilst his empire slipped out of his hands. The Caloró from Hind, Multán, or from whatever Trans-Caucasian or Cis-Himalayan province they set out from, ages ago, had come, and spreading over Spain, fixed themselves firmly in the part of Seville called the Triana, after the Emperor Trajan who was born there as some say, and where to-day they chatter Romany, traffic in horses, tell fortunes, and behave as if the world were a great oyster which they could open with their tongues, so wheedling and well hung.

So, on the evening of which I write, a Sunday in the month of May, the bull-fight was just over, leaving behind it that mixed air of sensuousness and blood which seems to hover over Seville after each show of bulls, as it may once have hovered, after a show of gladiators, about Italica in the old Roman days.

The fight was done, and all the tourists, after condemning Spanish barbarism, had taken boxes to a man, and come away delighted with the picturesqueness of the show.

Trumpets had sounded, and the horses, all of which had done more service to mankind than any fifty men, and each of whom had as much right, by every law of logic and anatomy, to have a soul, if souls exist, as had the wisest of philosophers, had suffered martyrdom. Hungry and ragged, they had trodden on their entrails, received their wounds without a groan, without a tear, without a murmur, faithful to the end; had borne their riders out of danger, fallen upon the bloody sand at last with quivering tails, and, biting their poor, parched and bleeding tongues, had died just as the martyrs died at Lyons or in Rome, as dumb and brave as they.

In the arena the light-limbed men, snake-like and glittering in their tinselly clothes, had capered nimbly before the bull, placing their banderillas deftly on his neck.

Waiting until he almost touched them, they placed one foot upon his forehead, and stepping lightly across the horns, had executed what is called *el salto de trascuerno*. Then leaping with a pole, they had alighted on the other side of him like thistledown, had dived behind the screen, had caught and held the furious beast an instant by the tail, and after having played a thousand antics, running the gamut, known to the intelligent as *volapie, galleo, tijerilla, veronica*, and *chatré,* escaped as usual with their lives.

The *espada* had come forward, mumbled his *boniment* in Andaluz, swung his montera round his shoulder towards the presidential throne, and after sticking his sword, first in the muscles of the neck, from which it sprang into the air, and fell, bloody and twisted, on the sand, taking another from an attendant sprite, butchered his bull at last, mid thunders of applause.

Blood on the sand; the sun reflected back like flame from the white walls; upon the women's faces cascarilla: a fluttering of red and yellow fans; lace veils on glossy hair, looking like new-fallen snow on a black horse's back, all made a picture of the meeting of the east and west to which the water-sellers' voices added, as they called *Agua*, in a voice so guttural, it sounded like the screaming of a jay.

A scent of blood and sweat rose from the plaza, and acted like an aphrodisiac on the crowd.

Bold-looking women squeezed each other's hands, and looked ambiguously at one another, as if they were half men. Youths with their hair cut low upon their foreheads, loose, swinging hips, and eyes that met the glance as if they were half girls, pressed one against the other on the seats. Blood, harlotry, sun, gay colours, flowers, and waving palm trees, women with roses stuck behind their ears, mules covered up in harness of red worsted, cigar girls, gipsies, tourists, soldiers, and the little villainous-looking urchins, who, though born old, do duty in the south, as children, formed a kaleidoscope. The plaza vomited out the crowd, just as the Roman amphitheatre through its *vomitorium* expelled its crowd of blood-delighting Roman citizens, *Civis Romanus sum*, and all the rest of it.

The stiff, dead horses, all were piled into a cart, their legs sticking out, pathetic and grotesque, between the bars. A cart of sand was emptied on the blood, which lay in blackening pools here and there in the plaza, and then the *espada*, smoking a cigar, emerged like Agag, delicately, and drove off, the focus of all eyes. Girls swarmed in the streets, sailing along with their incomparable walk unrivalled in the world, and in the Calle de la Passion the women of the life, stood against open, but barred windows, painted and powdered, and with an eye to business as they scanned passing men.

Lovers stood talking from the streets by signs to girls upon the balcony, their mother's presence hidden behind the curtain in the dark, and the space intervening, keeping their virtue safe.

Sometimes a man leaned up against the grating and whispered to his sweetheart through the bars, holding her hand in his. The passers-by affected not to see them, and either stepped into the street or looked with half-averted eyes, at the first act in life's great comedy.

In the great palm-tree planted square the salmon-coloured plaster seats were filled with men, who seemed to live there day and night, contributing their quota to the ceaseless national expenditure of talk. On this occasion they discussed, being all *intelligentes*, each incident and action of the fight, the old men deprecating modern innovation and sighing for the times and styles of Cucháres, or el Zeño Romero, he who first brought the art of bull-fighting from heaven, as his admirers say. If a girl, rich or poor, a countess from Madrid, or maiden of the Caloró from the Triana, chanced to pass, they criticised her, as a prospective buyer does a horse or as a dealer looks down a slave at Fez. Her eyes, her feet, her air, each detail of her dress were all passed in review, and if found pleasing, then came the approving, Blessed be your mother! with other compliments of a nature to make a singer at a Paris *café-concert* blush. The recipient took it all as a matter of everyday occurrence, and with a smile or word of thanks, according to her rank, pursued the uneven tenour of her way with heightened colour, and perhaps a little more *meneo* of her hips and swaying of her breasts.

In the Calle Sierpes, the main artery and chief bazaar, roofed with an awning right from end to end, the people swarmed like ants, passing, and then repassing in a stream. *Cafés* were gorged with clients, all talking of the bull-fight, cursing the Government, or else disputing of the beauty and the nature of the women of their respective towns. The clubs, with windows of plate glass down to the ground, showed the *haute gomme* lounging in luxury upon their plush-upholstered chairs, stiff in their English clothes, and sweating blood and water in the attempt to look like Englishmen, and to keep up an unconcerned appearance under the public gaze. Girls selling lemonade, *horchata, agráz,* with the thick, sticky sweetmeats, and the white, flaky pastry flavoured with fennel and angelica, left by the Moors in Spain, went up and down crying their wares, and offering themselves to anyone who wished to venture half a dollar on the chance. The shops were full of all those unconsidered trifles, which in Spain alone can find a market, cheap and abominably nasty, making one think that our manufactories must be kept running with a view to furnish idiots or blind men, with things they do not want.

After the gospel comes the sermon; sherry after soup, and when the bloodshed of the day has stirred men's pulses, they drift instinctively towards the dancing-houses, just as a drunkard in the morning turns back again to drink, to give another fillip to the blood. Men streamed to the Burrero, at whose narrow doors sat ancient hags selling stale flowers and cheaply painted matchboxes, pushing and striving in the narrow passage to make their way inside. The temple of the dance was an enormous building, barn-like and dusty, and with its emptiness made manifest by oil-lamps stuck about the walls.

The floor was sanded and in the middle of it, at little wooden tables, seated on rickety cane chairs, was the fine flower of the rascality of Spain, whilst round the walls stood groups of men, who by their dress might have been Chulos or Chalanes, loafers or horse-copers, all with their hair brushed forward on their foreheads and plastered to the head.

All wore tight trousers moulded to the hips, short and frogged jackets, and all had flat felt hats with a stiff brim, which now and then they ran their fingers round to see if it was straight.

Others were wrapped in tattered cloaks, and mixed with them were herdsmen and some shepherds, with here and there a bull-fighter and here and there a pimp.

In the crank, shaky gallery was a dark box or two, unswept and quite unfurnished, save for a bunch or two of flowers painted upon the plaster, and a poor lithograph of the reigning sovereign, flanking a bull-fighter. One was quite empty, and in the other sat two foreign ladies, come to see life in Seville, who coughed and rubbed their eyes in the blue haze of cigarette smoke, which filled the building, just as the incense purifies a church with its mysterious fumes.

Set in a row across the stage, like flowers in a bed, were six or seven girls. Their faces painted in the fashion of the place, without concealment, just like the ladies whom Velazquez drew, gave them a look of artificiality, which their cheap boots, all trodden down at the heel, and hair dressed high upon the head, with a comb upon the top and a red flower stuck behind the ear, did little to redeem.

Smoking and pinching one another they sat waiting for their turn, exchanging jokes occasionally with their acquaintances in front, and now and then one or the other of them rising from her chair walked to the looking-glasses placed on each side of the stage, and put her hair in order, patting it gently at the side and shaking out her clothes, just as a bird shakes out its feathers after it rolls itself in dust.

On one side of the stage sat the musicians, two at the guitar and two playing small instruments known as bandurrias — a cross between the mandoline and a guitar, played with a piece of quill. The women suddenly began to clap their hands in a strange rhythm, monotonous at first, but which at length, like the beating of a tom-tom, makes the blood boil, quiets the audience, stills conversation, and focusses all eyes upon the stage. The strange accompaniment, with the hands swept across the strings, making a whir as when a turkey drags its wings upon the ground, went on eternally. Then, one broke out into a half-wild song, the interval so strange, the time so wavering, and so mixed up the rhythm, that at first hearing it scarcely seems more pleasing than the howling of a wolf, but bit by bit goes to the soul, stirs up the middle marrow of the bones, and leaves all other music ever afterwards, tame and unpalatable.

The singing terminated abruptly, as it seemed, for no set reason, and died away in a prolonged high note, and then a girl stood up, encouraged by her fellows with shouts of *"Venga Juana," "Vaya salerosa,"* and a cross fire of hats thrown on the stage, and interjections from the audience of *"Tu sangre"* or *"Tu enerpo" [sic=cuerpo]* and the inspiriting clap of hands, which never ceases till the dancer, exhausted, sinks down upon a chair. Amongst the audience, drinking their Manzanilla in little tumblers about the thickness of a piece of sugar-cane, eating their *boquerones*, ground nuts, and salted olives, the fire of criticism never stopped, as everyone in Seville of the lower classes is a keen critic both of dancing-girls and bulls.

Of the elder men, a gipsy, though shouting "*Salero!*" in a perfunctory manner, seemed discontented, and recalled the prowess of a dancer long since dead, by name Aurora, surnamed La Cujiñi, and gave it as his faith that since his time no girl had ever mastered all the mysteries of the dance. The Caloró, who always muster strong at the Burrero, all were upon his side, and seemed inclined to enforce their arguments with their shears, which, as most of them maintain themselves by clipping mules, they carry in their sash.

Then, just as the discussion seemed about to end, in a free fight, a girl stepped out to dance. None had remarked her sitting quietly beside the rest; still, she was slightly different in appearance from all the others in the room, both in her air and dress.

A gipsy at first sight, with the full lustrous eyes her people brought from far Multán, dressed in a somewhat older fashion than the rest, her hair brought low upon her forehead and hanging on her shoulders after the style of 1840, her skirt much flounced, low shoes tied round the ankle, a Chinese shawl across her shoulders, and with a look about her, as she walked to the middle of the stage, as of a mare about to kick. A whisper to the first guitar caused him with a smile to break into a Tango, his instrument well *requintado* striking the chords with every finger of his hand at the same instant, as the wild Moorish melody jingled and jarred out and quivered in the air.

She stood a moment motionless, her eyes distending slowly and focussing the attention of the audience on her, and then a sort of shiver seemed to run over her, the feet gently began to scrape along the floor, her naked arms moved slowly with her fingers curiously bent, and meant perhaps to indicate by their position, the symbols of the oldest of religions, and, as the gipsies say, she drew the heart of every onlooker into her net of love. Twisting her hips till they seem ready to disjoint, and writhing like a snake, dragging her skirt up on the stage, she drew herself up to her full height, thrust all her body forward, her hands moved faster, and the short sleeves slipped back exhibiting black tufts of hair under her arms, glued to her skin with sweat. Then she wreathed forwards, backwards, looked at the audience with defiance, took a man's hat from off the stage, placed it upon her head, put both her arms akimbo, swayed to and fro, but still kept writhing as if her veins were full of quicksilver. Little by little the frenzy died away, her eyes grew dimmer, the movements of the body slower, then with a final stamp, and a hoarse guttural cry, she stood a moment quiet, as it is called, *dormida*, that is, asleep, looking a very statue of impudicity and lust. The audience sat a moment spellbound, with open mouths like Satyrs, and in the box where were the foreign ladies, one had turned pale resting her head upon the other's shoulder, who held her round the waist. Then with a mighty shout, the applause broke forth, hats rained upon the stage, *Oles* and *Vayas* rent the air, and the old gipsy bounded on the table with a shout, "One God, one Cujiñi"; but in the tumult. La Cujiñi had disappeared, gone from the eyes of Caloró and of Busné, Gipsy and Gentile, and the Burrero never saw her more.

Perhaps, at witches' sabbaths she still dances, or perhaps in that strange Limbo where the souls of gipsies and their donkeys dree their weird, she writhes and dislocates her hips in the Romalis, or in the Óle, she drags her skirts on the floor, with a faint rustling sound.

Sometimes the curious may see her still, dancing before a Venta in the blurred outline of a Spanish lithograph, her head thrown back, her hair, *en catagon*, with one foot pointing to a hat to show her power over, and her contempt for all the sons of man, just as she did upon that evening when she took a brief and fleeting reincarnation to breathe once more the air of Seville, heavy with perfume of spring flowers, mixed with the scent of blood.

Un Autre Monsieur

I had lost sight of Elise, said my friend, until one day as I was walking past, I am not sure if it was Woolland's or some other shop, I met her face to face. She seemed a little thin, I thought, and though she walked as gracefully as ever, holding her skirt up in the way that only her compatriots ever can compass, she looked so pale I saw that she was ill.

"What is the matter, Elise?" I said; "is it an affection of the heart?" To which she answered with a side look at the window of the shop to see if her hat was straight, "No, not of the heart; you forget that we professionals [she pronounced the word 'professionelles'] are quite impervious in that region; it is the chest I suffer from. The doctors say it is the life I have to lead — but really I have had congestion of the lungs."

We went to lunch just opposite in the grill-room of the hotel, where she insisted upon taking what she called *"La table de l'adultère,"* for she declared as it was in a dark corner she had noticed several affairs ripen, as she expressed it, in the surrounding gloom.

She asked for mineral water, and consommé with an egg in it, and proceeded with her tale.

"Things had been bad with me . . . how, I don't know. . . . They go in cycles, I suppose; for at one time I had, as you know, half the Turf Club . . . how shall I put it ... on my books?" She made a gesture with her hand, graceful and gracious, to the waiter, who was offering her a dish, and bit her lip and smiled as a man passed in with his wife and daughter, whispering to me, "He is a client," and then coughing a little, began again to talk.

I looked at her with interest, and saw how she had fallen away, that her collar-bones made ridges in her light summer blouse. "Ah yes, I see why you are looking," she said; "it is dreadful to be thin, that is to say, in my line of business, for men seem to like women to be fat, and I am nothing but old bones.

"I think it was a cold I caught coming back from France, where I had been to see my mother. Yes, do not laugh, and please say nothing about *ma mère*; for I know you insularies [sic] see something comic about that.

Charity

We, on the other hand, are much more lovers of our family than you, though you think not. Of course, both men and nations always plume themselves on qualities they lack. Yes, I am quite a little of a philosopher, that is, since I was ill. Well, well, it was congestion, as I said, which nailed me to my bed. When you are young and strong and nearly six feet high, as I am," and here she straightened herself up with pride, looking a true descendant of the pirates (she came from Normandy), with her fresh colour, bright grey eyes, and masses of fair hair, "it is silly to be ill. Illness in our profession usually takes us soon to the end of our resources, for we, of course, must make a good appearance, and frequent good restaurants, then we are always robbed by all who deal with us.

"Illness too lifts the veil, or the veneer of chivalry which most of our friends assume to us, although, of course, it also brings out what is good.

"I become a moralist, you see, a dreadful thing in one who has to chatter always and be gay. Ah!" and an ashy look came on her cheeks, "those awful conversations about horses, bad plays, and books, and pictures that you would not use in a back kitchen as a screen. I think the frankly indecent even harasses me less. Your countrymen, you'll pardon me, I know, have little *talent de société,* or perhaps they keep it all for those they think that they respect, that is, if any Englishman really respects a woman in his heart. Chivalry, eh — bah, we see what that means. Either the idea is real, or else it is a fraud. If it is real, it should make a man the same to every woman, especially to us who minister to his pleasures and act as lightning conductors to his home. That sets me thinking"— and here that wintry smile she used as an armour flitted across her face — "why a man's home is to be pure and a woman's not so, for strange as it may seem I have a home, that is a house in which I live. When a man leaves me with his 'Good night, old girl,' I often wonder if he thinks his home is purified by what has taken place in mine. Well, well," and as she drank her coffee, her eyes wandered to the man she knew who, seated with his daughter and his wife, kept his face turned away.

"Yes," she said, "there is a man who, no doubt, in his own home is kind enough, as men are kind, if all goes right with them. You see, I and his daughter, are almost of one age . . . a pretty girl enough she is, and would look better if only she wore good stays. How strange it is, here in this island, you so often see expensive clothes ill-worn and spoiled by villainous bad stays or made ridiculous by a cheap pair of boots, or something of that kind.

"When I fell ill, and when the doctors said I must go home and not live as I had been doing, the father of that girl was one of those to whom I went for help. He never answered when I wrote him, nor for that matter did any of the men who used to like to take me to the theatres when I was well and was a credit to their taste."

She paused and waived *[sic]* away a cigarette, saying she did not want to look like a *bourgeoise en goguette*, and as the man she said she knew walked out behind his women-folk, fixed her eyes on him, till he reddened, as she put it, "at the back of his neck between the collar and the hair."

Then smiling and coughing now and then, she told how one of her friends had pawned her rings to send her home to France and, turning serious, said, "Now I will tell you of a trouble I am in. You know that women of our class, if by some accident we fall in love, love far more fiercely than those that you call honest. I know the Spanish proverb about our love — that it resembles nothing but a fire of straw — but, there, it was concocted by a man . . . *les hommes, ça vous abîment une femme.* Personally I have never felt it . . . that is, but once or twice at most, and each time have regretted it, both for myself and him. You smile when I say 'him,' but it is true. However, that is not now what troubles me, but this.

"I know I cannot follow up this life, nor wish to, and I have told you that it was my ambition to study Art and try and learn to paint. No, no, I do not think I am a genius . . . nothing of the sort, but still I think I might have made a living in the Art world had I but had the chance. Now, though, the thing for me is how to live at all. I think I told you that I was a *mannequin* in a great Paris shop. I am you see both tall and elegant. . . . No, don't laugh ... it is so; for I was born, although my family was poor, with an innate sense of elegance in dress . . . the sentiment of rags." This was so manifestly true, my friend said nothing, but merely nodded, wondering what she would say. "I cannot go back to that way of life; for during the past years I have lived in luxury, that is to say, I have enjoyed a luxury tempered by the ever-present dread of want, but still a luxury. I have read books and haunted the museums; I know the various schools of painting tolerably well, revel in Corot, adore Degas and Monet, think Whistler inspired, and therefore cannot go home and settle down, marrying some *Betrave* or another, perhaps a local cattle-dealer or something of the sort. Now, though, a chance has come into my life, and I can neither jump at it nor yet neglect it; for as I told you I am *très bonne fille*, and would not like to wreck the life of anyone, especially of one who says he loves me . . . yes, loves me as I am."

She put a falling hairpin back into her hair, played with her bag, taking it up and looking at the clasp. Then put it down and after having sipped her coffee, began again to talk.

"The thing is this way . . . I had a lover — a *vieux colonel*, not a bad sort of man, stiff, angular, and with his face reddened by whisky and the sun of India, just such a man as Loti talks about, honourable I think, and wearisome. He liked to spend long hours with me, drinking and telling me about himself, his life, his horses and the women that he thought that he had loved. *Cocasse, le Colonel*, but still a gentleman. One day he brought an officer of his to see me. He was, I think, from Lancashire, some kind of a provincial anyway, and above all a type.

"What was he like? Well, short and freckled; such feet and hands, and with a neck the colour of a lobster, with the sun. His clothes not bad, but with a note of something of *le gentilhomme campagnard* about them. For a watch-chain, a leather . . . lip strap, I think, you call the thing . . . it go beneath the curb, and he tell me it is for when the horse shakes his head, so that he cannot turn the bit, and run away with you. Over his boots little white gaiters; and gloves, such gloves — so thick, like the stuff you make a fencing-jacket. Fair hair, what of it was left — not that he was bald, but I mean what the barber he have left — a mouth with teeth like a shark, an eye-glass, and a perpetual transpiration on his skin. Not pleasant-looking, eh? That where you make a mistake, then. He did look pleasant, and a gentleman, although he never said a word but 'Aoh yes, awful pleased to meet yer,' with an occasional 'Ha,' which at first made me jump.

"Why the colonel brought him I never could make out, but from the first night I saw his junior officer had fallen in love with me.

"I am not as a rule nervous . . . well . . . under fire; but this man, his very bashfulness made me feel like a milkmaid when her lover sits upon a gate and whistles at her. Not a word did he say whilst his superior officer imbibed champagne, and talked of horses he had known thirty or forty years ago, except to interject a 'Ha' at intervals. At last, though, it seemed near ending, the colonel rose to go. He pulled me to him, and giving me a winy kiss or two, remarked, 'Good-bye, old girl, we're going now. Ta! ta! Be virtuous and you'll be unhappy,' or something of the kind.

"I turned, and saw to my amazement that the lieutenant, who had drunk little, that is for one of his great bulk, had turned quite pale, and glared with rage at his commanding officer.

"He let his eye-glass fall with a loud chink against his waistcoat buttons, and holding out his hand, said, 'Good-bye; some day I'll call again'; so like a gentleman I — I own, was surprised.

"After a day or two, I got a letter from him — not too well written, and with a fault or two in the orthography — saying he meant to come and see me to-morrow afternoon.

"Of course I thought it was the usual kind of thing, and when the time came dressed myself in a light peignoir, laced, and with views to the inside, as we say. It suited me, fair as I am, and with my yellow hair, for it was colour *eau de Nil*, and as the gladiators when they marched round the ring no doubt put on their best, I always like to look my best when I expect to be a sacrifice.

"Punctually at the time he said, my officer came in. I came to meet him, smiling, thinking perhaps that he would kiss me, after the fashion of his kind, who do not generally waste time in words or in preliminaries. However, he held out his hand, and said a little stiffly, 'Glad to see you looking well,' and, sitting down upon a chair, began to look at me. What an original, I thought, as he kept staring at me, until I half began to blush with his continued gaze.

"His eyes roved round the room, and now and then his monocle fell, and he would put it back again, with a contortion of his face, like something on the stage.

"At last he fixed his eyes upon a picture that I had . . . well, *un peu leste*, but nothing very shocking, and turning red, he pointed up at it, observing, 'What a beastly thing. Ha! yes, abominable.' I did not know if I should laugh or be angry, but going to it, turned it round against the wall, and said, 'Now are you satisfied?' Then with some difficulty and with a number of 'Ha's' to help him through his tale, he said he loved me. I had not heard a man say that for the last five years, and it took me by surprise, so I said nothing, and I think turned red a little. Still I did not take in his meaning, and made a motion as of rising, for I expected he was like the rest of them. 'Not that,' he said. 'By God! Ha! No, I really mean it. Miss Elise, I love you awfully.'

"Still I said nothing, for what on earth was there to say? After a little while he went away, but came again at intervals, always the same — stiff, red, and awkward, and with the same song on his lips.

Charity

"At last one day, quite *à brûle-pourpoint,* he asked me would I marry him, but quite respectfully, and in a way that rather made me like him . . . it was phenomenal. What could I say, especially as after saying what he had he took my hand and, looking at me through his monocle, said, 'Could you love a fellow?'

"I was sore put to it, for I saw that I had to do with quite another sort of monsieur to him I told you of before.

"Love and my officer were not to be carried in one bag. Well, I felt grateful to him, for I understood the sacrifice he was prepared to make far better than he did himself, poor innocent.

"When he had pressed me for an answer, I told him all that he would have to undergo if I said 'Yes' to him. His horses — I had not told you he was in the cavalry — would all have to be sold. He gulped a little comically, for he was a great polo player, but manfully agreed. As his own colonel knew me, he would have to change into another regiment. . . . I thought of foot. . . . Of course I had to do the thinking . . . and go to India. He said that it would be a wrench, and that the Grabbies were a beastly lot. However, he would do it all, if I would love a fellow.

"As he talked on and held my hand, at first half timidly and then as in a vice, I rather liked him: he was so childlike and original; but an original.

"Love — no, that was impossible, and so I told him. His face fell for a minute, but he returned again, back to the charge. He didn't care. Ha! no, not a bit. I was the only woman that he ever cared for, and if I only would consider, take time, er — he did not wish to hurry me . . . so like a gentleman."

Elise stopped for a moment, and then —

"I have taken time to think of it, and cross to-night to France, paying my passage with the money that my friend pawned her rings to get for me. His money I refused to take. . . . I, too, have honour . . . and the best thing for me is to go home to my own village Pont de l' Évêque, and try and get my health.

"Then I shall live *en paysanne,* go to bed early, and in the morning hear the swallows in the roof; there used to be a nest above my window three or four years ago. How good their morals are compared to ours . . . I mean the swallows. 'Tis quite an idyll to see them feed their young ones, and the male never looks at any bird, except his *légitime.*

"When I feel better I shall go to Mass, not that I am a firm believer, still less a practiser, but the thing does you good somehow — perhaps the singing, or perhaps the recollection of one's childhood, or something of the kind.

"So I am off, and in a day or two shall be perhaps wandering along the Chaussée, with its double rows of trees, silvery, and looking like a Corot against the fields of corn.

"I shall be thinking of what I told you, and of how difficult it is to love a fellow. Then, when I am better, who knows what I shall do? . . . Ah! *méchant*. No, never, I swear it; he said he never would till we were married . . . you see he was not in the least like you, or any other man."

Charity

Christie Christison

Of all the guests that used to come to Claraz's Hotel, there was none stranger, or more interesting than Christie Christison, a weather-beaten sailor, who still spoke his native dialect of Peterhead, despite his thirty years out in the Plate. He used to bring an air into the room with him of old salt fish and rum, and of cold wintry nights in the low latitudes down by the Horn. This, too, though it was years since he had been at sea.

Although the world had gone so well with him, and by degrees he had become one of the biggest merchants in the place, he yet preserved the speech and manners of a Greenland whaler, which calling he had followed in his youth.

The Arctic cold and tropic suns during the years that he had traded up and down the coast had turned his naturally fair complexion to a mottled hue, and whisky, or the sun, had touched his nose so fiercely that it furnished a great fund of witticism amongst the other guests.

Mansel said that the skipper's nose reminded him of the port light of an old sugar droger, and Cossart had it, that no chemist's window in Montmartre had any *flacon*, bottle you call him, eh? of such resplendent hue. Most of them knew he had a history, but no one ever heard him tell it, although it was well known he had come out from Peterhead in the dark ages, when Rosas terrorised the Plate, in his own schooner, the *Rosebud*, and piled her up at last, somewhere on the Patagonian coast, upon a trip down to the Falkland Islands. He used to talk about his schooner as if she had been one of the finest craft afloat; but an old Yankee skipper, who had known her, swore she was a bull-nosed, round-sterned sort of oyster-mouching vessel, with an old deck-house like a town hall, straight-sided, and with a lime-juice look about her that made him tired.

Whatever were her merits or her faults, she certainly had made her skipper's fortune, or at least laid the foundation of it; for, having started as a trader, he gradually began to act, half as a carrier, half as a mail-boat, going to Stanley every three months or so with mails and letters, and coming back with wool.

Little by little, aided by his wife, a stout, hard-featured woman, from his native town, he got a little capital into his hands.

When he was on a voyage, Jean used to search about to get a cargo for his next trip, so that when the inevitable came and the old *Rosebud* ran upon the reef down at San Julian, Christie was what he called "weel-daein," and forsook the sea for good.

He settled down in Buenos Aires as a wool-broker, and by degrees altered his clothes, to the full-skirted coat of Melton cloth, with ample side-pockets, the heather-mixture trousers, and tall white hat, with a black band, that formed his uniform up to his dying day. He wore a Newgate frill of beard, and a blue necktie, which made a striking contrast with his face, browned by the sun and wind, and skin like a dried piece of mare's hide, through which the colour of his northern blood shone darkly, like the red in an old-fashioned cooking apple after a touch of frost.

Except a few objurgatory phrases, he had learned no Spanish, and his own speech remained the purest dialect of Aberdeenshire — coarse, rough and racy, and double-shotted with an infinity of oaths, relics of his old whaling days, when as he used to say he started life, like a young rook, up in the crow's-nest of a bluff-bowed and broad-beamed five-hundred barrel boat, sailing from Peterhead.

Things had gone well with him, and he had taken to himself as partner a fellow-countryman, one Andrew Nicolson, who had passed all his youth in Edinburgh, in an insurance office. Quiet, unassuming, and yet not without traces of that pawky humour which few Scots are born entirely lacking in, he had fallen by degrees into a sort of worship of his chief, whose sallies, rough and indecent as they often were, fairly convulsed him, making him laugh until the tears ran down his face, as he exclaimed, "Hear to him, man, he's awfu rich, I'm tellin' ye."

Christie took little notice of his adoration except to say, "Andra man, dinna expose yourself," or something of the kind.

In fact, no one could understand how two such ill-assorted men came to be friends, except perhaps because they both were Scotchmen, or because Andrew's superior education and well-brushed black clothes appealed to Christison.

He himself could not write, but knew enough to sign his name, which feat he executed with many puffings, blowings, and an occasional oath.

Still he was shrewd in business, which he executed almost entirely by telegram, refusing to avail himself of any code, saying, "he couldna stand them; some day ye lads will get a cargo of dolls' eyes, when ye have sent for maize. Language is gude enough for me, I hae no secrets. Damn yer monkey talk."

His house at Florés was the place of call of all the ship captains who visited the port. There they would sit and drink, talking about the want of lights on such and such a coast, of skippers who had lost their ships twenty or thirty years ago, the price of whale oil, and of things that interest their kind; whilst Mrs. Christison sat knitting, looking as if she never in her life had moved from Peterhead, in her grey gown and woollen shawl, fastened across her breast by a brooch, with a picture of her man, "in natural colouring." Their life was homely, and differed little from what it had been in the old days when they were poor, except that now and then they took the air in an old battered carriage—which Christison had taken for a debt—looking uncomfortable and stiff, dressed in their Sunday clothes. Their want of knowledge of the language of the place kept them apart from others of their class, and Christison, although he swore by Buenos Aires, which he had seen emerge from a provincial town to a great city, yet cursed the people, calling them a "damned set of natives," which term he generally applied to all but Englishmen.

Certainly nothing was more unlike a "native" than the ex-skipper now turned merchant, in his ways, speech, and dress. Courtesy, which was innate in natives of the place, was to him not only quite superfluous, but a thing to be avoided, whilst his strange habit of devouring bread fresh from the oven, washed down with sweet champagne, gained him the name of the "Scotch Ostrich," which nickname he accepted in good part as a just tribute to his digestive powers, remarking that "the Baptist, John, ye mind, aye fed on locusts and wild honey, and a strong man aye liked strong meat, all the worrld o'er."

In the lives of the elderly Aberdeenshire couple, few would have looked for a romantic story, for the hard-featured merchant and his quiet home-keeping wife appeared so happy and contented in their snug villa on the Florés road. No one in Buenos Aires suspected anything, and most likely Christison would have died, remembered only by his tall white hat, had he not one day chosen to tell his tale.

A fierce pampero had sprung up in an hour, the sky had turned that vivid green that marks storms from the south in Buenos Aires. Whirlfire kept the sky lighted, till an arch had formed in the south-east, and then the storm broke, blinding and terrible, with a strange, seething noise. The wind, tearing along the narrow streets, forced everyone to fly for refuge.

People on foot darted into the nearest house, and horsemen, flying like birds before the storm, sought refuge anywhere they could, their horses, slipping and sliding on the rough, paved streets, sending out showers of sparks as they stopped suddenly, just as a skater sends out a spray of ice. The deep-cut streets, with their raised pavements, soon turned to watercourses, from three to four feet deep, through which the current ran so fiercely that it was quite impossible to pass on foot. The horsemen, galloping for shelter, passed through them with the water banking up against their horses on the stream side, though they plied whip and spurs.

After the first hour of the tempest, when a little light began to dawn towards the south, and the peals of thunder slacken a little in intensity, men's nerves became relaxed from the over-tension that a pampero brings with it, just as if nature had been overwound, and by degrees was paying out the chain.

Storm-stayed at Claraz's sat several men, Cossart, George Mansel, one Don José Hernandez and Christie Christison. Perhaps the pampero had strung up his nerves, or perhaps the desire that all men feel at times to tell what is expedient they should keep concealed, impelled him; but at any rate he launched into the story of his life, to the amazement of his friends, who never thought he either had a story to impart, or if he had that it would ever issue from his lips.

"Ye mind the *Rosebud*?" he remarked.

None of the assembled men had ever seen her, although she still was well remembered on the coast.

"Weel, weel, I mind the time she was well kent, a bonny craft. Old Andrew Reid o' Buckieside, he built her, back in the fifties. When he went under, he had to sell his house of Buckieside. I bought her cheap.

"It's fifteen years and mair, come Martinmas, since I piled her up. . . . I canna think how I managed it, knowing the bay, San Julian, ye ken, sae weel.

"It was a wee bit hazy, but still I thought I could get in wi' the blue pigeon going.

"I mind it yet, ye see you hae to keep the rocks where they say they ganakers all congregate before they die, right in a line with yon bit island.

"I heard the water shoaling as the leadsman sung out in the chains, but still kept on, feeling quite sure I knew the channel, when, bang she touches, grates a little, and sticks dead fast, wi' a long shiver o' her keel. Yon rocks must have been sharp as razors, for she began to fill at once.

"No chance for any help down in San Julian Bay in those days, nothing but ane o' they *pulperias* kept by a Basque, a wee bit place, wi' a ditch and bank, and a small brass cannon stuck above the gate. I got what gear I could into the boat, and started for the beach.

"Jean, myself, three o' the men, and an old Dago I carried with me as an interpreter.

"The other sailormen, and a big dog we had aboard, got into the other boat, and we all came ashore. Luckily it was calm, and the old *Rosebud* had struck not above two or three hundred yards from land. Man, San Julian was a dreich place in they days, naething but the bit fortified *pulperia* I was tellin' ye aboot. The owner, old Don Augusty, a Basque, ye ken, just ca'ed his place the 'Rose of the South.' He micht as well have called it the Rose of Sharon. Deil a rose for miles, or any other sort of flower.

"Well, men, next day it just began to blow, and in a day or two knockit the old *Rosebud* fair to matchwood. Jean, she grat sair to see her gae to bits, and I cursit a while, though I felt like greetin' too, I'm tellin' ye. There we were sort o' marooned, a' the lot of us, without a chance of getting off maybe for months; for in these days devil a ship but an odd whaler now and then ever came nigh the place. By a special mercy Yanquetruz's band of they Pehuelches happened to come to trade.

"Quiet enough folk yon Indians, and Yanquetruz himself had been brocht up in Buenos Aires in a mission school.

"Man, a braw fellow! Six foot six at least, and sat his horse just like a picture. We bought horses from him, and got a man to guide us up to the Welsh settlement at Chubut, a hundred leagues away.

"Richt gude beasts they gave us, and we got through fine, though I almost thocht I had lost Jean.

"Yanquetruz spoke English pretty well, Spanish of course, and as I tellt ye, he was a bonny man.

"Weel, he sort o' fell in love wi' Jean, and one day he came up to the *pulperia* and getting off his horse, a braw black piebald wi' an eye like fire intil him, he asked to speak to me. First we had Caña, and then Carlón, then some more Caña, and yon *vino seco*, and syne some more Carlón. I couldna richtly see what he was driving at. However, all of a sudden he says, 'Wife very pretty, Indian he like buy.'

"I told him Christians didna sell their wives, and we had some more Caña, and then he says, 'Indian like Christian woman, she more big, more white than Indian girl.'

"To make a long tale short, he offered me his horse and fifty dollars, then several ganaker skins, they ca' them *guillapices*, and finally in addition a mare and foal. Man, they were bonny beasts, both red roan piebalds, and to pick any Indian girl I liked. Not a bad price down there at San Julian, where the chief could hae cut all our throats had he been minded to.

". . . Na, na, we werna' fou, just a wee miraculous. Don Augusty was sort o' scared when he heard what Yanquetruz was saying, and got his pistol handy and a bit axe he keepit for emergencies behind the counter. Losh me, yon Yanquetruz was that ceevil, a body couldna tak fuff at him.

"At last I told him I wasna on to trade, and we both had a tot of square-faced gin to clean our mouths a bit, and oot to the *palenque*, where the chief's horse was tied.

"A bonny beastie, his mane hogged and cut into castles, like a clipped yew hedge, his tail plaited and tied with a piece of white mare's hide, and everything upon him solid silver, just like a dinner-service.

"The chief took his spear in his hand — it had been stuck into the ground — and leaning on it, loupit on his horse. Ye ken they deevils mount frae the off-side. He gied a yell that fetched his Indians racing. They had killed a cow, and some of them were daubed with blood; for they folk dinna wait for cooking when they are sharp set. Others were three-parts drunk, and came stottering along, with square-faced gin bottles in their hands.

"Their horses werna tied, nor even hobbled. Na, na, they just stood waiting with the reins upon the ground. Soon as they saw the chief—I canna tell ye how the thing was done — they widna mount, they didna loup, they just melted on their beasts, catching the spears out of the ground as they got up.

"Sirs me, they Indians just took flight like birds, raising sich yellochs, running their horses up against each other, twisting and turning and carrying on in sich a way, just like fishing-boats running for harbour at Buckie or Montrose.

"Our guide turned out a richt yin, and brocht us through, up to Chubut wi'out a scratch upon the paint.

"A pairfect pilot, though he had naething in the wide world to guide him through they wild stony plains.

"That's how I lost the *Rosebud*, and noo, ma freens, I'll tell you how it was I got Jean, but that was years ago.

"In my youth up in Peterhead I was a sailorman. I went to sea in they North Sea whaling craft, Duff and McAlister's, ye ken. As time went on, I got rated as a harpooner . . . mony's the richt whale I hae fastened into. That was the time when everything was dune by hand. Nane of your harpoon guns, nane of your dynamite, naething but muscle and a keen eye. First strike yer whale, and then pull after him. Talk of yer fox hunts . . . set them up, indeed.

"Jean's father keepit a bit shop in Aberdeen, and we had got acquaint. I cannot richtly mind the way o' it. Her father and her mother were aye against our marryin', for ye ken I had naething but my pay, and that only when I could get a ship. Whiles, too, I drinkit a wee bit. Naething to signify, but then Jean's father was an elder of the kirk, and maist particular.

"Jean was a bonny lassie then, awfu' high-spirited. I used to wonder whiles, if some day when her father had been oot at the kirk, someone hadna slippit in to tak tea with her mither. . . . I ken I'm haverin'.

"Weel, we were married, and though we lo'ed each other, we were aye bickerin'. Maistly aboot naething, but ye see, we were both young and spirited. Jean liket admiration, which was natural enough at her age, and I liket speerits, so that ane night, after a word or two, I gied her bit daud or two, maybe it was the speerits, for in the morning when I wakit I felt about for Jean, intending to ask pardon, and feelin' a bit shamed. There was no Jean, and I thocht that she was hidin' just to frichten me.

"I called, but naething, and pittin' on ma clothes, searchit the hoose, but there was naebody. She left no message for me, and nane of the neighbours kent anything aboot her.

"She hadna' gone to Aberdeen, and though her father and me searchit up and doon, we got no tidings of her. Sort o' unchancy, just for a day or two. However, there was naething to be done, and in a month or so I sold my furniture and shipped for a long cruise.

"Man, a long cruise it was, three months or more blocked in the ice, and then a month in Greenland trying to get the scurvy out of the ship's company, and so one way or another, about seven months slipped past before we sighted Peterhead. Seven months without a sight of any woman; for, men, they Esquimaux aye gied me a skunner wi' their fur clothes and oily faces, they lookit to be baboons.

"We got in on a Sabbath, and I am just tellin' ye, as soon as I was free, maybe about three o' the afternoon, I fairly ran all the way richt up to Maggie Bauchop's.

"I see the place the noo, up a bit wynd. The town was awfu' quiet, and no one cared to pass too close to the wynd foot in daylight, for fear o' the clash o' tongues. I didna care a rap for that, if there had been a lion in the path, same as once happened to ane o' the prophets. Balaam, I think it was, in the old Book. I wouldna hae stood back a minute if there had been a woman on the other side.

"Weel, I went up to the door, and rappit on it. Maggie came to it, and says she, 'Eh, Christie, is that you?' for she aye kent a customer. A braw, fat woman, Maggie Bauchop was. For years she had followed the old trade, till she had pit awa' a little siller, and started business for hersel'.

"Weel she kent a' the tricks o' it, and still she was a sort of God-fearin' kind o' bitch . . . treated her lassies weel, and didna cheat them about their victuals and their claithes. 'Come in,' she says, 'Christie, my man. Where hae ye come from?'

"I tellt her, and says I, 'Maggie, gie us yer best, I've been seven months at sea.'

" 'Hoot, man,' she says, 'the lassies arena up; we had a fearfu' spate o' drink yestreen, an awfu' lot of ships is in the port. Sit ye doon, Christie. Here's the old Book to ye. Na, na, ye needna look at it like that; there's bonny pictures in it, o' the prophets . . . each wi' his lass, ye ken.'

"When she went out, I looked a little at the book — man, a fine hot one, and then as the time passed I started whistlin' a tune, something I had heard up aboot Hammerfest. The door flees open, and in walks Maggie, looking awfu' mad.

" 'Christie,' she skirls, 'I'll hae na whistlin' in ma hoose, upon the Sabbath day. I canna hae my lassies learned sich ways, so stop it, or get out.'

"Man, I just lauch at her, and I says, 'The lassies, woman; whistlin' can hardly hurt them, considerin' how they live.'

"Maggie just glowered at me, and 'Christie,' she says, 'you and men like ye may defile their bodies; but whilst I live na one shall harm their souls, puir lambies, wi' whistlin' on His day. No, not in my hoose, that's what I'm tellin' ye.'

"I laughed, and said, 'Weel, send us in ane o' your lambies!' and turned to look at a picture of Queen Victoria's Prince Albert picnickin' at Balmoral. When I looked round a girl had come into the room. She was dressed in a striped sort of petticoat and a white jacket, a blouse I think ye ca' the thing, and stood wi' her back to me as she was speaking to Maggie at the door.

"I drew her to me, and was pulling her towards the bed — seven months at sea, ye ken — when we passed by a looking-glass. I saw her face in it, just for a minute, as we were sort o' strugglin'. Ma God, I lowsed her quick enough, and stotterin' backwards sat down upon a chair. 'Twas Jean, who had run off after the bit quarrel that we had more than a year ago. I didna speak, nor did Jean say a word.

"What's that you say?

"Na, na, ma ain wife in sichlike a place, hae ye no delicacy, man? I settled up wi' Maggie, tellin' her Jean was an old friend o' mine, and took her by the hand. We gaed away to Edinburgh, and there I married her again; sort of haversome job; but Jean just wanted it, ye ken. How she came there I never asked her.

"Judge not, the ould Book says, and after all 'twas me gien' her the daud. Weel, weel, things sort of prospered after that. I bought the *Rosebud* and as ye know piled her up and down at San Julian, some fifteen years ago.

"I never raised ma hand on Jean again. Na, na, I had suffered for it, and Jean if so be she needed ony sort of purification, man, she got it, standing at the wheel o' nichts on the old schooner wi' the spray flyin', on the passage out.

"Not a drop, thankye, Don Hosey. Good nicht, Mr. Mansel; bongsoir, Cossart, I'm just off hame. Jean will be waiting for me."

Charity

A Princess

Nothing is wilder than the long stretch of sandy coast which runs from the East Neuk of Fife right up to Aberdeen.

Inland, the windswept fields, with their rough walls, without a kindly feal upon the top, as in the west, look grim and uninviting in their well-farmed ugliness.

The trees are low and stunted, and grow twisted by the prevailing fierce east winds, all to one side, just like the trees so often painted by the Japanese upon a fan.

The fields run down, until they lose themselves in sandy links, clothed with a growth of bent.

After the links, there intervenes a shingly beach, protected here and there by a low reef of rocks, all honeycombed and limpet-ridden, from which streamers of dulse float in the ceaseless surge.

Then comes the sea, grey, sullen, always on the watch to swallow up the fishermen, whose little brown-sailed boats seem to be scudding ceaselessly before the easterly haar towards some harbour's mouth.

Grey towns, with houses roofed with slabs of stone, cluster round little churches built so strongly that they have weathered reformations and the storms of centuries.

Grey sky, grey sullen sea, grey rocks, and a keen whistling wind that blows from the North Sea, which seems to turn the very air a steely grey, have given to the land a look of hardness not to be equalled upon earth.

One sees at first sight that in the villages no children could have ever danced upon the green. No outward visible sign of any inward graces can be seen in the hard-featured people, whose flinty-looking cheeks seem to repel the mere idea of kisses, and yet down in whose hearts exists a vein of sentiment for which in other and more favoured lands a man might search in vain. As any district, country, or race of men must have its prototype, its spot or person that sums up and typifies the whole, so does this hard, grey land find its quintessence in the town of Buckiehaven, a windswept fisher village, built on a spit of sand.

Charity

Its little church is stumpier than all the other little churches of the coast. Its houses are more angular, their crowsteps steeper, and the gnarled plane trees that have fought for life against its withering blasts, more dwarfish and ill-grown. The fisherfolk seem ruddier, squarer, and more uncouth than are their fellows.

Their little wave-washed harbour looks narrower and still more dangerous than the thousand other little harbours that dot the coast from Kinghorn to St. Forts.

Still in the churchyard in which the graves of mariners, of old sea-captains (who once sailed, drank, and suffered, where their descendants, now sail, drink, and suffer), lie thick, each waiting for the pilot, the headstones looking to the sea, their Mecca, there is an air of rest. The graves all look out seawards, where their hearts lived, and yet most of the denizens returned to lay their bones in the old paroch [sic] where in their youth they must have run about, clattering like ponies on the grey causeway stones. Yet there are gravestones which relate that Andrew Brodie or George Anstruther, were buried in the deep and that their monument was raised by Agnes, Janet, or some other sorrowing wife, in the full hope of their salvation, with a text drawn from the minor prophets and unintelligible to any eyes but those of love and faith.

The lettering on the stones is cut so deeply that in that mossless land it looks as fresh as when the widow and the local stonemason stood chaffering for its price, surrounded by her flaxen-headed children, whom in good time the sea would claim, taking them from her as relentlessly as it had claimed her man.

Only a little lichen here and there, yellow and looking like a stain, shows that time and the weather have both wrought their worst and failed to get a hold, so hard the whinstone, and so good the workmanship.

In the low, wiry grass the graves look like a flock of sheep, the rough-built wall keeps them from straying, and the squat cock upon the spire, that creaks so harshly in the wind, looks down upon them and does not crow, because it knows the inmates are asleep.

So they sleep on, sleeping a longer watch below than any that they ever had on earth, when the shrill boatswain's whistle roused them at each recurring period of four hours, or a shout called them all on deck to shorten sail.

All round the churchyard wall are old-world tombs, of worthies of the places — Brodies and Griersons, Selkirks and Anstruthers — adorned with emblems of their trades, as mallets, shears, and chisels, with a death's-head and cross-bones crowning all, to show not only that the skeleton had sat unbidden at life's feast, but after a full meal still lingered with his hosts.

The whinstone church, hardly distinguishable from the rocks beside the harbour, in colour and in shape, the little burial-ground more like a sheep-pen than a cemetery, the high-pitched house-roofs in the steep stony staircases of streets, all give the idea of a corner of the world to which no stranger could have penetrated except by accident. If such a one there were, he must have felt himself indeed a foreigner in such an isolated spot.

Yet on the south side of the church, set perhaps by accident to catch the little sun that ever shines upon that drear East Neuk, there is a slab let in, or stuck against the wall.

Upon the granite tablet, edged round with a supposititious Gothic scroll, cut into flowers like pastry ornaments upon a pie, the letters poorly executed, showing up paltry in their shallowness, beside the lettering of the staunch old tombs amongst the grass, is written, "Here lies Sinakalula, Princess of Raratonga, the beloved wife of Andrew Brodie, Mariner."

What were the circumstances of their meeting the stone does not declare, only that the deceased had been a princess in her native land, and had died in the obscure east-country haven, and had been "beloved."

Nothing, but all — at least all that life has to give.

The simple idyll of the princess and Andrew Brodie, mariner, is writ on the red marble slab, in letters less enduring than their love, badly designed and poorly cut, and destined soon to disappear in the cold rains and steely blasts of the East Neuk of Fife, and leave the stone a blank.

How they met, loved, and how the mariner brought home his island bride, perhaps to droop in the cold north, and how he laid her in the drear churchyard to wait the time when they should be united once again in some Elysian field, not unlike Polynesia, with the Tree of Life for palms, the selfsame opal-tinted sea, angels for tropic birds, and the same air of calm pervading all the air, only the mariner, if he still lives, can say.

The princess, as Andrew Brodie first saw her, must have looked like the fair damsels Captain Cook describes, with perhaps just a slight tincture of the missionary school, but not enough to take away her grace.

Dressed in a coloured and diaphanous sacque, a wreath of red hibiscus round her head, her jet-black hair loose on her shoulders, bare arms and feet, and redolent of oil of cocoa-nut, she must have seemed a being from another world to the rough mariner.

How he appeared to her is harder to determine, perhaps as did Cortes to La Malinche, or as did Soto to the Indian queen amongst the Seminoles. True, we know what Cortes was like, how he rode like a centaur, was noble, generous, that he knew Latin, as Bernal Diaz says, and Soto was designed by nature to capture every heart. The Scottish sailor possibly appeared as the representative of a strange race, harder and fiercer, but more tender at the heart than her compatriots.

His steel-blue eyes may have appeared to her as hardly mortal; his rough and hairy hands, symbols of strength embodified; his halting speech, a homage to her charms. Then as he must have been an honest and true-hearted man, approaching her with the same reverence with which he would have courted one of the hard-faced, red-headed women of his native place, not in the fashion of the trader or the beach-comber, it must have seemed as if a being, superior by its strength, had thrown its strength aside, all for her love.

When his ship sailed, the sailor may have hidden in the hills, then when her topsails had sunk well beneath the waves, and he was sure the ship would not return, come out of hiding, and strolled timidly along the beach, until some trader or the missionary came out and sheltered him.

Naturally, chiefs and missionaries and all the foreign population looked on his love as an infatuation; but he, setting to work, trading in copra and bêche-de-mer, in coral and the like, gradually made himself a man of consequence. Schooners would come consigned to him, and cargoes of his own lie heaped in *baracoons*, thatched with banana leaves.

At last, when he had "gathered siller" and become a man of substance — for Brodie certainly was one of those who could not stoop to live upon his wife — he must have gone and seen the missionary. One sees him sweating in his long-shore togs, a palm-tree hat upon his head, toiling along the beach, and rapping at the door. The missionary, most likely a compatriot, bids him come in, and lays the "Word," which he has been translating into Polynesian, upon the table and welcomes him.

"I'm glad to see ye, Andrew. How time goes on. Now you're a man of substance, and will be sending for a wife . . . unless, indeed, you might think of Miss McKendrick, the new Bible-reader. A nice-like lass enough. No bonny, but then beauty, ye ken, is not enduring. . . . What, ye dinna say? I thocht ye had been cured o' all that foolishness. They island girls are a' like children. What sort of looking wife would she be to ye at hame, man Andrew?"

This may have passed, and then the wedding in the mission church, with the dusky catechumens looking stiff and angular in the death-dealing clothes of Christianity, the bride listening to the old-fashioned Scottish exhortation on the duties of her new estate, what time the chief, her father, a converted pagan, thought with regret of the marriage ceremonies that he had witnessed in his youth, so different from these.

It may have been that for a year or two the ill-assorted pair lived happily, the husband trading and watching his men work in his garden, whilst his wife swung in a hammock underneath a tree. As time went by the recollection of the grey village in East Fife would come back to the husband's mind and draw him northwards, whilst the wife wondered what it was he thought about, and why the steely eyes seemed to look through her as if they sought for something that she could never see.

At last would come the day when he first spoke of going home, timidly, and as if feeling somehow he was about to commit a crime. Her tears and expostulations can be imagined, and then her Ruth-like resolution to follow him across the sea.

The voyage and the first touch of cold, the arrival in the bare and stormy land, the disappointment of poor Andrew, when he found he was forgotten by the great part of his friends, and that the rest despised him for having brought a coloured woman home, all follow naturally.

All the small jealousies and miseries of a provincial town, the horrors of the Scottish Sabbath, the ceaseless rain, the biting wind, the gloom and darkness of the winter, the disappointment of the brief northern summer, the sea, in which none but a walrus or a seal could bathe, must have done their worst upon the island princess, now become in very truth the wife of Andrew Brodie, mariner. One sees her in her unbecoming European clothes, simple and yet accustomed to respect, exposed to all the harshness of a land in which though hearts are warm, they move so far beneath the surface that their pulsations hardly can be felt, except by those accustomed to their beat.

Then in the end consumption, that consumption that usually attacks a monkey when it passes north of forty, making its end so human and so pitiful, must have attacked her too.

Then the drear funeral, with Andrew and his friends in weepers and tall hats, which the east wind brushed all awry, making them look like ferrets; the little coffin with the outlandish name and date, and "in her thirtieth year" emb*lazo*ned on it in cheap brass lettering; and the sloping pile of shingly earth, so soon to be stamped down over the island flower.

Slowly the friends would go, after shaking Andrew by the hand. He, feeling vaguely that he had murdered her whom he loved best, would linger, as a bird hovers for a time above the place where it has seen its mate fall, a mere mass of bloodstained feathers, to the gun.

When he was gone the island princess would be left alone with the wind sweeping across the sea, sounding around the Bass, and whistling wearily above Inch Keith to sing her threnody.

El Jehad

Si-Taher-Ibu-Lezrac was discontented with everything he saw.

The world had altered since his youth, but he had never changed. Allah, he was certain, was still the same — the One, the Indivisible, the Laudable, the Beginner, the Restorer, the Victorious, the Merciful, the Compassionate; Mohammed, too, must certainly be still the Messenger of God, and if his glory was for the time eclipsed, he would shine forth again, just as the sun shines forth, after a passing shower.

Still all was wrong.

The Nazarenes were richer every day. The very faithful seemed to be resigned and to have grown less faithful than of yore. Some even shaved their beards, leaving a moustache upon their upper lips, after the Turkish style.

The women wore their veils so thin, that they were more an incentive than a hiding of their charms. They laughed and talked as they went through the streets holding each other's hands, and hence, under their *haiks* sometimes Si Taher fancied that the outline of their figures looked as if stays confined them, after the fashion of the Nazarenes. The electric light, the tramways, theatres, the railway station, and the port, where Moslems, Christians, Negroes, and Chinese all worked together, all the slaves of him who paid them, without distinction, either of creed or race, all seemed a menace to Islám.

The fault must be, he thought, a lack of faith; Allah still gave the victory, but gave it only to the men who fought, and so Si Taher passed his days pondering upon all he saw, and miserable, anxious and unquiet, like a wild beast deprived of liberty.

Types of his sort — fine Arab types that look as if they might have followed either The Praised One himself or Okba, Musa or Tarik — come from the desert, or from some *dúar* lost in the hills, no one knows how or whence.

It seems a miracle how little time has changed them from the first Arabs who came to Africa a thousand years ago.

They are the men marked out by nature and by fate for prophets, and if they have no following the fault is not with them but with the changing times.

Brown and hard-looking, as if cut out of walnut-wood; with a beard so thick it looked more like a setting than a beard, though it was flecked with grey; his long and wavy hair falling about his shoulders like the mane of a wild horse, all in Si Taher, showed his desert origin and his descent from the wild tribes that, centuries ago, poured out like locusts from the Hadramut to overspread the world.

From his whole being there exhaled an air of mystery, of fanaticism, of ferocity mixed with a savage simpleness.

His thin and muscular body which his *haik* veiled, but did not hide, showed glimpses of his legs and arms, hairy as are the limbs of an orang-outang. His feet were shod with sandals of undressed camel's skin. His strong and knotted hands looked like the roots of an old oak, left bare above the ground, both in their size and make.

He always carried in his hand a staff of argán wood, which use and perspiration had polished like a bone, during the years of his wanderings up and down the various countries of Islám. No one remembered when he had first appeared, or where he came from, although Algiers and Constantine, Tlemcen, and the cities of the coast had known him well for years. At times he passed whole days silent and motionless. At times he sat in the mosque court, but motionless; so motionless that it might well have happened, that which did happen to the Prophet (whom may God have pardoned) who, being in an ecstasy of prayer, remained so quiet, that a dove, lighting on his shoulder, laid an egg inside his hood. Though he said nothing, yet it was known he was an enemy of all the Christians, hating them mortally.

The Arabs say knowledge is from the desert, and in a certain measure they are right; for certainly more of the primitive instincts of the race are to be found amongst those born amongst its sands, than falls to those whose lives are passed within a labyrinth of bricks.

Not that the Arabs think of that when they enunciate their apothegm, with the same serious air of enunciating an experience of their own, habitual to them even in the most futile things of life.

Certain it is that in the desert all the remains of old-world science, and the traditions of their faith, are better far preserved than in the towns, where modern notions and conversation with the Infidel — who, as the Arabs say, came from the sea — corrupt their purity.

Names of the stars, as Betelgeux and Aldebáran, Sohail and Fomalhaut, Algol, Altair, and Ras Alháque; legends of the first dawning of Islám; the adventures of the four just men, the companions of the Prophet; the daily practice of the simple, healthy life that nomads lead; the respect that children owe to elders, even the classical speech of the tribe of the Khoresh, all is preserved, more pure and more intense, out in the Sáhara, than in these lands, spurned by the Christian's boots, where his hat is, as it were, a challenge to the Believers' eyes. On that account, when a man from the desert comes to town, men venerate him, as the most perfect incarnation of the race. So, the brown, rag-clad, turbanless Si Taher, with his thick curly mane, confined about his forehead, with a grey cord of camel's hair, was looked on as a saint, that is, a man who cared not for the world, but lived within himself, for amongst Arabs faith is everything. Good works are estimable, especially when they bring benefits, but faith is Allah's gift; he gives or he withholds.

Through streets and squares he wandered, looking at everything with the fixed eyes of the true desert-born, which take in everything, down to the smallest detail, though they seem quite opaque.

He saw, and hated all he saw; and above everything his soul revolted when he saw some little soldier striking a true Believer without cause, shouldering him off the pavement or, with a sudden pull, snatching his turban off, and leaving him ashamed, bald-headed, and a sport for children and for fools.

Then in his eyes there shone a flame as when a man turns on the electric light and shuts it instantly, or when a captive lion glares for a moment at some idiot, when he sticks his cane between his bars.

However, like a true Arab as he was, he had himself in hand, and the first fury over, knew how to dull his eyes, and leave his face expressionless and blank. Much did he ponder on the ancient glories of his race and on the vestiges of antique splendour still existing in the land that Arabs call the Andalós, naming it always with a sigh.

Well did he know the Tower of Seville, the mosque of Cordoba, Malaga and its citadel and, best of all, the Castle of the Pomegranate, called by the Infidel, Granada, the city of dreams.

"Oh Granada," he would say, "I thought to see thee as a bride in spring, but I have seen thee widowed and in sorrow; I thought to see thee with my heart full of joy, but instead my eyes have filled with tears."

In his youth he had wandered to Madrid, capital of the Infidel, whose women all are veilless, and who know neither faith nor law. "May God destroy them," he would piously observe, passing between his strong and hairy fingers the beads of a thick rosary of white bone, which he had always in his hand, after the fashion of his kind. In his youth he had been a shepherd, and well remembered the happy days, when lying with his head against a bush of dry palmetto, watching his goats, half sleeping and half waking, amongst the sandy pastures of the Sáhara, he played upon a reed, waiting with patience for the evening prayer, and when the day was longer than the shadow of a spear. He liked to muse upon the proverb, "No prophet, but was a shepherd in his youth"; and used to say with an air of self-satisfaction, "Mohammed was a shepherd, as was I; shepherds were Abraham and David; why, therefore, shall not I be one, if Allah and his Messenger give me their aid?" In fact, all that a man, shepherd or not, requires is but God's help, and this the Arabs know, larding their speech with pious phrases, such as "May God bestow a blessing on thee," "May God increase thy welfare," or "God strengthen thee."

At times the poet, who, it is said, sleeps in the heart of every man, and not infrequently in Arabs, in despite of their material life, woke in Si Taher, and he saw the empire of Islám once again flourishing, like a palm tree by a pool.

He saw the banner of the Nazarenes trampled beneath the feet of the Believers, and its dominion once more re-established, where it had flourished in the past. As in a dream, he used to stray about the streets, with his eyes fixed on vacancy. Little by little men began to say he was a saint, a condition easily acquired with the Arabs, amongst whom the dividing-line between saint and madmen is not so stringently drawn, as it is with ourselves. To them all things are natural, as all things come from Allah, and if he wishes that a man shall be a saint he breathes upon him, making him mad, a hero, or a prophet, and setting him apart. When Europeans passed him in the streets they felt a feeling of repulsion; almost of fear; the Arabs, on the other hand, an ecstasy of joy when they beheld the terror that he caused.

Rumours went round he was an emissary of the Sennusi, that Sheikh and prophet who, from the depths of his oasis, never ceased praying for the restoration of the faith. Others again averred he was a prophet, and waited for a sign, that sign for which the whole world of Islám is waiting anxiously. When they receive it, so tradition says, they will all rise: the husbandman will leave the plough, the camel-driver his long line of camels, shepherds their flocks, and from the hills and plains, thousands will march to drive the Runis to the sea.

Poor and without a friend, solitary like a naked sword without a sheath, Si Taher passed his life, now sleeping in the courtyards of the mosques, now by a camel-driver's fire, again upon the shore behind a boat, with the waves lulling him to sleep, now in the market-places watching the crowds, and walking through the press, absorbed and quiet, as he were walking in a wood.

Si Taher's brainpan, always as agitated as a pan of crickets, kept him alternatively plunged in the deepest contemplation, or else a prey to visions, which left him writhen and exhausted with their vividness and force.

At times, he saw himself on horseback, with his long flint-lock in his hand, standing up in the stirrups, leaning well back against the cantle, his long reins floating in the air, his burnous streaming like a flag, and close behind him the serried ranks of an innumerable army of the mysterious, blue-clad, close-veiled warriors, sprung from the desert sands, as in the time of the Almohades, when those fierce sectaries spread over Spain like locusts, shouting the name of God. Under the influence of such dreams, his fury knew no bounds, and from a peaceful, contemplative man leaning upon his staff, and watching everything without a word, he suddenly became a maniac, raving and foaming at the mouth, till with the very violence of his emotions, he would collapse upon the sand. At such times everything he saw was matter for his rage.

French soldiers, with their baggy trousers and short jackets, and worst of all their officers, dressed tightly, an indecency to the true Believer's eye, caused him to gnash his teeth, and mutter that their mothers were all shameless, veilless ones, who never had said No.

Europe with all its pomps and vanities, quick-firing guns, its telegraphs and telephones, railways and workhouses, its boots with paper soles, its women with tight stays and high-heeled boots, its men who shaved their chins, leaving their hair to grow, as if they had been Jinns, its justice which to him was tyranny, and its injustices which kept him still uncomprehending, all appeared as a bad dream.

He had not grasped that that which is, is the best that the world has known to those who live in it, and that true justice only can be found in some far country, unattainable by man.

Well understood, the Holy Land lies always just a little farther on, as did Manoa, Trapalanda, the city of the Cæsars and that enchanted city in the far-distant, opaline and sun-flushed mountains, above San Luis Potosí. For poor Si Taher, it was none of these, neither the Andalós, nor

Egypt, Bagdad, Irak-el-Hind, or far-off Nabothea, but in the humblest *dúar*, thatched hut, or circle of low, black tents of camel's hair where were maintained in their integrity the customs of the faith.

These usages, which seem as if even in the times of the *Arabian Night*, *[sic=Nights]* they were old and time-worn, and natural laws which dated from the childhood of mankind, and which the Arabs had received from those their ancestors, who in the Neje and the Hedjáz, wandered with flocks and herds by day and night upon the plains, were to Si Taher as the essence of his blood. The panorama of the bay, its ships and boats, the high white town set in its frame of greenest gardens, the Alcazába, aloof, mysterious and grim, the life of the bazaars, the open squares, in which the water-carriers bending beneath their bursting goat-skin, ringing a little brazen bell, the passing women, noiseless as spectres, and close veiled, seemed to say nothing to the wanderer, or perhaps said much, as may some well-remembered field say much or little to the animals.

At times the injustice of his lot made him indignant, as it has made indignant every outcast since the beginning of the world, and as in the future when the advance of progress has made man doubly a slave, will make those who have failed, still more indignant than of yore.

Then he would say, "Vice pitches her tent and fortune fixes the poles of it, whilst virtue travels with adversity as her sole follower"; then set himself to find the reason with that blind faith in God, which from the days of St. Augustine all Africans have shared. At last he thought he saw his way. Could he but purify mankind all would be well, and once again Allah would give the victory; but well he knew that though the world goes out to greet the conqueror, he must conquer first.

Since our first fathers left the fair garden by the Tigris, all prophets, mad and just men, and everyone who thinks upon the miserable condition of mankind, racked between rage and tears, has *[sic = have]* seen that man needed but purity of life to save himself.

Much did Si Taher ponder on the first step to take, feeling as every one of the long line of prophets in the East has felt, that if the world was to be saved, the task depended on himself.

His constant wanderings and fasts, prolonged till he saw visions, even at noontide, had reduced him to a skeleton, so that he was in a fit state to try and move the world, without a fulcrum for the lever of his soul.

Men saw him straying about the places, where those who in times past had given up their lives, fighting against the enemies of God, lay buried, with a rough stone to mark their resting-places.

At night he gazed upon the stars, and sat down listening to the sounding of the surf, the scent of orange flowers filling his nostrils as it floated down the breeze.

Tears dimmed his eyes, and he recited poems from the *Diwan-el-Faredi*, or from the *Seven Suspended Lamps of the Moallakat*. Hours would he ponder on Al Makhari, reading the records of his race, his studies and his musings in thought becoming still more melancholy, and still a little nearer to the thin line that separates madness from generosity, a line so thin that the most part of men can never see it, thinking all mad who are not as themselves.

When on the sands at powder-play, the horsemen passed like a hurricane, twisting their guns around their heads, just as their ancestors had whirled their javelins, Si Taher shouted as they passed and called upon God's name.

Stretched in the shade, he played his lute for hours, and sang to it, in a low voice, interminable songs, finishing every verse with a long-drawn-out "Allah!" that seemed the plaint of some Believer who had lost his faith, and mourned its obsequies.

When he smoked hemp he used to lie in that strange drunkenness or ecstasy that falls upon the smoker of the dark, pungent weed. What dreams passed through his brain he told to no one, or if he saw the *huris*, beautiful as fawns, moving like branches of the myrobolan, diffusing ambergris.

Most likely all his dreams were either on the glories of his race, the times of Othman and of Abu Bekr, or of that age when all the poor were rich in contentment, the rich all poor in spirit, and everyone was satisfied with his condition, underneath the sky. Given over to his dreams and wanderings, Si Taher grew more ragged every day. His fell of hair hung round his head and neck as if it were a sort of unkempt aureole, uncombed and dirty, and the strange air between a prophet and a fool, so common to men of his kind throughout the East, rendered him terrible and ridiculous at the same time, as he stalked glaring, through the streets.

Little by little the authorities got wind. Si Taher was a dangerous man. They watched him carefully, but he did nothing but wander through the streets, though it was known that many waited anxiously, looking for a sign, and the whole town was stirred, as any town throughout the East is stirred when it is rumoured that a prophet will arise.

Charity

At last one morning, one of those mornings in the spring, in which the town buried in verdure, all bathed in sun, and with the scent of blossom from the orange gardens make them appear like ante-rooms to Paradise, with the breeze gently ruffling the leaves, the sea and land wrapped in a veil of whitest light, intense and melancholy at the same time, as if the sun were tired with shining for so many thousand years on the same landscape, when everything was tranquil, as tranquil as in an island lost in the Pacific, Si Taher rushed into the street, proclaiming the Jehad, "Allahu Ackbas" the Holy War, quintessence of the religion of the sword, and the last word of all religions upon earth. Long years had passed since it last echoed through the town. It ran like quicksilver right to the hearts of those who heard it, and serious men seated, like idols in a temple, half sleeping in their shops, shivered and rose, and then half doubtingly walked towards the market-place. There they paused, hesitating, and one looking round furtively said to his friend, fingering his rosary the while, "My son, take heed thy mouth break not thy neck," and his friend, with his nostrils wide distended, and with his breath coming spasmodically, replied, "Yea, let the archer tarry ere he draw the bow, for the shaft when it leaves the string returns no more . . . but did you hear the cry?"

The water-carriers left their goat-skins on the sand, and from the "Marsa" a crowd of boatmen, grasping stretchers, and handling their knives, left their boats rocking at the quay, and flowed towards the market-place all shouting out "Jehad." The word of fear was mumbled by old men, and children, playing, shouted it aloud.

Throughout the city a vague murmur ran, as in some town, built on the slopes of a volcano, there runs a murmur, just before an earthquake, or a lava-flow.

Rich Arabs clad in spotless white, serious and imposing in their fleecy haiks, and swaying in their majestic walk, like camels, heard the cry, and taking their red praying cushions underneath their arms, stood undecided waiting for a sign.

Even the Spahis seated erect in their high saddles, despite their discipline, looked at each other furtively, afraid to meet each other's eyes.

The murmur grew, just as a mountain stream in flood grows as it rushes on, and at the head of a huge crowd, appeared Si Taher looking like one possessed.

Foam flecked his beard, his eyes flashed fire, and in his hand he bore a goat's head fresh cut off, from which fell drops of blood upon the faithful, when he raised his hand before commencing his harangue.

He raised his voice, looked up to heaven, and in the very act of speaking, stopped, as a horse stops checked by the Arab bit. He stopped and gazed as, pushing through the crowd, there came a functionary. Short, and in an ill-cut uniform that rendered him more vulgar still, he tripped along with the peculiar skipping movement of the French soldier, looking upon the Arabs, with the look a butcher gives at a fat sheep, just as he draws the knife.

His smoked-out cigarette hung to his under lip, and his short sabre beat against his legs, as he strode on with that peculiar air of arrogance which all authority confers.

Pushing his way amongst the crowd, he made his way amongst the Arabs, who half timidly and half ferociously stood waiting, as a tame lion waits, not daring to attack its keeper, because it fears the whip.

Striding up to the would-be Messiah, he looked him firmly in the face, and in a jargon, half Arabic, half French, said roughly, "Macanshi el Jehad; Si Taher, you are drunk, or have been smoking hemp."

Si Taher vacillated, clutched his knife firmly, then sheathed it, and then let fall the bloody goat's head, which left a bright red blotch upon the sand.

Obediently he followed the French soldier through the crowd, and all the Arabs quietly went home to wait the coming of another prophet, one to whom God should give the victory, and the white town returned to slumber in the sun.

Charity

La Pampa

All grass and sky, and sky and grass, and still more sky and grass, the Pampa stretched from the *pajonales* on the western bank of the Paraná right to the stony plain of Uspallata, a thousand miles away.

It stretched from San Luis de la Punta down to Bahia Blanca, and again crossing the Uruguay, comprised the whole republic of that name and a good half of Rio Grande, then with a loop took in the *misiones* both of the Paraná and Paraguay.

Through all this ocean of tall grass, green in the spring, then yellow, and in the autumn brown as an old boot, the general characteristics were the same.

A ceaseless wind ruffled it all and stirred its waves of grass. Innumerable flocks and herds enamelled it, and bands of ostriches (Mirth of the Desert, as the Gauchos called them) and herds of palish-yellow deer stood on the tops of the *cuchillas* and watched you as you galloped past.

Down in the south, the Patagonian hare, mataco, and the quiriquincho scudded away or burrowed in the earth. Towards the middle region of this great galloping ground, the greatest that God made . . . perhaps He could not possibly have made a better, even had He tried . . . great armadillos and iguanas showed themselves, and in the north, around the deep metallic-toned *isletas* of hard-wood *montés*, flocks of macaws — red, yellow, and bright blue — floated like butterflies. Up in the north, ant-eaters (the Tamandua of the Guaranis) and tapirs wandered, looking as if they had escaped from out the Ark.

Over the whole extent the "tero-tero" hovered, screamed, whistled, and circled just above your horse's head. From every *monté* and from every maize field flew chattering flocks of parakeets.

Tigers and pumas inhabited the woods, right from the Estero Ñembuco, which I have crossed so often with the mud and water to my horse's cinch, down to the Antarctic beech forests of Sandy Point.

In all the rivers nutrias and lobos and the carpincho, with its great red teeth, swam with their heads awash, laid flat upon the stream, just like a seal at sea.

Viscachas burrowed, and wise, solemn little owls sat at the entrance of their burrows making pretence to guard them, as does a sentinel before a palace door.

Locusts occasionally visited the Pampa, blackening the sun, devouring all the crops, and disappearing just as they had come.

"Where is the Manga?" was a familiar question on the plains, and grave and bearded men reined in their horses, their *poncho*s suddenly clinging to their sides, just as a boat's sail clings around the mast when it has lost the wind, and pointing with a lean, brown finger stained with tobacco juice, replied, *Por allacito, en los Porongos*, and then departed, just as ships speak each other on the sea. The north wind filled the air with cottony filaments, and the pampero, roaring like a whole *rodeo* that had taken fright, levelled the houses and the grass. The air was full in summer of a perpetual twittering of insects that hung invisible, whilst in the winter the white hoar-frost in early morning silvered the grass, and hung congealed upon the tops of stakes, just as it did in the old world in which the poet-king penned the "Cantar de los Cantares," two thousand years ago.

All that, was what the Pampa had inherited from nature. When I first knew it, it looked just as it must have looked on the morning of the seventh day in far-off Nabothea, that old-world Entre-Rios, when the Creator rested and, looking earthwards, saw that it was good.

Man had but little altered it, but for a peach grove here and there, a white *estancia* house, or a straw-coloured *rancheria* or *pulperia*, built either at the pass of some great river or on a hill, as that at the Cuchilla de Peralta, by which the mule-trail, used since the Conquest, led, winding upon its way towards Brazil.

Men passed each other seated upright on their *recaos* driving their horses in a bunch in front of them, swinging their whips around their heads.

They passed, shouting a salutation, or if too far off to be heard, waving a hand, and sank into the plain just as a vessel sinks into the sea, the body of the horse first disappearing, then the man, *poncho*, and, last of all, his hat. The waves of grass appeared to swallow him, and as men rode they kept their eyes fixed on the horizon, or, if at night, upon a star. When the night caught them on the plains, after first hobbling the mare, they tied a horse to a long *soga*, making, if neither stick nor bone were to be found, a knot in the rope's end, stamping it in, and lying down upon it.

They smoked a cigarette or two, looked at the stars a little, and took good care to place their heads in the direction towards which they had to journey, for in the mists of sunrise nothing was easier than to mistake the point you aimed at, and wander back upon the trail.

In that green ocean, as the proverb said, "he who wanders from the trail is lost"; and it was true enough, as many a heap of bones, to which a shred of tattered cloth still clung, most amply testified, as you came on them on a gallop, looking perhaps for horses stolen or strayed. Your companion might or might not rein up his horse, but certainly would point in passing, and remark, "See where the grass grows rank around the bones; there has a Christian died."

"Christian" was used more as a racial than a religious term, the Indians usually being called *Los Bravos*, *Los Infieles*, *Los Tapes*, the latter usually applied either to the descendants of the Charruas in the Banda Oriental, or to the Indian Mansos of the Missions of the north. How much the aforesaid *Infieles* and the *Tapes* had left their impress on the speech and the life of the Gauchos, might be seen by the national costume of the *poncho* and the *chiripá*. These, as the early writers tell us, were adapted from the "Infidel we found dwelling in all these plains, when first Don Pedro de Mendoza came with his following to conquer for his lord, and to proclaim the glory of the name of Him who, though born in a stable, is higher than all kings." In the current Pampa speech the words *bagual*, *ñandu*, *ombú* and *vincha*, *tatu*, *Tacuara*, and *bacaray*, with almost all the names of plants, of shrubs and trees, recalled the influence of the Indians, the Quichuas, and Guaranis, the Pampas and Pehuelches, Charruas, and the rest of those who once inhabited the land.

Las boleadoras, known to the Gauchos as *Las tres Marias*, was the distinctive weapon of the southern plains. With them the Indians slew many of Don Pedro de Mendoza's men at the first Christianising of the River Plate, and with them also did the fierce Gaucho troops who rose under Elio and Liniers crash in the skulls of various English, Luteranos — for so the good Dean Funes styles them in his history — who under Whitelock had attacked the town. Only upon the Pampa, in the whole world, was this tremendous weapon ever known. None of the Pampa tribes used bows and arrows, for with them the *bolas*, and in especial the single stone, fixed to a plaited thong of hide, and called *la bola perdida*, quite supplied their place.

In fact, for no land but the Pampa, that is, in the Americas (for it could well be used in Africa and Asia), are *las tres Marias* fit. In North

America the plains are bushy or the grass is long as hay, conditions which would militate against the throwing of a weapon which, often thrown a yard or two behind the quarry's legs, sprang from the ground and then entangled them.

Nothing could be more typical of the wild life of forty years ago upon the plains than was the figure of a Gaucho dressed in his *poncho* and his *chiripá*, his naked toes clutching the stirrups, his long iron spurs kept in position by a thong of hide, dangling below his heels, his hair bound back by a red silk handkerchief, his eyes ablaze, his silver knife passed through his sash and *tirador*, and sticking out just under his right elbow, his *pingo* with its mane cut into castles, and its long tail floating out in the breeze as, twisting *las tres Marias* round his head, he flew like lightning down a slope, which the mere European horseman would have looked on as certain death, intent to "ball" one of a band of fleet *ñandus* all sailing down the wind.

Letting the *bolas* go, so easily, it seemed as if his will and not his hand directed them, they hurtled through the air, revolving on their own axis sixty or seventy yards, and, when the *sogas* met the ostriches' neck, the centrifugal force being averted, the balls fell down and, wrapping tightly round the legs, soon threw the giant bird upon its side. Ten or twelve bounds brought up the hunter, who, springing from his saddle, his huge iron spurs clanking like fetters on the ground, either put hobbles on his horse, or if he felt quite sure of him, threw the long reins upon the ground, confident that it, trained by experience to know a step upon the reins involved a pull upon the mouth, would stand obediently.

Then, drawing his *facon*, the Gaucho either stuck it deeply into the bird, low down upon the breast, or if occasion served, drawing a spare set of *boleadoras* from around his waist, or taking them from underneath the *cojinillo* of the *recao*, crashed in his victim's skull. Sometimes, indeed, with a *revés* of the *facon* they used to cut the ostrich's head off at a blow; but this wanted a sharp and heavy knife, and an arm with which to wield it, strong beyond ordinary.

I have seen a Gaucho, hunting wild colts, or ostriches, in the very action of swinging the *bolas* round his head, have his horse fall with him, alight upon his feet, and without losing the command of the direction of his swing, catch his own horse as it, springing to its feet, was just about to leave him helpless afoot upon the plains.

Afoot upon the plains . . . that was indeed a phrase of fear upon the Pampas of the south. No mariner afloat upon the waves, his mainstay but a little boat, was in a worse condition than the man who, from some cause or other, found himself horseless in the vast sea of grass.

From having been as free as is a bird, he instantly became as helpless as the same bird with a wing broken by a shot.

If cattle saw him, they not infrequently attacked him, when his one chance of safety (on the open plains) was to lie down and, simulating death, to let them smell him, which when they had done, if he lay still enough, they turned and went away. When the pedestrian approached a house the troop of dogs that every Gaucho kept surrounded him like wolves, barking and snapping at his legs if it were daytime, or falling on him literally like wolves if it should happen to be dark. Small streams, which generally had muddy bottoms, and through which his horse had plunged, sinking down to the cinch, but always getting through, to the man afoot became impassable, making him wander up and down their banks, perhaps for miles, till he could find a "pass."

If by an evil chance he lost his way his fate was sealed, especially upon that portion where distances were great between *estancias*, and where marauding Indians on a *malón* would kill him if they saw him, just as a boy kills a young bird when it runs fluttering across his path. To lose one's horse and saddle was worse than bankruptcy; in fact, was so considered, as in the story of a Frenchman who seeing a Gaucho standing idly about, inquired why he did not go out and work.

"Work, *madre mia*," said the man, "how can I work when I am bankrupt?"

"What then," the Frenchman said, "you have been in commerce, and fallen upon a bad affair; poor man, I pity you." The Gaucho stared at him, and answered, "In commerce — never in my life, but at a *pulperia* some Infidel or other stole my horse and saddle, with *lazo*, *bolas*, and a *cojinillo* that I bought up in Rioja, and left me without shade."

Poor man, how could he work, afoot and saddleless? No doubt before the Conquest men crossed the plains afoot; but painfully, taking perhaps long years to go from the Atlantic to the Andes, groping along from stream to stream, as the first navigators felt their way from cape to cape, coasting along the bays.

The coming of the horse gave a new life to the vast plains; for nature seemed to welcome horses once again, from the long interval between the times in which the Tertian eight-footed horse roamed on the Pampas, which now are populated by the descendants of the thirteen mares and the three stallions that Pedro de Mendoza left behind when he sailed back to Spain, after his first attempt to colonise.

This is the way I recollect it. First came short grasses, eaten close down by sheep, then thistles that grew as high as a man's head, a wilderness, through which the cattle had made a labyrinth of paths; then coarser grasses, and by degrees wiry, brown bents, until at length almost all sign of grass was lost, where the Pampas joined the stony plains of Patagonia in the south.

Northwards, the waving grasses also grew sparser, till in the Jesuit Missions, clumps of *yatais* encroached upon the plains, which ended finally, in the dense woods of Paraguay.

Silence and solitude were equally the note of north and south, with a horizon bounded by what a man could see when sitting on his horse.

There were few landmarks, but in the southern and the middle districts a dark *ombú*, standing beside some lone *tapera* and whose shade fell on some *rancho* or *estancia*, although the proverb said, "The house shall never prosper upon whose roof is thrown the shade of the *ombú*."

Well did the ancient Quichuas name the plains, with the word signifying "space," for all was spacious — earth, sky, the waving continent of grass; the enormous herds of cattle and of horses; the strange effects of light; the fierce and blinding storms and, above all, the feeling in men's minds of freedom, and of being face to face with nature, under those southern skies.

A Hatchment

R. B. Cunninghame Graham

To Walter B. Harris of Tangier
Explorer, Writer and Friend.

Introduction

A Hatchment (1913) was first published by Duckworth & Co., London. The collection contains sixteen stories and sketches with a considerable variety of settings: Rome (1), North Africa (1), England (2), Spain (3), Scotland (4) and South America (5). The average length of each is 15-16 pages, about 3,300 words. The title of the collection needs some explanation. As revealed in the title story, "A Hatchment", the word 'hatchment' is a term coming from heraldry, describing the coat of arms of a dead person, shown within a black lozenge-shaped frame and usually displayed on the front of the deceased's house. What Graham intended by the choice of title for the whole collection is open to speculation. The derivation of this meaning is from Old French, *hacher*, to chop, referring to the shading of fine lines, or hatching, often used in heraldry. It is possible that Graham is making a point about the subject matter of so many of his stories, belonging to a past that is dead. Equally, he may be punning on the other meaning of 'hatch', coming from Old English, referring to a new hatch of eggs, the stories in this collection. Certainly we must be aware that Graham is choosing his title with a considerable degree of subtlety.

Though not appearing together, each Spanish piece involves a quest.

"A Belly God" (17 pages), apparently referring to an individual finding pleasure in gratifying his appetite, is set in Madrid. Against the advice of his Galician hall-porter Andrés, a South American diplomat representing Costalarga, a former Spanish colony, hires the destitute Englishman William Heyward as his secretary. A Spanish general is noncommittal when diplomat and secretary try to promote a new and pretty unpalatable style of compressed food for the Spanish army. When the diplomat returns from two months in Paris, the porter reports a smell of burning from the sealed office: the secretary, his weekly salary unpaid, over ten days has eaten the compressed food. The porter sees Heyward as a "perfect belly god." Heyward has disappeared – and may even have died.

The opening external narration gives way to the first-person voice of the diplomat and some vituperation from the porter. The real strength of the tale lies in characterisation, with the four characters being nicely contrasted. The diplomat is kind to Heyward and hostile to Spain as the reactionary ex-colonial power. The porter, devoted to his tender-hearted employer, is uncharitable towards the secretary. The Spanish general is grossly squat, cruel and venal. As for Heyward, the title is clearly ironic: he is not an epicure but a man starving to death in the introduction and again later as a result of his employer's forgetfulness. Heyward is a pathetically vulnerable individual caught vastly out of his depth in a foreign place.

"A Page of Pliny" at c.8000 words is very long, almost a novella. Graham's narrator, a friend called McFarlane, tells the listening Graham of how he went to Spain to seek a Roman goldmine. He and a hired mining engineer travelled to the village of Carraceido and collected soil samples. When the soil was assayed, there was no gold. There is a personal application of this story to Graham's own career. In efforts to clear family debts, Graham and his wife Gabriela had in 1894 searched unsuccessfully for an old Roman goldmine in northern Spain, so McFarlane is Graham at one remove re-working his authentic experience: the library in the damp old house, very likely Gartmore, Vigo town unchanged from a visit a generation before, the heat in Orense, the stagecoach to Carraceido and this village's inn, inn-keeper, inn fleas and anciently idyllic landscape are very well depicted. Withal, the introduction is over-long and too detailed.

Whereas the engineer and in time the villagers all believe in the goldmine, McFarlane, unconvinced from the beginning, lacks the absolute belief needed by the seeker of Eldorado. The villagers, convinced that the soil samples will contain gold, merrily celebrate McFarlane's and the engineer's return from the mine location. Their hopes will prove baseless. In a final twist, the elderly McFarlane still likes to fancy that he owns a secret fairy mine worth millions as he awaits "the day when the regenerated Carraceido shall bear my honourable name." At the last the unbeliever dreams of Eldorado.

In "At Sanchidrian", the plot is spare. A train crossing the northern meseta has stopped briefly at a small station. A rider arrives and asks the dining-car staff for a block of ice for his elderly father, dying of fever. The rider charges furiously back to his village with the ice but his father dies before he arrives. The somewhat unSpanish place-name, properly Sanchidrián, is a real location, set a distance east of La

Estación (The Station) on the railway linking Valladolid with Ávila and Madrid. Though Graham does not supply the detail just mentioned, the introductory scene-setting – the Castilian plain in high summer and the slow-moving train - is substantial and carefully wrought. The rider's desperate return to Sanchidrián occupies four dramatic pages as the ice as big as a large loaf melts and the horse comes close to collapse. In a first climax the priest reports the father to have died an hour earlier imagining the touch of the ice brought by his dutiful son. In the second climax the son touches his dead father's forehead and lips with the now apple-sized piece of ice. This – the final piece in the collection - is a virtually perfect piece of technically dispassionate yet powerful third-person narration that would film beautifully.

The search for food in "A Belly God" has been successful – for a time. In "A Page of Pliny", the quest for gold has failed. In "At Sanchidrian", the son finds and brings the ice – to a now dead father. The three quests bear little final fruit.

In "Upwards", Graham's setting is a Christian church in Rome built on the site of an ancient basilica. The sketch shows remarkable sympathy in Graham for popular Catholic rituals. The slum-dwelling and peasant parishioners process up a considerable staircase. Once inside, their popular Christmas rituals include a boy of twelve reciting, with a stumble or two, a Christmas prayer; a tiny child briefly invoking the Madonna; and a girl – a young, pious actress - telling the tale of the Christian maiden Agatha threatened by a young Roman knight. The crowd then moves to the Christmas crib with its plaster figures representing the stable in Bethlehem. Graham personally dislikes "progress" as manifested in the use of electric light and gaudily coloured modern stucco figures. He prefers old-style candlelight and figures that once seemed painted by Dolci or Guerino. He does recognise that for the poor parishioners the effect remained the same. Some seminarians and priests look down on the common folk's behaviour, though in Graham's thoughtful view Peter founded a church not on philosophy but on blind faith. He displays impressive handling of the throng round the crib – working folk dressed in rags, young girls, soldiers speaking country dialect and an old peasant and his wife "like two bundles of dried vines."

The popular nature of the event crystallises in the final image of two toy balloons bouncing back off the low basilica ceiling. The opening page hints at Graham's scepticism about organised religion but as the sketch progresses such reservations are not allowed to cloud a firm mainly third-person narration where Graham presents the simple faith-minded parishioners very sympathetically. Graham does not call on the deep historical resonances of this church, named only once as the Ara Coeli (Altar of Heaven): it is in fact an ancient religious site, set on the Palatine Hill in the very centre of the old city, and is the home church of Rome's town council. Graham's sense of history and concern for the loss of old customs mean that he regrets the loss of "… an older world, a world human, but outworn, lovable, and yet passing from our eyes…" Yet another Graham piece closes on a note of gilded nostalgia.

The three shortest pieces in the collection are "Bismillah", "Falkirk Tryst" and "Mist in Menteith."

"Bismillah" opens in a charmingly described, almost painterly coastal setting that is part-Classical and part-Old Testament: it includes a bay, a white town, a watch-tower, a rocky hill and fishing-boats. A goatherd's pipe recalls the Golden Age. The goatherd being an Arab boy, the setting is North Africa. In the flock one kid in particular seems very attached to the young goatherd. The comment about "that pathetic trust in man that Eastern animals seem to have… " warns of future drama. When the boy hands the kid over to a village elder, the elder, murmuring the invocation "In the name of Allah" ("Bismillah…."), slits its throat. Unmoved, the boy watches the kid die.

In "Bismillah", Graham suppresses his usual narrative *persona*, opting for classic third-person objective narration. If in a herding culture there can be little sentimentality towards animals, a kid's death may be viewed and presented matter-of-factly: no great commotion in nature follows. Most readers, though, will be beguiled by the idyllic setting and the apparent companionship between goatherd and kid. This mood carefully established, an utterly dispassionate description of the kid's death follows, with Graham using suggestive language in "the blood spirted out…" and "Slowly the kid's head sank and coggled limply…", the latter unit using a Scottish verb 'to wobble, to rock.' The boy's lack of emotional response seems shocking, recalling the cool detachment of the impassive gauchos watching the summary execution – also by throat-slitting - of a young gaucho by a fellow gaucho in "A Silhouette" (*Faith*, 1909).

Two sketches are set in England - "A Moral Victory" in Yorkshire and "A Hatchment" on the south coast. The two families portrayed are rural upper class gentlefolk. One tale is light-hearted in tone, the other finally more sombre.

"A Moral Victory" is an affectionate tribute to Graham's Aunt Alexia, a redoubtable Yorkshire gentlewoman, dead now these forty years but in life a pillar of county society. Graham draws humour from her little beard and class-based High Churchness. She married a man quite different to herself - General Hickman Currie, brought up in French ways and inclined to flirt and womanise, even in old age. Another aunt delights in telling the young Graham the comical anecdote of how the General, appointed to a short-term command in India, thought it unwise to take Alexia. Over weeks he prepared the ship. One day Alexia drove to the docks and in the General's cabin discovered two sea-cots: the General planned to have female company on the voyage. Alexia sends home for her baggage. The General arrives to face Alexia. When later another carriage arrives loaded with luggage, the carriage and unseen occupant are sent away. A spirited lady has stymied an errant husband in a lively, comical sketch.

A hatchment as a diamond-shaped coat of arms of a dead person suggests ancient lineage, and the mansion-house in "A Hatchment" is solidly grounded in its village and the land. Widowed early, the "squire in petticoats" known to Graham was adored for her faith and good works. On her death her son, a seaman and a colleague of Graham's on the pampa [perhaps George Mansel, Graham's companion on the venture described in the novella, "Cruz Alta"], assumes her role. The goodhearted son serves dutifully and comically as a magistrate and cleverly engineers the resignation of his High Church vicar. In old age this man of the limitless sea and pampa withdrew to his smoking-room. Like several other old houses in Graham's life and writing, this house too decayed and since his friend's death it lies tenantless. Graham's friend's ghost still looks out over the coast towards the south-west. Graham does not say so, but the ghost may still remember the *pampero* wind. If any message there be, it may be that neither mother nor son, however active and benign, has been able to arrest the process of economic and physical decay.

The four tales set in Scotland all look back in time - to 1698, to the 1750-1760s and to the mid-nineteenth-century. Two have a measure of action, two are more descriptive.

"Loose and Broken Men" draws from old documents at Gartmore to allow Graham to relate a tale of old-style Highland raiders who came south of the Highland Line into Graham lands to steal cattle and horses. In December 1698 one such group seized all the possessions and animals of the widow m'Cluckey. The inventory of her losses and their value is almost gleefully recorded by Graham in the old Scots speech in a footnote that stretches over two full pages. As the raiders returned north by a route well known to Graham and intimately described, they gradually disposed of the booty "in open day... barely fifteen miles away." The documents record reports from various individuals – some traditional enemies of the Grahams, one the wife of the rustlers' leader - informing on the selling-off of the booty. The old papers do not supply an ending to the incident.

Graham *qua* landowner must view such raiders as disruptive rogues and outlaws, yet in his recounting of the incident there is a jocular tone that perhaps hints at a certain admiration for poverty-stricken Highlanders taking clever if illegal advantage of the comparative wealth of the Lowlands. He is certainly amused by the various efforts to cast blame not just on the raiders but on the people who bought goods and cattle from them. More soberly, Graham reflects on Scotland around 1700 being in many places still roadless when in England Addison, Swift and Defoe were emerging as writers. The implication is that Scotland then was primitive whereas England was developing a sophisticated society and culture. In Graham's *envoi* the Loose and Broken Men have all gone: only the hills and their ancient names remain.

In "The Beggar Earl" the intriguing title and the opening sentence – "Many a shadowy figure has flitted through the valley of Menteith" – instantly engage the reader's interest. Though Graham's character initially seems a worthless "cadger", the beggar earl's death is so imprinted in Graham's mind that he feels bound to recount his life. In 1744, an Edinburgh University medical student's claim to be an earl was rejected. His claims repeatedly ignored or denied, he took to riding an old white pony through "his" ancestral lands in Lomondside. Still dreaming of recognition in old age, one winter's morning he was found dead on the moor above Loch Lomond, his beloved parchments in his hand and his old pony standing by.

Though Graham makes two passing criticisms of the English and of success, the character sketch stands up well. The Graham family's traditional association with the Earldom of Menteith does not prevent the sketch being an entirely credible fiction. In spite of announcing his character's death early and introducing him as a sponger with a "fixed, foolish purpose", Graham gradually develops the beggar earl as perhaps self-deluded yet admirably likeable in his incorruptible Quixotic steadfastness.

In "Falkirk Tryst" Graham, delighting in the word "Tryst", recalls the ponies and cattle from the Islands and the north arriving at the great Falkirk Tryst. The October dawn awakening of the old Highland drovers is satisfyingly exact. More mischievously, Graham berates the English dealers for their slowness of mind and for shouting to make themselves understood to Highlanders who in fact spoke purer English. Graham's detailed review of a typical day at the Tryst ends nostalgically: "They are all gone with the old world they lived in… "

The language here has a strong Scottish flavour: tryst (meeting arranged in advance); hurl (to transport in a driven vehicle); burns (streams); dykes (walls), surmounted by their feals (turf coverings); plaid (long tartan cloth worn over the shoulder); daundered (walked, ambled); collie (sheepdog); a stot (calf); Hogmanay (New Year's Eve); "above the pass" (north and west of the Highland Line); kyloes (small long-horned long-haired cattle from NW Scotland); glens (narrow deep valleys); island "machars" (also machair: sandy grassy land above the high-water mark); "… doots" (doubts); targets (shields); claymores (large two-edged swords); brogues (untanned shoes); and bealach (*Gaelic* 'Pass of the Cattle'). Graham's fluent control of this language and of the whole picturesque event makes this a very fine piece of costumbrist writing.

These three sketches – "Loose and Broken Men", "The Beggar Earl" and "Falkirk Tryst" - are dense with the past and with a sense of loss.

In "Mist in Menteith", the Vale of Menteith's main feature is less the peat moss than the strange autumn mist that creates another sometimes hostile world. The same mist can lend a peculiar charm to the Lake and its islands. The three paragraphs from "Peat smoke floats…" form a prose poem that perfectly captures this sodden world. In the mist "Nothing is stable… Men come and go, the Saxon speech replaces Gaelic; even traditions insensibly are lost." In a closing litany the mist conquers all and brings for Graham a perhaps surprising sense of rest.

Five pieces set in the River Plate area look back to the last years of Indian terrorisation of the open pampa, to the pampa and its gaucho cowherding culture before barbed wire and modernisation and to Buenos Aires before large-scale immigration delivered a population explosion.

In "A Retrospect", Graham evokes the still colonial Buenos Aires he first knew in the 1870s – a flat town, with colonial buildings still standing and horses everywhere. St. Dominic's Church held trophies from the English attacks in 1806. Hotels, few and poor, included

Claraz's hostelry, popular with "camp" men. Huge numbers of Italian and Spanish emigrants were beginning to arrive in a city then of 300,000 people where the brothels already provided prostitutes of every nationality. Though new suburbs were appearing, the pampa and the salting-plant to which Graham delivered cattle still lay close to the city. Rather than the great modern city he knows of in 1913, Graham prefers old-style Buenos Aires. How many other Graham pieces could carry the sub-title "A Retrospect"?

In "Los Indios" Graham portrays the wild Indians of the pampa in southern Buenos Aires Province. What could slip into a dry exercise in anthropology is instead filled with drama, insight and understanding and solid evidence of his ability to project this usually maligned culture. His slightly over-pitched use of "romance" and "Arcadia" as applied to the Indians is more than counter-balanced by his riveting description of Indians massing in advance of a raid. He handles well the drama of their journey over huge distances to wreak havoc upon the utterly terrified white settlers on the shifting, permeable frontier. Graham understands well that the best defence for Christian settlers was not old firearms but a surrounding ditch, for the Indians scarcely ever dismounted and came to plunder rather than kill. In a single raid Indians could seize tens of thousands of cattle and sheep and many white women. Captive women were usually treated badly, though some did achieve positions of influence. The similarity between tame and wild Indians, their physical type and basic customs are clearly shown. Indian Territory – "Tierra Adentro" ('Inside Land') – gave refuge to rebel Indian chiefs and to outlaw gauchos. He recognises clearly that Indians and gauchos were very alike in their contempt of death and their cruelty. From his time in the 1870s Graham recalls one particularly brutal raid, but the days of savage Indian raids in the south of Buenos Aires province are now over. The evidence now suggests that the Argentine governments of the day practised ethnic cleansing, systematically and brutally exterminating the Indian warrior castes and dispersing their women and children into Christian society, so that Graham's penetrating sketch is a fascinating memorial to a savage, lost society.

"El *Rodeo*" was a gathering-place on an *estancia* where cattle in large numbers could be counted, checked for disease and treated, and separated out for dispatch to the slaughterhouse. Graham delivers a detailed and expert description of a *rodeo* involving several thousand cattle. Himself an accomplished horseman, he shows how gauchos expertly gathered in the cattle, kept them quiet, turned errant cows back to the *rodeo* and delivered, slaughtered and skinned a cow for the ranch-house meat-store. He admits that the sight of a difficult animal with its hocks sliced across and bellowing was repulsive. The greatest danger came from a stampede. In one stampede Graham saw a single semi-Indian rider trying to head off the stampede. When his horse tripped at high speed and somersaulted, the gaucho landed on his feet still holding his reins and smoothly and instantly re-mounted in a superb display of horsemanship. Graham's expertise as a horseman and writer makes this fine action piece exciting, even for the non-rider.

"The Pass of the River" was a crossing-place on the river Yi in the central Uruguayan pampa, on the cattle-trails north towards Brazil. A flying bridge, a flat-bottomed boat hauled on pulleys backwards and forwards across the river, carried cattle, sheep and mules, as well as bullock-carts and the weekly stagecoach. The nearby *pulpería* (country store-cum-bar) attracted the usual drinking and brawling gauchos, and rural prostitutes too Christian to bathe much. Cattle that stampeded would be brought back only hours later. Animals refusing to enter the raft were forced to swim across. Graham expects that now – thirty-plus years later - a railway over a hideous iron bridge will hold passengers who have no conception of the old life that swarmed around this vital crossing-place.

In "Anastasio Lucena" Graham's friend Mansel recalls an almost story-less experience that made a deep impression upon him. Once, in a storm on the southern pampa, at night, on an exhausted horse, he had finally found an isolated *rancho* where he was welcomed by a blind gaucho. The hut interior is carefully and fully described. The gaucho's teenage son lies half-asleep on the floor. The blind gaucho accepts his blindness as God's will. Mansel is given shelter, food and mate. The blind gaucho is confident that at night he could escape any marauding Indians. The gaucho's wife and other family are off in town shopping. The gaucho takes care of Mansel's horse and lends him one of his own horses. Years later Mansel still feels gratitude.

This blind gaucho is not a nomad, but a man with a settled family life. He shows no anger about his affliction. Though blind, he feels able still to survive on the open and dangerous pampa. He shows kindness to the stranger and comports himself with a quiet dignity that hints of nobility. He is the opposite of any image of the gaucho as a criminal and refugee from justice. As his sightless eyes "take in the Pampa with its indomitable space", the reader may see the blind gaucho himself as indomitable.

Overall, the collection *A Hatchment* is a considerable testament to Graham's range of skills as a sketch-writer and as a story-teller.

(J.McI)

Contents

Preface

There is a something almost indecent, as it were, in setting forth all a man thinks and feels, without an explanation or at the least a prelude of some sort. A fencing master goes through the salute, a jockey takes a preliminary canter, even divines resort to incantations of some kind or other before they fall a-preaching, and when a speaker starts with "Mr. Chairman, Ladies and Gentlemen" and the farrago that goes to herald forth a speech, that is his preface.

Now, preludes, prefaces and explanations are of the nature of a stalking horse, by means of which writers may approach their readers on their blind side. If a man writes a treatise upon aviation, or astronomy, he naturally has no false shame, for no one writes upon such matters without full knowledge, and it is ten to one he knows a hundred times more of them than does the man who reads. If by mischance the writer on the subjects I have named makes a mistake of detail, he is easily excused, and no one thinks himself aggrieved.

Upon the other hand, a man who writes from his own imagination should he chance to err in taste (a fault that even critics sometimes fall into) or fail in interesting, make but the slightest slip in grammar or in style, he is held as one accursed.

Only a poet gets worse treatment, for he, if he should happen to turn out a genius, is straightway worshipped, almost held a god; but if he fail, or if he only should attain mere excellence, all those who read him, although most likely they never wrote a line of verse in all their lives (or even decent prose), treat him as if he had insulted all their female relatives, was a stealer of the sacrament, and had sinned against the Holy Ghost. This possibly is just as it applies to poets, for when they are really great they make humanity feel small, and to a degree the same applies to every writer who comes before the public with something of his own, I mean something that no one else in the whole world could possibly have written, let it be good or bad.

In a way no writer can complain. Suppose Columbus after all the coil he made, and after all the months that he had bothered both the

Catholic kings, when they, as they conceived it, were occupied before Granada, in the most important matter in the world, had sailed away upon the proceeds of Queen Isabella's jewels, and had returned again, having found nothing but a waste of water, just like eternity, with no end or beginning, what would the world have said?

There was no standard in those days by which to judge Columbus, and there is none today, or ever will be one (as far as I can see), by which to measure writers, except they write on history, or mathematics, or compile biographies.

This being so, writers have no ground of complaint if they are weighed by a different metric system to that by which they weigh themselves. All they can do is to write some kind of preface or another for their own satisfaction, and to explain themselves to themselves, for naturally no one pays any attention to anything they write.

When a friend comes up for election at a club we do not go about saying he is a swindler and a rogue (that would be actionable and hence immoral); but very quietly, after having said we hope that Jones will be elected, drop a black bullet in the urn. The same thing happens to a writer, and his friends and critics straightway fall upon him, frequently not because of anything he writes, but from political, religious, or from social prejudice, just like a hundredweight of bricks.

Therefore, why after all should any writer take the trouble to write a preface to his work? I take it that it is, as it were, an involuntary action, just as some men, as brave as lions, never can fire a gun without first closing both their eyes.

Writers there are who are so far removed above their fellow-men, either by talent, social position, or by an aptitude for golf or politics (for these things weigh with critics just as much as style, or as originality), that they are shut off in a tower of brass, and quite invulnerable.

Let these write on, conscious that everything they pen will be approved of; but the rout of scribblers always should have some little thing, such as a preface or the like, on which the critics may take off the keen edge of their wit, just as in times gone by in low-class schools they served the suet pudding out before the meat.

I pen this foreword, not that I hope in any way it may avert misapprehension, for that I know is sure, but because in a mameluke bit, in the high port, are not infrequently put several little rings ... so that the horse may champ upon them.

R. B. Cunninghame Graham.

A Hatchment

The house, covered with creepers, and roofed with slabs of old grey stone, kept in their place by ridges of cement that looked like surf upon a beach that had become congealed, was only cut off from the churchyard by a wall.

The wall was built of yellowish stone, and, as the slabs upon the roof, was so much weathered that it looked like leather. Out of the crevices sprung pellitory and valerian.

So close were house and church that on a summer afternoon from the low-arched front door the voices of the congregation singing "Rock of Ages" seemed to blend with the humming of the insects in the trees.

Manor and churchyard were as near to one another as life is to death, only a step divided them.

At the first glance you saw the house had long been lived in by men rooted in the soil. It had an air of being cut off from the world. although the entrance-gate opened upon the little village street.

Still, when you passed through the gate, and came to a flagged path between two pillars, each surmounted by a ball, you felt that you had come into an older life.

Certainly the house itself stood far removed from railways, and in years gone by you reached it either by a road that ran on windy downs and overlooked the sea, or by one through fields with an infinity of gates.

These gates I have got down to open scores of times, in the last thirty years, from a high dog-cart, in sunshine and in snow, in rain and in a south-west gale. You had to keep them open with a stone, and if the wind blew fresh they not infrequently shut to and grazed the wheel. The roads were poorly kept and flinty, and twisted in and out, now between hedges, all blown sideways by the prevailing south-west winds, till they had become a sort of mat of vegetation, hollow upon one side, and then came out into lush fields, or ran through copses, so that the world seemed almost remote, as in the Hebrides.

All this gave the peculiar feeling as of becoming, as it were, marooned, when you had closed the entrance-gate behind you, and come into the grounds, with their old mulberries, their golden yew, and the half-dozen flower-beds, set with geraniums and begonias. Things that you never noticed in the outside world became important, and you felt instantly you were identified in some strange way with the old mansion house, and that the affairs of those who owned it had in some manner now become your own.

Over the gable of the porch, set in cement, was a rough pot of earthenware. It stood a little leaning towards the churchyard, either as a perpetual *memento mori* to the dwellers in the house, or as a perpetual reminiscence of the carelessness of the masons who in the past had set it in its place.

You passed into the house through a front door, upon one side of which was a round hole cut in the masonry, just like a leper-squint in an old church, designed in times gone by to reconnoitre those who entered, and if required to fire upon them, if they appeared unfriends.

The hall was dark, paved with grey flags, and set about with animals and birds, all badly stuffed, and dusty and decayed. A smell of damp mixed with the scent of gun-oil and of honey, of stale tobacco and of lavender, greeted your nostrils when you opened the front door. This smell, peculiar to the house, became not disagreeable when you were used to it.

I shall remember it always, and if by chance something recalls it to me, the old house rises in my mind. Its blackened pictures, furniture with little trains of dust below them showing where the worms had been at work upon the softer portions of the wood, its cold stone floors, its creaking stairs that bent and cracked and seemed to be about to break as you walked up them, and the mysterious noises as of footfalls, in the night, on the dark passages, made it a fitting habitation for the men who lived in it.

As those who live in them mould houses to their own tastes, giving them the stamp of their own idiosyncrasies, so does a house influence its owners, and put its mark upon them.

If this is so, most certainly the manor-house had set its mark upon the lady who owned it, when I first knew the place, now nearly forty years ago.

Left widowed early in her life, with three small children to bring up, and in a place such as was the old manor-house, which fostered prejudices, secluded as it was in its deep valley far from the world, she had become, as it were, a squire in petticoats, gentle and kindly as to exterior but strong and resolute in the conduct of affairs.

Her dress was of no fashion in particular, but such as gentlewomen have worn with little change for the last fifty years in country places. Her hair, parted in the middle of her head and drawn down rather low about the ears, had not a single silver thread in it, though she had long passed middle age. The villagers — half agriculturists, half sailors and poachers to a man — adored, but stood in awe of her, and when they met her in the lanes, saluted her, with the old-fashioned wave of the right arm, doubling the right hand backward up against the chest and extricating it below the chin with the palm upwards in the air.

Kindness was in the marrow of her bones, but yet a kindness tempered with judgment, so that few of the villagers imposed upon her, though she was always ready to come to their assistance, if her help was required. Progress she looked at just a little bit askance, which was but natural in her position, as it was new to her, and generally took the form of uprooting some old custom which in her eyes was beautiful, and putting nothing in its place.

Still the advance of education was as great a source of satisfaction to her as the decline of courtesy in speech, a cause of pain mixed with some not unnatural wonder that the increase of learning seemed to bring in its train a corresponding falling-off in manners and in kindliness.

Faith she was plentifully endowed with, not to the exclusion of good works, for if a woman was about to be confined or a man fell from a ladder, she turned her household upside down in her anxiety to send them soups and jellies, and bottles of port wine.

Herself the daughter of a clergyman, she had by right of birth a sort of left-handed interest in church government, in the same way a captain's daughter may think she has an innate gift for navigation, though in her case her theory if it is put in practice may lead to serious results.

On Sundays, seated in the chancel — for the manorial pew was in the precincts usually kept sacred for the choir — she listened to the service with a rapt air, joining most conscientiously in the responses, which in those days were muttered rapidly by all the congregation, headed by the clerk.

Old-fashioned hymns, such as the long-forgotten "Oh, refresh us, travelling through this wilderness," sung usually to a dull grinding tune, were her especial favourites. She found them as she said more satisfying than the more modern ones, and more appropriate. The church in which she worshipped, and which stood so near her house, was a small Norman edifice, plain, but not quite devoid of blunt architectural beauty, with its pointed arches and its Elizabethan monuments, over one of which were hung the helmet, gauntlet, and a great jingling spur that once belonged to the dead warrior who kneeled in alabaster at the right-hand corner of the tomb.

The Creed and Ten Commandments were set up on each side of the altar, the words finely set forth in great white lettering, so that the wayfaring man although a fool need not err on the path toward salvation, if he had learned to read. Death took the lady of the manor, in her old painted bed-chamber adorned with scenes drawn by a wandering Dutch artist, setting forth men going out hunting, all riding rather leggy horses and followed by their hounds.

She died as she had lived, occupied to the last minute of her life with parish duties, her infant school, and with the cares of her estate. The villagers mourned her sincerely, feeling they had lost a friend.

Her family laid her to rest beneath the flagstones of the chancel, on which during her lifetime her feet had rested for so many Sundays, as she sat listening to the sermon, with her head turned a little sideways, so as not to miss a word.

Her son — after he had given up the sea and returned home from South America, where he had acquired a Spanish, which, as a friend in reply to his mother's question if he spoke the language just like English, answered "exactly" — had settled down in the old house. Once settled, to the surprise of everyone, he manifested the same kind of interest as had his mother in the affairs both of the parish and the church.

Nothing but the advent of a new vicar with High Church ideas ousted him from the chancel, and when the Ten Commandments and the Creed were taken down, when he was away from home, and put up in a corner, he had them back again, remarking, with a Spanish oath or two, "we are all Protestants." I had not thought during the many years we spent together in South America that Protestantism was very present to his mind; but after all it must have, as it were, lain dormant, as grains of wheat found in Egyptian tombs, when put into congenial soil, have fructified and taken root after a thousand years.

The old house had claimed him, and from henceforth there were to be no more wild rides on the south Pampa, no nights in boats lying outside the mouth of rivers on the Gold Coast, for my friend. England is full of country houses, houses in which the family has spent its manhood for generations only to keep the roof watertight and the garden weeded, and yet their owners have passed adventurous years of youth abroad, and now sit waiting, as it were, for the last Tally-ho, and judging poachers on the Bench. Not that my Protestant ex-partner thought his lot a hard one, or that he ever shirked his duty either in the hunting-field or at Quarter Sessions, for he was, as he might have said himself, "dog-game," and besides was sustained by the gift of humour, that gift which next to faith makes life endurable.

So when he stood, bound in his hat and hosen, and with top-boots on, at his own door, waiting for his horse, watching the rain descend and churn the gravel paths, he used to say, "Fancy a man who sat so many miserable nights herding stock out upon the plains doing this sort of thing for fun."

At Quarter Sessions he must have introduced an air almost of the outside world, according to the story which he used to tell of an exploit of his own. "You see, old man," he said, "there was a silly devil of a labourer, somewhere by Litton Cheney, who had some row or other with his wife. Perhaps she nagged at him — God knows! — anyhow the fool went and jumped down a well. When he got there" — this he said just as if the man had gone upon a journey — "there was about five feet of water in the place.

"His courage failed him, and he halloaed out for help, and someone heard him yelling, and went and fetched a rope. They got him out, and charged him with attempting suicide.

"Some of those fellows on the Bench took quite a serious view of it. Plug-headed idiots, if they'd seen as many horse thieves hung as we have — eh what, eh? but they began to jaw.

"One duffer wanted to send the poor brute off to the Assizes, and it looked as if the rest were going to agree, though one or two stood out.

"Then up got a sort of writing-fellow, lived near Dorchester, used to come out occasionally with the Catstock, reins in a bunch, you know, longish hair, that sort of thing, no seat, not a bad sort of man. He began talking nineteen to the dozen about the inalterable right a fellow has to control his destiny. . . . My God, quoted Marcus Aurelius to the Bench . . . if a fellow has a smoky house, you know . . . fancy that sort of chat to a lot of men who had been at public schools, and never knew a word of Latin in their lives. Good, eh, what?

"Well, he was just getting up their backs. I saw old Lord Debenham putting on the kind of face that he has when he reads the lessons in

Debenham Church; so I chipped in, first time I'd ever said anything
. . . last, too, for that matter, and I said let's look at the thing in a
reasonable way.

" 'This four-storied fool didn't know he was committing any crime;
what he did comes under the Trespass Act. . . . Yes, eh, trespassing in
another fellow's well. Fine him a shilling.' The writing-man was mad,
but I grabbed him by the coat-tails, and old Lord Debenham's face
relaxed a bit. Rest of the beaks laughed . . . and I paid the shilling, and
gave the man another, and told him he had most awful luck, and would
have to go back to his wife."

These exercises or sports kept my friend in good health without
laying too great a tax upon his intellectual powers, and left him time to
devote himself to the furthering of evangelical Christianity throughout
the neighbourhood. The vicar, who had removed the symbols of our
faith from their position guarding the altar, as Gog and Magog guarded
the Guildhall, soon moved his squire to wrath, for the familiar black
gown was no more seen on Sunday, nor were a good half-dozen collects
used before the sermon was begun. His misdoings culminated when
choral service was introduced, and the word "Vicarage" was painted on
the gate.

Seated one evening in his smoking-room, which contained relics of
his life in South America, such as a pair of *bolas* hung between two
prints of stage-coaches stuck in the snow, a silver-headed whip, and a
lazo neatly coiled and carefully greased, "You see," he said, "I like to keep
the thing in order, though you can get no ostrich grease to soften it, in
this God-forsaken place," he told how he had got the better of the vicar,
and forced him to resign. The room was low, and as the grate had always
smoked since it was first put in, and the green wood required a world of
paper and attention to keep it going, the ceiling was as black as is the top
of an Indian's *teepee*, or as a Gaucho's hut upon the plains. The prints,
chiefly of houses in the county, looked as if they had been executed in
a mist, and on the bookshelves, when you took down the *Black Assize*
or Camden's *Britannia* (both, of course, in folio), your fingers left their
impress, in the dust of years, upon them.

After having had the workmen in, to pay their wages, treating them
just as he would have treated privy councillors, asking them to be seated,
and handing them his own tobacco pouch, he launched into his tale.

"Old man," he said, "that vicar was too much, a regular Jesuit,
auricular confession, and all that sort of thing. I had to bolt him." He

spoke as if the clergyman had been a rabbit, "What do you think I did? Eh, what? I got the Yellow Van down . . . cost quite a lot of money, camped it outside his gate . . . 'Vicarage' painted on it, ugh! I used to go and listen to the rot they talked. Enough to make a brass monkey sick . . . regular four-storied, magnolia-scented, gilt-edged rot. Still, the fellow wouldn't go . . . got his off-stirrup, as you may say, and settled in his seat.

"People did begin to look a little shy of him, but still he stuck to it, sulking at the bottom of the hole.

"Then I had a brilliant inspiration, and got a dozen or two of the *Priest's Manual on Confession* — that's what they call the damned thing, I think — and gave 'em out all round the village: that had the desired effect. The villagers, you remember there were a beastly lot of Baptists amongst them, never went near the parish church, but still hated the idea of the confessional and all that sort of thing, used to call their children, and bang the doors in his face when the vicar walked down the street.

"He stood it for a month and then resigned. Now I've got a fellow, so to speak, of my own — Welshman, I think he is — a rotten preacher, not a bad sort of chap, and quite a Protestant."

Years passed, and by degrees my friend grew more confirmed in all his habits, if possible kindlier to all his servants and dependents, but more disposed to show himself a cynic in his dealings with the world.

To the last he thought he was a Liberal, but in reality no one could possibly have been more thoroughly conservative, but not reactionary in regard to politics. In literature and science he always kept abreast of all new movements to the last day of his life.

Little by little the old manor-house fell into decay, for narrow circumstances always prevented him from doing more than what he called "scraping along the bottom," and by degrees one room after another became untenantable. The first to go was one of the old painted chambers, over which the roof bulged in so ominously that no one could be found willing to occupy the room. Damp gained upon the house, and in the little room just on the right hand of the porch, which once had been a sort of boudoir, the paddle fell from the Indian maiden's hand, of the wax model of a Mexican canoe, piled up with vegetables.

Loneliness and seclusion from the world drew a dark cloud over my friend's last years, and he who had passed his life either at sea, or on his horse upon the plains, sat the whole day before the fire, reading and dozing in his smoking-room.

With his death came the closing of the chapter, and to-day the old house stands tenantless, and the long line of gentlefolks who once inhabited it is ended.

All of them now have taken the short journey past the manor-house to the damp churchyard, of which the passing bell during their lifetime must so often have reminded them . . . though they were not the kind of men whom death ever intimidated.

Damp gathers on the cobwebbed windows of the old stables, that stables towards which they turned their steps each morning after breakfast, almost with the air of one who goes to church.

In the deserted kitchen garden, bindweed climbs on the bushes, and groundsel has usurped the vegetable beds; only a row of posts shows where the beehives once stood in a well-ordered row.

If the ghost of my departed friend haunts the old house, where he once lived, I see it just as he was himself in life — short, active, dark, with the thick, sleek hair that he preserved till the last moment of his life, his eyes prominent, and a little bloodshot in the corners, his hands small and well-cared-for, and his feet disproportionately large.

I think if ghosts can walk, that there can be no reason that we can allege against their riding, so I imagine that his shade stands waiting at the door, until they bring his shadowy horse for him to mount. There he stands, muttering now and then, "Eh, what, eh, a damned long time they take to saddle up a horse," and then mounting him lightly in one motion as we used to do upon the plains, rides slowly up the hill till he arrives at the old Knoll House on the hill that overlooks the sea. There he dismounts, I fancy, and the horse vanishes, whilst he, lighting an insubstantial cigarette of ship's tobacco, sits down on the fine grassy turf, that flows up to the foundations of the ruined masonry, and gazes seaward, drinking in the view that he most loved in life. The wide expanse of down, nothing but grass and sky, like the south Pampa, stretches out to Portland Bill.

The pebbly beach, on which the water goes down sheer only a few yards from the edge, runs like a serpent all along the coast, up to the great lagoon of Abbotsbury.

Far in the offing fishing-boats dotted the sea with their white sails, just as the swans dotted the waters of the decoy.

All that he sees, and feels the fresh breeze on his cheek, coming up from the south-west.

Los Indios

No one who has not lived upon the southern Pampa in the days when a staunch horse was of more value in time of trouble than all the prayers of all the good men of the world, can know how constantly the fear of Indians was ever present in men's minds.

The Indiada of the old Chief Catriel was permanently camped outside Bahia Blanca. They lived in peace with all their neighbours; but on the sly maintained relations with Los Indios Bravos, such as the Pampas, Ranqueles, Pehuelches and the rest who, though they had their Toldos out on the Salinas Grandes, and dotted all the way along the foothills of the Andes right up to the lake of Nahuel-Huapi and down to Cholechél, occasionally burst like a thunder-cloud upon the inside camps, as suddenly as a *pampero* blew up from the south.

All their incursions, known to the Gauchos as *malones*, were made by the same trails. They either entered the province near the town of Tapalquén, by the great waste between the Romero Grande and the Cabeza del Buey, or through the pass, right at the top of the Sierra de la Ventana, the curious hill with the strange opening in it, from which it takes its name.

The terror and romance of the south frontier were centred in the Indian tribes. When they broke in amongst the great *estancias* of the south, all but the chiefs riding upon a sheepskin, or without even that, carrying a lance made of a bamboo, fifteen to twenty feet in length, the point a sheep-shear, fastened to the shaft by a piece of a cow's tail, or other bit of hide wrapped round it green, then left to dry till it became as hard as iron, and with a tuft of horse-hair underneath the blade, looking like a human scalp, the deer and ostriches all fled in front of them, just as the spindrift flies before a wave.

Each warrior led a spare horse, taught to run easily beside him, and leave his hand free for the spear. They rode like demons of the night, their horses all excited by the fury of their charge, leaping the small *arroyas*, changing their feet like goats upon a stony place, and brushing through the high grasses with a noise as of a boat crashing through reeds. Now and again they struck their hands upon their mouths to make their yells, a loud prolonged "Ah, Ah, Ah — a — a," more wild and terrifying.

Each warrior carried round his waist two or three pair of *bolas*; the two large balls hanging on the left side, and the small hand-ball, on the right, just resting on the hip. All had long knives or swords, which as a rule they shortened for convenience of carriage to about the length of a sword-bayonet, wearing them stuck between the girth and the skirt of the saddle, if they should chance to have a saddle, and if they had none, stuck through a narrow woollen sash made by their women in the Tolderias, worked in strange, stiff, concentric patterns, bound round their naked waists. All were smeared over with a coat of ostrich grease, though never painted, and their fierce cries and smell were terrifying to the Gauchos' horses, making them mad with fear. Some twenty paces in advance rode the *cacique*, sometimes upon a silver-mounted saddle, choosing if possible a black horse to set it off well, and with his silver reins, seven feet in length, held high in his left hand as, spurring furiously, he turned occasionally to yell out to his men, grasping his spear about the middle as he careered along.

To meet them thus, alone upon the plains, say when alone upon a lazy horse, out looking up strayed cattle, was an experience not easily forgotten . . . and one which he who had it remembered vividly, if he escaped their lynx-eyed scouting, up to his dying day.

Your only chance, unless, as was unlikely, you had a *pingo* "fit for God's saddle," as the Gauchos said, was to alight, and having led your horse into a hollow, to muffle up his head in the folds of your *poncho*, to stop him neighing, and keep as still as death. Then, if you had not been perceived, and little on the plains escaped an Indian's eye, you almost held your breath, until the thunder of the Indians' horses' feet had died away, and mounting with your heart thumping against your sides, cautiously stole up the hollow, and getting off again, holding your horse by a long rope, peeped stealthily over the brow to see if all was clear. If out upon the plains you saw the ostriches, the deer or cattle running, or dust arise without a cause, you had to get back to the hollow and wait a little. Lastly, when you were certain all had passed, you drew the *latigo* of the hide-cinch, placing your foot against the horse's side to get more purchase, till he was like an hour-glass with the strain. Then mounting, you touched him with the spur, and galloped for dear life, till you got to a house, shouting as you rode up . . . "*Los Indios*" ... a cry which brought every male Christian running to the door.

Quickly the tame horses would be driven up and shut in the corral; all the old arms loaded and furbished up; for, strange as it may sound, the Gauchos of the south, although they were exposed to constant inroads of the Indians, never had anything but an old blunderbuss or so, or a pair of flint-lock pistols, and those out of repair.

The Indians themselves, having no arms but spears and *bolas*, were seldom formidable except out on the plain. A little ditch, not five feet deep and eight or ten across, kept a house safe from them, for as they never left their horses, they could not cross it, and as they came to plunder, not especially to kill, they wasted little time upon such places, unless they knew that there were young and handsome women shut up in the house. "Christian girl, she more big, more white than Indian," they would say, and woe betide the unlucky girl who fell into their hands.

Hurried off to the Toldos, often a hundred leagues away, they fell, if young and pretty, to the chiefs. If not, they had to do the hardest kind of work; but in all cases, unless they gained the affections of their captor, their lives were made a burden by the Indian women, who beat and otherwise ill-used them on the sly.

Such were the Indians on the warpath, from San Luis de la Punta, right down to Cholechél. Stretches of "camp" now under corn were then deserted or, at the best, roamed over by manades *[sic=manadas]* of wild mares.

A chain of forts, starting upon the Rio Quinto and running north and south, was supposed to hold the Indians in check; but in reality did little, as they slipped through to plunder, quite at their own sweet will. The mysterious territory known by the name of "Tierra Adentro," began at Las Salinas Grandes, and stretched right to the Andes, through whose passes the Indians, by the help of their first cousins, the Araucanians, conveyed such of the cattle and the mares they did not want, to sell or to exchange for silver horse-gear, known to the Gauchos by the name of Chafalonia Pampa, and highly coveted as having no alloy.

In type and habits there was little difference between La Indiada Mansa of the Chief Catriel and their wild brethren of the plains. Both were a yellow coppery colour, not tall, but well proportioned, all but their legs, which were invariably bowed by their lives passed on horseback from their youth. Both sexes wore the hair long, cut square across the forehead and hanging down the back, and both had rather flat and brutal faces, and all the men had restless eyes, perpetually fixed on the horizon as if they lived in fear.

Their beards were sparse, their constitutions hardy, and men and women both went down to the stream and bathed before the sun rose, taking care to be prepared to pour a calabash of water on the ground when the first rays appeared.

I see them now, coming back in a long string from the water, and hear their salutation "Mari-Mari" as they passed dripping on their way, their long black hair, lustrous and heavy, hanging loose down their backs.

Tierra Adentro served the wilder Gauchos for a sure refuge in their times of trouble, to which to fly after some "trouble" or another, in which some man had lost his life, or to escape from serving in some revolutionary force or any other cause.

Jose Hernandez, in his celebrated *Martin Fierro*, has described how Cruz and his friend took refuge with the Indians, and well do I remember, for we all knew the whole book by heart, taking my turn for a hundred lines or so, round the camp fire, out on the Napostá. The wood engraving, primitive and cheap, in which Cruz and Martin were shown jogging on at the Trotecito wrapped in their *ponchos*, driving the *tropilla*; and with the foal, looking like a young camel, bringing up the rear, is quite as well fixed in my memory as is the picture of the Conde Duque, the Emperor Charles the Fifth at Mulhouse, Las Hilanderas, or any other work of art.

The line beneath it always impressed us, and we all tried to get the last verses to recite, so as to round up with the epic, "Al fin, por una madrugada clara, viceron *[sic = vieron]* las ultimas poblaciones," the *poblaciones* being, if I remember rightly, some low and straw-thatched ranchos, surrounded by a ditch.

Their subsequent adventures are they not set down with some prolixity in La Vuelta de Martin.

The serious side of Tierra Adentro was in the refuge it afforded to revolutionary chiefs. The brothers Saá and Colonel Baigoiria held a sort of sub-command for years, under the great Cacique Painé, and to them came all the discontented and broken men, whom they formed into a kind of flying squadron, ranging the frontiers with the Indians, as fierce and wild as they.

All kinds of Christian women, from the poor China girl, carried off like a mare from an *estancia*, to educated women from the towns, and once even a *prima donna*, journeying from Cordoba to Mendoza, were to be found in that mysterious Inside Land. On one occasion a lady carried off from San Luis found herself about to be the prey of several chiefs, who were preparing to settle matters by a fight.

Throwing herself about Baigoiria's neck, who happened to be there, she cried, "Save me, *compadre*" and he, after some trouble, took her to his house. There he had several other wives; but white women, prisoners amongst the Indians, were said never to quarrel, so that they lived with a white man. Their fate with Indians was not much to be envied, except as in the case of the great Chief Painé, who for ten years at least was ruled by a white girl he took at the sack of an *estancia*, somewhere near Tapalquén.

In the Arcadia of the Tolderias, especially in those close by the apple forests of the Andes, the life of those who dwelt in them must have been a survival of another age, without a parallel in all the world.

In North America, the Indian tribes all had traditions of their own, a polity and a religion, often complicated.

Amongst the Toldos of the Pampas, except a perfunctory sun-worship and a most real faith in the Gualichu, that evil spirit to which mankind in every age has paid at least as much attention as to the principle of good, nothing of old traditions had been left. They lived almost exactly like the Gauchos, with the exception that they grew a little maize, and fed on mare's flesh, instead of beef. The Indian's *toldo* was but little inferior to the Gaucho's hut. Most of the Indians spoke a little Spanish, Both Indian and Gaucho wore the same clothes (the Indians when they could get them) in time of peace. In time of war, they went about almost stark naked, save for a breech-clout, and generally the hat was, as it is to Arabs, the stumbling-block, the Indians preferring to have their long black locks well dressed with mare's grease, or with ostrich oil, as a protection from the sun. Their carelessness of life and their contempt of death exceeded that even of their first cousins and deadly enemies the Gauchos, of whom it is said that one of them coming to see his friend, found him in the agonies of rheumatic fever, and after having looked at him compassionately, said, "Poor fellow, how he suffers," and drawing out his knife took the sufferer by the beard and cut his throat. Cutting of throats was a subject of much joking both amongst Gauchos and the Indians. Amongst the former it was called to "do the holy office," and a coward was said to be mean about his throat if at the last he showed the slightest fear. The agonies and struggles of a dying man were summed up briefly, "he put out his tongue when I began to play the violin" (i.e. with the knife), phrases and actions which had their counterpart or origin amongst the Indians.

I who write this have seen the Indian children playing carnival, with hearts of sheep and calves for scent bottles, squirting out blood on one another in the most natural way.

At the rejoicings in the Tolderias, after a successful *malon* or raid in some *estancia*, the amount of mare's flesh that the Indians used to eat was quite phenomenal. Some of them hardly stopped to cook it, or at the best but scorched it at the fire. Some ate it raw, drinking the blood like milk, and when half drunk — for *caña* was never wanting in the Toldos — and well daubed over with the blood, it made one wonder whether the chain connecting man with the orang-outang had any link with them.

Their choicest delicacy was the fat piece along a young colt's neck; this they ate always raw, and I remember once having to taste it in response to a compliment addressed me by a young warrior, who yelling "There's a good Christian," thrust the fat dripping meat into my unwilling hand. The effect was lasting, and to this day I cannot look on a piece of green turtle fat floating in the soup without remembering the Indian delicacy.

Well, well, the Toldos, those on the edge of the great apple forests of the Andes, and those between Las Salinas Grandes and the Lago Argentino, all are gone. All the wild riders now ride in Trapalanda, the mysterious city in which no Christian ever breathes his horse. Over the treacherous Guadál, the Vizcachera, or through the middle of a Cangrejál, no more wild horsemen gallop, certain to fall upon their feet, if their horse step into a hole; or if they chanced to fail to land upon their feet, rise and leap on from the offside leaning upon their spear.

No longer, on a journey, will they, as it appeared without a cause, suddenly strike their hands upon their mouths and yell, and then when asked the reason, answer, "Huinca, he foolish; Auca do that because first see the sierra," as in the days of yore.

Round the Gualichu tree, no longer bands from north and south will meet, and whilst within its influence forbear to fight; even refrain from stealing a fine horse during the time they celebrate their medicine dance. In separating, no Indian now will tear a piece from off his *poncho* and stick it on a thorn; the tree was a Chañar if I remember right.

Men looking for strayed horses, sleeping beside some lonely river no longer have to shiver half the night on guard, and burn their feet against the fire, placed in a hollow, dug with their knives in the green turf, so as to show no light, till it was time to saddle up and march.

No one will travel, as I did with a friend, now riding as I hope in some mysterious Trapalanda of his own (fit for men of no faith, but in good works), from Tapalquén down to the Sauce Grande, passing no house that was not burned and sacked, except a chance *estancia* surrounded by a ditch and full of women and of wounded men. We started with an alarm of Indians at Tapalquén, the plaza full of men all arming, and with wild-eyed and yelling countrymen galloping in on foaming horses, calling out *"Los Indios"* what time the *comandante*, seated in a cane-chair, sat taking *maté* as he passed his rough recruits in an extemporaneous review.

We camped on the Arroyo de los Huesos, swam the Quequen Salado, buried a man we found dead at Las Tres Horquetas, and after a week's riding, through camps swept clear of cattle and of mares, came to the Sauce Grande just in time to take a hand in a brief skirmish and see the Indians drive off the few remaining horses in the place.

Those times are gone, and now the plough breaks up the turf that had remained intact and virgin since the creation of the world.

A Hatchment

A Retrospect

When they had let the anchor go with a loud splash into the yellow, muddy water, nothing was in sight. By degrees several steam-tugs and then a fleet of whale-boats, manned by Genoese, came bounding over the short choppy waves. They seemed to come from nowhere, as no land was visible as far as one could see. All round our ship lay other vessels, rolling about, almost to show their coppers, Genoese and French and English, with a great raking barquentine, hailing from Portland Maine. Until the tugs and whale-boats had appeared, one could not fathom why so many ships had anchored all together, out of sight of land, in such a choppy sea. Ten minutes' steaming in a whale-boat brought into sight the tops of churches, cupolas and towers, and a few tall palm trees, and then five minutes afterwards a town, white, flat-roofed, Oriental-looking, that seemed to spring out of the waves.

It gradually grew clearer, and to the west appeared a low *barranco*, but still the town had no foundation, till the steam-tug had gone a little further in. Then the whole town grew clear, that is to say, the portion of it nearest to the river-bank, for the ground was so flat *[that]* the nearest houses blocked the rest from sight, giving the effect of a long line of white against the yellow water, broken by several round and red-tiled cupolas.

Eventually, after a passage of some fifteen miles, which left the fleet of anchored steamers quite hull down, the muddy bank on which the town stood was revealed. A wooden mole, broken in places — it was a sempiternal joke in Don Patricio Mulhall's English paper, the *Buenos Aires Standard*, which he served up every week, under the heading of the "Hole in the Mole" — ran out a little, say, about a hundred yards, towards the sea.

The water generally was too shoal for the steam-launches to land their passengers, these usually sea-sick and wet, for the three leagues of water were nearly always rough, and the short, broad-beamed launches, knocked about and plunged like a wild horse. A swarm of shore boats, chiefly manned by Neapolitans and Genoese, came out and hung about the launches, just as they had hung about the ocean-going ships. Those

171

who were wise refused to enter them until they had struck a bargain with these pirates of the shore, for as there was no tariff, or if there was, no one attended to it, you might be asked five or six dollars for the few hundred yards. You landed at the slippery stairs, all overgrown with barnacles, and stumbled up upon the pier, when for the first time you had a full view of the town.

Mostly all heavy merchandise was transferred from shore-going boats to bullock-carts, primitive-looking in construction, and with solid wheels. The driver, usually a Basque, banged on the oxen's horns with a stout, wooden mallet as he sat cross-legged on the yoke. The effect of all these various transhipments was to make the landing goods almost as dear as the whole freight from Europe to the Plate. When you had run the gauntlet of the Custom House, which in those days was a most serious affair, you emerged upon some low, arcaded streets, inhabited almost entirely by Italians of the seafaring class. They sat in villainous dark cafés, all playing cards and drinking *grappa* and from the cafés came a babel of all the dialects of their peninsula.

What struck one, even there amongst those shell-backs, where everything was redolent of the sea, was that a horse or two was standing hobbled about the door of every house. When you emerged and entered one or other of the deep streets, running between raised pavements three or four feet high, you met more horses. Men selling milk on horseback, these were chiefly Basques; men carrying nets for fishing; men with reeking hides freshly stripped off spread on their horses' backs; sleek business men on English saddles, made of cheap leather and abominably cut — all passed you, riding, and every horse you saw at first sight had a mouth like silk, the kind of mouth a man in Europe dreams of but never sees; and here, even the horses that the poorest rode, all had it, and all bent their necks as if they had been put through all the airs of the best *manège* in the world. All of them had their manes cut into an arch, leaving a mounting lock upon the withers, about two spans in width, and all had tails that would have swept the ground had they not been just squared off at the pasterns to keep them from the mud.

The deep streets led up to the chief plaza, a huge arcaded square, with many old colonial buildings in it. The house of the Conquistador, Don Juan Garay, now swept away as ruthlessly as if it had been an old church in London, stood at one corner of the square. It was, if I remember rightly, a low, flat-roofed building, with overhanging eaves, built to resist all time, and should have been preserved in a land where few monuments exist, as carefully as an old beau preserves his last front tooth, as a memorial of the past.

Other old buildings there were none, except the cathedral, built at an inartistic time, and looking like almost every other church in the New World, from the Franciscan Missions in Arizona and in Texas down to that of Patagones, all of which even the great cathedrals of Mexico and Puebla were of Jesuit architecture, with a Græco-Roman façade and a great cupola, like a gigantic beehive, rising from the centre of the pile.

One church I had forgotten, and one no Englishman should pass, unnoticed, that of St. Dominic.

In it the kind and tutelary saint had placed the power to catch and hold, so that succeeding ages might see and marvel, the heretic cannonballs fired by the Lutheran General Whitelocke when he attacked the town. In days of greater faith, or perhaps before the masonry had given way, the church held dozens, but in my time there were but three, which *Ad Majorem Dei Gloriam* remained a witness to the faith, both of the present generation and the past.

Inside the church, high up in the west aisle, there used to hang, and I suppose still do so, the colours of three British regiments of the line. A timely warning, as I used to think, to pride, and one which when men were well filled with new wine I used to show them, inviting them to pat their diaphragms and whistle "Rule Britannia" with the best grace they could. Not that I was not a good patriot, but because I thought, then in my youth, just as I do to-day, that patriotism begins at home, and if St. Dominic appeared and really caught those balls, he did it not, as a saint, but as an Argentine, for saints, I take it, when the celestial telephone is rung, are of the nationality of those who pray to them. In those days, now so far off and forgotten, the city still preserved to some extent its old colonial look. The greater portion of the houses had flat roofs, though here and there an ugly block of modern buildings, generally overladen with detail, sprung up and dwarfed their fellows, looking like stucco icebergs in a great sea of bricks. One or two houses, such as those of the Auchorenas [sic] and the Lumbs, had just been built in a half-Italian style, with *patios* of marble, filled with palms, with fountains, and with a great opaque glass ball of enormous size, balanced or fastened to a marble pillar, reminding one that after all the world turns round upon its axis, and that the luck may change.

Meat was sold at about ten cents the kilo, and bread was dearer than it was in Paris. Flour was imported from Chile and the United States, whilst all clothes came ready-made from Europe, and were both bad and dear.

Almost the entire male population dressed in black, and nearly everyone wore turned-down collars, cut very low upon the neck, and kept in place by narrow neckties like a shoe-string, and no one carried sticks. In fact, a walking-stick was the mark of a new-comer, what was called in those days *un recien yegao*, for pronunciation of the language followed a system of its own. Men prided themselves upon the smallness of their feet, as if they had been women, although the race was most athletic, and except at Mass or at great social functions, all wore black floppy hats. After a rainstorm, all the side streets became fierce watercourses, owing to the height of the side walks, and men with planks, which they stretched over from one pavement to the other, reaped a rich harvest from those who wished to cross.

A mile or two above the town men fished on horseback, riding their horses deep into the water, and after having made a circle with the rope fastened to their girths, galloping to the shore. Tramways had been established for a few months, and yet abounded, for no one walked who possibly could ride, and twenty yards before each car galloped a boy upon a horse, blowing upon a horn.

One of the chief sights of the place as I remember then, was the great square before the Stock Exchange. Hundreds of horses stood about hobbled, all with their reins fastened behind the cantle of the saddle, making them arch their necks like rocking-horses. They seldom moved, as they were hobbled short by the forelegs, but now and then turned round, and now and then, one of them who was *baqueano*, with his hobbles, if he espied a friend, would raise his hobbled feet and hop across to him. Perhaps their conversation was as intelligent as was that of those who had brought them there, and of a surety was more innocent. To a newcomer it seemed perilous to adventure upon foot into a maelstrom of four-footed beasts, such as the one that stood before the Bourse, on almost every morning in those days. However, as one of the peculiarities of the breed was that they never bit and hardly ever kicked, one soon grew used to it, and pushed one's way between, quite as contemptuously as if they had been all endowed with reason and gamblers upon 'Change.

The hotels were few and relatively poor, and most of them were situated in or about the Calle Veinte Cinco de Mayo, from the fashionable "Argentino" down to Claraz's, a little hostelry kept by a Swiss, a man of learning though an hotel-keeper, since widely known by his flora of the

Pampa. "Camp" men, who often passed amongst their countrymen, if they were English, under the name of "Gentle Shepherds," sea captains, mining engineers, and foreign journalists were the chief pillars of the place. A usual sight was the arrival of some sunburned man dressed in a well-cut, but frayed tweed suit, a grey felt hat, a flannel shirt without a collar, and his *recao* tied in a bundle, and carried by a *changador*, which was the name that the Portenós gave to porters, who nearly all were Basques.

The Gentle Shepherd generally shouted "Claraz," and was met by the tall black-haired and black-bearded Swiss, like an old friend.

Paying his *changador*, he asked who else was in the house, and when he heard their names summoned them all to drink. Then after this half-sacramental action, he got down his portmanteau or his box, which Claraz always kept for him up in some attic, and dressed himself in his best clothes, always a little creased, and sallied forth either on business or to impart vermilion to the town; but always wearing his soft hat, the outward visible sign of the interior grace of the true "camp" man, come to town. The little hostelry was built upon the plan of a monastery, with rooms like cells opening out from a corridor. The last of them, which in those times was mine on the occasions when I was in town, looked right upon the river, and on fine days one saw the houses of La Colonia, in the Republic of Uruguay, some thirty miles away.

It was expedient not to sit reading late at night at Claraz's, for it might happen that a Gentle Shepherd coming back after an evening spent in merriment, might try to shoot your candle out, a thing that has happened at least once or twice to the writer of these lines.

Each nationality had its Claraz's Hotel, which though not owned by Claraz, yet was run more or less on the same lines, with due allowance for the national characteristics of the guests. The other hotels were, of course, much more cosmopolitan, but all of them, except the "Argentino," had a homely air, which has long disappeared from all hotels in every quarter of the globe. Society was then not so exclusive as it has become, and foreigners who spoke the language all were well received. Few Argentines spoke English, and not too many French, and with the exception of a few of the richer families who had been in Europe, an evening's entertainment was in the style I recollect in my youth, in Seville and throughout southern Spain. The ladies sat on chairs in a great circle round the room, and men lounged at the doors, and now and then one would advance and ask a girl to dance. This dance was generally a valse, danced very slowly to the music of a jingly piano, and when it finished you slowly led your partner to her seat, and stood beside her murmuring the most elementary compliments. At older-fashioned houses still they danced the *cielito* and the *pericon* — curious old-world and picturesque survivals of an older age, and which perhaps are just as worthy of remembrance as will be the "Cake-Walk" and the "One-Step" when they are obsolete.

Women, except those of the poorer classes, seldom walked about alone, but in the evening, under the care of fathers, mothers, and the like, they swarmed in the Calle Rivadavia, which in those days was the chief promenade of the town.

There, walking up and down, they listened to those *flores*, which have from time immemorial been the custom of the Spanish youth to offer to the fair.

In fact, in those days, Buenos Aires still was a colonial city, but just emerging from its past. Great lines of steamships were just beginning to dump their cargoes of Italians and of Basques. Still, there was little difference on the whole between the various classes, and balls were given in the ground-floor rooms of old colonial houses, through whose enormous grated windows the populace gazed, smoking, and criticized the dancers, sometimes appreciatively, at others adversely, and always something in the spirit of prospective buyers at a fair.

The theatres were good and large, and in those days better constructed and more modern than those of London or of Paris, although their prices were enormous, taking into consideration the simple life led by the citizens.

The coinage was depreciated, the paper dollar standing at twopence-halfpenny, and the chief silver, the Bolivian four-real piece, a coin which with its llama and its palm, rough execution, and strange colour, looked like an ancient Roman denarius, and was much counterfeited.

No view of Buenos Aires of those times would be complete without a glance at the side temples of the Paphian goddess, she who came from the sea-foam, according to the Greeks, but who the Christian Church averred to have had her origin in mud.

Few towns could have been better kept supplied than was the city of good airs, with raw material. Spaniards and Greeks, Italians, French, English, Mulattresses (all with the *catinga*), Algerian Jewesses and girls from Paraguay, gazed from the windows of the great *casa amueblada* in 25th of May Street.

176

In bars and in tobacco shops they swarmed, and that in spite of licensed houses by the score.

Some, such as the great *quilombo* at what the English know as "one, two, three," *Cerrito* (*Cerrito*, 123), were models in their way.

Inside them all was looking-glass, walls, tables, roofs, and chairs. Upon them lounged the priestesses, and it was fashionable in those days to take one's coffee after dinner there. I have seen an august personage, one set above his fellows by the popular vote, stroll in and sit down in a chair, light a cigar and drink his coffee, chatting the while with all the ladies of the place, so affably that you would not suspect by the enumeration of a few thousand noses, he had become a god.

Such was the city in those days, with but a population of three hundred thousand souls.

The suburbs, Palermo and Las Flores, were just growing, and at El Tigre and La Boca, the industries that have arisen since lay in the lap of time. But a short league or two away, stretched the flat camps of Quilmes and El Monte Grande, their grass short, sweet, and eaten down by sheep, green as an emerald in the early spring, then carpeted with La Flor Morada, with red verbena; a dusty brown in summer, but soon turning green again at the first autumn rain.

It was a city of good air, and the old Spanish captain, he who sailed with Don Pedro de Mendoza, that gentleman of Almeria, once Chamberlain to Charles V, was right when he first felt the wind coming across the Pampa from the south and looking round remarked, "Que buenos, son los aires de aqui."

Although we knew it not, being perhaps more occupied with life than with political economy, the city held within itself the germs of all it has become. I know that it is great and prosperous, wealthy beyond the dreams of avarice; that the great liners all tie up at stone-built docks, and passengers step from them into their motor-cars. All this I know, and I am glad, for *anche io fú pittore*, that is, I used to ride along the streets of the old Buenos Aires generally upon a little *doradillo*, that I had, with the great silver spurs just hanging off my heels when I rode up to Claraz's Hotel, after delivering a troop of cattle at the *saladero*, on the outskirts of the town.

So may a man who in his youth has seen a gipsy dancer, brown, active, thin, and has admired her from afar, when he has met her in his after life, married to a capitalist, splendid in jewels and in Paris clothes, still think that she looked better in her print skirt and frayed Manila shawl.

A Hatchment

El Rodeo

The vast, brown, open space, sometimes a quarter of a mile across, called El *Rodeo*, which bears the same relation to the ocean of tall grass that a shoal bears to the surface of the sea, was the centre of the life of the great cattle *estancia*s of the plains. To it on almost every morning of the year the cattle were collected and taught to stand there till the dew was off the grass. To *parar rodeo* was the phrase the Gauchos used, equivalent to the cowboys' "round up" on the northern plains.

An hour before the dawn, when the moon was down, but the sun not up, just at the time when the first streaks of red begin to fleck the sky, the Gauchos had got up from their *recaos*.* In those days it was a point of honour to sleep on the *recao*, the *carona* spread out on the ground, the *jergas* on it, the *cojinillo* underneath the hips for softness, the head pillowed upon *los bastos*, and under them your pistol, knife, your *tirador*, and boots, yourself wrapped up in your *poncho* and with your head tied up in a handkerchief. The Gauchos had looked out in the frost or dew, according to the season of the year, to see the horse they had tied up overnight had not got twisted in his stake-rope, and then returned to sit before the fire to take a *matecito cimarron* and smoke. Every now and then a man had left the fire, and, lifting the dried mare's-hide that served for door, had come back silently, and, sitting down again, taken a bit of burning wood, ladling it from the fire, upon his knife's edge, and lit his cigarette. At last, when the coming dawn had lit the sky like an Aurora Borealis lights a northern winter's night, they had risen silently, and shouldering their saddles, had gone out silently to saddle up.

Outside the horses stood and shivered on their ropes, their backs arched up like cats about to fight. Frequently when their intending rider had drawn the pin to which they were attached, and after coiling up the rope approached them warily, they sat back snorting like a steam-engine when it breasts a hill. If it was possible, the Gaucho saddled his horse

* Argentine saddle made in several pieces, which comprised the *carona, jergos [sic]*, and *cojinillo* and *los bastos*.

after first hobbling his front feet, although he was sure to throw the saddle-cloths and the *carona* several times upon the ground. When they were put firmly upon his back, the rider, cautiously stretching his naked foot under the horse's belly, caught up the cinch between his toes. Passing the *latigo* between the strong iron rings both of the *encimera* and the cinch, he put his foot against the horse's side and pulled till it was like an hour-glass, which operation not infrequently set the horse bucking, hobbled as he was.

If, on the other hand, the horse was but half-tamed, a *redomon* as the phrase was, his owner led him up to the *palenque*, tied him up firmly to it, and after hobbling and perhaps blindfolding him, saddled him, after a fierce struggle and an accompaniment of snorts. When all was ready, and the first light was just about to break, showing the Pampa silvery with mist and dew, and in the winter morning often presenting curious mirages of woods hung in the sky, the trees suspended upside down, the *capataz* would give the signal to set off. Going up gently to their horses, the Gauchos carefully untied them, taking good care no coil of the *maneador* should get caught in their feet, and then after tightening the broad hide girth, often eight or nine inches broad, led them a little forward to let them get their backs down, or buck if they so felt inclined. Then they all mounted, some of the horses whirling round at a gallop, their riders holding their heads towards them by the *bozal* in the left hand, and with the reins and pommel of the saddle in the right. They mounted in a way peculiar to themselves, bending the knee and passing it over the middle of the saddle, but never dwelling on the stirrup, after the European way, so that the action seemed one motion, and they were on their horses as easily as a drop of water runs down a window-pane, and quite as noiselessly.

Calling the dogs, generally a troop of mongrels of all sorts, with perhaps a thin black greyhound or two amongst the pack, the Gauchos used to ride off silently, their horses leaving a trail of footsteps in the dew. Some bucked and plunged, their riders shouting as their long hair and *poncho*s flapped up and down at every bound the horses made. They left the *estancia* always at the *trotecito*, the horses putting up their backs, arching their necks and playing with the bit, whose inside rollers, known as *coscojo*, jingled on their teeth.

Then after a hundred yards or so one would look at the others and say "Vamos," the rest would answer "Vamonos" and set off galloping, until the *capataz* would order them to separate, telling them such and such a "point" of cattle should be about the hill which is above the river of the *sarandis*, there is a bald-faced cow in it, curly all over; you cannot miss her if you try. Other "points" would have a bullock with a broken horn in them, or some other animal, impossible to miss . . . to eyes trained to the plains.

In a moment all the horsemen disappeared into the "camp" just as the first rays of the sun came out to melt the dew upon the grass. This was called *campeando*, and the owner or the *capataz* usually made his aim some "point" of cattle which was the tamest and fed closest to the house, and probably contained all the tame oxen and a milk cow or two. When he had found them he drove them slowly to the *rodeo*, which they approached all bellowing, the younger animals striking into a run before they reached it, and all of them halting when they felt their feet on the bare ground. Once there, the *capataz*, lighting a cigarette, walked his horse slowly to and fro, occasionally turning back any animal that tried to separate and go back to the grass.

Most likely he would wait an hour, or perhaps two, during which time the sun ascending gathered strength and brought out a keen, acrid smell from the hard-trodden earth of the *rodeo*, on which for years thousands of cattle had been driven up each day. The "point" of cattle already there would soon begin to hang their heads and stand quite motionless, the *capataz'* horse either become impatient or go off into a contemplative state, resting alternately on each hind leg.

Such of the dogs who had remained with him would stretch themselves at full length on the grass. At last faint shouts and sounds of galloping and baying dogs would be heard in the distance, gradually drawing near.

Then a dull thundering of countless feet, and by degrees, from north, south, east and west, would come great "points" of cattle, galloping. Behind, waving their *ponchos*, brandishing their short *rebenques* round their heads, raced the *vaqueros*, followed by the dogs. As each "point" reached the *rodeo* the galloping men would check their foaming horses so that the cattle might arrive at a slow pace and not cause a stampede amongst the animals that were already on the spot.

At last all the "points" had arrived. Three, four, five or ten thousand cattle were assembled, and the men who had brought them from the thick cane-brakes and from the *montes* of the deltas of the streams, after having loosed their girths and lit cigarettes, proceeded slowly to ride round the herd to keep them on the spot. The dogs lay panting with their tongues lolling out of their mouths, the sun began to bite a little, and now and then a wild bullock or light-footed young cow, or even a small "point"of cattle, would break away, to try to get back to its *querencia*, or merely out of fright.

Then with a shout a horseman, starting with a bound, his horse all fire, his own long hair streaming out in the wind, would dart out after them, to try to head them back. "Vuelta ternero," "Vuelta vaquilla," they would cry, riding a little wide of the escaping beast. After a hundred yards or so, for the first rush of the wild native cattle was swift as lightning, the rider would close in. Riding in front of the escaping truant, he would try to turn it back, pressing his horse against its side.

If it turned, as was generally the case, towards the herd, after three or four hundred yards of chase, the Gaucho checked his horse and let the animal return at a slow gallop by itself till it had joined the rest.

If it was a fierce bullock or a fleet-footed cow, and even after he had bored it to one side it started out again, or stopped and charged, he rode beside it beating it with the handle of his *arreador*. When all these means had failed, as a last resource he sometimes ran his horse's chest against its flank, and gave it thus a heavy fall. This was called giving a *pechada*, and if repeated a few times usually cowed the wildest of the herd, though now and then an escaping animal had to be lassoed and dragged back, and then if it broke out again the Gauchos used to rope it, and after throwing it, dissect a bit of skin between the eyes, so that it fell and blinded the poor beast and stopped him running off. These were the humours of the scene, till after half an hour or so of gently riding round and round, the *rodeo*, from having been at first a bellowing, kaleidoscopic mass of horns and hoofs, of flashing eyes and tails lashing about, like snakes, a mere confusion of all colours, black, white and brown, dun, cream and red, in an inextricable maze, became distinguishable, and you perceived the various "points," each recognizable by some outstanding beast, either in colour or in shape. The *capataz* and all the Gauchos knew them, just as a sailor knows all kinds of ships, and in an instant, with a quick look, could tell if such and such a beast was fat, or only in the state known to the adept as *carne blanca*, or if the general condition of the herd was good, and this with a *rodeo* of five thousand animals.

Their searching eyes detected at a glance if a beast had received a wound of any kind, if maggots had got into the sore, and sometimes on the spot the cow or bullock thus affected would be lassoed, cast, its wound washed out with salt and water, and then allowed to rise. Needless to say, this operation did not improve its temper, and as occasionally, in order to save trouble, the Gauchos did not rope it by the neck and put another rope on the hind legs, both horses straining on the ropes to keep them taut, but merely roped and cast and then put a fore leg above the horn, and let a man hold down the beast by pulling on its tail passed under the hind leg, the man who stood, holding the cow's horn full of the "remedy," was left in a tight place.

If he had not an easy horse to mount, the infuriated beast sometimes pursued him with such quickness that he had to dive beneath the belly and mount from the offside. If by an evil chance his horse broke away from him to avoid the charge, two Gauchos rushing like the wind, their iron-handled whips raised in the air like flails, ready to fall upon the bullock's back, closed in upon the beast and fenced him in between their horses, at full speed, and as they passed, thundering upon the plain, men, horses and the flying animal all touching one another and straining every nerve, the man in peril, seizing the instant that they passed, sprang lightly up behind the near-side rider, just as a head of thistledown stops for a moment on the edge of a tall bank, tops it, and disappears.

When the *rodeo* had stood an hour or so, if nothing else was in the wind, the *vaqueros* galloped home slowly, smoking and talking of the price of cattle in the *saladeros*, the races to be held next Sunday at some *pulperia* or other, "La Flor de Mayo," "La Rosa del Sur," or "La Esquina de los pobres Diablos," and the *rodeo*, when it felt itself alone, slowly disintegrated just as a crowd breaks up after a meeting in Hyde Park, and all the various "points" sought out their grazing grounds.

On days when they required fresh meat at the *estancia*, when it was necessary in Gaucho phrase to *carnear*, then the *capataz* and two *peones*, coiling their *lazos* as they went, rode into the *rodeo*, the cattle parting into lanes before them, and after much deliberation and pointing here and there, with sage remarks on the condition of the herd, he would point his finger at a beast. Then, cautiously, the two *vaqueros*, with the loop of their *lazo* trailing on the ground, taking good care to hold it in their right hands, high and wide, so that their horses did not tread in it, would close upon their prey. Watching him carefully, the horses turning almost before the men gave them the signal with the hand or heel, the cattle edging away from them, they would conduct the animal towards the edge of the *rodeo* with his head to the "camp."

When he was clear, with a shrill cry they spurred their horses and the doomed beast began to gallop, unless perchance he doubled back towards the herd, in which contingency the operation had to be gone through again. Once galloping, the efforts of the riders were directed to keep him on the move, which in proportion to his wildness was harder or more easy to achieve, for a wild cow or bullock generally "parts" more easily than a tame animal. Perhaps the distance was a mile, and this they traversed at full gallop, hair, *poncho*, mane, and tail all flying in the wind, with a thin cloud of dust marking their passage as they went. When they got near the house one rider looked up at the other and said, "Now is the time to throw." In an instant, round his head revolved the thin hide-plaited rope, the ring (the last six feet in double plait) shining and glistening in the sun. The wrist turned like a well-oiled machine, the horse sprang forward with a bound, and the rope, winding like a snake, whistled and hurtled through the air.

It fixed as if by magic round the horns, the rider generally keeping in his hand some coils of slack for any casuality *[sic]* that might occur. The instant that it settled round the horns the rider spurred his horse away to the left side, for it was death to get entangled in the rope. In fact, in every cattle district maimed hands and feet showed plainly how dangerous was the game. The check, called the *tirón*, came when the animal had galloped twenty yards or so. It brought him to a stop, his hind legs sliding to one side. The horse leaned over, straining on the rope, the victim bellowed and rolled its eyes, lashing its tail against its flanks and pawing up the turf.

If the position of the animal was near enough, so as to save the carriage of the meat, the last act straight began. If not, after avoiding dexterously a charge or two, keeping the rope taut, and free from his horse's legs or even sides or croup, unless he was a well-trained cattle horse, the other *peon* riding up behind, twisting his *lazo* round his head, urging his horse against the lassoed animal, rode up and drove him nearer in. Once within handy distance from the house, the man who had been driving threw his rope and caught the bullock by the heels. Sometimes they threw him down and butchered him; at other times, the man who had him by the horns, keeping his *lazo* taut, he and his horse throwing their weight upon the rope, called to his fellow to dismount and *carnear*.

If he was an expert, throwing his reins upon the ground, he slipped off quickly, and crouching like a jaguar about to spring, ran cautiously to the offside of the enlassoed beast, drawing his long *facón*. Avoiding any desperate horn-thrust, like a cat avoids a stone, and taking care not to get mixed up with the rope, he plunged his knife deep down into the throat. The gushing stream of blood sprang like the water from a fire-plug, and the doomed creature sank upon its knees, then rocked a little to and fro, and with a bellow of distress, fell and expired.

If, on the other hand, the animal was fierce, or the man did not care to run the risk, he advanced, and, drawing his *facón* across its hocks, hamstrung it, and brought it to the ground, and then came up and killed it, when it was rendered helpless. On such occasions it was terrible, and quite enough to set a man against all beef for ever (had there been any other food upon the plains, to see the bullock jumping upon its mutilated legs and hear it bellow in its agony.

Last scene of all, the horses either unsaddled or attached to the *palenque*, or else to a stout post of the corral, the slayers, taking off their *poncho*s or their coats, skinned and cut up the beast. So rapidly was this achieved, that sometimes hardly an hour had elapsed from the "death bellow," to the time when the raw joints of meat were hung in the *galpón*. The hide was stretched out in the sun, and the *chumangos* and the dogs feasted upon the entrails, whilst the wild riders, dusty and bloodstained, took a *maté* in the shade.

There was another and a wilder aspect of the *rodeo*, which, like a *pampero*, burst on the beholders so suddenly that when it passed and all had settled down again, they gazed, half stunned, out on the tranquil plain. It might be that a *tropero* was parting cattle for a *saladero*, his men cutting out cattle, riding them towards a "point" of working bullocks, held back by men about a quarter of a mile from the main body of the herd. All might be going well, the *rodeo* kept back by men riding round slowly. The parties might be working quietly, without much shouting; the day serene, the sun unclouded, when suddenly an uneasy movement would run through the cattle, making them sway and move about, after the fashion of the water in a whirlpool, without apparent cause.

If the *tropero* and the overseer or the owner of the place himself were men who knew the "camp," and few of them were ignorant of all its lore, they did not lose a moment, but calling as gently as possible to the *peones*, they made them ride as close to one another as they could, in a great circle round about the beasts. It might be that their efforts would pacify the animals, but in all cases the "cutting out" was over for the day.

A little thing, a hat blown off, a *poncho* waving, a horse suddenly starting or falling in a hole, would render all their efforts useless and as vain as those of him who seeks to keep a flight of locusts from lighting on a field. In an instant the cattle would go mad, their eyes flash fire, their tails and heads go up, and, with a surge, the whole *rodeo*, perhaps five or six thousand beasts, would, with a universal bellow, and a noise as of a mighty river in full flood, break into a stampede. Nothing could stay their passage — over hills, down steep *quebradas*, and through streams they dashed, just as a prairie fire flies through the grass. Then was the time to see the Gaucho at his best; his hat blown back, held by a broad black ribbon underneath his chin, and as he flew along, slipping his *poncho* off, the *capataz* galloped to head the torrent of mad beasts.

The *peones*, spreading out like the sticks of a fan, urged on their horses with their great iron spurs, and with resounding blows of their *rebenques* as they strove hard to close and get in front. Those who were caught amongst the raging mass held their lives only by their horses' feet, pushed here and there against the animals, but still unmoved, upright and watchful in their saddles, and quick to seize the slightest opportunity of making their way out. If by mischance their horses fell, their fate was sealed; and the tornado past, their bodies lay upon the plain, like those of sailors washed ashore after a shipwreck — distorted, horrible.

The men who at the first had spread out on the sides, now closing in, had got in front, and galloped at the head of the mad torrent, waving their *poncho*s and brandishing their whips. They, too, were in great peril of their lives, if the herd crossed a *viscachera* or a *cangrejál** That was the time for prodigies of horsemanship. If I but close my eyes, I see, at a stampede on an *estancia* called "El Calá" a semi-Indian rushing down a slope to head the cattle off. His horse was a dark dun, with eyes of fire, a black stripe down the middle of his back, and curious black markings on the hocks. His tail floated out in the wind, and helped him in his turnings, just as a steering oar deflects a whaleboat's prow. The brand was a small "s" inside a shield. I saw it as they passed. Down the steep slope they thundered, the Indian's hair rising and falling at each spring that the black dun made in his course. His great iron spurs hung off his heels, and all his silver gear, the reins, the *pasadores* of the stirrups, the *chapeao* and *fiadór*, and the great spurs themselves, jingled and clinked as he tore

* A *viscachera* was a place where *viscachas* burrowed. A *cangrejál* was a colony of land crabs. Both made very dangerous traps for riders.

on to head the living maelstrom of the stampeding beasts. Suddenly his horse, although sure-footed, keen, and practised at the work, stepped in a hole and turned a somersault.

He fell, just as a stone from the nippers of a crane, and his wild rider, opening his legs, lit on his feet so truly, that his great iron spurs clanked on the ground like fetters, as he stood holding the halter in his hand. As his horse bounded to his feet, his rider, throwing down his head and tucking his left elbow well into his side, sprang at a bound upon his back and galloped on, so rapidly that it appeared I had been dreaming, and only have woke up, thirty years after, to make sure of my dream. Sometimes the efforts of the *peones* were successful, and the first panic stayed, the cattle let themselves be broken into "points," and by degrees and with great management were driven back to the *rodeo* and kept there for an hour or two till they had quieted down. If, on the other hand, they kept on running, they ran for leagues, till they encountered a river or a lake, and plunging into it, many were drowned, and in all cases many were sure to stray and mix with other herds, or, wandering away, never returned again.

The whole impression of the scene was unforgettable, and through the dust, both of the prairie and the thicker dust of years, I can see still the surging of the living lava stream and hear its thunder on the plain.

A Hatchment

Upwards

The steep steps of the old church were thronged with peasants and with the dwellers in the Roman slums. The stair led upwards nearly as steeply as the legendary, perhaps, almost untrodden path that leads to heaven. Upon them a sort of semi-pious, semi-pagan fair was going on, and men and women cried their wares, cheap images of saints, scapularies and rosaries, their beads cut out of bone, with chains of leady-looking tin. A crucifix, stamped out by the hundred dozen in a mill, dangled from each of them. The symbol was the same as if it had been carved in ivory and every link of gold. No doubt, in their last hour to those who bought them the presentment of their Redeemer moulded in tin (or stamped) was as consoling to them as the finest work of the Renaissance. It also served them just as well when they swore falsely, with real tears in their eyes, calling upon the moulded figure to lift his hand and slay them if they were lying, as they pressed it to their lips and lied. Withal they were a merry, handsome, loud-voiced crowd, and freely bought the sweetmeats and the flaky pastry which were on sale, together with the pious objects of their faith, out of the superfluity of their penury. The crowd pushed up the steps, the younger men halting to breathe and spit at every flight; the elder men and women toiling on, their eyes upon the ground, their hearts perhaps fixed upon heaven, at a slow plodding walk. Most of them wore a look of pleased, but not excited expectation, such as a man has on his face when he returns to some spot well remembered, that he has known for years.

The old, brown church looked down and seemed to welcome them, with the straw, leather-bound screen before the door, triced up like a lateen. Where the church rose a temple once had stood, and no doubt also seemed to welcome its crowd of worshippers, for both were heaven's altars in their own way. In fact, so little had the ritual changed inside the church that a pagan worshipper would hardly have felt out of place had he awaked after a sleep of centuries and mingled with the crowd. The skin-clad shepherds, with their wild locks and shaggy beards, the bold-eyed women with their ample busts and wealth of coarse, black hair, would all have been familiar to him, and to complete the feeling of familiarity, a whiff of burned-out incense mingled with the scent of garlic floated from the church, just as it must have often floated from the temple of the gods. The thin and parchment-looking women, who generally sit outside the church, day in, day out, the whole year through, receiving alms with a certain condescension, for they know that without them the givers cannot attain to glory through their charity, had given up their posts as a bad job. Nothing blocked the entry to the church, and through the doors the crowd poured in, the men piously crossing themselves in the familiar, syncopated style of all men born in Catholic countries, the women stopping a moment after the pious movement to put a handkerchief upon their hair, following the injunction of S. Paul. The crowd passed in, joyous, but orderly, unwashed, yet bearing in every gesture the tradition of a culture that was old long before Britain was a name. Though women jostled against men, men against women, in the space between the door and the body of the church, no cry was heard, or any giggling protest, such as is certain to be raised in other countries when people press against each other in the dark. Good manners, or the lack of imagination inherent in the race, kept them all within bounds; but yet their bounds were drawn so wide that in any other land they would not have restrained.

Inside, the darkness of the church was intensified by scaffolding, which had been up so long its colour hardly was to be distinguished from the stone. Young priests from all the seminaries in Rome were scattered here and there; their gowns and cassocks, red, green and blue, made blotches of dull colour as they passed to and fro. They moved about in knots, holding their cassocks up a little, just as a woman holds her skirts, for the floor of the church had been strewed with box-leaves, and the passage of the crowd had turned them into mud. There was a look upon their faces half interested, half critical, such as an actor wears in a strange theatre. Tombstones, each with a figure carved in high relief upon it, composed the pavement, which made it difficult to walk, and the strong scaffolding with which the aisle was filled cut it off into sections, something like loose boxes. Upon the baulks of timber boys had climbed up to see the show, just as they do when a procession passes down a street. A crowd was gathered round a table by a great pillar in the aisle. On it stood children, girls and boys, who huddled close up to one another for mutual support, just as wild horses do in a corral. Some priests stood by, and a few women, each with an eye upon her child, regarding it with pride tinged with anxiety. Around the table the various seminarists had secured front places and stood expectant, their faces all suffused with mild excitement and with sympathy. The populace, although in general not used to giving place to anyone, but standing unmoved if right in the middle of a crowded street looking at drivers and remarking, "I am a Roman," instinctively had given way to the young priests, as if it recognized their claim. After some little urging, a boy about twelve years of age, dressed in his ordinary clothes, stood forward, and with a gesture, such as S. Paul made when he spoke to the men of Athens, calling for silence, took up his parable: "My brethren, the heart of Jesus always is open to the pure of spirit. Come to him. . . . Come, my brethren, and hear the words of innocence, I, though a child, speak to you, for my heart is pure, the blessed words which, from the time when first the mysterious star stood fast over the stable in the East, and the three kings entered and knelt before the manger, where the Babe was laid . . . the Babe was laid" — he faltered for a moment, and a priest prompted him with "Courage, my son," and the child began again, just like a phonograph that has stuck for a minute — "the Babe was laid. The blessed word, the tidings of great joy, that we speak every year at this the blessed season of goodwill on earth and peace to all mankind. Therefore, my brethren, let us pray." Then he knelt down, crossing himself, and prayed for grace, and, rising to his feet, stretched out his arms in a fine, untaught gesture, and said: "Therefore, my brethren, after our prayer all that I say is, lay yourselves upon the Saviour's heart and listen to a child." His little sermon over, he stepped back amongst the other children, hot and triumphant, and a subdued but audible murmur of applause broke out from the young priests. One of them, a tall German youth, hung on the youthful preacher's words, with a far-off look of rhapsody upon his face, such as a peasant wears when in a church he sees the relics of a saint displayed. He said, after a sigh, to a companion, "I often think that only children should be allowed to preach," a sentiment with which many who are not priests could well agree, if there were many preachers like the Italian boy.

After the boy, a tiny child was lifted up and bleated out that the Madonna never says "Go away, naughty children"; but always holds her arms out to them and calls them to her breast. When it was duly kissed and lifted down from its high perch, a girl stood up, in direct contradiction of S. Paul's dictum, and launched into a tale. Tall, slight, with a head of rippling dark brown hair, which gave a look to her as of a youthful Magdalen, she began, twisting her thin, brown hands about, a little tale of a Christian maiden of old times exposed to peril through the wickedness of a young Roman knight. In a high voice she told how Agatha prayed to the blessed Madonna in her peril, and how God's Holy Mother struck the wretch with blindness, which only was removed when, at the Christian maiden's exhortation, the wicked Roman was baptized. "Come, then, to the Madonna, our dear mother, she who has care of all us children, seeing in every one of us the image of her Son."

The child cast down her eyes, crossed herself, threw back her hair a little, and, turning, stood a moment for that admiration that she was well aware was due to her. The seminarists, though perhaps not so much edified as with the boy, were still human enough to look admiringly at the young, pious actress, and then they trooped away across the church towards the presentment of the manger, where ox and ass stood looking at the sleeping Babe, whilst the three kings laid gifts before his feet. Whether the piles of carrots, lettuces, potatoes, and of artichokes that were heaped up before the manger were the gifts of the three kings or those of pious members of the congregation was difficult to say. Still, there they were, giving an air of actuality that the plaster ox and ass, the figure of the shepherd with his gourd hanging from his waist, and all the other pious properties, a little took away. Progress, which had left untouched the sanitary condition of the little streets outside the church, had worked great changes on the presentment of the stable where was laid the Babe. The figures of the Madonna, of Joseph, and of the kings were all of stucco painted in gaudy colours, and evidently had come from France. Their costumes had a kind of accuracy, giving them the effect of pious chromolithographs in books on Palestine.

Far different was the presentation of the manger a generation since. In those days, instead of a white glare from the electric light, three or four candles shed a murky gleam upon the scene. Joseph was dressed in mediaeval clothes, the Blessed Virgin might have stepped from a canvas either of Carlo Dolci or Guercino; two of the Magi wore what their designer no doubt thought was Babylonian court dress; the third was painted blacker than the ace of spades, with an enormous turban and a scimitar. Progress had touched the manger in the Ara Coeli with its finger, making it up to date, more realistic and less natural; but the effect remained the same to the poor peasants and slum-dwellers who were looking on.

The spectacle, not being sentimental, held no attraction for the knots of seminarists who had pressed closely round the preaching children and stood enraptured at their words. They passed by, if not indifferent, yet half ashamed, one or two muttering, "These sort of things are of the nature of a kindergarten . . . fit for the poor and the uneducated." So may a modernist regard with loathing a poor peasant kissing the brazen toe of the statue of S. Peter, quite unaware that the kiss and the man who kisses form the backbone of the Church which Peter founded, not on philosophy, but on blind faith, without foreseeing that in these latter days mountains would rise and block the path to heaven of the poor worshipper.

So round the chapel, with its glare of light and paper rocks, its stucco figures, and its ox and ass looking as if they had been borrowed from a child's Noah's ark, there was a throng of humble folk. Ragged old cloaks, so frayed and worn that the edges looked as if they had been fringed, covered up rags, and knotted horny hands that all their lives had toiled to produce all that made life worth living for, for others, leaned upon iron-shod staves. Girls with a dirty pocket-handkerchief balanced upon their heads stood gazing, just as a deer in a park stands gazing at a motor when it passes with a roar. Two soldiers, freshly caught, whose uniforms looked as if they had been made of cardboard, and in whose faces was the stare of wonder that they had brought from some lost village in the Apennines, stood and admired, talking in a strange dialect of the hills.

Children ran in and out among their elders' legs, and on the base of a great pillar sat an old peasant and his wife. Years and hard fare had turned their skins to parchment. No water had defiled their bodies since the day that they were born, and their patched clothes were indefinable in hue, with perhaps a shade of dusky brown giving a note of colour to them, as they sat looking like two bundles of dried vines. They gazed intensely with the air of seeing nothing that is so frequent in aged people who have passed hard lives, and the old man, letting his hand fall gently on his companion's knee, said, "Where is the infant Jesus; I cannot see Him for the bright light that they have put over the Blessed Virgin's head; but the ox and ass I see quite plainly looking down at the Babe." He saw the ox and ass; the crowd saw all the figures of the *presepio* just as they saw their daily lives, without the understanding of them. The youthful preachers and the manger, the knots of seminarists, the country folk, and the old couple sitting like Philemon and Baucis on the stone base of the great pillar, the church itself, and the religion that it taught, all seemed legitimate descendants of the old worshippers who once had worshipped in the temple that had stood upon the place. Their joys and hopes and fears were of an older world, a world human, but outworn, lovable, and yet passing from our eyes, although we gazed upon it as the peasant gazed, striving to see the Babe.

Slowly the crowd dispersed, tramping out heavily in their nailed shoes, and leaving yet one or two women still looking at the chapel and carrying children in their arms. Over their heads floated two toy balloons, one red, one yellow, and with the children looking up at them as they floated in the air. They soared up heavenwards, and might have reached the sky had not the low roof of the church beaten them down again.

A Moral Victory

My Aunt Alexia, whom I remember vividly, though she died more than forty years ago, was a type of the Yorkshire gentlewoman now long extinct. Short, and dark-haired, with eyes that seemed to be upon the point of starting from her head, she had a strong and wiry moustache, and when by chance she did not pull it out a growth of beard upon her chin, which used to make me shudder when as a boy she kissed me and they grated on the skin. I do not think this outward, visible sign of masculine interior forces gave her much trouble or annoyance, for she would say with pride, "My cousins the Fitzgibbons all have beards, both women and men alike." Family pride was a strong point with my good aunt, as she was nearly related to almost all the county families of Yorkshire, which interparentage a Scottish aunt of mine used to term scornfully in speaking of her, "Alexia and her fatiguing relatives." She always dressed in black, carried eternally a bag embroidered with steel beads, and was a little deaf, but never used a trumpet, saying that nearly all her Yorkshire cousins were as deaf as she was, with considerable pride.

She was a Churchwoman, not because of any special partiality for the ritual of the Church, but because, born as she was a member of a county family, it would have been impossible for her to belong to any other faith. Ladies and gentlemen, as a rule, were Churchmen, unless they happened either to be eccentric in their tastes or Roman Catholics. The latter faith was, as it were, a visitation from on high which they had inherited from birth, in the same way as a hare-lip or a big purple blotch on one side of their face. To be eccentric was permissible if one was either born a Martin, or a Fitzgibbon, or any other of the hierarchy of the West Riding, such as a Mundell or a Milton-Rounde. A gamekeeper might be a dissenter, but not a coachman or a butler, for it was painful to sit behind a man who was not properly baptized, or to drink wine poured out by one who did not walk up the church on a Sunday as it were strewed with eggs.

My Aunt Alexia, either by reason of her deafness or descent, had a hard temper, much like the disposition of an Airedale terrier; in fact, all her relations said that she was "varmint," a term which in their mouths was laudatory, for they applied it indifferently to dogs and horses, animals at least as sacred in their eyes as was the cat to the Egyptians, as well as to mankind. Still, she was kind-hearted, through *[sic]* brusque and masculine, and not without a vein of tenderness. As a child I stood in awe of her, partly on account of her exterior, partly because she was so deaf; but she had humour, a gift that always wins the confidence of children in a way older people seldom understand.

As fate would have it, this lady, a pattern of propriety and commonplace, with all the virtues and the failings of her class, her strong self-will and great austerity of face and bearing, had for a mate a man as different from her as the day is from the night, or, as she would have said, as chalk from cheese, in her old-fashioned speech.

Born in a military prison at Verdun, General Hickman Currie had grown up, not only speaking French, but quite a Frenchman in his ideas and ways. Short and well-made, he must have been in youth what he called *un joli garçon*; but in the days when I remember him he was a wizened little man, alert and active, and with a chestnut wig that could have taken in nobody, and least of all a boy. Well over seventy, I remember him rolling his eyes and playing the guitar, as he sang love-songs in the Spanish tongue, which language he had acquired in youth, and spoke it volubly in the Gallic fashion, accentuating every syllable alike, so that it seemed a kind of gibberish more than a human speech.

His wigs were my delight, for he had three of them, and now and then, when he was staying at a country house, he would appear with one a little longer than the last, and after looking in the glass would say, "My hair has grown ridiculously long," and go off into town.

All his upbringing and his military life, for he had served with credit in several campaigns, were not much calculated to make him what is called "domesticated," and his chief object to the last day of his life was what he euphemistically styled gallantry, being, as he said, "equally at home with any one of them." How such a man, with all his graces and his wigs, his songs to the guitar, his love of women, and his way of looking at the world, could have endeared himself to Aunt Alexia, always puzzled me. They seemed to pull together passably, for he, no matter what his practice may have, been, always was outwardly discreet, and treated her with deference, and, though he made no secret of his tastes, never gave cause for scandal, and yet one felt that there was something not quite right between them, rather divined than seen. Their marriage had been one of inclination, for Aunt Alexia was by report in those days not ill-looking in an Amazonian fashion, and possibly less deaf. Money they neither of them had, though each had something, and of course the General had his pension, for in the days when I remember him he had long turned his sword into a walking-stick, and had become a pillar of the club in a small watering-place.

Nothing restrained the General from his universal love-making; but by the time that I remember him it had become rather an affair of making compliments and eyes than of what he called "pushing the attack." Still, the old spirit lingered in him, for at a picnic, when a lady had got into some difficulty, he turned to me and told me to go to her assistance, and when I, boy-like, said she did not seem to need my help, rejoined, "A woman always is in want of help, my boy . . . especially on occasions when there is no need of it." My aunt looked upon his vagaries leniently enough in those days, though in the past they must have been of some annoyance to her, as I learned from another aunt of mine, whom report said the General had offended, either by making or not making love to her.

"My dear," said this good lady, "your Aunt Alexia has had a great deal to put up with from the General."

I could not help thinking that perhaps the General also had had something to put up with, but said nothing, knowing that if I did my aunt would not impart the information that was trembling on her tongue. "You see, my dear," she said, "your Aunt Alexia was one of those who understood when it was politic not to see everything." No one could possibly have accused my Aunt Margaret of not seeing everything. She was an Ogilvy, she used to say with pride, in the same way she might have stated she was vertebrate, and one of the mammalia, and certainly she could weigh a person in the balance and find him wanting at a glance.

Aunt Margaret resumed: "Your Aunt and General Hickman, a person whom I never liked, for I could not abide his airs and graces, respected and possibly loved each other, for now that all is past see what a happy pair they are. Still, dear, your Aunt Alexia once was young, although to look at her to-day . . ." Aunt Margaret was a good seven years senior to my other aunt, and took snuff freely, drying her handkerchiefs before the fire after the operation, and at no epoch of her life could possibly have been attractive; but still remained a woman at the heart in matters that affected others of her sex. "You know it is galling for a woman to have her husband running after everyone, even if you have a moustache yourself, my dear." I agreed, and she resumed: "Your aunt always kept up appearances, and I think, in her secret heart, was rather proud of the General's reputation in the abstract; but yet, my dear, no one likes concrete things, no matter what they say. Your Uncle Arthur, although he said he was a Buddhist, swore fearfully when he had an attack of gout. So, dear, when any of her friends — you know what fearful gossips your dear Aunt Charlotte and your Cousin Rachel are — used to come to your Aunt Alexia with tales about her husband, she always said they were all lies. Still, like a prudent woman, she did not talk too much. You recollect our Scottish proverb, 'Juke and let the jaw gae by'?"

I thought my aunt kept, so to speak, her finger on the trigger for an unconscionable time; but knew that once primed she would fire at last and hit the bull's-eye, so I merely nodded, saying, "What a memory you have for proverbs. Aunt Margaret! Better than Sancho Panza, I believe." "Ah yes, Sancho," she rejoined, and set about to gather up the disjointed fibres of her tale.

"Where had I got to? Oh yes, your Aunt Alexia always kept a stout heart to a stae *[sic = Sc. stey=steep]* brae, as the saying is, and never noticed many a thing that perhaps was not worth the noticing. Perhaps she never saw, and what the eyes do not see the heart does not grieve for, so it may be that she was wise enough. Deaf people are hard to understand. You never know what or when they hear; but seeing is a different thing, and your aunt had a vision like a lynx. Well, well, the General was appointed to a command in India. In those days the passage round the Cape took ninety to a hundred days. All of a sudden he became so attentive to your aunt that everybody was surprised. He used to bring her flowers, and walk about with her just as he must have done before their honeymoon. Your Aunt Alexia never seemed at ease when, as she used to say, her husband was too French in his behaviour. Anyhow, the General said what could he do in India alone without his *chère petite Alexie*, and discoursed on the hardships of the voyage, for as the appointment was for a short time your aunt thought it was hardly worth her while to go so far afield. It was arranged that all goodbyes were to be said at home. The General said he could not bear to see his wife standing upon the shore and waving a wet handkerchief . . . a woman with her pocket-handkerchief rolled up into a ball, red eyes, and hair flying in the wind . . . he used to say *decoiffée*, but always translated it and every other French word that he used, for your Aunt Alexia spoke no language but her own."

My aunt turned towards me, and, looking at my expectant face, said: "I am not sure if it is altogether charitable to go on with my story, but it may serve you as a warning some day, so I will just go on." Aunt Margaret, being a Scotchwoman, had the saving gift of humour, so with a twinkle in her eye she went on with the story that she was bursting with desire to tell. "For several weeks — a voyage was a serious thing in those days — the General seemed to live down at the docks. He used to come back home to dinner worn out, as he said, with making proper preparations for his men. The soldier, he would say, lives through the stomach; feed him and he will follow you through fire; starve him and he will leave you in the lurch. Your Aunt Alexia, who I think had been captivated in the past by her husband's *bonhomie*, his easy manners, and his air of the complete man of the world, and who had always clung to him in spite of all his *fredaines*, as he called them, saying, 'Men will be men,' to which he answered, 'Yes, my life, and women women,' for he had no illusions as to woman's soulful love, now really began to respect him, as in her mind's eye she saw him labouring for the welfare of his men. As the time of sailing drew nearer day by day it seemed to Aunt Alexia as if she had been acting meanly in letting her husband take the voyage all alone. Though it had been agreed she should not come down to the ship to spare the General's feelings and her own at parting, as the day of his departure drew near, whether she suspected anything or whether she thought she ought to go and see if he was comfortable on board, she took a sudden resolution and drove down to the docks upon the morning of the day before the vessel sailed. The steward met her at the gangway, and as he ushered her below remarked 'We was on the look-out for you, Mum; the General's had the cabin done up beautiful, and only half an hour ago he sent a barrowful of flowers.'" What my aunt thought no one but she herself could possibly have told; however, she was *varmint*, and made no sign, and quietly followed the steward down below.

The first glance round the cabin must have shown her how the land lay, for evidently the General did not contemplate a solitary voyage. Fresh chintz and flowers with plate and pictures gave the cabin an air as of a yacht, and two sea-cots standing beside each other, an air of domesticity unusual in the cabin of a transport in those far-distant days.

My aunt looked round as if she had expected everything just as she found it, said, "It is all very nice, though the fresh paint and varnish is a little overpowering. . . . Send me a cup of tea." The plan of her campaign must have sprung to her brain at once intuitively, as to the brain of a consummate general in the field, for, taking off her bonnet and her wrap, she wrote a letter, which she sent back by the cab. After an hour or two the cab returned bringing her boxes, which she instantly unpacked. In the afternoon the General came down, whistling a little air, to see that all was right before he went off home to take a tearful farewell of his wife. What passed between them when they found themselves together in the cabin none ever knew but the two principals, and they never divulged a word.

Later in the afternoon another cab arrived piled high with luggage, but a mysterious note handed in by the steward caused it to turn about and return silently to town. Early next morning the vessel put to sea, and as my aunt was a bad sailor, perhaps the General had an easier time for the first week than by all rights he had deserved. As the mysterious lady who was to have occupied the cot in which my aunt reposed had never shown herself aboard, matters remained in a vague condition of conjecture, and my Aunt Margaret when she told the story always declared that she thought Aunt Alexia most probably never let her husband really know that she suspected anything was wrong. How she explained her unexpected presence in the ship Aunt Margaret had no idea, but she opined there must have been some awkward moments at the captain's table when conversation flagged, and when their cabin door was closed, and they retired to rest.

Bismillah

A flock of goats lay on the rocky hill, their parti-coloured backs looking like stones amongst the scrub of lentisk and low palm. The noonday sun had made them drowsy, even the whirring of a dragon-fly as it passed like a humming-bird, barely made them raise their heads. Below the hill spread out the bay, blue, calm, and looking almost artificial, or as if drawn by an indifferent painter, it was so conventional, with its white waves breaking upon a pebbly beach in a long, soothing swish. At one end of the bay rose the white town, surrounded by a ruined wall. The houses mounted up the hill in steps, flat-topped, and painted a pale pink or a metallic blue. One or two slender towers and a few palm-trees stood up here and there. No smoke defiled the atmosphere, and thus the town looked empty and unreal. So might Pompeii have appeared had it been left deserted and not overwhelmed. About the middle of the bay two or three fishing-boats lay becalmed, their high lateens sticking up straight, just as the bar of an old Arab draw-well, with its tall arm and heavy stone tied to its butt with an esparto rope, sticks up on a brown plain. A long white line, fleecy and sparkling in the sun, showed where a tide-rip crossed the straits, although so still was everything it might have been but painted by the inferior draftsman that had drawn the sea. The other arm of land that formed the bay was high and rocky, and was crowned by an old watch-tower standing on a cliff. Villages, shown by their cactus hedges, which cut them into squares like a vast chess- board, with here and there a round white dome that marked a saint's house springing up like a mushroom in a field, were almost indistinguishable from the scrub.

Sea, land, and hills, the patches of dark bush, the grove of fig-trees round the crumbling fort, in which the cannon all lay prone beside their carriages . . . the end of war is peace . . . were bathed in a white light, which cast black shadows on the sand. All was so quiet that you could almost hear the growth of plants, and the faint, twittering notes of the goatherd's pipe, cut from a green cane, seemed to fill all the air. A little sandy river ran beneath the fort.

Some ragged cattle, and thin mares with their feet hobbled with a palmetto cord, stood about listlessly. A knot of camels grazed on the sparse and wiry grass. Storks chattered on the thatched roofs of the village by the salt-pans, and the remains of an old Roman port still stood up stoutly after ten centuries of pillage and decay. All was so peaceful and so primitive that if Theocritus had come to life again, he could not but have taken up his pen to write another idyll, to prove the golden age had never passed away.

All round the hillock, upon which, amongst palmetto bushes and the rocks, the goats were lying, ran like a lake a tract of sandy ground, white with the efflorescence of the salt that flowed out from the pans. On it the grass grew sparely, and little flowers, pink and procumbent, appeared between its stalks. The guardian of the flock lay with his head under a clump of dwarfish palm, his two brown legs, tanned with the sun that he had fought with all his life and that his ancestors brought in their blood from the far Yemen or the Hejáz, looked like the roots of the thick bushes that the sand had left uncovered at his feet. His dark and liquid eyes were not unlike those of the goats he herded, and as he played upon his pipe a strange wild air, the intervals so wild and so uncertain that a bird might have been deceived by it and flown about him, thinking that one of its own kind was in distress, a little kid, white but for a spot or two about its nose, nestled up to his side. Now and again he patted it, and the two seemed but a little separated from one another, in nature or degree.

As the day wore on the goats slowly began to rise and feed; the boy got up, leaving a little hollow in the sand where he had lain by the palmettos, and, drawing out his sling, lazily sent a stone or two whistling towards the goats. As the stones struck the ground near to the animals they drew their feet together in a bunch, jumped to one side, and then, after stretching out into a long line, dispersed about the stones to graze. A flight of cranes, looking like aerial camels, passed overhead, their shrill, harsh cries lost in the stillness of the air. Nature awoke after its midday torpor, and in the valley the lean Arab mares, dragging their hobbled feet slowly along or rising in a sort of stifled rear, turned their heads towards the breeze as they began to feed. Their foals, that had lain looking as if half dead, rose to their feet, and, shaking off the sand, whinnied and trotted after them, their stilt-like legs giving them an air of those strange animals drawn by the cave-dwellers upon the rocks.

Slowly the little river filled. Stones on the sandy flat were covered as if by magic by the incoming tide, so imperceptibly that you could no more mark the rising of the flood than follow the slow movement of the hands of a cathedral clock as they eat time before your eyes. The droning of the insects ceased, save for the sharp metallic chirp of crickets, and caravans of asses and of mules that had arrived too late to pass the river were turned back to the grass to feed or struck a winding path between high bushes to seek another ford. As the goats fed, the small, white kid followed the little goatherd like a dog, stopping to eat, then trotted up to him to rub its nose against his legs. He took its innocent caresses just as a man acknowledges those of his dog, as if they were his due; but at the same time something he prides himself upon as testifying to his worth. All day the goats fed happily amongst the stones or browsed upon the thorns. Sometimes they ran along the trunk of a fallen tree like tight-rope dancers, to reach its branches, or bounding on a rock, stood for an instant motionless, and leaping down again, began again to feed, with just the air that a man wears upon his face after some sudden foolish action into which he is betrayed.

By slow degrees the sun began to slant, gilding the mosque towers in the town across the bay, painting the sails of fishing-boats and throwing ever-lengthening shadows on the sand. The massive walls of the deserted Roman port turned to a dullish yellow in its rays, and the far-off mountains above Tetuán seemed to draw nearer as the light haze raised by the heat was slowly dissipated. As the sun sank, tribesmen returning from the town, all dressed in white as if they had been shrouded for their own burial, came trooping homewards, crossing the river seated on their mules. One would go forward with his white garments tucked up, sounding the water with a stick. Then came the caravan, some mounted, some on foot, the women passing with their garments held up round their necks, but with their faces all veiled chastely, for, as the Arabs say, the devil enters at the mouth. The mules' and ponies' feet, in the swift, running walk that they affect, seemed not to leave the ground, and yet the riders, rocked by the motion, swayed in their seats just as a man does on a camel, as it slides through the sand. They brushed through beds of the palmettos making a noise as of the opening of a fan. Passing the little plain, in the midst of which stood the steep hillock where the goats had lain amongst the stones, they disappeared down the rough path that crossed a stream, and reappeared upon the bush-clad hill, looking like a flock of sheep in their white clothes, then faded out of sight.

Sometimes, instead of these white friar-like figures, a knot of men from the far highlands, dressed in their short brown cloaks, their scarlet flannel gun-cases wound turban-like about their heads, passed at a swinging trot. They bore their rifles in their hands and danced along like fauns, occasionally firing a shot or two or simulating a hill-fight, whirling their guns about and uttering wild cries. As they passed on their way, either on foot or mounted, the little flock of goats, with that pathetic trust in man that Eastern animals seem to have above all others of their kind, scarcely avoided them, and now and then a pony's tail seemed to be whisked to brush the flies off, it passed so near their heads.

Their little shepherd stood playing on his reed or plaiting a palmetto cord, his two brown feet, with their prehensile toes holding the ground just as a monkey's paws curve around a rope. At last all the returning village folk had gone, the sun sank lower, and the boy, gathering his flocks together, walked towards home in front of them piping on his reed.

In a long line they followed, the kids occasionally stopping to browse upon the cytisus and the lentiscus bushes. The milk-white kid followed the closest at his heels. The little river, from which the tide had now retired, was almost empty, and the flock passed it with the water scarcely up to their knees. They threaded through the open gateway of the old Roman port, passed by the salt-pans and drew near to an Arab village, built of reeds and thatched with thistle stalks, giving the huts the look as of the nest of some gigantic bird. Upon a little plot of grass outside the village sat several elders, men of grave mien, bearded and formal in their manners, who by their appearance should have been discoursing on religion, the unity of God or on his attributes; but who were probably talking about the price of grain. An air of peace, such as one fancies reigned on earth when Boaz courted Ruth, hung over everything. Girls lingered at the well and talked, and then, their slender water-jars filled up, and with a tuft of tender canes or reeds floating on the top, went homeward, stepping like deer upon their naked feet and swaying with their load. Bells tinkled on the kine, and now and then a homing stork circled about the huts and dropped into its nest.

Over the straits was stealing by degrees a greenish light that made the hills in Spain still more intensely vivid, flushed as they were with red. The fishing-boats began to look mysterious as the day faded, and the town to stand out white and unnatural-looking, like a dead city in the moon. As the flock and its shepherd reached the village one of the grave and bearded men arose. He stopped the boy, and speaking to him in sonorous Arabic said something, and the boy, reaching out a lean brown hand, caught the white kid and held it for a moment. The village elder felt its neck, and then drawing out a knife, after a pious "In the name of God," rapidly cut its throat. The kid uttered a little cry, and from its neck the blood spirted out in a stream upon the grass. One little jet fell on the boy's brown foot, and as he watched the last contortions of the dying kid with interest, but without feeling for his playmate's loss, dried in the warm sea breeze and looked as if a vein had been exposed.

Slowly the kid's head sank and coggled limply, and with a heaving motion of its flanks its life was finished. Mystery of mysteries! Still the same air of peace hung over everything, and as the flock passed to its pen the call to prayer was wafted up to heaven from the village mosque, fitful and quavering.

A Hatchment

Mist in Menteith

Some say the name Menteith meant a peat moss in Gaelic, and certainly peat mosses fill a third of the whole vale. However that may be, its chiefest attribute is mist. Shadows in summer play on the faces of the hills, and snow in winter spreads a cold carpet over the brown moss; but the mist stays the longest with us, and under it the semi-Highland, semi-Lowland valley puts on its most familiar air.

When billowing waves wreathe round the hills, and by degrees encroach upon the low, flat moors, they shroud the district from the world, as if they wished to keep it from all prying eyes, safe and inviolate. Summer and spring and winter all have their charms, either when the faint green of the baulked vegetation of the north breaks out, tender yet vivid, or when the bees buzz in the heather in the long days of the short, nightless summer, or when the streams run noiselessly under their shroud of ice in a hard frost. The autumn brings the rain, soaking and blurring everything. Leaves blotch and blacken, then fall swirling down on to the sodden earth.

On trees and stones, from fences, from the feals upon the tops of dykes, a beady moisture oozes, making them look as if they had been frosted. When all is ready for them, the mists sweep down and cover everything; from the interior of the darkness comes [sic] the cries of wild ducks, of herons as they sit upon the trees, and of geese passing overhead. Inside the wreaths of mist another world seems to have come into existence, something distinct from and antagonistic to mankind. When the mist once descends, blotting out the familiar features of the landscape, leaving perhaps the Rock of Stirling floating in the air, the three black trees upon the bare rock of the Fairy Hill growing from nothing, or the peak of the Cobbler, seeming to peer above enormous mountain ranges, though in reality nothing more vast than the long shoulder of Ben Lomond intervenes, the change has come that gives Menteith its special character.

There are mists all the world over, and in Scotland in particular; mists circling round the Western Islands, filling the glens and boiling in the corries of the hills, mists that creep out to sea or in towards the land from seawards, threatening and dreadful-looking; but none like ours, so impalpable and strange, and yet so fitting to our low, flat mosses with our encircling hills. In older days they sheltered the marauders from the north, who in their gloom fell on the valley as if they had sprung from the night, plundered and burned and harried, and then retreated under cover of the mist, back to their fastnesses.

As they came through the Glen of Glenny, or the old road behind Ben Dhu, which comes out just a little east of Invertrossachs, when the wind blew aside the sheltering wreaths of steam, and the rare gleams of sun fell on the shaggy band, striking upon the heads of their Lochaber axes, and again shifted and covered them from sight, they must have seemed a phantom army, seen in a dream, just between consciousness and sleep.

The lake, with its three islands, its giant chestnuts, now stag-headed and about to fall, the mouldering priory, the long church with its built-up, five-light window, the castle, overgrown with brushwood, and with a tree springing up from the middle hall, the heronry, the rope of sand the fairies twisted, which would have made a causeway to the island had they not stopped just in the nick of time, the single tree that marks the gallows, and the old churchyard of the Port, all these the mist invests with a peculiar charm that they lack when the sun shines and shows them merely mouldering ruins and decaying trees.

So of the Flanders Moss. It, too, in mist seems to roll on for miles; its heathy surface turns to long waves that play against the foot of the low range of hills, and beat upon Craigforth as if it were an island in the sea. Through wreaths of steam, the sullen Forth winds in and out between the peat hags, and when a slant of wind leaves it clear for an instant it looks mysterious and dark, as might a stream of quicksilver running down from a mine. When a fish leaps, the sound re-echoes like a bell, as it falls back into the water, and rings spread out till they are lost beneath the banks.

After a day or two of gloom life begins somehow or another to be charged with mystery; and, walking through the woods, instinctively you look about half in alarm as a roe bounds away, or from a fir-tree a capercailzie drums or flies off with a noise as if a moose was bursting through the trees.

Peat smoke floats through the air from cottages a mile away, acrid and penetrating, and fills the nostrils with its scent. The little streams run with a muffled tinkle as if they wished to hide away from sight; rank, yellow ragweeds on their banks, bowed down with the thick moisture, all hang their heads as if they mourned for the lost sunshine and the day. Now and then leaves flutter down slowly to the ground like dying butterflies. Over the whole earth hangs, as it were, a sounding-board, intensifying everything, making the senses more acute, and carrying voices from a distance, focussed to the ear.

So through our mists, a shepherd's dog barking a mile off, is heard as loudly as if it were a yard or two away, although the sound comes slowly to the hearing, as when old-fashioned guns hung fire and the report appeared to reach one through a veil. Thus does the past, with its wild legends, the raiders from the north, the Broken Men, the Saxon's Leap, the battles of the Grahams and the McGregors, come down to us veiled by the mist of time. In the lone churchyards, whose grass is always damp the whole year round, whose earth, when a new grave is dug, is always wet, so wet that not a stone rolls from it to the grass; the tombstones, with the lettering overgrown with lichens, only preserve the names of the old enemies who now lie side by side, in a faint shadowy way. The sword that marks the resting-place of the men of the most turbulent of all the races of that borderland is usually only the shadow of a sword, so well the mist has done its work, rounding off edges and obliterating chisel marks.

Boats on the Loch o' the Port, with oars muffled by the cloud of vapour that broods upon the lake, glide in and out of the thick curtain spread between the earth and sky, the figure of the standing fisher in the stern looming gigantic as he wields his rod in vain; for, in the calm, even the water-spiders leave a ripple as they run. In the low, mossy "parks" that lose themselves in beds of bulrushes before they join the lake, the Highland cattle stand at gaze, the damp congealing on their coats in whitish beadlets, and horses hang their heads disconsolately, for no matter in what climate they are born, horses are creatures of the sun. Under the shroud of gloom it seems that something strange is going on, something impalpable that gives the valley of Menteith its own peculiar air of sadness, as if no summer sun, no winter frost, no fierce March winds, or the chill cold of April, could ever really dry the tears of moisture that it lays up under the autumn mist. So all our walls are decked with a thick coating of grey lichen on the weather side that looks like flakes of leather, and on the lee side with a covering of bright, green moss.

Thatch moulders, and from it springs a growth of vegetation; a perpetual dripping from the eaves opens a little rill below it, in which the pebbles glisten as in a mountain stream.

Along the roads the scanty traffic rumbles fitfully, and on the Sabbath, down the steep path towards the little church, knots of fantastic figures seem to stalk like threatening phantoms. When they draw near, one sees that they were but the familiar faces of MᶜKerrochar of Cullamoon, Graham of Tombreak, Campbell of Rinaclach, and Finlay Mitchell, dressed in their Sunday clothes. They pass the time of day, daunder a little in the damp kirkyard, so heaped with graves they have to pick their way between them just as sheep pick their way and follow one another on a steep mountain path, or when they cross a burn.

Although their talk runs on their daily life — the price of beasts at the last market or the tryst, upon bad seasons and the crops, all in the compassed and depreciatory vein characteristic of their calling and their race, they once have been fantastic figures towering above the dry-stone dykes that edge the road. That glory nothing can take away from them, or from the valley where they dwell.

Nothing is stable. Snows melt and rain gives place to sun, and sun to rain again; spring melts into summer, then autumn blends insensibly with winter, and the year is out. Men come and go, the Saxon speech replaces Gaelic; even traditions insensibly are lost.

The trees decay and fall, then they lie prone like the great hollow chestnut trunks, blackened by tourists' fires, in Inchmahome. Our hills and valleys all have changed their shapes under the action either of fire or ice. Life, faiths, ideals, all have changed. The Flanders Moss that was a sea is now crossed by a railway and by innumerable roads. What, then, shall we, who have seen mists rising up all our lives, feared them as children, loved them in riper years, cling to, but mist?

Refuge of our wild ancestors, moulder of character, inspirer of the love of mystery, chief characteristic of the Keltic mind, spirit that watches over hills and valleys, lochs, clachans, bealachs and shaggy baadans, *[sic = Gael. baidean, a flock of sheep]* essence compounded of the water of the sky and earth, impalpable, dark and threatening, Fingal and Bran and Ossian, and he who in outstretching Ardnamurchan strung his harp to bless the birlinn of Clanranald, all have disappeared in thy grey folds.

Whether thou art death stealing amongst us, veiled, or life concealed behind a curtain, or but an emanation from the ground, which the poor student, studying in Aberdeen, working by day upon the wharves and poring over books at night, can explain as easily as he can solve all other mysteries, with his science primer, who shall say?

All that I know is that when the mantle of the damp rolls down upon us, battling with the rough oak copse upon Ben Dearch or Craigmore till all is swallowed up and a smooth surface stretches out over what, but half an hour before, was a thick wood of gnarled and secular trees that stood like piles stand up in an embankment, eaten by the sea, the mist has conquered.

Somehow, I think, its victory brings a sense of rest.

A Hatchment

The Pass of the River

The river spread out broad, but swift and deep, just underneath the little town, which stood upon a sandy bank, the whitewashed, flat-roofed houses, appearing from the far side of the pass, buried in gardens and in trees. To the east, the river's banks were buried in a forest of *ñandubay*, of *coronillo* and *chañár*. In the great bend it formed, the *monte* grew so thickly that when you penetrated it in search of horses, or to put up strayed cattle, to the *rodeo*, it seemed you were in another world from that of the open grassy prairies, only a league away.

Paths ran about between the thickets, passing round clumps of cactus, and avoiding pools. The scent came from the blossoms of the *espinillo de olor*, and from the *arasá*, filling the nostrils with a perfume almost of the tropics; the creeping plants in places bound the thickets in a net of living cordage — impenetrable, mysterious, and as if nature had set a challenge to mankind, saying, "Thus far . . , but there are secrets that you shall not solve."

Birds, as the little black-and-white *viudita*, with its forked, twitching tail; the plump, metallic-looking, purple-winged *jacú*; the francolin, and half a hundred others, flashed across the path. From overhanging boughs the nests of the hornero hung. Humming-birds poised themselves, brighter than jacinths, more iridescent than the beryl, as they sucked the honey from the great trumpet-shaped and dark-red, fleshy cactus flowers. Closer to the river, cormorants sat meditating on bald boughs, and in the stream aigrettes and herons fished, whilst gorgeous kingfishers flitted across the surface of the water and disappeared into the sedge.

Mares, with long, ropy manes, stood feeding in the clearings: then bounded back into the bush with a sharp snort at the first sight of man. Domestic cattle that had gone wild, bellowed and pawed the ground as you passed on your way, as if they somehow, in some mysterious way, remembered that their ancestors had one day been as free as were the forest deer — shyest of all the animals in the River Plate.

Such was the river on the east.

Towards the north, a line of stony hills, not high, but steep, extended towards the frontiers of Brazil. The grass was wiry, and the stones seemed to have been strewn by accident; between them sprung up tufts of thorny bush.

The hills ended about a league or two from the river-bank, leaving a space of open prairie to the west, which gradually shelved down towards the Pass.

Tracks, like those that the Arabs make all through the desert, made their appearance several hundred yards before the last descent; tracks not made by wheels, for nothing but the weekly diligence and a rare bullock cart or two ever passed on the road. Horses and mules and cattle, flocks of sheep and still more horses, mules and cattle and more flocks of sheep, were what had made the tracks; and yet the prairie was so wide, the carpet of long grass so strong, that almost all tracks ceased when once the trail had come out on the plain. From the last little rise, one saw the river, yellowish green, and swirling quietly in its channel, making smooth whirlpools here and there. It ran so silently, that it looked like oil, and now and then small landslips, either of sand or mud, fell with a splash into the stream that undermined the banks. Occasionally a fish sprang from the water and then fell back with a loud crash, and now and then a water tortoise raised its head. The pass itself spread out about a quarter of a mile in width, and on the land side to the west stood several straw ranches and a white flat-topped *pulperia*, known as the "Twenty-Fifth of May."

A row of posts for hitching horses were driven deep into the ground before the door, and at them all the day stood horses blinking in the sun. The *cojinillos* of the saddles were doubled forward over the pommel to keep the seat cool in hot weather or dry in rain. The reins were tied back to the cantle of the saddle to prevent them falling down and being stepped upon. Sometimes a man, emerging from the *pulperia*, with a gin bottle in his hand, or a bag of *yerba*, placed them in his saddle-bags, and carefully undoing his hide halter, girthed up his horse, putting his foot against its side, then, mounting, struck into the road towards the "camp" at a fox-trot, which after a hundred yards or so he changed to the slow gallop of the plains, his right arm moving rhythmically up and down as he allowed his whip to dangle on his horse's flanks to keep him to his pace.

Some of the horses at the hitching posts were saddled with old *recaos* covered with sheep-skins, and others blazed with silver, and now and then a wild-eyed *redomon* sat back and snorted when an incautious stranger came too near.

Occasionally three or four men came out together, some of them half drunk; but in an instant all had mounted lightly, and so to speak took wing, just like a flight of birds. No diving for their stirrups, and no snatching at the reins, no sticking out the body in an undignified position as they got up, and no resounding whack of the leg on the off-side of the horse, after the European style, ever occurred amongst these centaurs as they rode slowly off. Occasionally a man who had drunk too freely of *Carlón* or of *Cachaza*, and topped up with some gin, swayed in his saddle, but his horse seemed to catch him as he swayed, so perfect was his balance, and so firm his grasp between the thighs.

A stout stockade of posts of *ñandubay* set touching one another was thrown about the house, leaving the entrance narrow enough to close with a long pole, a precaution which at times was not unneeded, when some Gaucho tried to ride into the court.

The actual door led into a low room in which a counter ran from wall to wall, surmounted by a railing of light wood, in which a little trap was cut; through it the owner passed the drinks, the boxes of sardines, the packages of raisins or of figs, which constituted his chief articles of trade.

Outside the counter lounged the customers, for in those days the *pulperia* was a sort of unofficial club to which the idlers of the district all resorted, to while away their time. The clank of spurs sounded like fetters on the hard mud floor, and night and day a cracked guitar, with either every string fashioned of wire, or else the catgut mended up with strips of hide, twangled eternally. The *payador,** if so be that there was one present, took it of right, and after tuning up — an operation which generally took some time — played silently for a few bars, usually only a few simple chords, and then struck into a wild song, sung in a high falsetto, prolonging all the vowels and finishing upon the highest note he could attain. These songs almost invariably dealt with love, and were of the most melancholy complexion, according strangely with the fierce look and wild appearance of the singer and the grim faces of the listeners.

Occasionally a man would rise, and coming to the window in the railing say "Carlón," and would receive the dark red, heady Catalonian wine in a tin mug that held about a pint, and pass it round to all the loungers, beginning always with the *payador*.

* Improvisatore.

In North America, upon the prairies in similar circumstances, you kicked the counter and said "How," with perhaps the addition of "Boys, here's the hair off your heads"; but at the *pulperia* upon the Yi the etiquette was to take the mug and murmur "Gracias," or if you were a man of parts some pretty phrase or other, for though all men the whole world over are the slaves of etiquette, in different lands, it takes a different form, just as one star differs from another in brightness and in size.

Men would come in, and, after salutations, drink silently and go, touching their hats, and others instantly plunge into a conversation about the almost certain revolution or any other topic of the "camp," just as men do in clubs, where some make friends and others pass their lives hedged in behind their collars, speaking to nobody. Occasionally a fight would come about after a quarrel, and sometimes two known *valientes* would challenge one another to fight until first blood, the loser to pay a pint of wine or something of the kind.

That was the time for elaborate preparations. Spurs would be taken off and given to the *pulpero* and *ponchos* rolled about the arm. Then some authority would instruct the combatants where the knives should be held, leaving an inch, two inches, or the half blade beyond the hand, and the two heroes would begin. These contests were more formal than when they fought in earnest, and body blows were barred. Usually, after springing to and fro like cats, parrying, passing and crouching low, catching the blows upon their arms defended by their summer *ponchos*, they would pause for breath, whilst the assistants criticized the strokes. As all the cuts were levelled either at the arm or face, the contest sometimes lasted five or six minutes, and when at last the blood was drawn the beaten man, calling for wine, handed it courteously to his opponent, who passed it back to him, with many compliments. This was the summer weather, so to speak, of *pulperia* life, but now and then a sudden fury, after a bout of drink or any cause, would make some man get up vociferating like a maniac and drawing his *facón*.

Such a sight I remember once, not at the *pulperia* on the Yi, but near Bahia Blanca, where a grim old man, his long grey hair hanging a foot or more upon his shoulders, suddenly bounded on the floor, and drawing his long knife, beat furiously upon the counter and the walls, yelling out, "Viva Rosas, mueran los unitarios Salvajes," and foaming at the mouth. He looked so terrible that most of those assembled either drew their arms, or sliding out like cats to the *palenque* took the hobbles off their horses, and stood waiting by their sides. The *pulpero* hurriedly drew down his window, then taking his revolver in his left hand, carefully placed some empty bottles in a row upon the counter, ready to throw upon the crowd. After a minute, which, I confess, seemed longer than an hour, and after having menaced everyone with death unless they cried out "Viva Rosas," the old man's knife fell from his hand upon the ground, and he himself, tottering towards a seat, sat silent, rocking himself to and fro, and mumbling in his beard. The Gauchos sheathed their knives, and one of them muttered, "He is thinking of the deaths he owed when he was young. Leave him in peace."

The owner of the *pulperia* on the Yi was one Eduardo Peña, a sort of cross between a Gaucho and a townsman, wearing a coat and waistcoat, but no shirt collar, and with his loose *bombachas* tucked into high riding-boots with patent leather tops, worked with an eagle in red thread. Tall and athletic, the lump inside his coat by his right elbow showed where his pistol was, and everybody knew in politics he was a Blanco, although he generally kept his opinions pretty quiet, being, as he said, "a kind of a guitar for all to play upon."

No one had ever seen him with a good horse to ride, which he explained by saying he was half a sailor, being the owner of the *balsa* on the Pass.

The *balsa*, a flying bridge, worked by men pulling on a rope, which was swept across the river by the action of the stream, gave Eduardo Peña a position of importance midway between the dignity of an *estanciero* and of a merchant in the town.

Although there was a ford in average weather. three or four hundred yards above the flying bridge, few used it, as it was deep and dangerous, the bottom full of holes, and after several hours of rain became impassable.

Lounging about the river's edges stood the *balseros*, generally Correntinos, an amphibious race of men, as much at home in a canoe as on a horse's back, tall, slight, and Indian-looking, talking a curious dialect of Spanish, all mixed with Guarani.

A colony of little huts, some made of straw and others out of old tin cans, was set about a hundred yards from the water-side. In them lived several *chinas*, who drove a thriving trade in love amongst the passers-by. One or two of them, such as "Boton de Oro" and "Molinillo de Cafe," and in especial a half-Indian girl known as "La Laucha," almost deserve a place in history, considering the time they lived about the place and their resisting powers.

All of them on occasions were ready with their knives, and it would have been a bold man indeed who tried to better them at playing *monte* or *la taba*, or any of the games, so called of chance, played by the *habitués* of the Pass.

As all the whole world over extremes meet, it was curious to see how the old customs of the Greeks were to be seen in the straw *ranchos* near the *balsa* on the Yi. If any of the *chinas* were employed on what for want of a more explicit term we may refer to as *l'ouvrage de dames*, she dropped the mare's hide which served as door, and no one troubled her, just as in Hellas ladies of the same profession were wont to close their doors. All the night long the tinkling of guitars came from the *ranchos,* and usually by day the occupants slept and recuperated until the evening, when they came out and sat at the receipt of custom, and hence the name of *Las Murciélagas*, by which they all were known. Although the river ran within a hundred yards of their straw *ranchos*, no one had ever seen one of these "bats" bathe or do anything but draw a can of water from its stream. Had they been asked, it is not improbable that they had answered, "Only Indians bathe. We are Christians and clean," or something of the kind. So does the pride of race blind people to their welfare, and take away all of our senses, including that of smell. Day in, day out, horses and cattle waited at the Pass, their owners hailing the *balsa*, which was safe to be upon the other side, and sitting, with one leg crossed on the pommel of the saddle, smoking their cigarettes.

A fine green dust, composed of every kind of animal manure, filled all the air upon fine days, and as there were no trees within a quarter of a mile, the heat was tropical, and the few sheds which stood about for shelter from the sun, sure to be occupied.

The cattle hung their heads as if they had been on *rodeo*, and the peons, placed upon the bank for fear of a stampede, slumbered upon their saddles, though with one eye always half open for the first sign of movement in the herd. Sometimes a troop of mules, wild and unbroken, going to Brazil, gave more excitement, for the first sight of the great *balsa* arriving at the bank was sure to frighten them, when in a moment, in a cloud of dust, they disappeared into the camp, the negro peons from Rio Grande rushing to head them back. Sometimes the owner or his *capataz*, a dark Brazilian riding a horse covered with silver trappings, his saddle kept in place by a crupper — a most unusual thing amongst the Gauchos of the plains — wearing a sword stuck through his girths, and with a pair of silver-mounted pistols at his saddle-bow, by dint of galloping was able to head the troop into a swamp or angle of the river, or against some wood, and gradually get them calmed down and manageable. All generally went well as long as the frightened animals could be kept all together, but if they separated and cut out into "points," days might elapse before the troop again was got up to the Pass. As mules that once had been stampeded were always liable to stampede again, the utmost care was needed to make them by degrees, and twenty at a time, enter the *balsa* and allow themselves to be transported to the other side.

Occasionally all efforts were in vain. Then came the time for Don Eduardo Peña and his men. Two Correntinos in canoes, one up the stream and one below, lay on their paddles ready to keep the swimming animals from getting washed away. Gently, and with infinite precaution, they were conducted to the ford, and when at last they all were huddled on the bank and stood there terrified, the mounted men closed in upon them with a shout. Forcing their horses up against the mules, they yelled, and swung their *lazos* and their whips. At last some mule, bolder or more experienced than the rest, would stretch its ears out towards the water and take a cautious step. Then was the time for noise to cease, for mules are twenty times more self-reliant than are horses, and it was ten to one if the first mule should enter, the rest would follow him.

If the first mule took his decision and began to swim, others soon followed, and by degrees the troop would take the water, their heads sticking out straight like camels, and a faint line of back appearing as they swam.

In their canoes the Correntinos splashed water with their paddles to keep the animals together, and when the whole were swimming, paddled beside them to prevent them turning back. The Brazilian negroes crossed, swimming on their horses, and the *capataz*, when he had seen them land and gather up the mules into a bunch, rode slowly to the *balsa*, and forcing in his horse by dint of spurring was taken over dry.

Sometimes he too had his adventures, as one who, I remember, riding a half-tamed horse, had it jump with him on its back over the railing of the *balsa* in the middle of the stream. Swearing in Portuguese, and spouting water like a whale, he clambered back again, but, like a perfect Gaucho as he was, still holding fast the reins. His horse swam after him, and the fierce current carried it sideways till it lay helpless, when it was towed along.

His *cojinillo* was turned back, showing a pair of *boleadoras* which he had placed across the saddle underneath the seat. Little by little the current washed them off, amidst the laughter of the people on the raft. Just as they seemed about to disappear, a Gaucho, sitting on his horse, threw himself sideways, and, hanging by his heel, caught them upon the end of his *facón*.

The discomfited Brazilian, both his hands occupied in keeping up his horse's head, murmured a "*muito obrigado*," amid the laughter of the crowd.

All day the *balsa* journeyed to and fro, and Don Eduardo Peña lounged about, smoking and taking his receipts, varying his occupation by an occasional visit to his *pulperia*, to take a vermouth or a *vino seco* with a friend.

All day the stream of life, going northward to Brazil and south towards the capital, was focussed at the Pass.

Horsemen as still as statues waited for their turn, the only sign they were alive being when their horses shook their heads, making the *oscojo* of the bit rattle against their teeth.

Horsemen came up at a slow *trotecito*, their horses playing with the bit, the riders' hands holding the reins as lightly as they had been silk threads, and other riders came up with a succession of wild snorts and bounds, their half-wild horses shying from the *balsa* and only entering it after a stubborn fight. Great herds of cattle, flocks of sheep, long trains of bullock carts loaded with wool, and, once a week, the diligence, drawn by six horses, with a boy riding a seventh fastened by a *lazo* from the cinch to a great iron hook upon the pole, passed with a rattle of glass windows, in a dense cloud of dust.

Such were the humours of the Pass, focus and brief epitome of Gaucho life in Uruguay.

Now without doubt a hideous iron bridge stretches across the Yi. Trains pass and rumble, and out of them lean passengers who look out at the Pass, which once was the chief interest of all life between Durazno and San Fructuoso, in a perfunctory way, then ring the bell and ask how long a time they have to wait before the dinner hour.

Anastasio Lucena

We lay so near the shore in a steam tug that we could hear the noises of the city, and see the lights that looked so close it seemed that you could touch them by stretching out your hand. The watchmen called each hour, informing us that the night was serene, after having hailed the Blessed Virgin in a long-drawn-out wail.

Though we had lain there for three days in quarantine, none of us could sleep, partly on account of the mosquitoes and partly from the uneasy pitching of the tug-boat in the muddy current of the River Plate.

Three of us whiled away the time by fishing and by telling stories, the travellers' resource at such times, as we sat and smoked. Our budget was exhausted, and after having sat a long time silent in the sweltering heat, Mansel said suddenly: "I have told you all my yarns, but I can recollect a thing, there is no story in it, that left a strong impression on my mind."

We looked towards him gratefully as he sat cutting tobacco on his riding boot, with a long silver-handled knife. Tall, dark, and nervous, with round, prominent eyes, a sparse moustache, a skin tanned by the sun to a brick-dark red, his thick, brown hair cut short like a French soldier's, or, as he called it, "all the same dog's back," although he wore the loose black merino trousers worn by all "camp-men" in those days, shoved into patent leather riding-boots, and slept, as we said, in his spurs, you saw he once had been a sailor, at the first glance. The sea leaves marks upon its votaries that even time never entirely rubs out, perhaps because, being an element so hostile to mankind, the difficulty of accustoming oneself to all its moods alters a man for life.

Rough-tongued and irascible, he was one of those who in their dictionaries had never come upon the verb "to fear."

He slowly rolled his cigarette and sheathed his silver-handled knife behind his back, leaving the haft just sticking out below his elbow on the right side. After expelling through his mouth and nostrils a sort of solfatara of blue smoke, he said: "Yes, call my yarn a memory, a recollection . . . for it is not a story, only a circumstance that I remember vividly, just as one never can forget an object seen in a flash of lightning . .

. perhaps the word should be . . ." One of us interjected "An Impression"; he nodded and began his tale: —

"Night caught me, miles from a house, on a tired horse, and with a storm of wind and rain, such as you only see upon the plains. At first I galloped, hoping to arrive at some place where I could pass the night under a roof, and then as the darkness thickened, my horse, impervious to the spur, slackened down to a jog, which in these parts they call a *trotecito*. An hour or so of stumbling through the darkness, broken occasionally by lightning that seemed to run along the ground, of being suddenly brought up against a stream which seemed impossible to pass, and having to ride up banks to find a crossing, and the jog-trot became a walk.

"No matter how I spurred, nothing could move my horse; but just as I was thinking that I should have to pass the night out in the 'camp,' I thought I heard the distant barking of a dog. My horse had heard it too, and, turning him towards the sound, I felt him quicken up again to a slow, shuffling trot. It seemed I rode for hours, until at last the barking grew more furious, and in the distance a feeble light gleamed rather than shone, just like a vessel's mast-head light at sea. I brushed through some tall thistles, and by dint of whip and spur drove my horse, now so tired he could scarcely drag himself along, towards the barking of the dogs.

"At last my horse emerged out of the long, rough grass that clothes the southern Pampas, on to the open space before a house. Though it was dark I felt the difference at once, and the soft rustling of the wild grasses that sounds at night almost as if you rode through water ceased, and I began to hear my horse's footfall on the hard-trodden ground. The folded sheep were bleating in the *chiquero*, and when I turned towards it, I divined rather than saw the piles of cut, dried thorns, ranged in a circle, after the fashion that one sees amongst the Arabs, forming the corral, from which an acrid smell, rising from all the fleeces closely packed together, floated on the night air.

"Advancing still a little further, I saw the house, a mud and wattle *rancho*, with its low thatched roof. Through the interstices of the walls came the reflection of the fire, which burned right in the middle of the floor. It seemed as if at last, after long years of battling with the storm, that I had reached a haven of some sort. The *rancho* stood forlorn upon the open space. No tree, no shrub, no garden, or any patch of cultivated ground cut it off from the plain, that seemed to flow right up to it on every side.

"A dried and crumpled mare's hide formed the door. As the wind beat on it and got in between it and the jambs, it surged about, reminding me of a boat heaving at a wharf. Right opposite the door, and twenty yards or so away, stood a hitching post of *ñandubay*, at which to fasten horses, and spurring up to it, I called out, 'Ave Maria purissima,' and received the answer, 'Sin Pecado Concebida.' A man seemed to rise from the darkness by my side, and saying in a gentle voice, 'Welcome, get off and let your horse loose, he is too tired to stray,' called off the pack of barking dogs and led me by the hand into the house. The mare's hide swung to behind us stiffly, blotting out the night, and the bright glare from the blazing hearth was almost blinding to my eyes, fresh from the storm and rain. 'Sit, down upon one of those bullocks' heads,' said my entertainer, 'your horse cannot go far, and if he is too tired to travel in the morning I will give you one of mine.'

"He spoke, and as he stood before the fire that burned on the low hearth, erect and sinewy, with his long mane of jet-black hair, a little flecked with grey, falling down on his shoulders, I saw that he was blind. His eyes appeared quite perfect, but evidently saw nothing, and as he moved about the *rancho* he now and then touched with his shoulder or his head some of the horse gear that hung from pegs upon the walls. He must have somehow felt I saw his great calamity — for out upon the plains what cross could possibly be heavier to bear? — for he said, 'Yes, I am blind. The visitation came from God, only three years ago. It crept upon me by degrees, no one knows how, although a doctor in the town said it was paralysis of the optic nerve; not that I cared much what he said, for when a man is blind it comes from God, like death or any other ill.'

"He paused and motioned with his hand towards me, just as if he saw, towards the bullocks' heads, and when I squatted down, he too took his seat on one of them. 'Take off your boots,' he said, 'and dry yourself, and throw some wood upon the fire — it is there in the corner; my son, he who sleeps there on his *recado*, took care to pile up plenty, for I smelt the coming of the storm.'

"I had not seen the boy, who now turned on his elbow and looked up. His father went on, 'He is tired, for at this moment we are alone here in the *rancho*; my wife and family have gone to town, and he has had to be on horseback all the day, from the time when the false dawn streaks the sky, till sundown, doing all the work.' As I piled the wood upon the fire my host looked towards me and said, 'How tall you are!' And when I asked him how he knew, said, 'The voice comes from the rafters, as it were. We blind think much on things that in our seeing days we took no notice of.'

"The storm still raged outside, and as my things dried before the fire of bones and *ñandubay*, that feeling of contentment that comfort brings with it after exposure to the weather for long hours, stole over me. The boy upon his saddle had turned his face away from the glowing embers, and the hut felt like a ship at sea; and I, a passenger under the guidance of a pilot who was blind, felt myself listening to his talk, as if he were a friend of years, as happens in the plains when men meet casually, just as it happens with the other animals. A horse puts out its head and snuffles, and his fellow instantly becomes his friend, or at least he is not actively his enemy, and the same thing occurs with men.

"Under the directions of my host, I put a side of mutton down to roast, skewering it upon an iron spit, which he said I should find stuck in the thatch. The roast crackled and sputtered, and the rich juices fell into the fire and made it fiercer, and as it roasted slowly, we passed round the *maté*, I having put the kettle and the bag of *yerba* into the blind man's hand. Practice had made it just as easy for him to pour the water into the hole cut in the gourd as it is for a man who wears a sword to sheathe it in the dark. So after having filled the gourd, and taking a long pull of it to see that it was working properly, he passed it to me, and I sucked the hot, bitter mixture with the avidity of a man who has been storm-tossed and has not eaten since the early dawn.

"My host had not the unnatural curiosity of a defenceless man upon a frontier to know if there was any recent movement amongst the Indians, for his fate would not have been uncertain if at any time — even upon the night we sat and talked — a raiding party of the Tchehuelches or the Pampas had happened to pass by. 'Our lives,' he said, 'are in God's hand,' a truism which it was hard to controvert, though at the same time, situated as we were, the intervention of a good and speedy horse might have assisted fate. Still, when he listened now and then, and held the *maté* half-way to his lips, and gave that strained attention that makes the attitude of listening in blind men seem, as it were, to indicate some extra sense in them, I watched him with some trepidation till he said: 'It is nothing, only a stallion rounding up his mares. Each night,' he said, 'I saddle up a horse and leave him tied under a shed behind the house, and if I could but get my hand upon his mane I might yet lead the Indians a dance.' He felt my look of wonder, and rejoined: 'I should ride keeping the wind upon my cheek, and as the night is dark, I and the Indians would be on an equality. In fact, I think that if there were any advantage, it would be upon my side, for I know all the "camps" for leagues on every side, so well, that I can cross them easily, even though I am blind.'

"I looked at him, and thought what a fine figure he would look wrapped in a double darkness, with his hair flying in the wind, and his eyes open, but unseeing, as he galloped through the night. When the roast was ready, I took the horn in which was kept the salt and water, from a peg and sprinkled it, and then, with a courteous gesture, my host pointed towards the meat, and we fell to, cutting great chunks off with our knives and holding one end in our teeth, cut them down to our lips. We talked about the usual topics of the 'camp,' the marks of horses, Indian incursions, the accursed ways of government, the locusts, and the things that in such countries replace the reports of parliaments and police-courts, and all the villainies of city life.

"Then we lay down upon our saddles, after the tall, blind Gaucho, whose name I learned was Anastasio Lucena, had said the rosary.

"Morning broke fine and clear, with a slight film of frost upon the grass. In the *chiquero* the sheep were bleating to be let out, and cattle on the hills got up and stretched themselves, looking like camels as they stood with their heads high and their hind-quarters drooping to the ground. A distant wood behind a little hill was hung suspended in the sky, with the trees growing towards the earth by an effect of mirage, and from the world there came a smell of freshness and a sensation of new birth. My horse was not in a fit state to travel, and when the boy had driven the *tropilla* up to the corral, Anastasio Lucena unsaddled and let loose the horse he always kept tied up at night for fear of Indians, which rolled and neighed and then galloped off to seek its fellows in the 'camp.' We stood in the corral, and, as I swung the *lazo* round my head two or three times to see it had no kinks, I said to Anastasio, 'Which of the horses may I catch?'

"He looked towards them just as if he saw them perfectly, and answered, 'Anyone you like except the little *doradillo*. He is my wife's and she will soon be back again from town, where she has gone to buy the children clothes.'

"As the *tropilla* galloped round the corral I marked a cream-coloured with a black tail and mane, and threw the *lazo*, which uncoiled just like a snake and settled round his neck.

" 'Which have you caught?' asked Anastasio; and I answered, 'The black-cream-colour.' He smiled and said: 'A little quick to mount, but a good horse — well, let him loose to-night just after dark, when you get to the *Estancia* de la Cascada, a short ten leagues away, and by the morning he will be back at home. Your horse I will have collared to the mare, and you can send for him in a week or so, when he is rested and fit again for work.'

"I saddled up, thanked Anastasio Lucena for his hospitality, who answered that he was my servant, and that his house was mine whenever I might pass. Then mounting, not without difficulty, for the black-cream-colour was quick as lightning in the turns he made the instant that you raised your foot towards the stirrup, and started with a rush. After the first bound or two was over and the horse settled to a steady lope, I turned and looked back towards the *rancho* where I had passed the night. Upon the threshold stood its owner, tall and erect; his long black hair just flecked with grey, falling down on his shoulders, reminded me somehow of pictures of Christ that I had seen. His head was turned towards the sound of the black-cream-colour's hoofs, and his eyes, open but sightless, seemed to take in the Pampa with its indomitable space."

Mansel stopped, passed his own hand across his eyes as if they pained him with the intensity of the impression they had received long years ago, and then, as if he were talking to himself, said:

"Adios, Anastasio Lucena — or perhaps I ought to say 'so long.' Perhaps he has now taken the long *galopito* on which his want of sight was not a hindrance to him, or perhaps he now sees better than we do ourselves. *Quien sabe?* Anyhow, he has come back to me to-night, and I am glad to thank him once more for his hospitality, and his good cream-colour with the black tail and mane."

A Page of Pliny

My friend McFarlane lived in a curious old house, far from the world. When you had driven up the long, neglected avenues, you felt that you could pass your life there happily, just as some kind of sailors must have felt when they had been marooned upon a lonely island lost in the South Seas. He and his wife, a studious woman, but yet with an adventurous strain, lived quietly as was befitting to their narrow circumstances, due to the fall in agricultural values, which in those days had just begun.

Tall, thin, and freckled, McFarlane had no Scottish accent in his speech, only that faint and whining intonation which reminds one of the wind running out of the chanter of a bag-pipe after a Lament. "I would like to tell you," he once said, "of my one excursus into mining — that is, if when you have heard the tale you think it worthy of the name." I had known miners up and down the world; had seen them in the Sierra Madre, in Arizona, at the Real de Famatima, in Spain, in Portugal, and in Africa, and knew they all imagined that they held Golconda at the sharp end of their picks, if they were poor, and that their mine was the best in the whole world if they were rich.

So I pricked up my ears, and said, "Go on, let's hear about it." McFarlane, after he had lighted up his pipe, slowly began to talk.

"In my old house there were two upright bookcases in the recesses of the long, low Adams' room, with its four pillars, its double fireplaces, its five great windows, and its lookout on the steep terraces and rushy parks, in which grew islands of sycamores and limes, with here and there a wind-swept birch, whose roots, laid bare by winter rains, were honeycombed with rabbit-holes. Beyond the belts of planting, between which ran the public road, was a round hill planted with beech-trees, and further on, or rather flowing up against its side, as if it were a sea, a billowing, brown moss.

"Time sometimes hung a little heavy on my hands in the long spells of rain which visited that portion of the world . . . although you know," my friend observed, after the fashion of so many of his countrymen, "our climate is no worse than that of England, after all.

"The damp exuded from the walls and furniture all 'bloomed' . . . that was the word the housemaids used to use . . . showing a kind of bluish moisture, and grates turned red with rust. At such times, far from a town, and when old favourites had been read, re-read, and put away, one set about exploring one of those books that all men have upon their bookshelves, which they have never read, and yet know the outside, the binding, and the lettering on the backs so well that they have but to shut their eyes to see them in their own particular place in some old room, although the books themselves have long been sold, and perhaps now lie blistering in the sun upon a tray outside a shop . . . they that in times gone by were dusted once a week, and cared for almost as if they were alive.

"Such a book there was, in folio, which always stood upon a lower shelf between Sir Walter Raleigh's *History of the World* and Gerarde's *Herbal*.

"Parkinson stood a little further on, with Sir James Hope's *Scottish Fencing Master*, *The Parfait Mareschal*, and a tall Montaigne, which had been bought in Paris from a lead box upon the quays.

"Andrade's *Arte da Cavalheiria,* and Garcilasso de la Vega's *History of Peru*, a folio Bible (seldom read), Douglas's *Peerage*, and Nisbet's *Heraldry*, almost made up the shelf.

"The book in question (two volumes folio) was bound in sheepskin, with the name on the back done with a thick quill pen, a rose below the lettering as an ornament, and a small piece of sheepskin gone from near the top of Volume II, leaving the threads that bound the leaves together exposed to daylight, an accident which, like the sticking of the curtain at a theatre, always seems to let you peer, as it were indelicately, into the secrets of a life which, to be held at its true value, should be inviolate.

"The hand-drawn lettering set forth in Spanish that the two bulky volumes were the works of Pliny. Inside, upon the title-page, it appeared that in addition to the *Natural History* were commentaries by Fray Geronimo de Huerta, Familiar of the Holy Office of the Inquisition. These commentaries were in the way of additions, and contained facts that the heathen writer did not know, as they had happened after his decease.

"Books like the Spanish Pliny are not to be embarked upon without consideration, so I, the owner of it, after unfastening the little loops of catgut into which fitted two small shells as buttons, looked at the title-page and saw that the Holy Office had approved and certified the work.

"In addition, the Rector of Salamanca of that day, the King's confessor, and several, reverend Churchmen had read the book and had approved it, finding, as they said, 'that although written by a heathen, it contained nothing subversive of morality, or anything which we find ourselves forced to condemn, so that it may go forth and be sold here in the Court, and generally throughout the Spains, the Indies, and in the other realms of his most gracious Majesty the King.'

"Four or five prefaces and forewords from various scholar-clerics introduced one by degrees to Pliny's work; but slowly and as if the writers only stopped because had they gone on they would have written the whole book. In a spell of bad weather no book could possibly be more appropriate than was the Pliny with its two portly tomes.

"Long had I swithered, as we say beyond the Tweed, about the matter, being well aware that, in any case, probably it was not only the first step that counted, but that the second and each succeeding one would be as heavy as the last. Long did I dally with the first volume, reading the various prefaces and the 'censuras,' and wondering how anyone could possibly have piled so many words on one another without at last being forced to say something or other, if only by mistake.

"Then looking at the introduction, and being struck, as always is the case when I now look at the old book and smile at the adventure which grew out of my first attempt at reading it, by the fact that Pliny was a gentleman, I turned the leaves over in the perfunctory way that one is apt to fall into upon a rainy day. I remember too, how, given the state of natural history of the time, it struck me that the knowledge Pliny had about the various birds and beasts, plants, planets, stones, and minerals that he describes, was accuracy itself compared to the additions of the Spanish monk, who thought that he was bringing Pliny up to date, with his dull commentaries.

"I soon got tired of reading it, and made it over to my wife. She read and annotated, after her custom, and in a day or two asked me if I remembered hearing of a Roman gold mine in Galicia, upon a journey we had made.

"The thing had slipped my memory, though when she spoke of it I thought I had heard something of the sort, in a vague kind of way.

"So she took up the Spanish Pliny and read me out a passage, in which the writer talked of a gold mine in Lusitania, which, of course, in his days comprised Galicia. Then I remembered how the country people used to go down to the sands upon the River Sil and wash for gold, and an infinity of stories we had heard, near Carraceido, a little village by a lake, not very far from Villa Franca in the Vierzo, a most neglected part of Spain, twenty or thirty years ago.

"Well, well, my wife in half a moment had perceived the connection, intimate and quite complete, between the page of Pliny and the tales the Spanish peasantry had told us on the River Sil." He said this, proud of his clever wife, not that for a single moment he appeared to have been deceived by her quick jump to the end of the long chain and her omission of the links. These he saw clearly were all wanting; but yet he knew his wife's perception and quick intuition were superior to his own, and he was Scotch enough to know when he was outclassed, although no doubt in the realm of things that can be acquired he thought himself omniscient after the fashion of his race.

So he resumed, half smiling, and yet pleased both with himself and her. "Nothing would content my wife but that I should go at once and find the gold mine, which she was certain by the system that she had of mental triangulation would be there waiting for me.

"She said, not without reason, I confess, that nobody in Spain had ever heard of Pliny but as a troublesome historian about whom boys were bothered when at school, and that although throughout the district, which she remembered now was called the Val de Orras, traditions lingered, no one had thought of making a survey. I, who knew Spain as well as she did, thought there was something in her arguments, but still was unconvinced about the mine.

"Yet, there is something in the confidence of one you live with that, if it does not at once impel belief, still keeps your mind upon the stretch. In the evening, several days later, when we were sitting in the long drawing-room, which on the one side of the house was flush with the carriage-drive, and on the other raised ten or twelve feet above the terraces, the petroleum lamps casting dark shadows, for we had done away with our gasometer (my father's joy) as not being artistic, and sat in semi-darkness, blowing the half-green logs of wood that seethed and spluttered in the grate, we fell a-talking of the passage that my wife had found.

"Man," said my friend, with one of those half lapses into the vernacular that Scotchmen use amongst themselves when they wish either to disarm criticism or capture sympathy, "it may have been the loneliness of the old house, the moonlight streaming in at one of the five windows — neither myself nor yet my wife ever drew blinds or curtains — or maybe it was that by the firelight a proposition seems more convincing than in the light of day . . . at least, I think so.

"All that I do know is that we agreed that evening that I should go and find the place where Pliny said the Romans drew much of their gold in Spain.

"We laughed, I mind it well, although it was so many years ago, and my wife had not a single silver thread in that bonny head of hair of hers, as black as a crow's wing.

"Time flies," and as he spoke he looked into the glass above the mantelpiece, as if he wished to mark its hand upon himself; and then, as one who, after gazing in a crystal ball, sees a sad vision in it, sighed and took up his tale.

"How well I see us sitting by the fire in our old lonely house that evening, with all our dogs about us. When we had once got the thing settled in our minds, the next step was to get a mining engineer, for I knew nothing about mines, though I had lived in places in Mexico where mysterious strangers used to come up to you, and, after looking round to see that no one had their eye upon them, produce a dirty packet from the recesses of their rags, and after taking off a dozen bits of paper, show you a piece of dull red-looking rock, and say that it was '*plata piña,*' the richest specimen known to the world, and that for a consideration they would impart its whereabouts and make you a rich man. They never would explain, when they had a treasure such as they swore they knew of, why they were always in such poverty. so I concluded they were all philanthropists and did not care for gold.

"My wife knew of an engineer, one Thomas Garnard, whom she had met in some forgotten place in Spain. As he lived in Madrid, and fortune had not smiled upon him, he seemed the very man.

"He wrote and said that he would meet me at Orense, for with the care that people quite inexperienced in business always take in matters such as these, we had not informed him, but in vague terms, of our projected search.

"I confess when I found myself on board the steamer bound for Vigo, with a treatise upon placer-mining in my bag, I felt inclined to laugh.

"I read the mining treatise, and made little of it, and then took out my pocket-book and conned the passage we had copied out of Pliny, and found it vaguer in the full light of day than it had seemed at home in the dark Georgian room. However, there was nothing to be done, and in a twinkling, as it seemed, the vessel passed the narrow channel between the islands that guard Vigo harbour, and ran into the bay. Little by little she opened up the town clustering upon its hill, and dominated by the two fangless castles, looking like blind lions, impotent, but awful to behold.

"The great black rock of the Cabrón, the long and winding channel up to the Lazaretto, I saw just for a moment, as the vessel turned and steamed up to her anchorage, and then the Monte de la Guia, crowned with its hermitage, seemed to project and shut them out of view. I went ashore, almost, as we say, in a dwawm, and heard mechanically the boys who always cluster round a foreigner, all screaming out, 'I say.' Nothing had altered. The Guardias Civiles stood in their glazed three-cornered hats and their green worsted gloves, impassive, motionless, and looking like the law embodified. *[sic]* No one could possibly have ever been so law-respecting as they looked. The bullock-carts, with their high wicker sides and solid wheels, looking like Roman carts upon a coin of Hadrian, still creaked along, although, as I was told, the new Alcalde contemplated putting out an order that the axles should be greased. Still, as of yore, some horses played upon the green beside the sea, although a nasty, little public garden, with young magnolias, dusty oleanders, a stuccoed fish-pond and a fountain with a boy struggling with a goose, so much distorted that the boy looked like an abortion in a jar, and the goose seemed like a bladder full of lard, had filched a portion of the ground. The usual dollar passed me through the custom-house, and sitting down upon a plaster bench in the new garden, I observed with pleasure that the wreck of the three-masted schooner, which I knew had lain just at high-water mark upon the shore for the last twenty years, was still almost intact, although some of her copper had been torn away, leaving a rent upon her side. Gone was the Alameda, with its tall elm-trees, and in its place a walk the natives called El Bulevar, with a tin kiosk, where newspapers should have been sold had there been anyone to buy them, and on its paths a man or two wandered about discontentedly, carrying those tall tin cylinders with a small roulette board upon the top, selling the wafers known as *barquillas*, the joy of nurserymaids and their attendant swains in every Spanish town.

"These signs of want of progress gave me courage, for I argued, if here in Vigo, in this place, which after all is a provincial capital, things never seem to change, how much less likely is there to be change out in the district where the mine was situated. So after breakfast, which, though the waiter told me that it would be ready shortly after twelve, was only served at half-past one, I took the train for Orense, where I had arranged to meet my mining engineer.

"The line followed the harbour, running by Redondela and breaking off through some wild moors, past oak woods, maize fields, vineyards and little brown-roofed towns; now passing mountain Calvaries, with their stone crosses overgrown with lichen, and then by streams upon whose banks women were washing in the sun.

"We passed by Rivadavia, which lay sweltering in the heat, and towards evening, in a cloud of dust, slowly steamed into Orense, with the rough jolting on the ill-closed points, well known on Spanish trains. A grateful coolness was just setting in as I drove rattling and jingling through the streets, passing the lofty bridge, one of the wonders of the place. The proverb says, 'Three things Orense has, the like of which are not in Spain. Its Bridge, its Christ, and its three Boiling Springs, the Burgas'; and it is true enough.

"The heat was tropical, and the inhabitants all were sitting at their doors, exhausted by their battle with the sun, to catch the evening breeze.

"Men sat on chairs, tilted against the walls, with their shirt collars loosened, and women leaned from windows, pale and exhausted, while in the shade lay panting yellow dogs, snapping occasionally at flies as they buzzed round their jaws. I reached the inn begrimed with perspiration and with dust, and as I did so I was greeted by a man, who grasped my hand and welcomed me to Orense, which he remarked was just as hot as Lima or as the hob of hell. I guessed that he was Garnard, and in a moment he had introduced himself, shoving a limp and dirty card into my hand. On it I read, in faintish lettering, the legend, 'Tomas Garnard,' and an address in Lima, which had had a pen drawn through it, and 'Horno de la Mata, 17 Madrid,' inserted in its stead.

"When I had read it carefully and handed him my own, we went into the inn, dined and then talked, until the small hours of the night, about the Roman mine.

"Don Tomas Garnard was a man to whom life was a fairy tale. Nothing astonished him if it was only wild enough; but on the other hand the merely credible did not appeal to him, and he subjected it to strict examination, finding it, as a general rule, impossible, and not worthy of belief.

"He had met my wife at an hotel in Lima . . . I mean Madrid, he added . . . and talked with her about the district where we now found ourselves, and she had told him of the legends she had heard amongst the peasantry. He knew no Latin, except the names of minerals, but when I read the passage I had copied out at home he became fired at once, though I confess, each time I read the words, they seemed less definite.

"Next morning saw us in the diligence, on a hot morning, one of the hottest I remember in my life, jolting towards the Val de Orras, but luckily seated beside the driver in what is known as the *pescante*, a kind of hood, from which he kept up a perpetual fire of oaths and blows and cigarettes, lighting a fresh one from the last one smoked, all through the livelong day. His assistant, an active-looking lad, got down occasionally, even although the coach was going at full speed, and taking out a handful of well-chosen pebbles from his sash, threw them with great precision at the mules, and then laying one hand upon the rail, leaped back into his seat. Inside, the unlucky passengers were packed like sardines, and all day long, across the dusty plains, up barren hills, on which the stones reflected back the heat, we jingled noisily. Now and again the old rope harness broke, and we stopped half an hour to get it spliced, and then jogged on again.

"Sometimes we crawled along at a foot pace, and then again rushed down a hill-side madly, the diligence swaying and rocking like a ship at sea and lurching on the stones. When we changed horses we all got down, and smoked and drank a little *aguardiente*, tossing it off and swallowing water after it, for it was hot as fire.

"We stopped and dined in a small inn at a four-cross-road, and as the food was cooking at a huge, open fireplace in the great dining-room, I listened to the vicissitudes of my new friend's life in the Andean mining camps, and gathered that he had brought more treasure home from the New World in knowledge of mankind than in mere specie. However, he appeared skilled in his own profession, and certainly was most agreeable as a travelling companion, and well endowed with all that optimism which but intensifies in every miner as he gets on in life.

"Late in the evening the diligence jogged into a little town, the horses and the mules dead beat, and all the passengers shaken like walnuts in a sack, stiff, bruised and sore, dusty and travel-stained."

My friend McFarlane paused in his tale, and looking at me said, "I wish you could have seen me with my mining engineer, seated at the long table under the evil-smelling lamp, with the heterogeneous company that assembles for dinner in the best inn of a small Spanish town. Three Government officials, an officer or two, with several commercial travellers and a priest, were the sole company on this occasion, and, as was not unnatural, their curiosity was aroused as to the reason that could have brought two foreigners, evidently not travelling to sell goods, to a place so remote.

"We bumped into the little village of Carraceido in the afternoon, and saw the diligence go on, after it had changed horses, with something of the feeling that a man on a raft must have when a ship passes without perceiving him and leaves him to his fate.

"I tell you," said McFarlane, "I felt just like the Scotchman who was going to be hanged . . . you know the story . . . disgusted with the whole proceedings . . . there, on that afternoon.

"The whole thing was so utterly absurd, to have come so far about a mine that it was twenty-five to one never existed, or if it had, was worked out centuries ago and clean forgotten by mankind.

"However, there we were, I and my mining engineer, in the remote and tiny Spanish village, and the best thing we had to do was to take up our bags and walk into the inn. We watched the diligence on the straight, dusty road till it had vanished, and then turned to the innkeeper, a fat, broad-shouldered man in a short jacket edged with imitation astrakhan, a wide black sash round his tight trousers, and his feet shod with *alpargatas*, who gravely greeted us. Following him through the great store-room on the ground floor, which led into the stables at one end, we stumbled up a stair steep as a ladder, and were ushered to a room.

"Two iron beds, with vignettes of the Madonna at the head in coloured tin, the mattresses stuffed with dried maize leaves, two rickety rush-bottomed chairs, a wooden table, and a small wash-stand were the adornments of the place — not much, but yet sufficient for the wants of the stray guests who visited the inn.

" 'Here can your worships rest,' our host remarked, and left us to ourselves. Don Tomas Garnard, as by this time I called the mining engineer, rose to the occasion, and after saying that a tambo in the Andes of Peru was ten times worse, and that at least we had the sun in Carraceido, opened the window, and we looked out upon the hills.

"Groves of great chestnut-trees covered them, clothing the slopes with a thick veil of green. Through the thick copse, the bright red soil appeared as if the ground was bleeding, and above the trees stretched the brown hill-side, covered with cistus and with thyme, which gave a scent so pungent and so keen that it filled all the air. Upon the other side the lake of Carraceido lay, broad, dark, and motionless. Great banks of bulrushes seemed to fence it in, and through them lanes were cut, in which lay several flat-bottomed boats, and, nearer to the shore, cattle were standing knee-deep in the water, with their tails lashing off the flies.

"In the far distance rose the Asturian mountains, whilst a small river running near the inn tinkled amongst the stones.

"It was a lovely landscape, just like an idyll by Theocritus; in it the vines hung from stone trellises, the husbandman at evening, shouldering his plough, made from a piece of wood and tipped with iron, slowly walked homewards, smoking, and shepherds who piping on a reed were followed by their sheep without a dog to bark and worry at their heels, as in more favoured lands."

McFarlane sighed, and his mind seemed to dwell upon the sight of flocks in England driven towards the slaughter-houses with blows and curses, two or three bob-tailed dogs, far more humane, if not so human as their masters, urging them on to death.

He did not give his thoughts expression, and no doubt in every case the sheep's fate is to be eaten, just as the swimmer's is to be taken by the sea. "You mind," he said, "the Roman legionaries, when they got to the place — for after all the Val de Orras is not far from the famed river that they took for Lethe — refused to cross, sat down, and but for their commanders would have beat their short broadswords either to ploughshares or to reaping-hooks."

I nodded, and he went on:

"Next morning, after a night I shall not easily forget, although the landlord denied with oaths that there were fleas, as if we thought of them, having seen the far too friendly little faces of much greater wonders of the insect world peer out at us from every quarter of the room, we dressed and wandered out.

"The Roman mine was a tradition of the place, well known to everyone, and in the River Sil after a flood people occasionally washed out a pan or two and got a little gold. This set my friend afire, and all the day he wandered up and down, jotting down what he heard in a crushed note-book, greasy and dog-eared, in order, as he said, to strike an average of the lies when he had panned them out.

"I wonder at myself," remarked McFarlane. "I do so now! I did so then! But by degrees the whole fantastic thing — scheme, expedition, or adventure, call it what you will — took hold of me, and I began half to believe I was about to make a fortune, half to believe I was a fool. Never in all my life, since my brief sojourn at the Zacatecas Mines, did I hear so much mining talk. Pay-dirt and bed-rock, gold in the quartz, in placer-diggings, and many other terms of which I had no real idea of the true value, were always in my head. One morning Don Tomas came rushing in, roaring 'Eureka!' but luckily more suitably attired than Archimedes, and explained that he had found a man who knew the Roman gold-mine, that it was three leagues off amongst the hills, and by the account must have been a great placer-working in the old Roman times.

"For some strange reason, which I forget or disremember, for the two states of memory are very different* we arranged to start about an hour before the sun went down and camp amongst the hills. We left the village mounted on mules, with a man following upon a donkey carrying provisions, late in the afternoon.

"Most of the inhabitants stood at their doors to see us start, for every living soul knew of our expedition, and the Roman mine had been a household word to all of them from their earliest youth, not much believed in, but still ever present to their minds.

"With the grave cynicism of Spanish peasants, they looked on us as madmen; but with the materialism of their race were quite prepared to take advantage of the fruits of our mad brains. In the meantime, the hire of the mules had been a godsend to them, for in the village hardly any money circulated, although for all that the inhabitants were as ready at a bargain as if they had been brought up on the Stock Exchange.

"Don Tomas Garnard . . . as he now styled himself with pride . . . went about making preparations as if he thought the mine was found, the money got together to exploit it, and that we were in some way benefactors of mankind, and deserved well of Spain. Speaking but little Spanish, and understanding less, he was immune from the disparaging remarks that fell so freely from the villagers, who, as is usually the case the whole world over, were critical just in proportion to their ignorance — a reflection artists of every kind may take for their own consolation when they read hostile comments on their work set forth with circumstance. Our landlord, who was a man who had a certain knowledge of the world, having often been in Lugo, and even visited Leon, looked on himself as an authority. We heard him saying, 'No, friends, I do not think these men are mad. They paid my bill in good, sound money, for I tested every piece. The madman does not pay. Therefore I think they must be really engineers, these Frenchmen, and it may be they will discover something beneficial to us all. Myself, I understand them well, having seen many of the French in Lugo, and I can vouch they both are honourable men.'

"This testimony did us much good, and I believe we started out upon that scorching afternoon, leaving the villagers in the same spirit of half-respectful admiration, tinged a little with contempt, that the inhabitants of Palos manifested towards Columbus, as he walked down to the beach to sail for the New World.

"The track we followed in the sweltering heat led upwards for a mile or two through chestnut woods, the bright, red soil covered with banks of cistus in the open places, whose flowers looked like a flight of great white butterflies. The scent of thyme and rosemary penetrated to our souls, poignant and aromatic, as our beasts stumbled on the stones. Behind us, calling out 'Arré!' in a perfunctory way, our guide walked by his loaded donkey, smoking. and singing now and then a Ribeirana in a falsetto key. About half-way, just as we rested for a moment by a projecting rock, the light began to fail, and from the village rose the Angelus, just as a sheep-bell tinkles in the hills to warn the sheep that may be wandering, that it is folding-time.

"The moon rose brilliantly, casting strange shadows on the wild path that we were following. Stones turned to boulders, dead stumps of trees to threatening figures pointing strange weapons at us in her distorting rays; and frogs and crickets filled the night with melody.

"After an hour or two of struggling upwards, the path got easier to travel, and led us out into a little open glade amongst some chestnut trees.

"Our guide dismounted, for he had clambered up upon his beast and had been sitting side-ways on the pack, let loose his donkey, hobbled its feet, and, drawing out his flint and steel, soon had a bright fire burning underneath a tree.

"When we had made some tea and smoked a cigarette, we strolled across the little clearing, and a most wondrous view, made still more marvellous by the moon's glittering beams, lay stretched beneath us, for the green glade ended abruptly in a precipice. Sheer down it went, and seemed unfathomable. It looked as if a monstrous bowl had been dug out of the red earth about a quarter of a mile across. A chestnut wood, dark and mysterious in the moonlight, covered the bottom of the bowl. The depth and the false perspective that the moonlight gave to everything, made it look like a carpet. Here and there in patches you could see the ground, and from the patches towered great pinnacles of dark red earth three or four hundred feet in height.

"Upon their tops grew bushes, making them look like some fantastic vegetable. The moon-beams played upon them, magnifying and distorting them, and striking here and there upon a pebble in their sides, which sparkled brilliantly. So still was everything that we stood looking, awestruck, till the guide, advancing cautiously up to the hedge, held out a lean, brown finger and said, 'That is the Roman mine.'

"I almost had to pinch myself to be sure I was awake, the whole thing was so strange. Here I was a relatively sensible man, who after having left his house a thousand miles away, upon the wildest wild-goose chase imaginable, without an indication but a vague passage in a book written nearly two thousand years ago, and yet I heard our guide's remark, which he proffered quite as a thing of course, and with my eyes I gazed into the mighty chasm in the hill that I at once saw was in some way or other the work of human hands. Don Tomas Garnard, on the contrary, saw at a glance the whole affair, and with a shout exclaimed, 'A placer-working! What wonderful men the Romans were. In some way that I cannot see from here, they had washed down the whole hill-side just as we do to-day'"

"I wandered up and down the clearing, smoking, but always coming back to the edge of the chasm, listening occasionally to Don Tomas, who had become almost ecstatic in his joy. 'To-morrow, when it is light,' he said, 'we must get down from this place where the idiot of a guide has brought us to, and get to work at once.' The night wore on, and just about the dawn the howling of a wolf deep in the hills just reached us, but clear enough to startle both the mules, who strained upon their ropes and trembled, and would have broken loose had we not quieted them.

"The world seemed just as far away as the fixed stars, and we ourselves felt as if all its inhabitants had disappeared, leaving alive only ourselves and the three animals, under the starry sky.

"Early next morning we began our work, after having got down to the level of the great placer-digging by a winding path made by the goats in the hill-side.

"We found our guide, for reasons known but to himself, had brought us to the highest point, though on the other side of the great basin there was no precipice. Perhaps he thought the effect was better from the height, but anyhow the view into the corrie was magnificent, and from no other point could we have had the same sensation when he said 'There is the Roman mine,'

"We had to move our camp, for the goats' track was not the most convenient path to use in going up and down. So we established ourselves under a spreading chestnut-tree, and sent the guide back on a mule for more provisions, and then began to look the proposition (as Don Tomas said) in the face.

"At the first glance, that is, at the first glance to a man experienced in such things, the place had been worked systematically. Don Tomas pointed out the cuttings, waterways, and places where he said the Romans had their sluices, and I said 'Yes' to everything, and by degrees began to think that I was mad.

"Enthusiasm is so catching," said McFarlane, and smiled, half at himself, half at humanity in general. "Without it, where would have been the founders of religions, discoverers, prophets, and leaders of all kinds, who, after all, when they stood out and shouted 'follow me,' had nothing to depend upon except the trust that they excited in themselves? Anyhow, for the next day or two we washed out countless pans of dirt, hoping always that the Romans, who, I was assured by Don Tomas, must have worked in a primitive though scientific way — that is, for the times in which they lived — had left enough gold in the ground to make it worth our while to go and what is called denounce the mine, and claim it for ourselves. We washed and worked, prospecting all the ground as thoroughly as possible, Don Tomas walking over the whole basin just as a spaniel quarters a cover, and talking volubly about our prospects of success.

"He said if we could get only the colour. which I understood to mean the smallest particle of gold, that we should have enough to make our fortunes twenty times over, for in the hollow where the ancient workings lay there must have been ten acres at the least. Each time we washed a pan towards the end the same thing happened: Don Tomas grew excited, swearing that this time we were certain of it; and when each time nothing but fine red sediment remained, mixed with some little pebbles, he was quite sure that the next try was certain to give something better, and so the time wore on.

"For my part, the first day was quite sufficient; and though the enthusiasm of my companion had worked a little on my mind, and the site of the ancient placer-digging certainly stirred a vaguish kind of hope, I had had enough of it, and my back ached with washing out the pans. I had not told you that a small stream ran through the middle of the working, and on its edge we stood and washed until I grew to hate the very sight of the whole place, and it seemed that in all my life I had done nothing else but wash out mud in a tin pan, and then begin again.

"Still Don Tomas was not discouraged, for he maintained that the Romans, who had evidently disposed of water-power by damming up all the streams in the district, for in our rambles we had found remains of ancient dams, had worked the surface dirt so clean that there was nothing we could get at by our rude attempts; but for all that, a scientific assay might reveal the presence of some gold.

"He argued that in the columns which were left standing, columns which neither of us could explain, there must be earth which never had been touched. Therefore, if in that basin there had once been gold, in the parts of it that never had been worked, some gold must still remain if we could hit upon it.

"As this seemed reasonable, we loaded up a mule with two great sacks of earth dug from the heart of one of the tall pillars, and after having taken a last look at the great corrie in the hill, its groves of chestnut trees, its bright red soil, its growth of cistus, and its banks of thyme, germander, and of rosemary, we loaded up our beasts with the remains of the provisions, our pots and kettles, our blankets and the abominable tin pans, and took our way to Carraceido, tired, eaten by mosquitoes, sun-burned, with our hands blistered, and in that state of mind in which a man will quarrel with his dearest friend about the colour of a mule. However, Don Tomas was not a man to quarrel with, and as he sat upon his mule, his knees almost upon a level with his chin, his gaiters half unbuttoned, a stick cut from a bush in his right hand, and the reins in his left all in a bunch, tugging continually at the beast's mouth, he looked so comical, with his red face, surrounded by a frill of greyish whisker, his keen grey eyes peering out on the world as if it were a mine to be prospected, one could not help but laugh, however much you were annoyed.

"All his talk ran upon what we should do in Lima, for he could never get out of his head that he was not still in Peru, and of the probabilities of our success. I let him talk, feeling that our success lay but in the experience we had acquired, and the possession of the view of the old Roman working, first seen by moonlight, from the lone clearing in the woods. Nothing could ever stamp that out, nothing destroy the wildness of the sound of the long-drawn-out howling of the wolf heard on that moonlit night.

"Soon we drew near the village, and if our setting out had been received but coldly, nothing could well have been more cordial than our welcome on our return. The villagers went immediately from one extreme right to the other, and when they saw the laden mule, the wildest rumours as to our success were set about at once. The little street was full — women stood at the doors, and children ran about like rabbits, whilst men stepped forward to congratulate us on having found the mine.

"The innkeeper hailed us as the saviours of the district, and after we had washed and had a meal, the precious sacks, having been put beneath the beds and the door locked, a sort of deputation of the chief inhabitants, with the priest at its head, appeared to interview us on all that we had seen.

"We sat down in the *patio* and called for wine, after having sent out to the *estanco* for cigars. The priest stepped forward, and, taking off his hat, harangued us briefly on the ancient Romans, on British energy, and on the wealth that he supposed would flow into the town when we had got the mine in order and once begun to work. He said that, owing to bad government, the state of parties, and the lack of confidence existing betwixt man and man, so contrary to the principles of our holy faith, Spain had gone through a period of decay. This, as a patriot, he deplored, and trusted that with the well-known energy of Englishmen . . . Spain, he observed, had always been the friend of England since Vilanton had come to help the Spaniards to expel the French . . . we should at least in Carraceido . . . that Carraceido which had always been well known for its patriotic principles . . . be enabled to remove the curse that lay upon our land.

"He thanked us both — me for my public spirit, and Don Tomas for that hard-headed shrewdness and engineering knowledge that distinguished him — and hoped that when Pactolus had poured a stream of gold into the place, two of the streets of the new town that would arise should bear our honourable names.

"The miller was more brief, and merely said he knew we had the gold, for he had seen the sacks upon the mule. No one could come to him, as he said, with celestial music; he was a practical and a hard-working man, but seeing is believing, and so he wished us luck, remarking that he cared little for the ancient Romans, who he had always understood were hardly better than the Moors; but in all cases, if they had been so foolish as to leave their gold up in the hills, it was a right and proper thing Christians should profit by their carelessness.

"We then drank gravely to the health of England and of Spain in a rough, heady, new, red wine, tasting of earth and pigskin, and lighting our cigars, long rolls of blackish-looking leaf that burned as if they had been dipped in nitre, tilted our chairs against the wall and fell a-talking as we smoked. Much did we say about the badness of the Government, the infamy of those in high estate, the price of bullocks at Brañuelas market, and other topics of the kind, till someone went and fetched the music, which consisted of a man who played on a shrill pipe called the *dulzaina*, to the accompaniment of a little drum, on which the executant beat with his right hand just as the Arabs beat a tom-tom, and with his left scratched on the parchment with a stick. The noise was terrible, and echoed in the courtyard until the very walls appeared to tremble, and lasted for a full hour, until the players ceased as suddenly as they began, and, after tossing off their wine, deigned to accept of half a dollar, and retire, leaving us stupefied. As the performers went down the village street their deafening harmony by degrees became assuaged, and, in the silent air, gradually blended into a curious mixture of the singing of a cricket and of the noise made by a water-mill, not disagreeable and quite in character with the half-savage nature of the place.

"Next morning found us with our luggage and our sacks waiting to take the diligence as it passed by the little inn. The landlord, who had been so surly and indifferent, had now become a friend. He shook us warmly by the hand, asking us to remember that Ildefonso Lopez was our friend and servant, and that he trusted on our return we would not forget him, for upon his part he accompanied us in spirit upon our mission to the Court, and wished us great success.

"When we had piled our things into the rickety, old coach, drawn by its four thin mules and an apocalyptic horse, and it began to jingle off, I looked back on the place which I had visited under such curious circumstances with the feeling of regret mingled with joy with which a shipwrecked sailor, who has been rescued by a passing ship, might look upon the island where he has spent so many lonely months, as it sinks back into the sea.

"Of course, I knew that the whole thing was finished, and was half sorry; but Don Tomas was still enthusiastic, and remained so until we watched the final process of the assay in the Mining College of Madrid.

"Needless to say, it proved infructuous, *[sic]* though I will not deny, as we watched the final firing down of our two sacks till they became a handful of red dust in the last crucible, that I was stirred by hope and fear in an unconscionable way."

McFarlane ceased. In the smoking-room of his old Georgian house the fire burned low upon the hearth, and its light flickered on the faces of his grim-visaged ancestors whose effigies adorned the walls and seemed to smile at him.

From the terraces outside came the low belling of a roe, and the long branches of the cedars, stirred gently by the breeze, looked almost human, as if their fingers wished to clutch at something, as they swayed to and fro.

McFarlane sighed, and, as he lit another cigarette, said quietly:

"Sometimes as I sit here alone, watching the moonbeams mingle with the fire, I fancy that I own a mine in which there are no shareholders, no calls for money, and which has no quotations of its stock. I work it, only by moonlight and with the help of the old Romans, and it yields millions to me, both in experience and recollection, as I await the day when the chief street in the regenerated Carraceido shall bear my honourable name."

The Beggar Earl

Many a shadowy figure has flitted through the valley of Menteith. Just as the vale itself is full of shadows, shadows that leave no traces of their passage, but, whilst they last, seem just as real as are the hills themselves, so not a few of those who have lived in it seem unsubstantial and as illusive as a ghost.

Perhaps less real, for if a man detects a spectre with that interior vision dear to the Highlanders and to all mystics, Highland or Lowland, or from whatever land they be, he has as surely seen it, for himself, as if the phantasm was pictured on the retina of the exterior eye.

Pixies, trolls, and fairies, the men of peace, the dwellers in the Fairy Hill that opens upon Hallowe'en alone, and from which issues a long train, bringing with them our long-lost vicar Kirke of Aberfoyle. True Thomas, and the rest of all the mortals who forsook their porridge three times a day, for the love of some elf queen, and have remained as flies embedded in the amber of tradition, are in a way prosaic. Men have imagined them, ending them with their own qualities, just as they have endued their gods with jealousy and hate. Those born in the ordinary, but miraculous, fashion of mankind, who live apparently by bread alone, and yet remain beings apart, not touched by praise, ambition, or any of the things that move their fellows, are the true fairies after all.

Such a one was the beggar earl. All his long life he lacked advancement, finding it only at the last, as he died, like a cadger's pony, by a dykeside in the snow. That kind of death keeps a man's memory fresh.

Few can tell to-day where or in what manner died his ancestors — the mail-clad knights who fought at Flodden, counselled kings, with the half-Highland cunning of their race, and generally opposed the Southrons, who, impotent to conquer us in war, yet have filched from us most of our national character by the soft arts of peace. A mouldering slab of freestone here and there, a nameless statue of a Crusader with his crossed feet resting upon his dog, in the ebenezerised cathedral of Dunblane; a little castle on a little reedy island in a bulrush-circled lake, some time-stained parchments in old muniments preserve their memory, . . . to those who care for memories, a futile and a disappearing race.

His is preserved in snow. Nothing is more enduring than the snow. It falls, and straight all is transfigured. All suffers a chromatic change: that which was black or red, brown, yellow or dark grey, is changed to white, so white that it remains for ever stamped on the mind, and one recalls the landscape, with its fairy woods, its stiff, dead streams, its suffering trees and withered vegetation, as it was on that day.

So has the recollection of the beggar earl remained, a legend, and all his humble life, his struggles and his fixed, foolish purpose been forgotten; leaving his death as it were embalmed in something of itself so perishable that it has had no time to die.

No mere success, the most vulgar thing that a man can endure, would have been so lasting, for men resent success and strive to stifle it under their applause, lauding the result, the better to belittle all the means. His life was not especially eventful, still less mysterious, for the poor play out their part in public, and a greater mystic than himself has said, "The poor make no noise."

Someone who knew him said he was "a little man; a little clean man, that went round about through the country. He never saw him act wrong. . . . He was — just a man asking charity. He went into farmhouses and asked for victuals; what they would give him; and into gentlemen's houses."

This little picture, drawn unconsciously, shows us the man he was after ill-fortune overtook him. For a brief season he had been well known in Edinburgh. In 1744, when he was studying medicine, he suddenly appeared at the election of a Scottish peer and told the assembly who he was, and claimed the right to vote.

From that time till his death, he never dropped his claim, attending all elections of a Scottish peer till he got weary of the game. Then disillusion fell on him, and he withdrew to beg his bread, and wander up and down his earldom and the neighbouring lands, until his death.

Once more he came into public view, in the year 1747, when he published his rare pamphlet, *The Fatal Consequences of Discord,* dedicated to the Prince of Wales. In it he says "that there can be no true unity without religion and virtue in a State."

This marks him as a man designed by nature to be poor, for unity and virtue are not commodities that command a ready sale.

He had not any special gift, but faith, and that perhaps sustained him in his wanderings. Perhaps he may have thought that he would sit some day in a celestial senate, and this belief consoled him for his rejection by an earthly house of peers. One thing is certain, even had the House of Lords, that disallowed his claim, although he voted several years in Edinburgh, approved him as a peer, it would not have convinced him of his right one atom more; for if a man is happy in conviction, he had it to the full.

It is said he bore about with him papers and pedigrees that he would never sell. No bartering of the crown for him, even for bread. A little, grey, clean-looking man, mounted upon an old white pony, falling by degrees into most abject poverty and still respected for his uprightness, and perhaps a little for his ancestry, for in those days that which to us is but a mockery, was real, just as some things which with us are valued, in those days would have been ridiculous.

So through the valley of Menteith, along the Endrick, and by Loch Lomond side, past the old church at Kilmaronock, through Gartocharn, and up and down the Leven, he took his pilgrimage.

Over the wild track on the Dumbarton moor, and past the waterfall at the head of the glen of Galingad, he and his pony must have wandered many times, reflecting that the lands he passed over should have been all his own, for he was really Earl of Menteith by right and by descent, no matter though his fellow peers refused to recognize him. He talked at first, in any house he came to, of his rights, and people having little news to distract them in those days, were no doubt pleased to hear him and to inveigh against injustice in the way that those who had themselves received it all their lives are always pleased to talk.

So does a goaded ox lower his head and whisk his tail, and then, after a glance thrown at his fellow, strain once again upon the yoke. Then, when the novelty was over they would receive his stories with less interest, driving him back upon himself, until most likely he bore his wrongs about with him, just as a pedlar bears his pack, in silence, and alone. So did he, when the first efforts to obtain his title and his rights had spent their force, quit Edinburgh as it had been a city of the plague when there was any election of a peer.

Whilst he was wandering up and down the parishes of Kilmaronock and of Port, Scotland was all convulsed with the late rising of '45. Parties of soldiers, and bands of Highlanders, retreating to the north, must have passed by him daily, and yet he never seems to have had the inclination to change sides. Staunch in his allegiance to the Government, and with a faith well grounded in the Protestant Succession, as his pamphlet shows, most probably he was a Church and State man, as he would have said, up to his dying day.

Of such, as far as kings and rulers are concerned, are the elect, and thrones are founded on this unquestioning belief, more strongly than on armies or in Courts.

As the years passed, and he still wandered up and down Menteith, losing by degrees the little culture that his studies had implanted in him when he attended the Edinburgh schools, the farmers must have begun to treat him, first as one of themselves, and then just as they would have treated any other wandering beggar-man. Still, on the few occasions when he had to write a letter he always signed "Menteith," especially to begging letters, and the signature, no doubt, consoled him many a time for a refusal of his plea.

Few could have known all the traditions of the district as did the wandering earl; but he most probably, living amongst them, thought them not in the least remarkable, for it needs time and distance to make old legends interesting.

He and his pony must have been familiar figures on the roads, and when he came to a wild moorland farm, no doubt they welcomed him, expecting news from the outside world, and were a little disappointed when he sat silent in the settle, gazing into the smouldering peats, brooding upon his wrongs.

At such times, most likely he drew out his cherished papers from his wallet and pored upon them, though he must long ago have known them all by heart, and as he read them all his pride in his old lineage revived, and the long day upon hill tracks may have seemed light to him as he sat nodding by the fire. His hosts, with the old-fashioned hospitality of those times, would set before him a great bowl of porridge, which he must often only have eaten for good manners' sake, and then gone off to sleep beside his pony on the straw.

How many years he wandered through the mosses and the hills, how many times he saw the shaws in April green upon the Fairy Hill, or the red glow upon the moor in autumn, is not quite clear; but all the time he never once forsook his wanderings. Offers were made him, by many of his friends, to settle down; but either the free life held something for him that no mere dwelling in a house could give, or else he thought himself more likely to attain his object by being always on the road, travelling, as it were, like a Knight of the Holy Grail, towards some goal unseen that fascinated him, still always further on.

No doubt the darksome thickets by loch sides, in which he and his pony must have passed so many summer nights, were pleasanter than a smoke-infested Highland shieling. Sleeping alone in them he could hear all the mysterious voices of the night; hear wild ducks whirring overhead, the cries of herons in the early morning, the splash made by the rising trout, and watch the mist at dawn creeping upon the water as he lay huddled in his plaid.

All our old tracks, so long disused, but visible to those who look for such things, by their white stones, on which so many generations of brogue-clad feet have passed, and by the dark green grass that marks them as they meander across uplands or through the valleys, he must have known as well as did the drovers coming from the north.

Lone wells, that lie forgotten nowadays, but of which then the passers-by all knew and drank from, he too had drunk from, lying upon his chest, and with his beard floating like seaweed in the water as he lay.

Mists must have shrouded him, as he rode through the hills, and out of them strange faces must have peered, terrible and fantastic to a man alone and cut off from mankind.

Possibly to him the faces seemed familiar and more kindly than were those he generally saw upon his pilgrimage. If there were fairies seated on the green knolls, he must have seemed to them one of themselves, for certainly he was a man of peace.

Cold, wind and rain and snow must have beat on him as they do upon a tree, but not for that did he once stay his wanderings up and down. As age drew on him it was observed that by degrees he seldom left his native parish, Kilmaronock, where he was known and understood by all.

There is a tract of moorland, high-lying and bleak, from which at the top you see Loch Lomond and its islands lying out as in a map beneath. The grey Inch Cailleach, and dark Inch Murren with its yews float in the foreground like hulks of ships, and the black rock of Balmaha rises above a little reedy bay. Just at the bleakest part of the bare moor the wandering earl was seen by some returning drovers on a cold winter's night. Light snow was falling, and as they passed him on the wild track that leads down to the vale of Leven, huddled up on his pony, they spoke to him, but he returned no answer, and passed on into the storm. All night it snowed, and in the morning, when the heritors were coming to the old kirk of Bonhill parish, they found him with his back against a dry stone dyke, and his beloved parchments in his hand. Not far away his old white pony, with the reins dangling round his feet, stood shivering, and in the snow where he had thrust his muzzle deeply down to seek the grass were some faint stains of blood.

A Belly-God

The Minister of Costalarga lived at the corner of a gaunt, new square, just at the back of the old convent of Las Salesas, in Madrid. The enormous red brick building, now turned into a law court, filled one corner of the square.

Well did the Madrilenian people say it was a barbarous affair, built in a barbarous style, by a barbarian queen.

Dwindling acacias, burned by the sun and wind, with a few clumps of dusty oleanders, stood forlornly here and there, and in the cables of the tramway line, the tails of kites were always to be seen entangled, draggled and dirty, and looking like dead birds.

The nymph that stood upon a dolphin in the middle of the stuccoed fountain basin seemed to be taking medicine through the conch-shell which was stuck into her mouth, and pointed at the sky. One longed to take it from her lips, throw it away, and tell her she had had enough of it.

Over the doorway of the house in which the representative of Costalarga lived was hung the shield of the Republic, barred in broad strips of blue. In the chief quarter of the shield appeared a chain of mountains, on one of which was hung a cap of liberty. Over the last peak of the chain, the sun was rising with a grin. All the compatriots of the Minister, who were marooned, as it were, from want of funds, asked their way to the house on which the arms of the Republic were displayed.

On almost every day, at office hours, that is, between eleven and three, one or two olive-coloured men were certain to appear. Andrés, the old Galician hall-porter, looked on them with great disfavour, observing, "There goes another Indian in a top-hat; he is safe to touch our Minister for money! That's all they come about"; then he would curse their mothers, quite in the Oriental style, calling them sons of sitters at the windows, on the look-out for men.

His fears were not ill-founded, for in addition to his compatriots, there was a constant influx of distressed literary men, who came to the

Legation knowing the Minister himself was known, as they would say, in the Republic of the Muses, and for a tender-hearted man.

Standing, and looking from his window in the square, one day he saw a man reading a newspaper. At the first glance, he knew he was a foreigner, ragged and miserable. The man folded his newspaper, which fell into its folds as if it were a map, stuffed it into his pocket, dusted his trousers, pulled up his collar, and fastening up his coat, began to walk towards the house. Then he went back, and sitting down again, once more drew out his dirty newspaper.

"I watched him," said the Minister, "half-compassionately! that is to say half in compassion for myself, for I was married and had children, half in compassion for his misery, for I discerned at once that in the end he would choke down his shyness and his pride and come and call on me.

"At last he did so, and having run the gauntlet of Andrés, was ushered up to where I sat, in a room filled with papers and with books, which perhaps gave him courage to speak out, by their familiar air. Before he spoke he had reminded me of the protagonist in an old Spanish comedy. *El Vergonzante en Palacio [sic = vergonzoso]*, he was so ill at ease and shy and awkward in his ways. Beginning in a halting Spanish, with all the verbs in the infinitive, he lapsed at once into his native tongue, when I addressed him in it, after having read his card. On it was written 'Mr. William Heyward' — why do you English alone of all the world, put 'Mr.' on your cards, I wonder? — and the address of a poor boarding-house kept by an Englishwoman, one Señora Smith. I looked at Mr. Heyward as he sat twisting his hat round in his hands. Instantly I seemed to read his history . His thin and undecided-looking hands had several warts upon them, and his whole air showed he was fed on tea and bread and butter, which had turned his skin to a faint muddy colour, something like a frog.

"Withal, I saw he was a man of education, and so when I had given him a cigarette, I asked what it was I could do for him, although I knew he wanted work and food. 'Your Excellency,' he said, and when I said 'For God's sake do not call me Excellency,' he began again, 'Your Excellency, I have ventured . . . ventured to call upon you, though it has cost me a great deal.'

"I knew about his effort, for I had seen it, and knew exactly in which pocket the crushed and much-read newspaper reposed, but merely smiled at him in as encouraging a way as possible.

" 'Your Excellency,' he went on, 'the fact is, I am almost beat. There is nothing for an educated man to do, at least an educated foreigner, here in Madrid. I have been a tutor, teaching English in a family, but lost the job, partly on account, I think, of my bad clothes, and partly because I have no aptitude for teaching anything. I have done a little in the office of an agent for patent medicines, and I have kept Señora Smith's accounts. She is the owner of the boarding-house where I am staying, but now she tells me that she cannot afford to keep me on, and so I have been wandering about looking for literary work . . . to the Consulate, the Embassy, and all the bookshops, but they all bowed me out.'

"I looked at him and did not wonder, for you know what Madrid is like. Everyone writes and no one reads, and even natives of the place have a hard fight to live. A fight, yes, that is the word, for life; there is a battle with the climate to begin with, and then with everyone. To make a long story short, I took him into my employment, for I was then at work upon a thousand things. I think I had a book on Costalarga and its resources, mineral and agricultural, and as a field for emigration, on the stocks; some poetry of my own, a novel, and no end of work which rightly should have fallen to the Consul, if we had had one in Madrid.

"Poor Mr. Heyward was profuse in thanks, and I soon found him useful enough for work requiring no initiative. Naturally he could not write shorthand, knew little French, was quite impossible in Spanish, and what I had often found in educated Englishmen, had not the least idea of English grammar or of style. As I paid him every week, he by degrees got into better case, bought a few clothes, and even had a little colour in his cheeks, and I once heard him whistling a 'Tango,' but grossly out of tune.

"Andrés, my porter, never was reconciled to him, and used to speak of him as 'the foundling Englishman the Minister has got to serve as secretary.' I think I told you that Andrés was a Galician, with all the vices and the virtues of his race. No one, not born a millionaire, could possibly have had the sentiment of property better developed than Andrés.

"Though he had never had much property himself, he looked on it as something sacred, and on me, though I confess I could hardly be called a man of property, as his especial charge.

"He used to reason with me, about putting money in a bank, an institution which, as he said, is liable to break, whereas if put into a stocking between two mattresses, or buried in a hole, money is safe, unless a man finds out the hiding-place.

"Nothing that Mr. Heyward possibly could do removed the suspicions of Andrés, who always looked on him in some way as an interloper, and used to ask me, 'Are there not plenty of poor Spaniards, men who understand the pen, but that you must take a foreigner, making your house a foundling hospital?' My porter had the spirit of the province and the town so strongly rooted in his blood, that almost everyone he looked on as a potential enemy, in the same way, no doubt, his Celt-Iberian and Suevian ancestors had looked upon mankind. Two years of service in his youth in Ceuta had but intensified the feeling, though now and then he used to say he had met honest Moors, 'men of one word,' as he expressed it, although but infidels. As regards human sympathy, he was, just as I fancy are so many Spaniards, far more in sympathy with the Moors than with North Europeans, and certainly a Moor in their streets does not attract half so much criticism as would a Swedish countryman, clothed in his native dress,

"However, quite unconscious of the enmity he had evoked, Heyward went on writing my letters, helping me with my translations, for even if a man knows English pretty well, as I do, there are always niceties that he must miss in a work of long breath."

In point of fact, the Minister's command of English, Heyward used to say, was quite uncanny, and made him feel as if he were the foreigner, and his employer was the Englishman.

"As time went on, I got to like the fellow, and to understand his Anglo-Saxon and his special reticences.

"Sometimes he used to bring crushed, rather withered-looking flowers for my wife, and sweetmeats for the kids. He even would have given cigarettes to the hall-porter had he met with the least encouragement. In fact, he had the milk of human kindness in his blood, and to myself was grateful in so heartfelt a way, it used to make me quite uncomfortable. You know amongst us Latins envy replaces your hypocrisy, and to oblige a man is generally to make an enemy.

"One thing there was about my secretary that was a constant wonder and a source of pity to me. We, you know, have still preserved a little more formality in our address in Spanish countries than you have in the north. Whenever any of these long salutations inquiring as to his health and that of all his family was addressed to him, Heyward would colour up, flush, and become confused, and never find the right reply, but trip up in his speech.

"This attitude was incomprehensible to Spaniards, who used to call him proud and speak of him as being of a despotic character, and a despiser of the poor. When he first learned this, it pained him to the heart, for if he had to help a dog to jump upon a chair, he did it with humility, as if he did not wish to show the animal that it was in the least inferior to him, even in degree. Little by little he became extremely useful to me, and I used to put off on to his shoulders things that I ought to have looked into personally, about the Embassy.

"A countryman of mine of an inventive turn of mind sent several cases to Madrid of some sort of compressed food that he wanted me to press upon the Government to take up for the troops. I can see the stuff arrive in three middling-sized cases, abnormally heavy, and soldered down with lead.

"Heyward and I opened them, and took note of the contents. I remember thinking if there was anything in the world that possibly could make a soldier's life more ignominious, it was to have to eat such horrid-looking stuff and read the misleading adjective 'palatable' stamped upon each slab. After a week of constant writing, I heard from the War Office that General Cañaheja would be glad to see me on a day, his secretary wrote, that would be convenient to him.

"I very nearly did not go, the form of his communication was so insolent, but after all, I thought, I do not want anything myself, so I will bear it for my countryman, and if his food is so deleterious as it looks, at least it will kill some of them. 'Another Spaniard gone to hell,' as we used to say when we killed one of them during our wars for independence, in my grandfather's time.

"Accompanied by Heyward, for he understood the stuff better than I did, we visited the General at the War Office. The house, which was the palace of Godoy, Prince of the Peace (and lover of the Queen), in the days when Napoleon was about to receive the first kick, here in Spain, that showed mankind that he was vulnerable, was an enormous, red brick building with the windows faced in stone. It stood upon a little hill, in the middle of a garden, and day and night sentries paced up and down before its doors. When it so happened that a regiment of cavalry had to furnish men, the additional ridicule was added of a man walking to and fro in spurs, and looking like an alligator when he waddles on the sand. The enormous mass, which, as I said, in old days was the town house of Godoy, and now the focus of all that is most reactionary in

Spain, impressed me disagreeably from the first moment that I entered it. One felt that constitutional liberty was left behind outside its iron gate, and that a heavy, but a stupid, hand lay over everything. Orders were shouted even if the men to whom they were delivered stood but a yard away, and the same man who stood so quietly to listen to them, turned and repeated them in the same voice and key to his inferior, who roared to someone else.

"One official passed us on to another, and at last we stood, after climbing innumerable stairs, in the presence of the great man. He received us civilly enough, and promised — I had been a Minister myself in my own country, and know what a man in that position has to say — to look into the matter of the stores. As I looked at his short, squat figure, his blood-shot eyes and bristly moustache, his hairy hands, his ill-made civilian clothes, and recollected that it was he who had shot so many prisoners in cold blood, tortured a few, and finally returned from the last war a millionaire without seeing a shot fired, a mad desire came over me to spring and strangle him.

"Then I laughed at myself, for I reflected that, short-sighted as I was, all I should do would be perhaps to upset the inkstand, and that the General only had to call and I should be conducted out with ignominy, and in the morning the papers would appear with leaded types and with the headline, 'Sudden insanity of a Minister, and a Field-Marshal's calm.'

"So, after thanking General Cañaheja, I withdrew, taking my secretary, and certain that the incident was closed, and the General would have forgotten all about the stores before I well had got into the street. However, I had complied (as we say), and now could write with a clear conscience to my poor friend at home.

"A few days afterwards, I received a sudden telegram calling me with all my family to Paris, and I remember now, as we walked up and down the station waiting for the train to start, that my poor secretary seemed to be struggling to say something; but I was occupied, and articulate speech was never his strong point, poor fellow, at any time of day. I see him now, as the train slowly drew out of the station, standing, as it were, framed in the rapidly diminishing glass arch, just like a miniature.

"Two months went by, in which I was so occupied in Paris that all thoughts of my secretary or of Madrid were quite obliterated. When I returned at last, as the train slowly jolted through Castile, passing the rocky desert between Avila and the Escorial, stopping at little stations where no one ever was known either to get in or out, all seemed familiar and yet strange to me. Spain has a hold on me that I believe no other country takes, life is so primitive and yet so intense, it seems as if you touched the Middle Ages and the most ultra-modern life, when you stretch out your hands.

"Andrés, the porter, welcomed me with a long string of most minute inquiries as to my health, that of my wife and child, and as to how we had got through the journey, the whole concluding with his congratulations on our being once more in the Court. Nothing was to be seen of Mr. Heyward; but on my writing-desk was a long consular report I had asked him to draw out, carefully done and put where I could not have missed it; but without a word from him who drew it up. None of my servants could, or would, tell me about him, till I bethought me of Andrés.

"He came up, bursting with his subject, and informed me that he had something to impart that would astonish me.

" 'That secretary,' he said, 'was nothing but a thief, a stealer of the sacrament. I never liked him from the first. A man that blushed and could not look you in the face when you but said good morning or good evening in Castilian to him; that made me think about him evilly. Your Excellency, pardon me, not being a son of the country, was too confident. My father always told me, "Andrés, never be confident, do not facilitate a rogue. A rogue is like a Moorish horse; when things are going well, all of a sudden he spies a mare, sets up his back and squeals, and then where are you?" My father, too, had served, as I have, against the infidel.

" 'Yes, Excellency, I will be brief. After a week or two, I remember this John, for I will not now give him the treatment of Don, which he has forfeited, seemed to fall back again into his old ways. He got more shy than ever — "Never trust a shy man, a friar, or a male mule," the proverb says — and never changed his shirt.

" 'With licence, I may say, I think he had no shirt, and by degrees he used to bring in newspapers, handfuls of straw and sticks, that he had gathered in the streets, and other nastiness. One would have thought he was an ostrich about to build a nest. There used to be a smell of burning, and when I tried to look through the keyhole, I found it was plugged up.

" 'Time went on so, and I each day more ill at ease, for, Excellency, I feared the man was plotting something; at last, after ten days or so, myself just like S. Lawrence on his grid-iron, he went away; and from that moment I have never looked upon his face. After a day or two I went into your study, for I had been so put about I was unable to attend to anything . . . even my duties to your Excellency. What a sight was there . . . a heap of ashes in the grate, and all your Excellency's boxes of compressed food standing quite empty, excepting one that had been burned to cook his delicacies. I saw it at a glance, this unlucky John had eaten everything. A wolf, your Excellency, a perfect belly-god. A man born without shame.'

"He stopped at last, and stood with a pleased look upon his face, certain that he had done his duty, and waiting for a word of compliment from me on his fidelity.

"A light broke in upon me, and a tingling, running from my toes, passed up my spinal marrow, making my very hair feel stiff and my skin turn as rough as sandpaper.

"Now I saw why Mr. Heyward's speech had remained undelivered when he came to see me off, despite the throes as of a parturition, which had so shaken him.

"You see, I used to pay him every Saturday, poor devil, and in the two long months that I had been away he had been famishing."

The Minister of Costalarga passed his hand over his sleek black hair uneasily, as he walked up and down the room; then, going to the window, he threw it open with a jerk and gazed out anxiously. No one was seated on the stucco benches of the great, deserted plaza, except a soldier of the Princesa's regiment, in his blue uniform guarded with silver lace. He sat, with a burned-out cigarette just hanging on his lips, in animated conversation with a girl carrying a basket on her arm, who, on her way to market, had stopped a moment, most probably to talk of military matters, with the warrior. The nymph, standing dejectedly upon her dolphin in the water-basin, was the sole witness of their interview. The conch-shell, seen from the side on which they sat, looked a little like an ear-trumpet which she had turned to spy upon their talk and catch their confidences. They did not heed it, and as a light air from the Guadarrama stirred the acacia leaves, making them shiver, and the dry oleanders rustle mournfully, the Minister, coming back into the room, shut to the window, murmuring, "I had half hoped that he might have been there, on the look-out for me."

Falkirk Tryst

In these days when every vestige of old custom and old speech is being rapidly submerged in the dumb waves of progress, the word "Tryst" should be preserved by Act of Parliament. How well it figures in the Border Ballads — "Atte the Reidswire, the Tryst was set," "Gailie she came to the Trysting Tree," and half a hundred other instances, show what a fine poetic word it is. None other in the language could supply its place, . . . the trysting oak, at which Wallace is said to have convened his merry men in the Blane Valley, would sound poor enough, as poor as the Holy Scriptures, put into the modern vulgar tongue. Besides all this, it is a word that to Scotchmen (such as have no Gaelic) gives an air of superiority over the mere Englishman. Many years ago I crossed with a lady who always had maintained that between English and Lowland Scotch there was no difference, from the West Ferry to Dumbarton, in the ferry-boat.

It was raining cats and dogs, and, as we waited in the rain beside the rickety old pier below the castle, a cab drove slowly up. We eyed it curiously. I asked the driver to take us to the railway station. He rather surlily refused. Whereupon one of a host of long-shore youths who were standing, heedless of the rain, watching a full-rigged ship being towed down the Clyde (being moved apparently by the air of discomfort which the lady who was with me showed), remarked, "Hurl them up, Jimmy." Jimmy relaxed his features, and answered in an apologetic way, "I canna, man, I'm trysted."

We tramped up to the station in the rain, but never afterwards did my companion maintain that the two languages were identical.

During my boyhood, Falkirk Tryst was an event to be looked forward to, for droves of ponies from the Islands and the north used to be driven down the pass by an old drove road which passed Aberfoyle. Thin and wild-eyed, with ropy manes and tails that swept the ground, they strayed along.

Chestnuts and piebalds, duns with a black stripe down their back and markings like a tiger on the hocks, cream-colours with dark tails and manes, skewbalds and bays (never a single roan), they used to remind me of the troops of mustangs that I had read of in Mayne Reid. Behind them on a pony, with his knees up to his mouth, a broken snaffle bridle, and in his hands a long, crooked hazel stick, the drover followed, always enveloped in his plaid. A dog or two hung at his pony's heels, and in a language that was strange to us as Telegú, he used to shout anathemas at beasts that lagged behind.

Slowly they trailed along, for time was what the driver had most at his command, stopping to crop the grass, or drink at the broad, shallow crossing of the mountain burns, standing about in knots knee-deep, and swishing with their tails, just as in after life I have seen wild horses do in both Americas. Foals trotted by their mothers' sides, and the whole road was blocked between its dry-stone dykes, surmounted by their feals.

Usually these herds of ponies, collected from the far Highlands and the Islands, were the first sign of the approaching Tryst. Sometimes, however, early in the morning if we were going out to fish, at one of those broad, grassy spaces, which in those days existed at the crossing of four roads, one used to come upon men lying round a fire. Wrapped in their plaids on which the frost showed white, or the dew shone just as it does upon a spider's web, their sticks laid near their hands, they slumbered peacefully. Around them grazed West Highland cattle, black, dun, or chestnut, their peaceful disposition belied by their long, curving horns and shaggy foreheads, and as you passed, one of the men was sure to rise upon his elbow, pull his plaid off his head, and after looking around to see the cattle had not strayed, throw wood upon the fire, and then lie down to sleep again, after muttering a salutation either in Gaelic or in the sing-song English which in those days men of his kidney spoke. Great flocks of blackfaced sheep were also to be met with coming southwards to the Tryst, driven by men who daundered on behind them with that peculiar trailing step that only those who passed their lives upon the road were able to acquire. Generally two or three accompanied the herd, dressed usually in homespun tweeds, which smelt of wool and peat smoke, and were so thick that those who wore them looked like bears, as they lounged heavily along.

All of them had a collie, which if he was not trained, they led tied by a cord, without a collar round his neck, and fastened to a button on their coats. The dogs looked lean and wolfish, for it was long before the times when they were fashionable as pets, and at a sign, or in response to some deep guttural Gaelic order, they turned back straying sheep so dexterously, one used to wonder where the line that separated their instinct from their master's reason, ended or began.

As the droves slowly took their passage through the land, the drovers often would sell a pony-beast, or a stot that had got footsore, to farmers on the way. These sales were not concluded without expenditure of time and whisky and an infinity of talk.

Then the tired colt or calf was led into the byre, and the long line of ponies or of cattle started again, filling the road from side to side and leaving as it passed a wild, warm smell of mountain animals.

Such were the outward visible signs of Falkirk Tryst as I remember them, so many years ago, before the railways and the weekly sales reduced it to a mere cattle market, shorn of importance and of historic connection with the past. The country folks in upland farms and grazing districts looked on it as one of the important functions of the year,

"So many weeks from the October Tryst," "It would be aboot the Tryst that Andra married Jean," "I canna pay ye till the Tryst," were all familiar sayings, and the date itself was as well known to all, as Hallowe'en or Hogmanay, or even the New Year.

In those days Christmas was not held as a holiday except in districts such as Strathglass, Morar, or Moidart, or in the islands where the old faith prevailed, and where the phrases "if you please" and "thank you" were usual accidents of speech, which to a free and self-respecting man were not derogatory.

Mankind, however, must have festivals, and thus the Tryst had somehow crept into the Scottish Colin Clout's Calendar.

The drovers and the droves, coming as they did from the mysterious regions "above the pass," brought with them something of romance, and, in fact, as they strayed along our roads they always called to my recollection etchings by Callot of the Hungarian gipsies which, bound in an old crushed morocco cover, used to lie in the drawing-room and be shown to us as children on Sundays and wet afternoons.

It may be, too, that, unknown to themselves, the Lowland ploughmen working in the fields looked at the drovers as a man accustomed to office work looks on a sailor as he passes by, with feelings oscillating between contempt and envy of his adventurous life.

Certain it was that the old Highland drovers would not have changed their mode of life for anything. To wake up on a bright morning in

October, and shake the hoar frost from one's clothes, collect the cattle, and having sent the whisky bottle round, once more to find oneself upon the road, with the scene changing constantly as you strolled along, must have been pleasanter by far than settled occupation with its dull daily round.

To travel round the Highlands buying a pony here, another there, three or four ewes or stots on one farm, and then setting out upon the trip to Falkirk, sleeping by the herd, and after perhaps a fortnight arriving at the Tryst, to find the booth set up, the other drovers gradually dropping in, exchanging notes on prices, and on the incidents of the march, produced a kind of [man] that Scotland knows no more.

The "parks" by Larbert where the Tryst was held presented on the fateful day the aspect of a fair, with the tents and the crowd of country people.

Sheep bleated and cows lowed, and, as it generally was raining, a smell of tar and wool hung in the air. Knots of men wrapped in plaids, their clothes showing the signs of having camped by the roadside, their faces tanned or reddened by the sun, their beards as shaggy as the coats of the rough kyloes that they passed their lives with, chatted with Lowland shepherds from the Cheviots.

Dealers from England, better dressed but slower in their minds and speech than any Scotsman possibly can be, surveyed the animals, poking them with their sticks, and running down their points after the fashion of the intending buyer in every country of the world. Rough-looking lads, but with that air of supernatural cunning that commerce with the horse imparts, ran ponies up and down.

Beefy-faced cattle-dealers from the Midlands roared at Highlanders whose English was defective, thinking to make them understand by noise; and Highlanders, who themselves understood English almost as well as they did, and spoke it far more purely, pretended to mistake their meaning to get more time to think what they should say.

When, after an infinity of haggling, a price was reached, to which the seller gave assent, both parties would adjourn to one or other of the tents, to wet the bargain, and sit down at a white, deal table, placed upon the grass, and swallow whisky in a way that no one not connected with the cattle trade could possibly achieve. On them it had no more effect than milk, unless to make the fiery faces of the Yorkshire dealers a thought redder, and set the Highlanders a-talking still more fluently than when they had gone in.

Quarrels were rare, and drunkenness not common with such seasoned vessels; but on the rare occasions when the whisky had proved stronger than the head, they lay down peacefully to sleep it off, beside their animals, with their heads buried in their plaids.

The day wore on, amidst the lowing of the beasts and noise of bargaining, and towards evening the roads were full of strings of animals being driven off, either towards the railway, or on the way to their new homes. I often wondered if they missed the rough and shaggy men, so near to them in type, or thought about the upland pastures in the glens, or the sweet, waving grass of island "machars" in the lush Lowland fields.

It pleases us and stills our conscience to say that animals know no such feeling, but yet "I hae my doots," and the wild winnyings [*sic*] and jerks back on the halter must mean something, . . . but after all they have no souls.

Not that such speculations ever entered anybody's head at Falkirk Tryst. Well, well, the Tryst, that is as I knew it in my boyhood, has slipped away into the realms of old, forgotten, far-away memories.

It formed a link between the modern world and times when kilted drovers with their targets at their backs, girt with their claymores, their feet shod in the hairy brogues by which they gained the name of the Rough-Footed Scots, drove down their kyloes and their ponies through the very bealach [*=pass*] that I remember in my youth. They are all gone with the old world they lived in; but still the shadows fall upon the southern slopes and creep into the corries of the Ochils that overlook the historic parks by Larbert in which the Tryst was held. Heavy-nailed boots now press the grass that once was brushed so lightly by the Highland brogues. No one now sleeps beside the roads, nor, rising with the dawn, wrings out the dew-drops from his plaid.

The life that once was real, now seems fantastic; not half so real as the shadows on the hills, and even they only endure whilst the sun shines, chasing one another up and down till it peeps in again.

A Hatchment

Loose and Broken Men

I found the other day an old bundle of papers docketed as above in my own hand.

Many years ago I must have come on them at Gartmore, and as in those days it was what the people called a "sort o' back-lying place," traditions of the doings of loose and broken men still survived, though vaguely and as in a mist. The loose and broken men, whose fame still echoed faintly in my youth, were those who after the "Forty-five" either were not included in the general amnesty, or had become accustomed to a life of violence.

Once walking down the avenue at Gartmore with my old uncle Captain Speirs, we passed three moss-grown lumps of pudding-stone that marked the ancient gallows-tree. Turning to it he said:

" 'Many's the broken man your ancestor, old Laird Nicol, hangit up there, after the 'Forty-five.'" He also told me, just as if he had been speaking about savages, "When I was young, one day up on Loch Ard-side, I met a Hielandman, and when I spoke to him, he answered 'Cha neil Sassenach' I felt inclined to lay my whip about his back."

Even then I wondered why, but prudently refrained from saying anything, for the old Captain had served through the Peninsular Campaign, had been at Waterloo, and, as the country people used to say, he had "an eye intil him like a hawk."

This antipathy to Highlandmen which I have seen exhibited in my youth, even by educated men who lived near to the Highland Line, was the result of the exploits of the aforesaid loose and broken men, who had descended (unapostolically) from the old marauding clans.

The enemy came from "above the pass" to such as my old uncle, and all the glamour Scott had thrown upon the clans never removed the prejudice from their dour Lowland minds.

Perhaps if we had lived in those times we might have shared it too.

One of the documents in the bundle to which I have referred is docketed "Information for Mr. Thomas Buchanan, Minister of

Tullyallan, heritor of Gouston in Cashlie." Gouston is a farm on the Gartmore estate, on which I, in years gone by, have passed many long and wet hours measuring drains and listening to complaints : 'Laird, ma barn flure's fair boss," "Ye ken a' the grips are wasted," "I havena got a gate in the whole farm," with much of the same kind; complaints no doubt all justified, but difficult to satisfy without Golconda or the Rand to draw upon, are ever present in my mind.

The document itself, one of a bundle dealing with the case, written I should judge by a country writer (I have several documents drawn up by one who styles himself "Writer in Garrachel," a farm in Gartmore barony), is on that thick and woolly but well-made paper used by our ancestors, and unprocurable to-day. The writing is elegant, with something of a look of Arabic about its curving lines. It states that:

"Ewan Cameron, Donald McTavish in Glenco, Allen Mackay in thair ["in thair" seems what the French would call "*une terre vague*" but has a fine noncommittal flavour in a legal document], John and Arch. McIan, his brethren, Donald McIan alias Donachar, also Paul Clerich, Dugald and Duncan McFerson in Craiguchty, Robert Dou McGregor and his brethren, John and Water McWatt, *alias* Forrester, in Ofference of Garrochyle belonging to the Laird of Gartmore . . . came violentlie under cloud of night to the dwelling-house of Isabell McCluckey, relict of John Carrick, tenant in the town of Gouston with this party above mentioned and more, on December sixteen hundred [the date is blank, but it occurred in 1698], and then on the same night, it being the Lord's Day, broke open her house, stript [another document on the case says "struck," which seems more consonant to the character of the Highlanders] and bound herself and children contrarie to the authoritie of the nation, and took with them her whole insicht and plenishing,* utensils and domicil, with the number of six horses and mares, sixteen great cows, and their followers, item thirty-six great sheep and lambs and hogs equivalent, and carried them all away violentlie, till they came to the said Craiguchty, where the said Ewan Cameron cohabited."

---

* *The subjoined Inventory, dated 1698, which follows here, shows how thoroughly the work was done. It also shows what a careful housewife Isabell McCluckey was, and that she was a past mistress of the science of making a "poor mouth."*

Ane particular List of what goods and geir utencills and domicills was taken and plundered from Issobell McLuckie Relict of the decest John Kerick by Eun Cameron and his Accomplices as it was given up by her self:

In primis there was Ane gray meir estat to	040 00 0
Item other three meirs estat to 20 lib p.p. is	060 00 0
It Ane flecked horse and ane black horse estat to 24 lib p.p	048 00 0
It there was taken away ten tydie Coues estat to p.p. 24 lib is	240 00 0
It three forrow Cowes giving milk estat to p.p. 20 lib is	060 00 0
It two yeild Cowes estat to 12 lib p.p. is	024 00 0
It two two yeirolds estat to 8 lib p.p. is	016 00 0
It there was taken away thirtietwo great south-land	
Sheep estat to thre pound Scots p pice is	096 00 0
It there was fourtein hogs estat to 2 lib 10 sh: p.pis is	021 00 0
It of Cloath and wolen yairn estat to	035 00 0
It Eight plyds viz four qrof double and four single estat to	048 00 0
It ane pair of wollen Clats estat to	001 16 0
It Ane pair of Cards estat to 2 mk is	001 6 8
It two heckles viz Ane fyne & ane courser estat to	003 18 0
It of mead neŭ harn in shirts 30 elns estat to	012 00 0
It of neŭ Linning in Shirts 24 elns estat to	012 00 0
It ten petticoats estat to	030 00 0
It four westcoats for women estat to	004 6 0
It thre gouns for women estat to	012 00 0
It on ax two womels a borrall & a hamer estat to	002 10 0
It two brass pans estat	003 12 0
It two dozen & a half of spoons estat to	001 18 0
It on pair of sheetts & and on pair of blanqwets estat to	005 00 0
It on Covering estat to	004 00 0
It two bibles estat to	003 10 0
It on pair of tongs estat to	000 10 0
It 2 pair shoes & 2 pairs stockings estat to	005 08 0
It two green aprons estat to	003 00 0
It Ane pair of plou Irons and plough graith estat to	012 00 0
It Ane pistoll and a firelock estat to	010 00 0
It of readie Cash	013 06 8
It ane buff belt	001 04 0
It two plyds estat to	016 00 0
It of Muslin and Lining and oyr fyn Close estat to	020 00 0
It ten elns of new black felt in yearn & wool	010 00 0
It Sick Sack of tueling four elns each	008 00 0
It a canvas eight eln	002 13 04
It a quarter of Butter & a half ston	002 00 0
I flacked horse 4 year old	
1 bell broun horse 3 whyt feet 8 year old	
2 bell broun mares whyt foted whyt nosed 7 year old	
Merk of her sheep	
prope in ye far lug & only cloven in ye near lug-	
Loss of 20 bols of red land whyt corn sowing	33 13 04
It a hundred cups of sheep muck	09 00 00
It Sixtie cups of cows muck	02 00 00
It of silver rent	60 00 00
It of Lorne meal ten bols	80 00 00
It of expenses wt. McLuckie at sevrel trysts	10 00 00
It of spy money	10 00 00

	204.13.4

A Hatchment

I fancy that in Craiguchty, which even in my youth was a wild-looking place, the "authoritie of the nation" had little sway in those days. From another document in the bundle, it appears that not content with driving off the stock and bearing away the "insicht and the plenishing," the complainants and their servants "were almost frichted from their Witts, through the barbarous usadge of the said broken and loose men."

However, the "mad herdsmen," as the phrase went then, drove the "creagh" towards Aberfoyle. The path by which they carried it was probably one that I once knew well.

It runs from Gartmore village, behind the Drum, out over a wild valley set with junipers and whins, till after crossing a little tinkling, brown burn, it enters a thick copse. Emerging from it, it leaves two cottages on the right hand, near which grow several rowans and an old holly, and once again comes out upon a valley, but flatter than the last. In the middle of it runs a larger burn, its waters dark and mossy, with little linns in which occasionally a pike lies basking in the sun.

An old-world bridge is supported upon blocks of pudding-stone, the footway formed of slabs of whin, which from remotest ages must have been used by countless generations of brogue-shod feet, it is so polished and worn smooth. Again, there is another little copse, surrounded by a dry-stone dyke, with hoops of withies stuck into the feals, to keep back sheep, and then the track comes out upon the manse of Aberfoyle, with its long row of storm-swept Spanish chestnuts, planted by Dr. Patrick Graham, author of *Sketches of Perthshire*. From this spot, Ewan Cameron, Donald McIan (*alias* Donachar) and Robert Dhu McGregor might have seen, though of course they did not look, being occupied with the creagh, the church and ancient churchyard of Aberfoyle, and the high-pitched, two-arched bridge, under which runs the Avon-Dhu.

All this they might have seen as "Ewan Cameron cohabited at Craiguchty," near the Bridge of Aberfoyle. Had they but looked they would have seen the clachan with its low, black huts looking like boats set upside down, the smoke ascending from the wooden box-like chimneys — these they did not mark, quite naturally, as they were the only chimneys they had ever seen; nor did the acrid peat-reek fill their nostrils, accustomed to its fumes, with the same smell of wildness as it does ours to-day.

Craigmore and its White Lady was but a ruckle of old stones to them, and if they thought of any natural feature, it may have been the Fairy Hill to which the Rev. Robert Kirke, their minister, had retired only six years before, to take up habitation with the Men of Peace.*

Most probably they only scrugged their bonnets, shifted their targets on their backs, called out to any lagging beast, or without stopping picked up a stone to throw at him. The retiring freebooters "lay there (Craiguchty) the first night." One can see them, going and coming about the little shieling, and Ewan Cameron's wife and children, with shaggy hair and uncouth look, coming out to meet them, just as the women of an Arab *duar* come out to meet a marauding party, raising their shrill cries.

Some of the men must have been on guard all night to keep the animals from straying and to guard against surprise, and as they walked about, blowing upon their fingers to keep them warm, the cold December night must have seemed long to them.

They would sleep little, between the cold and fear of an attack. Long before daylight they would be astir, just as a war party of Indians, or cattle-men upon an expedition in America, who spend the colder hours before the morning seated around the fire, and always rise just before dawn to boil their coffee pots. We know what took the place of coffee with Ewan Cameron and his band, or can divine it at the least.

Next night they reached Achray, "in the Earl of Menteith's land, and lay there in the town." By this time the "said hership" (that is, the stolen beasts) must have been rather troublesome to drive, as the old trail, now long disused, that ran by the birch copse above the west end of Loch Dunkie, was steep and rocky, and ill adapted for "greate cowes."

Both at Craiguchty and Achray they had begun to sell their booty, for the tenants there are reported as not having been "free of the hership."

In fact, "Walter and John McLachlin in Blairwosh" bought several of the animals. Their names seem not to have been concealed, and it appears the transaction was looked upon as one quite natural.

One, Donald Stewart, "who dwells at the west end of Loch Achray," also "bought some of the geare," with "certaine" of the sheep, and "thereafter transported them to the highland to the grass."

Almost unconsciously, with regard to these sheep, the Spanish proverb rises to the mind, that says, "A sardine that the cat has taken, seldom or never comes back to the plate."

* See the *Secret Commonwealth of Elves, Fairies and Fauns,* written in 1691 (?) and supposed to have been first published in 1815. It was reprinted in 1893, with Introduction by Andrew Lang.

So far, all is clear and above-board. Ewan Cameron and his band of rogues broke in and stole and disposed of such of the booty as they could, sharing, one hopes, equitably between them the sum of "fiftie six pounds, six shillings and eight pennies" (Scots) that they found in the house, reserving naturally a small sum, in the nature of a bonus, to Ewan Cameron, for his skill in getting up the raid.

As I do not believe in the word "stripping," and am aware that if we substitute the homelier "striking" for it, no great harm would probably be done in an age when the stage directions in a play frequently run "beats his servant John," when speaking of some fine, young spark, all hitherto seems to have been conducted in the best style of such business known on the Highland line.

Now comes in one "Alexander Campbell, *alias* McGrigor," who "informs"; oh, what a falling off was there, in one of the Gregarach.

This hereditary enemy of my own family, and it is chiefly upon that account I wish to speak dispassionately . . . *sed magis amicus Veritas* . . . informed, that is he condescended to give his moral support to laws made by the Sassenach, "that Duncan Stewart in Baad of Bochasteal, bought two of the said cowes." Whatever could have come into his head? Could not this Campbell, for I feel he could not have been of the sept of Dougal Ciar Mor, the hero who wrought such execution on the shaveling band* of clerks after Glen Fruin, have left the matter to the "coir na claidheamh"?

So far from this, the recreant McGregor, bound and obliged himself "to prove the same by four sufficient witnesses" — so quickly had he deteriorated from the true practice of his clan. His sufficient witnesses were "John Grame and his sub-tenant in Ballanton, his neighbour Finley Dymoch, and John McAdam, Osteleir in Offerance of Gartmore." A little leaven leaveneth the whole, and the bad example of this man soon bore its evil fruit.

We find that "Robert Grame in Ballanton" (that is not wonderful, for he was of a hostile clan and had received none of the spoil as justifiable hush money) also came forward, with what in his case I should soften

* I am well aware that gentlemen of Clan Gregor have indignantly denied that Dougal Ciar Mor was the author of the slaughter of the students in Glen Fruin. If though we hold him innocent, how is he to be justified in the eyes of fame, for he seems to have done nothing else worthy of remark, . . . except of course being the ancestor of Rob Roy, an entirely unconscious feat of arms on his part.

into "testimony." Far more remains to tell. "Jean, spouse to the said Ewan Cameron," that very Ewan who so justly received a bonus as the rent of his ability, also came forward and informed. She deponed "that Walter McWatt was of the band," although we knew it all before.

It is painful to me to record that the said McWatt was "tenant to said Laird of Gartmore," for it appears, according to the evidence of Ewan Cameron's wife, that "he brocht the said rogues to the said house, went in at ane hole in the byre, which formerly he knew, opened the door and cutted the bands of the said cowes and horse." This man, who after all neither made nor unmade kings, but only served his lord (Ewan Cameron), "got for his pains, two sheep, a plyde, a pair of tow-cards, two heckles and a pair of wool cleets, with ane maikle brass pan and several other thinges." The harrying of the luckless Isabell McCluckey seems to have been done thoroughly enough, and in a business-like way. However, punishment possibly overtook the evil-doers, as Thomas McCallum, "who changed the said brass pott with the said McWatt for bute,"* testified in confirmation of the above.

"Item Janet Macneall giveth up that she saw him take the plough irons out of a moss hole the summer thereafter with ane pott when he flitted out of Offerance to the waird, and that he sent the plaid and some other plenishing that he got to John Hunter his house in Corriegreenan for fear of being known. Item the said Walter McWatt died tenant to the Laird of Gartmore, and his spouse and the said John Hunter took and intromitted with the whole geir. Item Elizabeth Parland spouse to umquhile *[for a time]* George McMuir, Moorherd in Gartmore, informs, she being ane ostlere, that they gave a cow that night they lifted the hership to Patrick Graeme in Middle Gartfarran in the byegoing betwixt himand his brother Alexander Graeme in Borland and also that the said Robert McGrigor and his brethern with the said John McWatt met them in the way, although they came not to the house.

"Item that they sold the rest of the geir at one Nicol McNicol's house in the Brae of Glenurchy and the said Nicol McNicol got a flecked horse for meat and drink from them and lastly Dugald McLaren and his brother Alexander got aquaviti among them. This is the true information of the said persons that I have endeavoured to get nottrie att, and if they be not material bonds and grounds of pursuit in it I give it over, but as I think the most material point is in the third article."

* Bute = spoil or exchange.

So ends the document, leaving us in the dark as to what happened in the end, just as is usually the case in life.

The names of nearly all the witnesses, as Elizabeth Parlane, John Ffisher, Robert Carrick, Robert McLaren, Thomas McMillan, the pseudo-McGregor, and of course the Grames, were all familiar to me in the Gartmore of my youth.

All the place-names remain unchanged, although a certain number of them have been forgotten, except by me, and various old semi-Highlanders interested in such things, or accustomed to their sound. Ballanton, Craiguchty, Cullochgairtane (now Cooligarten), Offerance of Garrachel, Gouston of Cashlie, Bochaistail, Gartfarran, Craigieneult, Boquhapple, Corriegreenan, and others which I have not set down, as Milltown of Aberfoyle, though they occur in one or other of the documents, are household words to me.

What is changed entirely is the life. No one, no one alive can reconstruct a Highlander of the class treated of in my document as Loose and Broken Men.

Pictures may show us chiefs; song and tradition tell us tricks of manner; but Ewan Cameron, Robert Dou McGrigor, and their bold compeers elude us utterly. A print of Rob Roy, from the well-known picture once in the possession of the Buchanans of Arden, hangs above the mantelpiece just where I write these lines. He must have known many a "gallowglass" of the Ewan Cameron breed; but even he was semi-civilized, and of a race different from all my friends. Long-haired, light (and rough) footed, wild-eyed, ragged carles they must have been; keen on a trail as is an Indian or a Black-boy in North Queensland; pitiless, blood-thirsty, and yet apt at a bargain, as their disposal of the "particular goodes, to wit, four horses and two mares," the sheep and other "gear," goes far to prove.

The mares and horses are set down as being worth "thirttie six pound the piece overhead," and I am certain Ewan Cameron got full value for them, even although the price was paid in Scots, for sterling money in those days could not have been much used "above the pass." It must have been a more exciting life in Gartmore and in Aberfoyle than in our times, and have resembled that of Western Texas fifty years ago. In London, Addison was rising into fame, and had already translated Ovid's *Metamorphoses*. Prior was Secretary to the Embassy in Holland, Swift was a parish priest at Laracor, and in the very year (1698) in which Ewan Cameron drove his "creagh" past the Grey Mare's Tail, on the old road to Loch Achray, Defoe published his *Essay on Projects*, and two years later his *True Englishman*.

Roads must have been non-existent, or at least primitive in the district of Menteith. This is shown clearly by the separation, as of a whole world, between the farm of Gouston, near Buchlyvie, and the shores of Loch Achray, where it was safe to sell, in open day, beasts stolen barely fifteen miles away.

Men, customs, crops, and in a measure even the face of the low country through which those loose and broken men passed, driving the stolen cows and sheep, have changed. If they returned, all that they would find unaltered would be the hills, Ben Dearg and Ben Dhu, Craig Vadh, Ben Ledi, Schiehallion, Ben Voirlich, distant Ben More, with its two peaks, and Ben Venue peeping up timidly above the road they travelled on that December night; the Rock of Stirling, the brown and billowy Flanders moss, and the white shrouding mists.

A Hatchment

At Sanchidrian

It was full harvest-time throughout Castile.

The corn, short in the stalk and light, as is all corn that ripens early, stood ready to be reaped. In places it had been already cut, and lay in sheaves upon the ground. In others it was cut and carried, and again, between some patches, carts loaded high were creaking through the fields, if the word field can be applied to ground that has no hedges or divisions visible to any other eyes than those accustomed from their birth to the brown plains. Across the dusty, calcined steppe the Sud-Express had crawled since daybreak, stopping at every wayside station, jolting and creaking like a bullock wagon. The passengers had long ceased to look out, and sat perspiring in their darkened berths, for the Castilian plain in summer is not for eyes accustomed to see beauty only in places where even nature puts on a sort of easy, meretricious dress, and decked in pine woods, set with hills and waterfalls, seems to invite the applause of travelling photographers. Castile only reveals itself to those who know it under every aspect, wind-swept and drear in winter, sun-baked in summer, and at all times adust and stern, a mere wide steppe bounded by distant clearly cut hills, from which nothing is to be expected but strange effects of light.

On every side, right up to where it joined the distant hills, stretched the brown plain. The sun had scorched the very trunks of the trees till they appeared to suffer and to be about to burst, just as they crack and suffer in a frost. The only flowers left alive were a few yellow thistles and some clumps of artemisia, which reared their heads, as it were, in defiance of the sun. Long lines of men mounted on donkeys crossed between the fields of stubble and of corn. The Castilian summer had turned them black as Arabs, and their sad, high-pitched songs, as they kept on their way indomitably in the fiery heat, seemed to complete the likeness to the men from whom they had inherited all that they knew of agriculture.

Over the steppe, the narrow line of railway formed the connecting link with the outside world, the world of newspapers, of motor-cars, of aviation, and of telephones. Glistening bright in the sun, like a steel ribbon, ran the line. It passed by little tile-roofed towns, each clustering round its church, brown and remote — towns where a sandy, unpaved street ran out until it lost itself in the great plain; towns only joined to one another by a narrow track meandering through the corn fields, or the sparse round-topped pine woods, tracks that avoided all the obstacles, passing round, stony hills and following watercourses till they came on a shallow place to cross. Often the towns were only visible like ships hull down, the church towers seemingly hung in the air without foundations, they were so far off from the line. The train jogged on, passing by Ataquines, Palacios de Goda, Arévalo, Adanero and other little stations, where no one possibly could have got in or out since first the line was laid. It entered them and stopped under some dust-laden acacias or China-trees. A man emerged and called the station's name, adding "a minute" or "two minutes" as the case might be, although the train was just as likely to stop ten minutes or a quarter of an hour, whilst the electric bell twittered so faintly that at times one was not sure if it was really an electric bell that sounded or only crickets in the sand chirping metallically. Sometimes a horse stood blinking in the sun tied to a post, a gun upon the heavy old-world saddle and a brown blanket hanging from the pommel, almost to the ground; sometimes some charcoal-burners' mules stood waiting to be unloaded, and generally some ragged-looking fowls, half buried in the sand, were squatted at the lee-side of the round, mud-topped oven, striving to dodge the heat. Occasionally a half-dressed woman peeped from a window, her blue-black hair wild as a pony's mane, holding the blind between her teeth as she looked out upon the train. Such were the stations, mere islands in a sea of brown; each one the faithful copy of the other, and every one of them cheaply constructed and sun-bleached till they had all become as much a part and parcel of the landscape as the mud houses with their red-tiled eaves.

So from one little, ill-built point of contact with the world, to the next, as ill-built as the last, the train crept on, the heat increasing and the subtile *[sic]* air becoming more diaphanous, so that the distant mountains almost appeared to be transparent, and the dead haulms of fennel and of mullein to stand out so clearly that they looked like trees.

Herds of black cattle stood by dried-up water-holes, occasionally a bullock licked the earth where it appeared almost like china, polished and glazed as it had dried and baked, and then stamping and bellowing, slowly walked back into the herd. Brown shepherds stood immovable as posts, their shadows forming a refuge for their dogs, their flocks all huddled in a ring, with their heads crouched low upon the ground, to escape their enemy, the sun. Nature stood silent in the violet haze, and as the train rattled across the ill-closed catch-points outside another little station, a porter called out in a long-drawn melody, "Sanchidrian, five minutes," and the express came alongside the platform, the engine throbbing as if it were something living and glad to be at rest. A goods train standing just outside the station bore the inscription, written with a piece of chalk, "No water in Velayos," and the whole plain looked parched and suffering as if the rain of fire that fell from heaven upon it had burned into its heart. No passengers stood waiting, even the little groups of country people that generally throng Spanish stations, making the platform a public promenade, were missing, for Sanchidrian itself was distant from the line.

The weary stationmaster in his gold-laced cap and uniform frock-coat was, with the porter who had called the station's name, the only living thing except two nearly naked children, sitting by the draw-well, and a lean yellow dog. The five minutes that the train ought to have remained might just as well have been abridged to one, or, on the other hand, drawn out to twenty, and no one would have cared, had not, emerging from a cloud of dust, a rider come up to the hitching-post, dismounted hurriedly, and holding in his hand his saddle-bags, walked quickly to the open door, at which the cooks and waiters of the dining-car stood trying to catch a little air. "Friends," he said, taking off his hat and passing his brown hand across his forehead, "have you any ice?" They stared at him as he stood in his short black jacket edged with imitation astrakhan, his tight, grey trousers strapped inside the leg with the same cloth from which they had been made, his black serge sash showing beneath his waist-coat with its silver buckles, and his red-worsted saddle-bags, tasselled and fringed, thrown over his right shoulder and hanging down his back.

"Ice, why of course we have it," said the waiter. "Who in this heat could live without it shut in the hot train?" answered the conductor, interested and glad to have the opportunity of a chance word with anyone outside his little world.

The horseman, who looked anxiously at the somnolent train out of the corner of his eye as if it were a colt that might spring forward at any minute and leave him in the lurch, began again: "You could not live without ice here in this train, you say, eh? My father cannot die without it. For days the fever has consumed him, and in the night, listening to every hour the watchman calls, he says 'Miguel,' that is my name — Miguel Martinez, at your service — 'I could die easier if I had some ice . . . a little ice to put upon my forehead and between my lips.' Ice in Sanchidrian! As well go out to gather artichokes at sea. To-day he seemed just going, and the priest said to me, 'Miguel, saddle the Jerezano and go down and meet the train; there they have ice, for certainly those who travel by it must drink cool.' So I have come; say, can you spare me a lump of ice, for what I spoke about?"

The electric bell stopped twittering, and the porter called "Passengers aboard," but still the train stood at the platform, although the engine-driver had clambered slowly to his post. He whistled, and the couplings tightened with a jerk, just as a waiter holding a lump of ice about as big as a large loaf came to the door, wrapping it, as he walked, in straw. He gave it to the horseman, who stood waiting in the sun. "A thousand thanks," he said. "A son thanks you in his father's name. What is the value of this piece of ice?" The man who gave it, and the little knot of cooks and waiters standing at the open door of the long dining-car as the train began to move, looked at each other, and one said, "Friend, we do not sell our ice, it is not ours to sell. Moreover, may it relieve your father." Miguel, now walking swiftly by the moving train, said, "Once again, a thousand thanks; take, then, this packet of cigars," and handed to the last man he could reach one of those bundles of ill-rolled salitrose-looking *[sic = Sp. salitroso]* parcels of cigars sold in the *estancos* of small Spanish towns.

The train swung on and rumbled past him, leaving him standing for a moment in the heat, waving his hand to the white-clad cooks and waiters grouped on the platform of the dining-car. Miguel stood waiting till it had cleared the station, and then, walking outside to where his horse stood waiting, unhitched him and threw the saddle-bags across the saddle, then gathering his reins in his left hand he mounted in one motion, and settling himself, drew out an olive switch which he had left sticking between the pommel and his horse's back; then having felt the lump of ice with his right hand, touched his horse with the spur and set his face towards his home. Putting the butt-end of his cigarette behind his ear, Miguel struck out into the road. The thick, white dust lay on the narrow track like snow, dulling the horse's footfalls and giving him the look of shuffling in his gait, although Miguel, holding his reins high and a little to the near side of the high pommel, and with his spurs dangling behind the cinch, kept him up to the full stretch of the Castilian pace.

His olive face, under his broad-brimmed, grey, felt hat with its straight brim, looked anxiously ahead, and when his little, nervous horse had got well warmed and the dried sweat melted again upon the skin, Miguel, pressing him with his legs, put him to a slow gallop, now and again putting his hand behind the saddle to feel how the precious lump of ice was standing the fierce sun.

A constant dripping through the worsted saddle-bags warned him to hurry, so he pressed on, passing long lines of mules laden with charcoal or with great nets of straw, and men on donkeys, who looked at him with wonder as he flew past them at three-quarter speed upon the road. Some of them merely said "Adios," and others shouted inquiries as to his haste, but he in every case answered with a wave of his hand and pressed his spurs into the cinch. He passed through groves of olive trees, silvery, gnarled and secular, under whose scanty shade men sat, eating their midday meal, their broad-brimmed hats lying beside them on the ground, their close-shaved heads wrapped in old-fashioned, blue-checked handkerchiefs, tied in a knot behind.

As he passed in a cloud of dust, pointing to their olives and their bread and to their leathern skins of wines, they made the gesture of inviting him to eat, and he returned their courtesy by a movement of his hand, taking a pull upon his horse as the track grew steeper and stonier, as it ran through an aromatic waste of cistus and wild thyme. His heavy Arab stirrups brushed through the sticky cistus which grew on each side of the narrow, sandy path, till they became all coated with their gum and everything stuck to them as if they had been smeared with birdlime.

Butterflies hovered over the great, white flowers, and lizards ran up tree-trunks, pausing and looking round just before they disappeared from view. From the recesses of the waste came an incessant hum of insects, and now and then a flight of locusts shot across the path, and plunged into the bushes, just as a school of flying fish sinks into a wave.

The hot half-hour between the bushes, struggling through the sand, had told its tale upon the gallant, little horse, whose heaving flanks, distended nostrils and protruding eyes showed that he had almost had enough. When they emerged again into the plain and saw the little brown-roofed town, only a short league away, Miguel dismounted for a moment, and after slackening his cinch anxiously secured his saddle-bags, from which large drops of moisture fell upon the ground. Tightening his girth again, he mounted, and the Jerezano, who had stood head to wind, responding to the spur, struck into a short gallop, his rider holding him together and pressing him with both legs into his bit.

They passed a threshing-floor, on which a troop of mares was being driven round to thresh the corn, followed by a man seated upon a hurdle laid on a heavy stone. The floor itself was white and shiny, and seemed as hard as marble, trodden by the horses' feet. Near it some sun-burned men threw grain into the air with wooden spades to winnow it, and as Miguel passed by upon the road they called out to him, giving him the time of day and asking how his father was; but to them all he only waved his hand and pressed his spurs into his horse's sides, which now were red with blood.

Outside the town the track passed through the bed of a dry stream, and came out on the other bank on a paved causeway set with pebble-stones that led into the town. A heavy stumble on the stones showed him his horse was failing, and he pulled him back into a trot. Passing the straggling cottages, each with its corral for goats, he came into the little street, and as he rode by the church door he touched his hat and crossed himself as his horse slithered on the stones. Turning out of an angle of the dusty *plaza* with its stucco seats and dwarfed acacias, he came into a street in which the houses seemed of a richer sort of folk, his horse now beaten to a walk. As he neared one which had a roughly sculptured coat of arms over the doorway a sound of wailing fell upon his ears. He stopped, and getting off his horse, he threw the reins mechanically on the ground. A priest came out to meet him. "Miguel," he said, "your father, may God have pardoned him, has left this vale of tears more than an hour ago. The Lord in his great mercy, for the fever burned like fire in his veins, was pleased to make his parting easy, and for an hour before he died he murmured now and then, 'How cool the ice is! It stills the throbbing of my forehead and slakes my thirst — my son Miguel rode for it to the train.'"

Miguel turned to his horse, and taking from the saddle-bags the lump of ice, now little bigger than an apple, followed the priest into the great bare room, where on his bed his father's body lay. Round it stood weeping women, and the children in a corner of the room holding each other's hands gazed stolidly at the brown face that looked like walnut-wood against the linen of the bed.

Falling upon his knees, Miguel kissed the thin hands crossed on the chest, and then after a prayer he rose and put the precious lump of ice first on his father's forehead and then upon his lips. He crossed himself, and after having said some words of consolation to the women, went out again to where in the hot sandy street his horse stood waiting, with his legs stretched a little forward and his head hanging to the ground. The sweat had made a little pattern in the sand as it dropped from his belly and his flanks, Miguel slowly undid the girths, and taking off the bridle, led the horse into the stable, and after throwing hay upon the manger, went back into the room.

The priest was praying, and the sobbing of the women sounded like surf upon a beach, whilst from outside the crickets' chirping filled the air with its wild melody. Far to the south the Sud-Express still crept along its narrow ribbon of bright rails towards Madrid.

Brought Forward

R. B. Cunninghame Graham

Introduction

When *Brought Forward* was published in 1916, Cunninghame Graham had recently been working for the War Office in his old haunts in Uruguay on the sad business of selecting and shipping horses for British military use back in Europe. He had reached the age of sixty-four and the valedictory note of his preface anticipated, wrongly as it turned out, that this would be his final collection of sketches. Its fifteen pieces of writing are characteristically varied in location, period, topic and form. Six of the sketches are set in South America, three in Scotland, three in England, and one each in Morocco, France and Spain. In time they range from the contemporary back to the 16th century, but almost all must have been written between the years 1914-1916. The typical Graham sketch as represented in this volume mutates in form, focus and pace, sometimes quite disconcertingly, mingling historical reconstruction, travelogue, journalism, autobiography, philosophical musings and fictional narrative.

Despite this apparently wilful diversity, however, the powerful impact on Graham of the Great War gives the work a unifying elegiac tone. This tone may be heightened in retrospect by the fact that the book is dedicated to Commander Charles Cunninghame Graham, his younger brother, who, after a career in the Royal Navy and with the lifeboat service, was to die the following year, 1917. The Preface, while barely mentioning the war, foreshadows this sombre mood in its account of the discovery of the corpse of a long dead Apache Indian in a secluded valley of the Mexican Sierras, "I liked the manner of his going off the stage."

The title of the first item, "Brought Forward", a short story with a contemporary Scottish setting hints ironically at connotations of bookkeeping and legal transactions, underlined by Geordie's laconic parting words, "Well, someone's got to account for it." It touches on themes that recur in other pieces in the collection. The locale is Beardmore's Parkhead Forge, a huge steel complex in the east end of Glasgow which during the war employed 2000 men producing armaments and armour plate for warships. This also became a stronghold of the workers' radical movement later to be known as 'Red Clydeside'. David Kirkwood, one of its leaders, worked at Parkhead and would be known to Graham through their early involvement in Scottish Labour politics. Previously, as an MP in the 1880s, Graham had made a mark by actively espousing the cause of various groups of exploited workers.

The writing moves economically through the bleak industrial landscape to focus on a brassfitters' workshop and its occupants. It highlights the male camaraderie of the group and particularly the bond between Jimmy and Geordie, and their reactions as news from the front reaches them. The fitters are shown as alertly opinionated on matters of politics, religion and the progress of the war. Unfortunately, however, Graham's uncertain command of Glasgow dialogue leaves their lunchtime discussions embarrassingly like the efforts of the Kailyard writers whom he elsewhere attacked so sharply. Probably the most effective touch in the tale is the linked pathos of the requisitioned Clydesdale workhorses and the parade of enlisted soldiers.

Graham's almost religious love and compassion for horses emerge in five other pieces in the collection. In two of his longer autobiographical sketches, "Los Pingos" and "Bopicuá", he impressionistically evokes episodes in his recent military work in Uruguay. His feelings have their most moving expression in "Bopicuá", in his hope that God will care for slaughtered horses in an equine heaven-haven, and "they will feed in prairies where the grass fades not and springs are never dry." His was a heartfelt angry despair of the kind felt also by his contemporary, the composer Edward Elgar. "Los Pingos" opens on the shore of a desolate inlet by the Uruguay river. A cosmopolitan bunch of waiting gauchos and sailors are shown in telling little vignettes. When eventually a tug arrives towing two lighters with a freight of horses, the process of disembarking begins, and interest gradually focuses on the pingos, 'good horses', enjoying their release and swimming in the bay. The sketch ends in admiration of these happy creatures and Graham's melancholy rhetorical question, "Where are they now?" Bopicuá was a settlement north of the meatpacking port of Fray Bentos where Graham was based. His sketch of that title complements "Los Pingos" by detailing how the best horses brought in by the gauchos are examined, selected and purchased for the British army. The behaviours of the encamped gauchos and the corralled horses are both described. Graham is particularly sensitive to the individualities of the horses and their reactions in groups as they are driven at sundown towards pasture by a railway siding. In the half light a sympathetic gaucho pronounces their elegy: "Eat well [. . .] the grass in Europe all must smell of blood."

"In a Backwater" registers Graham's recent encounter with an elderly farmer in a rural corner of the Home Counties. He is operating the same old-style disorganised, peasant style of agriculture of which Graham had had experience, and mixed feelings, on his own estate in Menteith. The man, who is described rather condescendingly as "a simple soul", is obsessed and disturbed by the war news which reaches him via his newspaper and information from passers-by. Graham sets this distress against the idyllic background of a long-settled English countryside in midsummer. The farmer is particularly horrified by the thought that commandeered farm horses such as his own are being mown down in Belgium among the harvest crops. His poetic lament for "dead 'orses and dead soldiers lying by 'undreds in the standing corn" is a moving culmination to this short sketch.

The ambitious narrative "Feast Day in Santa Maria Mayor", draws upon Graham's youthful experiences of Paraguay in the 1870s, when he developed an interest in the history of abandoned Jesuit mission stations ('reductions') in the region. The greatest of these had been that of Santa Maria Mayor. His account of a day-long festival in that decayed settlement traces the lively rhythms of the festivities as all sorts of local people begin to arrive, and a depleted form of Mass is celebrated. Much eating, drinking and ragged music ensue. Yet again horses play their part, for the feast's events centre on a display of gaucho horsemanship, the age-old equestrian contest of riding at the ring. As the day ends, silence and mist descend on the community. The title of the sketch, "Hippomorphous" appears to be Graham's own coinage, suggesting the transfiguration of a horse into a deity. Drawn from extensive reading of earlier historians, this is his take on the bizarre story of how the favourite black warhorse of the conquistador Cortes came to be worshipped as a deity by Indians in Yucatán. Graham's sardonic anticlerical conclusion is that the zealotry of Franciscan missionaries contrived to destroy a primitive, innocent horse cult, whose Godhead, the statue of Cortes's defunct charger, had done less harm than any other god, Christian or otherwise. The topic is revisited in his later work, *Horses of the Conquest* (1930).

As already suggested, undertones of the Great War shadow this whole 1916 collection; and universal aspects of conflict - brutality, heroism, patriotic enthusiasm and the pity and folly of war - also emerge in "Mudejar", "Uno dei Mille" and "Elysium".

The Spanish term, 'Mudéjar', relates to a style of architecture blending Moorish and Spanish features. This sketch, which draws on Graham's knowledge and experience of Spain, is a tour de force in his allusive narrative style which assumes in the reader an unlikely range of reference concerning an obscure incident. It takes the form of an imaginative reconstruction of a savage episode in the city of Saragossa during the short life of the Spanish Federal Republic of 1873-74. A government army is trying to flush out remnants of die-hard anarchists, the 'Intransigents', who are holed up in the city's historic Torre Nueva, which is a gem of Mudéjar architecture. As the horrific siege develops, we see on both sides examples of stubborn and heroic courage culminating in the suicidal self-sacrifice of a friar. Finally the colonel leading the attacking force is required by his CO to explain why he had not simply pounded the old tower to pieces with his big guns in order to minimise his own losses. The colonel's reply, highlighting one of the dire dilemmas of war, is an aesthetic justification, "It is Mudejar of the purest architecture."

"Uno Dei Mille" is one of Graham's pieces of personal reportage that open on a wide-angled panorama and close in on a particular event and individual. Though the location is not clearly identified, the city seems to be Rio de Janeiro, which had a large concentration of Italian immigrants. The time is the beginning of the Great War before Italy formally entered the conflict, and the "Mille" of the title recalls the legendary thousand patriots whom Garibaldi had recruited in 1860 in his efforts to unify Italy. The frail old flag-draped figure at the centre of the sketch, an immigrant survivor of that campaign, is being honoured by hundreds of youthful Italians who are now excitedly sailing back home to join the fight against Germany. The infectious war fever of these volunteers is balanced in Graham's account by the Italian Consul's sober reflections on their likely fate as cannon fodder.

In "Elysium", we are offered a fleeting glimpse of one young soldier in another great city, London, on brief leave from the front. Still in combat gear and marked by the mud of the trenches, he has two naively adoring women on his arms, his sweetheart and his sister. Graham, the onlooker, nurses a curmudgeonly judgement on the "miserable, cheap finery" that the girls are wearing, but the lad is proudly, possessively, showing them some of the sights in Westminster, Pall Mall and Clubland. As they pass the Army and Navy Club (the 'Rag') their self-absorbed happiness is observed wistfully by two elderly officers. The implied contrast is between the threesome's momentary euphoria and the horrors to which the warrior must return in the far from Elysian fields of Flanders.

Gauchos, the solitary, rough-riding drovers of the South American pampas, have a significant place in the *Brought Forward* sketches, and they are central to two pieces, "Heredity" and "El Tango Argentino". There seems to have been attributes in these horsemen to which Graham aspired — probably their style, their skills with weapons, their hauteur and their austere loyalty to the old ways. The nicely judged short story "Heredity" opens on a historical survey of the cultures on both sides of the disputed territory between Uruguay and Brazil, invoking parallels with the Scottish/English borderlands. From this account emerges the "slight and graceful figure" of Jango Chaves who embodies many of these qualities as he rides forth with nonchalant bravado deliberately to shoot up his neighbours across the frontier. With his statuesque poise he might well be Don Roberto himself hacking along Rotten Row.

"El Tango Argentino" is formally the most ambitious sketch in the volume. Here Graham speaks autobiographically of his experiences in Paris and Uruguay. He starts in a luxury Paris hotel around 1913 when the Tango dance craze first hit European high society, then via the awkward device of a dream he moves back in time, to a primitive rancho in Uruguay, but finally awakes to discover himself still in Paris. This powerful piece dramatises the differences between what Graham sees as the effetely indecent form of the dance in Paris and the raw stylish force of its gaucho origins: "Gravity was the keynote of the scene." The switch in tone within the sketch is striking: the description of the wealthy hotel guests is judgmental and bitterly sarcastic with, remarkably, traces of misogyny and anti-Semitism; whereas the gaucho's sexual honour killing is recorded vividly without any explicit moralising.

There are in this collection four very different pieces in which Graham exemplifies, however obliquely and ironically, certain elements of a personal creed of ethical values. These are "A Minor Prophet", "El Masgad", "With the North East Wind" and "Fidelity".

The minor prophets of the Old Testament were notable for scolding man's sins and follies and predicting the terrible wrath of Jehovah, but in Graham's sketch, "A Minor Prophet", his improbable visionary has a very different message, the pure Corinthian gospel of the universal power of Love. The episode occurs on Sunday in the centre of a manufacturing town in West Yorkshire, probably Bradford. Graham in his anticlerical mode briefly savages the hypocrisies of churchgoing, then turns his ridicule on the colourful collection of orators peddling their flaky theories at the local Speakers' Corner. Towards the end of the day as the crowds diminish, a shabby Chaplinesque figure, forlorn but resolute, takes the stand and proclaims his powerful doctrine of Love with increasing confidence to an almost non-existent audience. The impact of the sketch comes from the bizarre juxtaposition of the pathetic orator and the genuine force of his Blakean vision of a future England. In "El Masgad", a meandering narrative set in south west Morocco, the local Sherif, by definition a descendant of Muhammad, is a similarly unlikely prophet, dirty and unprepossessing in appearance, but according to Graham, revered as genuinely holy since Allah has ordained it so. He is in conversation with a urbane European consul long experienced in Arab ways of thinking. The virtue that the Sherif recommends fervently to the Consul is Faith, simple, unquestioning trust in the infinite power of the Creator. He illustrates his point with reference to the fable of a small lizard, El Masgad, to whom Allah assigned the duty of praying for all the animal kingdom, and who faithfully turns his head to Mecca at the time of prayer: "it is a little animal of God [...] and we too are in His hand [...]."

Graham rounds off this collection as he began, in Scotland. He is good on funerals, and his volumes of sketches include tributes to distinguished acqaintances such as William Morris and Joseph Conrad. In this vein "With the North-East Wind" is a very fine, moody piece of obituary commentary. It records the cremation of his old friend Keir Hardie, the miners' leader and co-founder with Graham of the Scottish Labour Party. The locale is the same raw industrial Glasgow that the reader encountered in the title sketch, "Brought Forward"; and the period is the same, for Hardie died in 1915. The mourners recall him with respect and affection, for his courageous struggle in the cause of underprivileged workers. Graham himself sees Hardie as a man "who was simple and yet with something of the prophet in his air, and something of the seer. Effective yet ineffectual." Another minor prophet? What after all did he achieve? For answer we are left with the faint blue smoke fading into the atmosphere, and the Kilpatrick hills in the background.

In "Fidelity", Graham comes even closer to home. His host, the meditative laird in a country house overlooking the Clyde, seems a displaced *alter ego* of Graham himself in his later years at Ardoch. The autumnal, melancholy ambience of the old house with its adjacent woods and moorland is nostalgically evoked, and the laird's animal parable is poignant in the extreme. The instinctive, helpless loyalty of the whaup to its fatally wounded mate is, like the lizard El Masgad's faith, an object lesson for mankind.

Four ineffectual minor prophets, the little preacher, the Sherif, the miners' leader and the laird? And Graham's preferred virtues would seem to be love, faith, courage and fidelity - "but the greatest of these is Love."

Finally then, assessing the volume *Brought Forward* as a whole, we may conclude that while at first glance it could seem a random selection thrown together by a prolific writer as a routine publishing ploy, in fact it has its own distinctive harmony. Composed largely between 1914 and 1916, it can be appreciated as a moving conjunction of themes and tones - horses, war, gauchos, minor prophets - infused with Cunninghame Graham's deeply felt responses to the first years of the Great War. It deserves to be valued as a unique and major Scottish contribution to the literature of that period.

(JNA)

To
Commander Charles E.F. Cunninghame Graham, R.N.

Contents

Preface

Luckily the war has made eggs too expensive for me to fear the public will pelt me off the stage with them.

Still after years of writing one naturally dreads the cold potato and the orange-peel.

I once in talking said to a celebrated dancer who was about to bid farewell to her admirers and retire to private life, "Perhaps you will take a benefit when you come back from finishing your last tour." She answered, "Yes . . ."; and then added, "or perhaps two."

That is not my way, for all my life I have loved bread, bread, and wine, wine, not caring for half-measures, like your true Scot, of whom it has been said, "If he believes in Christianity he has no doubts, and if he is a disbeliever he has none either."

Once in the Sierra Madre, either near the Santa Rosa Mountains or in the Bolson de Mápimi, I disremember which, out after horses that had strayed, we came upon a little shelter made of withies, and covered with one of those striped blankets woven by the Návajos.

A Texan who was with the party pointed to it, and said, "That is a wickey-up, I guess."

The little wigwam, shaped like a gipsy tent, stood close to a thicket of huisaché trees in flower. Their round and ball-like blossoms filled the air with a sweet scent. A stream ran gently tinkling over its pebbly bed, and the tall prairie grasses flowed up to the lost little hut as if they would engulf it like a sea.

On every side of the deep valley — for I forgot to say the hut stood in a valley — towered hills with great, flat, rocky sides. On some of them the Indian tribes had scratched rude pictures, records of their race.

In one of them — I remember it just as if now it was before my eyes — an Indian chief, surrounded by his friends, was setting free his favourite horse upon the prairies, either before his death or in reward of faithful services. The little group of men cut in the stone, most probably with an obsidian arrow-head, was life-like, though drawn without perspective, which gave those figures of a vanished race an air of standing in the clouds.

The chief stood with his bridle in his hand, his feather war-bonnet upon his head, naked except the breech-clout. His bow was slung across his shoulders and his quiver hung below his arm, and with the other hand he kept the sun off from his face as he gazed upon his horse. All kinds of hunting scenes were there displayed, and others, such as the burial of a chief, a dance, and other ceremonials, no doubt as dear to those who drew them as are the rites in a cathedral to other faithful. The flat rock bore one more inscription, stating that Eusebio Leal passed by bearing despatches, and the date, June the fifteenth, of the year 1687. But to return again to the lone wickey-up.

We all sat looking at it: Eustaquio Gomez, Polibio Medina, Exaltacion Garcia, the Texan, two Pueblo Indians, and I who write these lines.

Somehow it had an eerie look about it, standing so desolate, out in those flowery wilds.

Inside it lay the body of a man, with the skin dry as parchment, and his arms beside him, a Winchester, a bow and arrows, and a lance. Eustaquio, taking up an arrow, after looking at it, said that the dead man was an Apache of the Mescalero band, and then, looking upon the ground and pointing out some marks, said, "He had let loose his horse before he died, just as the chief did in the picture-writing."

That was his epitaph, for how death overtook him none of us could conjecture; but I liked the manner of his going off the stage.

'Tis meet and fitting to set free the horse or pen before death overtakes you, or before the gentle public turns its thumbs down and yells, "Away with him."

Charles Lamb, when some one asked him something of his works, answered that they were to be found in the South Sea House, and that they numbered forty volumes, for he had laboured many years there, making his bricks with the least possible modicum of straw, just like the rest of us.

Mine, if you ask me, are to be found but in the trails I left in all the years I galloped both on the prairies and the pampas of America.

Hold it not up to me for egotism, O gentle reader, for I would have you know that hardly any of the horses that I rode had shoes on them, and thus the tracks are faint.

Vale.

R. B. Cunninghame Graham

Brought Forward

The workshop in Parkhead was not inspiriting. From one week's end to another, all throughout the year, life was the same, almost without an incident. In the long days of the Scotch summer the men walked cheerily to work, carrying their dinner in a little tin. In the dark winter mornings they tramped in the black fog, coughing and spitting, through the black mud of Glasgow streets, each with a woollen comforter, looking like a stocking, round his neck.

Outside the dreary quarter of the town, its rows of dingy, smoke-grimed streets and the mean houses, the one outstanding feature was Parkhead Forge, with its tall chimneys belching smoke into the air all day, and flames by night. Its glowing furnaces, its giant hammers, its little railway trucks in which men ran the blocks of white-hot iron which poured in streams out of the furnaces, flamed like the mouth of hell.

Inside the workshop the dusty atmosphere made a stranger cough on entering the door. The benches with the rows of aproned men all bending at their work, not standing upright, with their bare, hairy chests exposed, after the fashion of the Vulcans at the neighbouring forge, gave a half-air of domesticity to the close, stuffy room.

A semi-sedentary life quickened their intellect; for where men work together they are bound to talk about the topics of the day, especially in Scotland, where every man is a born politician and a controversialist. At meal-times, when they ate their "piece" and drank their tea that they had carried with them in tin flasks, each one was certain to draw out a newspaper from the pocket of his coat, and, after studying it from the Births, Deaths, and Marriages, down to the editor's address on the last page, fall a-disputing upon politics. "Man, a gran' speech by Bonar Law aboot Home Rule. They Irish, set them up, what do they make siccan a din aboot? Ca' ye it Home Rule? I juist ca' it Rome Rule. A miserable, priest-ridden crew, the hale rick-ma-tick o' them."

The reader then would pause and, looking round the shop, wait for the answer that he was sure would not be long in coming from amongst such a thrawn lot of commentators. Usually one or other of his mates would fold his paper up, or perhaps point with an oil-stained finger to an article, and with the head-break in the voice, characteristic of the Scot about to plunge into an argument, ejaculate: "Bonar Law, ou aye, I kent him when he was leader of the South Side Parliament. He always was a dreary body, sort o' dreich like; no that I'm saying the man is pairfectly illiterate, as some are on his side o' the Hoose there in Westminister. I read his speech — the body is na blate, sort o' quick at figures, but does na take the pains to verify. Verification is the soul of mathematics. Bonar Law, eh! Did ye see how Maister Asquith trippit him handily in his tabulated figures on the jute business under Free Trade, showing that all he had advanced about protective tariffs and the drawback system was fair redeeklous . . . as well as several errors in the total sum?"

Then others would cut in and words be bandied to and fro, impugning the good faith and honour of every section of the House of Commons, who, by the showing of their own speeches, were held to be dishonourable rogues aiming at power and place, without a thought for anything but their own ends.

This charitable view of men and of affairs did not prevent any of the disputants from firing up if his own party was impugned; for in their heart of hearts the general denunciation was but a covert from which to attack the other side.

In such an ambient the war was sure to be discussed; some held the German Emperor was mad — "a daft-like thing to challenge the whole world, ye see; maist inconsiderate, and shows that the man's intellect is no weel balanced . . . philosophy is whiles sort of unsettlin' . . . the felly's mad, ye ken."

Others saw method in his madness, and alleged that it was envy, "naething but sheer envy that had brought on this tramplin' upon natural rights, but for all that he may be thought to get his own again, with they indemnities."

Those who had studied economics "were of opinion that his reasoning was wrong, built on false premises, for there can never be a royal road to wealth. Labour, ye see, is the sole creative element of riches." At once a Tory would rejoin, "And brains. Man, what an awfu' thing to leave out brains. Think of the marvellous creations of the human genius." The first would answer with, "I saw ye coming, man. I'll no deny that brains have their due place in the economic state; but build me one of your Zeppelins and stick it in the middle of George Square without a crew to manage it, and how far will it fly? I do not say that brains did not devise it; but, after all, labour had to carry out the first design." This was a subject that opened up enormous vistas for discussion, and for a time kept them from talking of the war.

Jimmy and Geordie, hammering away in one end of the room, took little part in the debate. Good workmen both of them, and friends, perhaps because of the difference of their temperaments, for Jimmy was the type of red-haired, blue-eyed, tall, lithe Scot, he of the *perfervidum ingenium*, and Geordie was a thick-set, black-haired, dour and silent man.

Both of them read the war news, and Jimmy, when he read, commented loudly, bringing down his fist upon the paper, exclaiming, "Weel done, Gordons!" or "That was a richt gude charge upon the trenches by the Sutherlands." Geordie would answer shortly, "Aye, no sae bad," and go on hammering.

One morning, after a reverse, Jimmy did not appear, and Geordie sat alone working away as usual, but if possible more dourly and more silently. Towards midday it began to be whispered in the shop that Jimmy had enlisted, and men turned to Geordie to ask if he knew anything about it, and the silent workman, brushing the sweat off his brow with his coat-sleeve, rejoined: "Aye, ou aye, I went wi' him yestreen to the headquarters o' the Camerons; he's joined the kilties richt eneugh. Ye mind he was a sergeant in South Africa." Then he bent over to his work and did not join in the general conversation that ensued.

Days passed, and weeks, and his fellow-workmen, in the way men will, occasionally bantered Geordie, asking him if he was going to enlist, and whether he did not think shame to let his friend go off alone to fight. Geordie was silent under abuse and banter, as he had always been under the injustices of life, and by degrees withdrew into himself, and when he read his newspaper during the dinner-hour made no remark, but folded it and put it quietly into the pocket of his coat.

Weeks passed, weeks of suspense, of flaring headlines in the Press, of noise of regiments passing down the streets, of newsboys yelling hypothetic victories, and of the tension of the nerves of men who know their country's destiny is hanging in the scales. Rumours of losses, of defeats, of victories, of checks and of advances, of naval battles, with hints of dreadful slaughter filled the air. Women in black were seen about, pale and with eyelids swollen with weeping, and people scanned the reports of killed and wounded with dry throats and hearts constricted as if they had been wrapped in whipcord, only relaxing when after a second look they had assured themselves the name they feared to see was absent from the list. Long strings of Clydesdale horses ridden by men in ragged clothes, who sat them uneasily, as if they felt their situation keenly, perched up in the public view, passed through the streets. The massive caulkers on their shoes struck fire occasionally upon the stones, and the great beasts, taught to rely on man as on a god from the time they gambolled in the fields, went to their doom unconsciously, the only mitigation of their fate. Regiments of young recruits, some in plain clothes and some in hastily-made uniforms, marched with as martial an air as three weeks' training gave them, to the stations to entrain. Pale clerks, the elbows of their jackets shiny with the slavery of the desk, strode beside men whose hands were bent and scarred with gripping on the handles of the plough in February gales or wielding sledges at the forge.

All of them were young and resolute, and each was confident that he at least would come back safe to tell the tale. Men stopped and waved their hats, cheering their passage, and girls and women stood with flushed cheeks and straining eyes as they passed on for the first stage that took them towards the front. Boys ran beside them, hatless and barefooted, shouting out words that they had caught up on the drill-ground to the men, who whistled as they marched a slow and grinding tune that sounded like a hymn.

Traffic was drawn up close to the kerbstone, and from the top of tram-cars and from carts men cheered, bringing a flush of pride to many a pale cheek in the ranks. They passed on; men resumed the business of their lives, few understanding that the half-trained, pale-faced regiment that had vanished through the great station gates had gone to make that business possible and safe.

Then came a time of waiting for the news, of contradictory paragraphs in newspapers, and then a telegram, the "enemy is giving ground on the left wing"; and instantly a feeling of relief that lightened every heart, as if its owner had been fighting and had stopped to wipe his brow before he started to pursue the flying enemy.

The workmen in the brassfitters' shop came to their work as usual on the day of the good news, and at the dinner-hour read out the accounts of the great battle, clustering upon each other's shoulders in their eagerness. At last one turned to scan the list of casualties. Cameron, Campbell, McAlister, Jardine, they read, as they ran down the list, checking the names off with a match. The reader stopped, and looked towards the corner where Geordie still sat working silently.

All eyes were turned towards him, for the rest seemed to divine even before they heard the name. "Geordie man, Jimmy's killed," the reader said, and as he spoke Geordie laid down his hammer, and, reaching for his coat, said, "Jimmy's killed, is he? Well, some one's got to account for it."

Then, opening the door, he walked out dourly, as if already he felt the knapsack on his back and the avenging rifle in his hand.

Brought Forward

Los Pingos

The amphitheatre of wood enclosed a bay that ran so far into the land it seemed a lake. The Uruguay flowed past, but the bay was so land-locked and so well defended by an island lying at its mouth that the illusion was complete, and the bay appeared to be cut off from all the world.

Upon the river twice a day passed steam-boats, which at night-time gave an air as of a section of a town that floated past the wilderness. Streams of electric light from every cabin lit up the yellow, turgid river, and the notes of a band occasionally floated across the water as the vessel passed. Sometimes a searchlight falling on a herd of cattle, standing as is their custom after nightfall upon a little hill, made them stampede into the darkness, dashing through brushwood or floundering through a marsh, till they had placed themselves in safety from this new terror of the night.

Above the bay the ruins of a great building stood. Built scarcely fifty years ago, and now deserted, the ruins had taken on an air as of a castle, and from the walls sprang plants, whilst in the deserted courtyard a tree had grown, amongst whose branches oven-birds had built their hanging nests of mud. Cypresses towered above the primeval hard-wood, which grew all gnarled and horny-looking, and nearly all had kept their Indian names, as ñandubay, chañar, tala and sarandi, molle, and many another name as crabbed as the trunks which, twisted and distorted, looked like the limbs of giants growing from the ground.

Orange trees had run wild and shot up all unpruned, and apple trees had reverted back to crabs. The trunks of all the fruit-trees in the deserted garden round the ruined factory were rubbed shiny by the cattle, for all the fences had long been destroyed or fallen into decay.

A group of roofless workmen's cottages gave an air of desolation to the valley in which the factory and its dependencies had stood. They too had been invaded by the powerful sub-tropical plant life, and creepers covered with bunches of bright flowers climbed up their walls. A sluggish stream ran through the valley and joined the Uruguay, making a little natural harbour. In it basked cat-fish, and now and then from off the banks a tortoise dropped into the water like a stone. Right in the middle of what once had been the square grew a ceiba tree, covered with lilac flowers, hanging in clusters like gigantic grapes. Here and there stood some old ombús, their dark metallic leaves affording an impenetrable shade. Their gnarled and twisted roots, left half-exposed by the fierce rains, gave an unearthly, prehistoric look to them that chimed in well with the deserted air of the whole place. It seemed that man for once had been subdued, and that victorious nature had resumed her sway over a region wherein he had endeavoured to intrude, and had been worsted in the fight.

Nature had so resumed her sway that buildings, planted trees, and paths long overgrown with grass, seemed to have been decayed for centuries, although scarce twenty years had passed since they had been deserted and had fallen into decay.

They seemed to show the power of the recuperative force of the primeval forest, and to call attention to the fact that man had suffered a defeat. Only the grass in the deserted square was still triumphant, and grew short and green, like an oasis in the rough natural grasses that flowed nearly up to it, in the clearings of the woods.

The triumph of the older forces of the world had been so final and complete that on the ruins there had grown no moss, but plants and bushes with great tufts of grass had sprung from them, leaving the stones still fresh as when the houses were first built. Nature in that part of the New World enters into no compact with mankind, as she does over here in Europe to touch his work kindly and almost with a reverent hand, and blend it into something half compounded of herself. There bread is bread and wine is wine, with no half-tints to make one body of the whole. The one remaining evidence of the aggression of mankind, which still refused to bow the knee to the overwhelming genius of the place, was a round bunch of eucalyptus trees that stood up stark and unblushing, the colour of the trunks and leaves so harshly different from all around them that they looked almost vulgar, if such an epithet can be properly applied to anything but man. Under their exiguous shade were spread saddles and bridles, and on the ground sat men smoking and talking, whilst their staked-out horses fed, fastened to picket-pins by rawhide ropes. So far away from everything the place appeared that the group of men looked like a band of pioneers upon some frontier, to which the ruins only gave an air of melancholy, but did nothing to dispel the loneliness.

As they sat idly talking, trying to pass, or, as they would have said, trying to make time, suddenly in the distance the whistle of an approaching steamer brought the outside world into the little, lonely paradise. Oddly enough it sounded, in the hot, early morning air, already heavy with the scent of the mimosas in full bloom. Butterflies flitted to and fro or soared above the scrub, and now and then a wild mare whinnied from the thickets, breaking the silence of the lone valley through which the yellow, little stream ran to the Uruguay.

Catching their horses and rolling up the ropes, the men, who had been sitting underneath the trees, mounted, and following a little cattle trail, rode to a high bluff looking down the stream.

Panting and puffing, as she belched out a column of black smoke, some half a mile away, a tug towing two lighters strove with the yellow flood. The horsemen stood like statues with their horses' heads stretched out above the water thirty feet below.

Although the feet of several of the horses were but an inch or two from the sheer limit, the men sat, some of them with one leg on their horses' necks; others lit cigarettes, and one, with his horse sideways to the cliff, leaned sideways, so that one of his feet was in the air. He pointed to the advancing tug with a brown finger, and exclaimed, "These are the lighters with the horses that must have started yesterday from Gualeguaychú, and ought to have been here last night." We had indeed been waiting all the night for them, sleeping round a fire under the eucalyptus grove, and rising often in the night to smoke and talk, to see our horses did not get entangled in their stake ropes, and to listen for the whistle of the tug.

The tug came on but slowly, fighting her way against the rapid current, with the lighters towing behind her at some distance, looking like portions of a pier that had somehow or another got adrift.

From where we sat upon our horses we could see the surface of the Uruguay for miles, with its innumerable flat islands buried in vegetation, cutting the river into channels; for the islands, having been formed originally by masses of water-weeds and drift-wood, were but a foot or two above the water, and all were elongated, forming great ribbons in the stream.

Upon the right bank stretched the green prairies of the State of Entre-Rios, bounded on either side by the Uruguay and Paraná. Much flatter than the land upon the Uruguayan bank, it still was not a sea of level grass as is the State of Buenos Aires, but undulating, and dotted here and there with white *estancia* houses, all buried in great groves of peach trees and of figs. On the left bank on which we stood, and three leagues off, we could just see Fray Bentos, its houses dazzlingly white, buried in vegetation, and in the distance like a thousand little towns in Southern Italy and Spain, or even in Morocco, for the tower of the church might in the distance just as well have been a minaret.

The tug-boat slowed a little, and a canoe was slowly paddled out to pilot her into the little haven made by the brook that flowed down through the valley to the Uruguay.

Sticking out like a fishing-rod, over the stem of the canoe was a long cane, to sound with if it was required.

The group of horsemen on the bluff rode slowly down towards the river's edge to watch the evolutions of the tug, and to hold back the horses when they should be disembarked. By this time she had got so near that we could see the horses' heads looking out wildly from the sparred sides of the great decked lighters, and hear the thunderous noise their feet made tramping on the decks. Passing the bay, into which ran the stream, by about three hundred yards, the tug cast off one of the lighters she was towing, in a backwater. There it remained, the current slowly bearing it backwards, turning round upon itself. In the wild landscape, with ourselves upon our horses forming the only human element, the gigantic lighter with its freight of horses looked like the ark, as set forth in some old-fashioned book on Palestine. Slowly the tug crept in, the Indian-looking pilot squatted in his canoe sounding assiduously with his long cane. As the tug drew about six feet of water and the lighter not much more than three, the problem was to get the lighter near enough to the bank, so that when the hawser was cast off she would come in by her own way. Twice did the tug ground, and with furious shoutings and with all the crew staving on poles, was she got off again. At last the pilot found a little deeper channel, and coming to about some fifty feet away, lying a length or two above the spot where the stream entered the great river, she paid her hawser out, and as the lighter drifted shorewards, cast it off, and the great ark, with all its freight, grounded quite gently on the little sandy beach. The Italian captain of the tug, a Genoese, with his grey hair as curly as the wool on a sheep's back, wearing a pale pink shirt, neatly set off with yellow horseshoes, and a blue gauze necktie tied in a flowing bow, pushed off his dirty little boat, rowed by a negro sailor and a Neapolitan, who dipped their oars into the water without regard to one another, either as to time or stroke.

The captain stepped ashore, mopping his face with a yellow pocket-handkerchief, and in the jargon between Spanish and Italian that men of his sort all affect out in the River Plate, saluted us, and cursed the river for its sandbanks and its turns, and then having left it as accursed as the Styx or Periphlegethon, he doubly cursed the Custom House, which, as he said, was all composed of thieves, the sons of thieves, who would be certainly begetters of the same. Then he calmed down a little, and drawing out a long Virginia cigar, took out the straw with seriousness and great dexterity, and then allowed about a quarter of an inch of it to smoulder in a match, lighted it, and sending out a cloud of smoke, sat down upon the grass, and fell a-cursing, with all the ingenuity of his profession and his race, the country, the hot weather, and the saints.

This done, and having seen the current was slowly bearing down the other lighter past the sandy beach, with a last hearty curse upon God's mother and her Son, whose birth he hinted not obscurely was of the nature of a mystery, in which he placed no credence, got back into his boat, and went back to his tug, leaving us all amazed, both at his fluency and faith.

When he had gone and grappled with the other lighter which was slowly drifting down the stream, two or three men came forward in the lighter that was already in the little river's mouth, about a yard or so distant from the edge, and calling to us to be ready, for the horses had not eaten for sixteen hours at least, slowly let down the wooden landing-flap. At first the horses craned their necks and looked out on the grass, but did not venture to go down the wooden landing-stage; then a big roan, stepping out gingerly and snorting as he went, adventured, and when he stood upon the grass, neighed shrilly and then rolled. In a long string the others followed, the clattering of their unshod feet upon the wood sounding like distant thunder.

Byrne, the Porteño, stout and high-coloured, dressed in great thigh boots and baggy breeches, a black silk handkerchief tied loosely round his neck, a black felt hat upon his head, and a great silver watch-chain, with a snaffle-bridle in the middle of it, contrasting oddly with his broad pistol belt, with its old silver dollars for a fastening, came ashore, carrying his saddle on his back. Then followed Doherty, whose name, quite unpronounceable to men of Latin race, was softened in their speech to Duarte, making a good Castilian patronymic of it. He too was a Porteño[1], although of Irish stock. Tall, dark, and dressed in semi-native clothes, he yet, like Byrne, always spoke Spanish when no foreigners were present, and in his English that softening of the consonants and broadening of the vowels was discernible that makes the speech of men such as himself have in it something, as it were, caressing, strangely at variance with their character. Two or three peons of the usual Gaucho type came after them, all carrying saddles, and walking much as an alligator waddles on the sand, or as the Medes whom Xenophon describes, mincing upon their toes, in order not to blunt the rowels of their spurs.

Our men, Garcia the innkeeper of Fray Bentos, with Pablo Suarez, whose negro blood and crispy hair gave him a look as of a Roman emperor of the degenerate times, with Pancho Arrellano and Miguel Paralelo, the Gaucho dandy, swaying upon his horse with his toes just touching his heavy silver stirrups with a crown underneath them, Velez and El Pampita, an Indian who had been captured young on the south Pampa, were mounted ready to round the horses up.

They did not want much care, for they were eating ravenously, and all we had to do was to drive them a few hundred yards away to let the others land.

By this time the Italian captain in his tug had gently brought the other lighter to the beach, and from its side another string of horses came out on to the grass. They too all rolled, and, seeing the other band, by degrees mixed with it, so that four hundred horses soon were feeding ravenously on the sweet grass just at the little river's mouth that lay between its banks and the thick belt of wood.

Though it was early, still the sun was hot, and for an hour we held the horses back, keeping them from the water till they had eaten well.

The Italian tugmaster, having produced a bottle of trade gin (the Anchor brand), and having drank *[sic]* our health, solemnly wiped the neck of the bottle with his grimy hand and passed it round to us. We also drank to his good health and voyage to the port, that he pronounced as if it were written "Bono Airi," adding, as it was war-time, "Avanti Savoia" to the toast. He grinned, and with a gesture of his thick dirty hand, adorned with two or three coppery-looking rings, as it were, embedded in the flesh, pronounced an all-embracing curse on the Tedeschi, and went aboard the tug.

1 *Porteño*, literally a man born in the port of Buenos Aires, but is also applied to any one born in the province of Buenos Aires.

When he had made the lighters fast, he turned down stream, saluting us with three shrill blasts upon the whistle, and left us and our horses thousands of miles away from steam and smoke, blaspheming skippers, and the noise and push of modern life.

Humming-birds poised themselves before the purple bunches of the ceiba[1] flowers, their tongues thrust into the calyx and their iridescent wings whirring so rapidly, you could see the motion, but not mark the movement, and from the yellow balls of the mimosas came a scent, heady and comforting.

Flocks of green parroquets flew shrieking over the clearing in which the horses fed, to their great nests, in which ten or a dozen seemed to harbour, and hung suspended from them by their claws, or crawled into the holes. Now and then a few locusts, wafted by the breeze, passed by upon their way to spread destruction in the plantations of young poplars and of orange trees in the green islands in the stream.

An air of peace gave a strange interest to this little corner of a world plunged into strife and woe. The herders nodded on their horses, who for their part hung down their heads, and now and then shifted their quarters so as to bring their heads into the shade. The innkeeper, Garcia, in his town clothes, and perched upon a tall grey horse, to use his own words, "sweated blood and water like our Lord" in the fierce glare of the ascending sun. Suarez and Paralelo pushed the ends of the red silk handkerchiefs they wore tied loosely round their necks, with two points like the wings of a great butterfly hanging upon their shoulders, under their hats, and smoked innumerable cigarettes, the frontiersman's specific against heat or cold. Of all the little company only the Pampa Indian showed no sign of being incommoded by the heat. When horses strayed he galloped up to turn them, now striking at the passing butterflies with his heavy-handled whip, or, letting himself fall down from the saddle almost to the ground, drew his brown finger on the dust for a few yards, and with a wriggle like a snake got back into his saddle with a yell.

The hours passed slowly, till at last the horses, having filled themselves with grass, stopped eating and looked towards the river, so we allowed them slowly to stream along towards a shallow inlet on the beach. There they stood drinking greedily, up to their knees, until at last three or four of the outermost began to swim.

1 *Benbax ceiba*, a large tree with spongy, light wood, that has immense bunches of purple flowers.

Only their heads appeared above the water, and occasionally their backs emerging just as a porpoise comes to the surface in a tideway, gave them an amphibious air, that linked them somehow or another with the classics in that unclassic land.

Long did they swim and play, and then, coming out into the shallow water, drink again, stamping their feet and swishing their long tails, rise up and strike at one another with their feet.

As I sat on my horse upon a little knoll, coiling my *lazo*, which had got uncoiled by catching in a bush, I heard a voice in the soft, drawling accents of the inhabitants of Corrientes, say, "Pucha, Pingos."[1]

Turning, I saw the speaker, a Gaucho of about thirty years of age, dressed all in black in the old style of thirty years ago. His silver knife, two feet or more in length, stuck in his sash, stuck out on both sides of his body like a lateen.

Where he had come from I had no idea, for he appeared to have risen from the scrub behind me. "Yes," he said, "Puta, Pingos," giving the phrase in the more classic, if more unregenerate style, "how well they look, just like the garden in the plaza at Fray Bentos in the sun."

All shades were there, with every variegation and variety of colour, white, and fern noses, chestnuts with a stocking on one leg up to the stifle joint, horses with a ring of white right round their throats, or with a star as clear as if it had been painted on the hip, and "tuvianos," that is, brown, black, and white, a colour justly prized in Uruguay.

Turning half round and offering me a cigarette, the Correntino spoke again. "It is a paradise for all those pingos here in this rincón:[2] grass, water, everything that they can want, shade, and shelter from the wind and sun."

So it appeared to me — the swiftly flowing river with its green islands; the Pampas grass along the stream; the ruined buildings, half-buried in the orange trees run wild; grass, shade, and water: "Pucha, no . . . Puta, Pingos, where are they now?"

1 *Pingo* in Argentina is a good horse. *Pucha* is a euphuism *[sic = euphemism]* for another word.
2 Elbow of a river.

Fidelity

My tall host knocked the ashes from his pipe, and crossing one leg over the other looked into the fire. Outside, the wind howled in the trees, and the rain beat upon the window-panes. The firelight flickered on the grate, falling upon the polished furniture of the low-roofed, old-fashioned library, with its high Georgian overmantel, where in a deep recess there stood a clock, shaped like a cross, with eighteenth-century cupids carved in ivory fluttering round the base, and Time with a long scythe standing upon one side.

In the room hung the scent of an old country-house, compounded of so many samples that it is difficult to enumerate them all. Beeswax and potpourri of roses, damp, and the scent of foreign woods in the old cabinets, tobacco and wood smoke, with the all-pervading smell of age, were some of them. The result was not unpleasant, and seemed the complement of the well-bound Georgian books standing demure upon their shelves, the blackening family portraits, and the skins of red deer and of roe scattered about the room.

The conversation languished, and we both sat listening to the storm that seemed to fill the world with noises strange and unearthly, for the house was far from railways, and the avenues that lead to it were long and dark. The solitude and the wild night seemed to have recreated the old world, long lost, and changed, but still remembered in that district just where the Highlands and the Lowlands meet.

At such times and in such houses the country really seems country once again, and not the gardened, gamekeepered mixture of shooting ground and of fat fields tilled by machinery to which men now and then resort for sport, or to gather in their rents, with which the whole world is familiar to-day.

My host seemed to be struggling with himself to tell me something, and as I looked at him, tall, strong, and upright, his face all mottled by the weather, his homespun coat, patched on the shoulders with buckskin that once had been white, but now was fawn-coloured with wet and from the chafing of his gun, I felt the parturition of his speech would probably cost him a shrewd throe. So I said nothing, and he, after having filled his pipe, ramming the tobacco down with an old silver Indian seal, made as he told me in Kurachi, and brought home by a great-uncle fifty years ago, slowly began to speak, not looking at me, but as it were delivering his thoughts aloud, almost unconsciously, looking now and then at me as if he felt, rather than knew, that I was there. As he spoke, the tall, stuffed hen-harrier; the little Neapolitan shrine in tortoise-shell and coral, set thick with saints; the flying dragons from Ceylon, spread out like butterflies in a glazed case; the "poor's-box" on the shelf above the books with its four silver sides adorned with texts; the rows of blue books, and of Scott's Novels (the Roxburgh edition), together with the scent exuding from the Kingwood cabinet; the sprays of white Scotch rose, outlined against the window blinds; and the sporting prints and family tree, all neatly framed in oak, created the impression of being in a world remote, besquired and cut off from the century in which we live by more than fifty years. Upon the rug before the fire the sleeping spaniel whined uneasily, as if, though sleeping, it still scented game, and all the time the storm roared in the trees and whistled down the passages of the lone country house. One saw in fancy, deep in the recesses of the woods, the roe stand sheltering, and the capercailzie sitting on the branches of the firs, wet and dejected, like chickens on a roost, and little birds sent fluttering along, battling for life against the storm. Upon such nights, in districts such as that in which the gaunt old house was situated, there is a feeling of compassion for the wild things in the woods that, stealing over one, bridges the gulf between them and ourselves in a mysterious way. Their lot and sufferings, joys, loves, and the epitome of their brief lives, come home to us with something irresistible, making us feel that our superiority is an unreal thing, and that in essentials we are one.

My host went on: "Some time ago I walked up to the little moor that overlooks the Clyde, from which you see ships far off lying at the Tail of the Bank, the smoke of Greenock and Port Glasgow, the estuary itself, though miles away, looking like a sheet of frosted silver or dark-grey steel, according to the season, and in the distance the range of hills called Argyle's Bowling Green, with the deep gap that marks the entrance to the Holy Loch. Autumn had just begun to tinge the trees, birches were golden, and rowans red, the bents were brown and dry. A few bog asphodels still showed amongst the heather, and bilberries, dark as black currants, grew here and there amongst the carpet of green sphagnum and the stag's-head moss. The heather was all rusty brown, but still there was, as it were, a recollection of the summer in the air. Just the kind of day you feel inclined to sit down on the lee side of a dry-stone dyke, and smoke and look at some familiar self-sown birch that marks the flight of time, as you remember that it was but a year or two ago that it had first shot up above the grass.

"I remember two or three plants of tall hemp-agrimony still had their flower heads withered on the stalk, giving them a look of wearing wigs, and clumps of ragwort still had a few bees buzzing about them, rather faintly, with a belated air. I saw all this — not that I am a botanist, for you know I can hardly tell the difference between the Cruciferæ and the Umbelliferæ, but because when you live in the country some of the common plants seem to obtrude themselves upon you, and you have got to notice them in spite of you. So I walked on till I came to a wrecked plantation of spruce and of Scotch fir. A hurricane had struck it, turning it over almost in rows, as it was planted. The trees had withered in most cases, and in the open spaces round their upturned roots hundreds of rabbits burrowed, and had marked the adjoining field with little paths, just like the lines outside a railway-station.

"I saw all this, not because I looked at it, for if you look with the idea of seeing everything, commonly everything escapes you, but because the lovely afternoon induced a feeling of well-being and contentment, and everything seemed to fall into its right proportion, so that you saw first the harmonious whole, and then the salient points most worth the looking at.

"I walked along feeling exhilarated with the autumn air and the fresh breeze that blew up from the Clyde. I remember thinking I had hardly ever felt greater content, and as I walked it seemed impossible the world could be so full of rank injustice, or that the lot of three-fourths of its population could really be so hard. A pack of grouse flew past, skimming above the heather, as a shoal of flying-fish skims just above the waves. I heard their quacking cries as they alighted on some stooks of oats, and noticed that the last bird to settle was an old hen, and that, even when all were down, I still could see her head, looking out warily above the yellow grain. Beyond the ruined wood there came the barking of a shepherd's dog, faint and subdued, and almost musical.

"I sat so long, smoking and looking at the view, that when I turned to go the sun was sinking and our long, northern twilight almost setting in.

"You know it," said my host, and I, who often had read by its light in summer and the early autumn, nodded assent, wondering to myself what he was going to tell me, and he went on.

"It has the property of making all things look a little ghostly, deepening the shadows and altering their values, so that all that you see seems to acquire an extra significance, not so much to the eye as to the mind. Slowly I retraced my steps, walking under the high wall of rough piled stones till it ends, at the copse of willows, on the north side of the little moor to which I had seen the pack of grouse fly after it had left the stooks. I crossed into it, and began to walk towards home, knee-deep in bent grass and dwarf willows, with here and there a patch of heather and a patch of bilberries. The softness of the ground so dulled my footsteps that I appeared to walk as lightly as a roe upon the spongy surface of the moor. As I passed through a slight depression in which the grass grew rankly, I heard a wild cry coming, as it seemed, from just beneath my feet. Then came a rustling in the grass, and a large, dark-grey bird sprang out, repeating the wild cry, and ran off swiftly, trailing a broken wing.

"It paused upon a little hillock fifty yards away, repeating its strange note, and looking round as if it sought for something that it was certain was at hand. High in the air the cry, wilder and shriller, was repeated, and a great grey bird that I saw was a whaup slowly descended in decreasing circles, and settled down beside its mate.

"They seemed to talk, and then the wounded bird set off at a swift run, its fellow circling above its head and uttering its cry as if it guided it. I watched them disappear, feeling as if an iron belt was drawn tight round my heart, their cries growing fainter as the deepening shadows slowly closed upon the moor."

My host stopped, knocked the ashes from his pipe, and turning to me, said: —

"I watched them go to what of course must have been certain death for one of them, furious, with the feelings of a murderer towards the man whose thoughtless folly had been the cause of so much misery. Curse him! I watched them, impotent to help, for as you know the curlew is perhaps the wildest of our native birds; and even had I caught the wounded one to set its wing, it would have pined and died. One thing I could have done, had I but had a gun and had the light been better, I might have shot them both, and had I done so I would have buried them beside each other.

"That's what I had upon my mind to tell you. I think the storm and the wild noises of the struggling trees outside have brought it back to me, although it happened years ago. Sometimes, when people talk about fidelity, saying it is not to be found upon the earth, I smile, for I have seen it with my own eyes, and manifest, out on that little moor."

He filled his pipe, and sitting down in an old leather chair, much worn and rather greasy, silently gazed into the fire.

I, too, was silent, thinking upon the tragedy; then feeling that something was expected of me, looked up and murmured, "Yes."

Brought Forward

"Uno Dei Mille"

A veil of mist, the colour of a spider's web, rose from the oily river. It met the mist that wrapped the palm-trees and the unsubstantial-looking houses painted in light blue and yellow ochre, as it descended from the hills. Now and then, through the pall of damp, as a light air was wafted up the river from the sea, the bright red earth upon the hills showed like a stain of blood; canoes, paddled by men who stood up, balancing themselves with a slight movement of the hips, slipped in and out of sight, now crossing just before the steamer's bows and then appearing underneath her stern in a mysterious way. From the long line of tin-roofed sheds a ceaseless stream of snuff-and-butter-coloured men trotted continuously, carrying bags of coffee to an elevator, which shot them headlong down the steamer's hold. Their naked feet pattered upon the warm, wet concrete of the dock side, as it were stealthily, with a sound almost alarming, so like their footfall seemed to that of a wild animal.

The flat-roofed city, buried in sheets of rain, that spouted from the eaves of the low houses on the unwary passers-by, was stirred unwontedly. Men, who as a general rule lounged at the corners of the streets, pressing their shoulders up against the houses as if they thought that only by their own self-sacrifice the walls were kept from falling, now walked up and down, regardless of the rain.

In the great oblong square, planted with cocoa-palms, in which the statue of Cabrál stands up in cheap Carrara marble, looking as if he felt ashamed of his discovery, a sea of wet umbrellas surged to and fro, forging towards the Italian Consulate. Squat Genoese and swarthy Neapolitans, with sinewy Piedmontese, and men from every province of the peninsula, all had left their work. They all discoursed in the same tone of voice in which no doubt their ancestors talked in the Forum, even when Cicero was speaking, until the lictors forced them to keep silence, for their own eloquence is that which in all ages has had most charm for them. The reedy voices of the Brazilian coloured men sounded a mere twittering compared to their full-bodied tones. "Viva l'Italia" pealed out from

317

thousands of strong throats as the crowd streamed from the square and filled the narrow streets; fireworks that fizzled miserably were shot off in the mist, the sticks falling upon the umbrellas of the crowd. A shift of wind cleared the mist off the river for a moment, leaving an Italian liner full in view. From all her spars floated the red and white and green, and on her decks and in the rigging, on bridges and on the rail, men, all with bundles in their hands, clustered like ants, and cheered incessantly. An answering cheer rose from the crowd ashore of "Long live the Reservists! Viva l'Italia," as the vessel slowly swung into the stream. From every house excited men rushed out and flung themselves and their belongings into boats, and scrambled up the vessel's sides as she began to move. Brown hands were stretched down to them as they climbed on board. From every doorstep in the town women with handkerchiefs about their heads came out, and with the tears falling from their great, black eyes and running down their olive cheeks, waved and called out, "Addio Giuseppe; addio Gian Battista, abbasso gli Tedeschi," and then turned back into their homes to weep. On every side Italians stood and shouted, and still, from railway station and from the river-side, hundreds poured out and gazed at the departing steamer with its teeming freight of men.

Italians from the coffee plantations of São Paulo, from the mines of Ouro Preto, from Goyaz, and from the far interior, all young and sun-burnt, the flower of those Italian workmen who have built the railways of Brazil, and by whose work the strong foundations of the prosperity of the Republic have been laid, were out, to turn their backs upon the land in which, for the first time, most of them had eaten a full meal. Factories stood idle, the coasting schooners all were left unmanned, and had the coffee harvest not been gathered in, it would have rotted on the hills. The Consulate was unapproachable, and round it throngs of men struggled to enter, all demanding to get home. No rain could damp their spirits, and those who, after waiting hours, came out with tickets, had a look in their eyes as if they just had won the chief prize in the lottery.

Their friends surrounded them, and strained them to their hearts, the water from the umbrellas of the crowd trickling in rivulets upon the embracer and the embraced.

Mulatto policemen cleared the path for carriages to pass, and, as they came, the gap filled up again as if by magic, till the next carriage passed. Suddenly a tremor ran through the crowd, moving it with a shiver like the body of a snake. All the umbrellas which had seemed to move by their own will, covering the crowd and hiding it from view, were shut down suddenly. A mist-dimmed sun shone out, watery, but potent, and in an instant gaining strength, it dried the streets and made a hot steam rise up from the crowd. Slouched hats were raised up on one side, and pocket handkerchiefs wrapped up in paper were unfolded and knotted loosely round men's necks, giving them a look as of domestic bandits as they broke out into a patriotic song, which ceased with a long drawn-out "Viva," as the strains of an approaching band were heard and the footsteps of men marching through the streets in military array.

The coloured policemen rode their horses through the throng, and the streets, which till then had seemed impassable, were suddenly left clear. Jangling and crashing out the Garibaldian hymn, the band debouched into the square, dressed in a uniform half-German, half-Brazilian, with truncated pickel-hauben on their heads, in which were stuck a plume of gaudy feathers, apparently at the discretion of the wearer, making them look like something in a comic opera; a tall mulatto, playing on a drum with all the seriousness that only one of his colour and his race is able to impart to futile actions, swaggered along beside a jet-black negro playing on the flute. All the executants wore brass-handled swords of a kind never seen in Europe for a hundred years. Those who played the trombone and the ophicleide blew till their thick lips swelled, and seemed to cover up the mouthpieces. Still they blew on, the perspiration rolling down their cheeks, and a black boy or two brought up the rear, clashing the cymbals when it seemed good to them, quite irrespective of the rest. The noise was terrifying, and had it not been for the enthusiasm of the crowd, the motley band of coloured men, arrayed like popinjays, would have been ridiculous; but the dense ranks of hot, perspiring men, all in the flower of youth, and every one of whom had given up his work to cross the ocean at his country's call, had something in them that turned laughter into tears. The sons of peasants, who had left their homes, driven out from Apulean plains or Lombard rice-fields by the pinch of poverty, they now were going back to shed their blood for the land that had denied them bread in their own homes. Twice did the band march round the town whilst the procession was getting ready for a start, and each time that it passed before the Consulate, the Consul came out on the steps, bare-headed, and saluted with the flag.

Dressed in white drill, tall, grey-haired, and with the washed-out look of one who has spent many years in a hot country, the Consul evidently had been a soldier in his youth. He stood and watched the people critically, with the appraising look of the old officer, so like to that a grazier puts on at a cattle market as he surveys the beasts. "Good stuff," he muttered to himself, and then drawing his hand across his eyes, as if he felt where most of the "good stuff" would lie in a few months, he went back to the house.

A cheer at the far corner of the square showed that the ranks were formed. A policeman on a scraggy horse, with a great rusty sabre banging at its side, rode slowly down the streets to clear the way, and once again the parti-coloured band passed by, playing the Garibaldian hymn. Rank upon rank of men tramped after it, their friends running beside them for a last embrace, and women rushing up with children for a farewell kiss. Their merry faces set with determination, and their shoulders well thrown back, three or four hundred men briskly stepped along, trying to imitate the way the Bersaglieri march in Italy. A shout went up of "Long live the Reservists," as a contingent, drawn from every class of the Italian colony, passed along the street. Dock-labourers and pale-faced clerks in well-cut clothes and unsubstantial boots walked side by side. Men burnt the colour of a brick by working at the harvest rubbed shoulders with Sicilian emigrants landed a month or two ago, but who now were going off to fight, as poor as when they left their native land, and dressed in the same clothes. Neapolitans, gesticulating as they marched, and putting out their tongues at the Brazilian negroes, chattered and joked. To them life was a farce, no matter that the setting of the stage on which they moved was narrow, the fare hard, and the remuneration small. If things were adverse they still laughed on, and if the world was kind they jeered at it and at themselves, disarming both the slings of fortune and her more dangerous smiles with a grimace.

As they marched on, they now and then sketched out in pantomime the fate of any German who might fall into their hands, so vividly that shouts of laughter greeted them, which they acknowledged by putting out their tongues. Square-shouldered Liguresi succeeded them, with Lombards, Sicilians, and men of the strange negroid-looking race from the Basilicata, almost as dark-skinned as the Brazilian loungers at the corners of the streets.

They all passed on, laughing, and quite oblivious of what was in store for most of them — laughing and smoking, and, for the first time in their lives, the centre of a show. After them came another band; but this time of Italians, well-dressed, and playing on well-cared-for instruments. Behind them walked a little group of men, on whose appearance a hush fell on the crowd. Two of them wore uniforms, and between them, supported by silk handkerchiefs wrapped round his arms, there walked a man who was welcomed with a scream of joy. Frail, and with trembling footsteps, dressed in a faded old red shirt and knotted handkerchief, his parchment cheeks lit up with a faint flush as the Veteran of Marsala passed like a phantom of a glorious past. With him appeared to march the rest of his companions who set sail from Genoa to call into existence that Italy for which the young men all around him were prepared to sacrifice their lives.

To the excited crowd he typified all that their fathers had endured to drive the stranger from their land. The two Cairoli, Nino Bixio, and the heroic figure, wrapped in his *poncho*, who rides in glory on the Janiculum, visible from every point of Rome, seemed to march by the old man's side in the imagination of the crowd. Women rushed forward, carrying flowers, and strewed them on the scant grey locks of the old soldier, and children danced in front of him, like little Bacchanals. All hats were off as the old man was borne along, a phantom of himself, a symbol of a heroic past, and still a beacon, flickering but alight, to show the way towards the goal which in his youth had seemed impossible to reach.

Slowly the procession rolled along, surging against the houses as an incoming tide swirls up a river, till it reached the Consulate. It halted, and the old Garibaldian, drawing himself up, saluted the Italian colours. The Consul, bare-headed and with tears running down his cheeks, stood for a moment, the centre of all eyes, and then, advancing, tore the flag from off its staff, and, after kissing it, wrapped it round the frail shoulders of the veteran.

With the North-East Wind

A north-east haar had hung the city with a pall of grey. It gave an air of hardness to the stone-built houses, blending them with the stone-paved streets, till you could scarce see where the houses ended and the street began. A thin grey dust hung in the air. It coloured everything, and people's faces all looked pinched with the first touch of autumn cold. The wind, boisterous and gusty, whisked the soot-grimed city leaves about in the high suburb at the foot of a long range of hills, making one think it would be easy to have done with life on such an uncongenial day. Tramways were packed with people of the working class, all of them of the alert, quick-witted type only to be seen in the great city on the Clyde, in all our Empire, and comparable alone to the dwellers in Chicago for dry vivacity.

By the air they wore of chastened pleasure, all those who knew them saw that they were intent upon a funeral. To serious-minded men such as are they, for all their quickness, nothing is so soul-filling, for it is of the nature of a fact that no one can deny. A wedding has its possibilities, for it may lead to children, or divorce, but funerals are in another category. At them the Scottish people is at its best, for never more than then does the deep underlying tenderness peep through the hardness of the rind. On foot and in the tramways, but most especially on foot, converged long lines of men and women, though fewer women, for the national prejudice that in years gone by thought it not decent for a wife to follow to the grave her husband's coffin, still holds a little in the north. Yet there was something in the crowd that showed it was to attend no common funeral, that they were "stepping west." No one wore black, except a minister or two, who looked a little like the belated rook you sometimes see amongst a flock of seagulls, in that vast ocean of grey tweed.

They tramped along, the whistling north-east wind pinching their features, making their eyes run, and as they went, almost unconsciously they fell into procession, for beyond the tramway line, a country lane that had not quite put on the graces of a street, though straggling houses were dotted here and there along it, received the crowd and marshalled it, as it were mechanically, without volition of its own. Kept in between the walls, and blocked in front by the hearse and long procession of the mourning-coaches, the people slowly surged along. The greater portion of the crowd were townsmen, but there were miners washed and in their Sunday best. Their faces showed the blue marks of healed-up scars into which coal dust or gunpowder had become tattooed, scars gained in the battle of their lives down in the pits, remembrances of falls of rock or of occasions when the mine had "fired upon them."

Many had known Keir Hardie in his youth, had "wrocht wi' him outby," at Blantyre, at Hamilton, in Ayrshire, and all of them had heard him speak a hundred times. Even to those who had not heard him, his name was as a household word. Miners predominated, but men of every trade were there. Many were members of that black-coated proletariat, whose narrow circumstances and daily struggle for appearances make their life harder to them than is the life of any working man before he has had to dye his hair. Women tramped, too, for the dead leader had been a champion of their sex. They all respected him, loving him with that half-contemptuous gratitude that women often show to men who make the "woman question" the object of their lives.

After the Scottish fashion at a funeral, greetings were freely passed, and Reid, who hadna' seen his friend Mackinder since the time of the Mid-Lanark fight, greeted him with "Ye mind when first Keir Hardie was puttin' up for Parliament," and wrung his hand, hardened in the mine, with one as hardened, and instantly began to recall elections of the past.

"Ye mind yon Wishaw meeting?"

"Aye, ou aye; ye mean when a' they Irish wouldna' hear John Ferguson. Man, he almost grat after the meeting aboot it."

"Aye, but they gied Hardie himself a maist respectful hearing . . . aye, ou aye."

Others remembered him a boy, and others in his home at Cumnock, but all spoke of him with affection, holding him as something of their own, apart from other politicians, almost apart from men.

Old comrades who had been with him either at this election or that meeting, had helped or had intended to have helped at the crises of his life, fought their old battles over, as they tramped along, all shivering in the wind.

The procession reached a long dip in the road, and the head of it, full half a mile away, could be seen gathered round the hearse, outside the chapel of the crematorium, whose ominous tall chimney, through which the ashes, and perchance the souls of thousands have escaped towards some empyrean or another, towered up starkly. At last all had arrived, and the small open space was crowded, the hearse and carriages appearing stuck amongst the people, like raisins in a cake, so thick they pressed upon them. The chapel, differing from the ordinary chapel of the faiths as much as does a motor driver from a cabman, had an air as of modernity about it, which contrasted strangely with the ordinary looking crowd, the adjacent hills, the decent mourning coaches and the black-coated undertakers who bore the coffin up the steps. Outside, the wind whistled and swayed the soot-stained trees about; but inside the chapel the heat was stifling.

When all was duly done, and long exordiums passed upon the man who in his life had been the target for the abuse of press and pulpit, the coffin slid away to its appointed place. One thought one heard the roaring of the flames, and somehow missed the familiar lowering of the body . . . earth to earth . . . to which the centuries of use and wont have made us all familiar, though dust to dust in this case was the more appropriate.

In either case, the book is closed for ever, and the familiar face is seen no more.

So, standing just outside the chapel in the cold, waiting till all the usual greetings had been exchanged, I fell a-musing on the man whom I had known so well. I saw him as he was thirty years ago, outlined against a bing or standing in a quarry in some mining village, and heard his once familiar address of "Men." He used no other in those days, to the immense disgust of legislators and other worthy but unimaginative men whom he might chance to meet. About him seemed to stand a shadowy band, most of whom now are dead or lost to view, or have gone under in the fight.

John Ferguson was there, the old-time Irish leader, the friend of Davitt and of Butt. Tall and erect he stood, dressed in his long frock-coat, his roll of papers in one hand, and with the other stuck into his breast, with all the air of being the last Roman left alive. Tom Mann, with his black hair, his flashing eyes, and his tumultuous speech peppered with expletives. Beside him, Sandy Haddow, of Parkhead, massive and Doric in his speech, with a grey woollen comforter rolled round his neck, and hands like panels of a door. Champion, pale, slight, and interesting, still the artillery officer, in spite of Socialism. John Burns; and Small, the miners' agent, with his close brown beard and taste for literature. Smillie stood near, he of the seven elections, and then check-weigher at a pit, either at Cadzow or Larkhall. There, too, was silver-tongued Shaw Maxwell and Chisholm Robertson, looking out darkly on the world through tinted spectacles; with him Bruce Glasier, girt with a red sash and with an aureole of fair curly hair around his head, half poet and half revolutionary.

They were all young and ardent, and as I mused upon them and their fate, and upon those of them who have gone down into the oblivion that waits for those who live before their time, I shivered in the wind.

Had he, too, lived in vain, he whose scant ashes were no doubt by this time all collected in an urn, and did they really represent all that remained of him?

Standing amongst the band of shadowy comrades I had known, I saw him, simple and yet with something of the prophet in his air, and something of the seer. Effective and yet ineffectual, something there was about him that attracted little children to him, and I should think lost dogs. He made mistakes, but then those who make no mistakes seldom make anything. His life was one long battle, so it seemed to me that it was fitting that at his funeral the north-east wind should howl amongst the trees, tossing and twisting them as he himself was twisted and storm-tossed in his tempestuous passage through the world.

As the crowd moved away, and in the hearse and mourning-coaches the spavined horses limped slowly down the road, a gleam of sunshine, such as had shone too little in his life, lighted up everything.

The swaying trees and dark, grey houses of the ugly suburb of the town were all transfigured for a moment. The chapel door was closed, and from the chimney of the crematorium a faint blue smoke was issuing, which, by degrees, faded into the atmosphere, just as the soul, for all I know, may melt into the air.

When the last stragglers had gone, and bits of paper scurried uneasily along before the wind, the world seemed empty, with nothing friendly in it, but the shoulder of Ben Lomond peeping out shyly over the Kilpatrick Hills.

Elysium

The Triad came into my life as I walked underneath the arch by which the sentinels sit in Olympian state upon their rather long-legged chargers, receiving, as is their due, the silent homage of the passing nurserymaids. The soldier in the middle was straight back from the front. The mud of Flanders clung to his boots and clothes. It was "deeched" into his skin, and round his eyes had left a stain so dark, it looked as if he had been painted for a theatrical make-up. Upon his puttees it had dried so thickly that you could scarcely see the folds. He bore upon his back his knapsack, carried his rifle in his hand all done up in a case, which gave it, as it seemed to me, a look of hidden power, making it more terrible to think of than if it had shone brightly in the sun. His water-bottle and a pack of some kind hung at his sides, and as he walked kept time to every step. Under his elbow protruded the shaft of something, perhaps an entrenching tool of some sort, or perhaps some weapon strange to civilians accustomed to the use of stick or umbrella as their only arm. In himself he seemed a walking arsenal, carrying his weapons and his baggage on his back, after the fashion of a Roman legionary. The man himself, before the hand of discipline had fashioned him to number something or another, must have looked fresh and youthful, not very different from a thousand others that in time of peace one sees in early morning going to fulfil one of those avocations without which no State can possibly endure, and yet are practically unknown to those who live in the vast stucco hives either of Belgravia or Mayfair.

He may have been some five-and-twenty, and was a Londoner or a man from the home counties lying round about. His sunburnt face was yet not sunburnt as is the face of one accustomed to the weather all his life. Recent exposure had made his skin all feverish, and his blue eyes were fixed, as often are the eyes of sailors or frontiersmen after a long watch.

The girls on either side of him clung to his arm with pride, and with an air of evident affection, that left them quite unconscious of everything but having got the beloved object of their care safe home again. Upon the right side, holding fast to the warrior's arm, and now and then nestling close to his side, walked his sweetheart, a dark-haired girl, dressed in the miserable cheap finery our poorer countrywomen wear, instead of well-made plainer clothes that certainly would cost them less and set them off a hundredfold the more. Now and again she pointed out some feature of the town with pride, as when they climbed the steps under the column on which stands the statue of the Duke of York. The soldier, without looking, answered, "I know, Ethel, Dook of York," and hitched his pack a little higher on his back.

His sister, hanging on his left arm, never said anything, but walked along as in a dream; and he, knowing that she was there and understood, spoke little to her, except to murmur "Good old Gladys" now and then, and press her to his side. As they passed by the stunted monument, on which the crowd of little figures standing round a sledge commemorates the Franklin Expedition, in a chill Arctic way, the girl upon the right jerked her head towards it and said, "That's Sir John Franklin, George, he as laid down his life to find the North-West Passage, one of our 'eroes, you remember 'im." To which he answered, "Oh yes, Frenklin"; then looking over at the statue of Commander Scott, added, " 'ee done his bit too," with an appreciative air. They gazed upon the Athenæum and the other clubs with that air of detachment that all Englishmen affect when they behold a building or a monument — taking it, as it seems to me, as something they have no concern with, just as if it stood in Petrograd or in Johannesburg.

The homing triad passed into Pall Mall, oblivious of the world, so lost in happiness that they appeared the only living people in the street. The sister, who had said so little, when she saw her brother shift his knapsack, asked him to let her carry it. He smiled, and knowing what she felt, handed his rifle to her, remarking, " 'Old it the right side up, old girl, or else it will go off."

And so they took their way through the enchanted streets, not feeling either the penetrating wind or the fine rain, for these are but material things, and they were wrapped apart from the whole world. Officers of all ranks passed by them, some young and smart, and others paunchy and middle-aged; but they were non-existent to the soldier, who saw nothing but the girls. Most of the officers looked straight before them, with an indulgent air; but two young men with red bands round their caps were scandalised, and muttering something as to the discipline of the New Army, drew themselves up stiffly and strutted off, like angry game-cocks when they eye each other in the ring.

The triad passed the Rag, and on the steps stood two old colonels, their faces burnt the colour of a brick, and their moustaches stiff as the bristles of a brush. They eyed the passing little show, and looking at each other broke into a smile. They knew that they would never walk oblivious of mankind, linked to a woman's arm; but perhaps memories of what they had done stirred in their hearts, for both of them at the same moment ejaculated a modulated "Ha!" of sympathy. All this time I had walked behind the three young people, unconsciously, as I was going the same road, catching half phrases now and then, which I was half ashamed to hear.

They reached the corner of St. James's Square, and our paths separated. Mine took me to the London Library to change a book, and theirs led straight to Elysium, for five long days.

Brought Forward

330

Heredity

Right along the frontier between Uruguay and Rio Grande, the southern province of Brazil, the Spanish and the Portuguese sit face to face, as they have sat for ages, looking at, but never understanding, one another, both in the Old and the New World.

In Tuy and Valenza, Monzon and Salvatierra, at *Poncho* Verde and Don Pedrito, Rivera and Santa Ana do Libramento, and far away above Cruz Alta, where the two clumps of wood that mark old camps of the two people are called O Matto Castelhano and O Matto Portuguez, the rivalry of centuries is either actual or at least commemorated on the map.

The border-line that once made different peoples of the dwellers at Floriston and Gretna, still prevails in the little castellated towns, which snarl at one another across the Minho, just as they did of old.

"Those people in Valenza would steal the sacrament," says the street urchin playing on the steps of the half fortalice, half church that is the cathedral of Tuy on the Spanish side.

His fellow in Valenza spits towards Tuy and remarks, "From Spain come neither good marriages nor the wholesome winds."

So on to Salvatierra and Monzon, or any other of the villages or towns upon the river, and in the current of the native speech there still remains some saying of the kind, with its sharp edges still unworn after six centuries of use. Great is the power of artificial barriers to restrain mankind. No proverb ever penned is more profound than that which sets out, "Fear guards the vineyard, not the fence around it."

So Portuguese and Spaniards in their peninsula have fought and hated and fought and ridiculed each other after the fashion of children that have quarrelled over a broken toy. Blood and an almost common speech, for both speak one Romance when all is said, have both been impotent against the custom-house, the flag, the foolish dynasty, for few countries in the world have had more foolish kings than Spain and Portugal.

That this should be so in the Old World is natural enough, for the dead hand still rules, and custom and tradition have more strength than race and creed; but that the hatred should have been transplanted to America, and still continue, is a proof that folly never dies.

In the old towns on either side of the Minho the exterior life of the two peoples is the same.

In the stone-built, arcaded plazas women still gather round the fountain and fill their iron-hooped water-barrels through long tin pipes, shaped like the tin valences used in wine-stores. Donkeys stand at the doors, carrying charcoal in esparto baskets, whether in Portugal or Spain, and goats parade the streets driven by goatherds, wearing shapeless, thickly-napped felt hats and leather overalls.

The water-carrier in both countries calls out "agua-a-a," making it sound like Arabic, and long trains of mules bring brushwood for the baker's furnace (even as in Morocco), or great nets of close-chopped straw for horses' fodder.

At eventide the girls walk on the plaza, their mothers, aunts, or servants following them as closely as their shadows on a sunny afternoon. In quiet streets lovers on both sides of the river talk from a first-floor balcony to the street, or whisper through the window-bars on the ground floor. The little shops under the low arches of the arcaded streets have yellow flannel drawers for men and petticoats of many colours hanging close outside their doors, on whose steps sleep yellow dogs.

The jangling bells in the decaying lichen-grown old towers of the churches jangle and clang in the same key, and as appears without a touch of *odium theologicum*. The full bass voices boom from the choirs, in which the self-same organs in their walnut cases have the same rows of golden trumpets sticking out into the aisle.

One faith, one speech, one mode of daily life, the same sharp "green" wine, the same bread made of maize and rye, and the same heaps of red tomatoes and green peppers glistening in the sun in the same market-places, and yet a rivalry and a difference as far apart as east from west still separates them.

In both their countries the axles of the bullock-carts, with solid wheels and wattled hurdle sides, like those upon a Roman coin, still creak and whine to keep away the wolves.

In the soft landscape the maize fields wave in the rich hollows on both sides of the Minho.

The pine woods mantle the rocky hills that overhang the deep-sea lochs that burrow in both countries deep into the entrails of the land.

The women, with their many-coloured petticoats and handkerchiefs, chaffer at the same fairs to which their husbands ride their ponies in their straw cloaks.

At "romerias" the peasantry dance to the bagpipe and the drum the self-same dances, and both climb the self-same steep grey steps through the dark lanes, all overhung with gorse and broom, up to the Calvaries, where the three crosses take on the self-same growth of lichen and of moss. Yet the "boyero" who walks before the placid oxen, with their cream-coloured flanks and liquid eyes of onyx, feels he is different, right down to the last molecule of his being, from the man upon the other side.

So was it once, and perhaps is to-day, with those who dwell in Liddes or Bewcastle dales. Spaniard and Portuguese, as Scot and Englishman in older times, can never see one matter from the same point of view. The Portuguese will say that the Castilian is a rogue, and the Castilian returns the compliment. Neither have any reason to support their view, for who wants reason to support that which he feels is true.

It may be that the Spaniard is a little rougher and the Portuguese more cunning; but if it is the case or not, the antipathy remains, and has been taken to America.

From the Laguna de Merin to the Cuareim, that is to say, along a frontier of two hundred leagues, the self-same feeling rules upon both sides of the line. There, as in Portugal and Spain, although the country, whether in Uruguay or in Brazil, is little different, yet it has suffered something indefinable by being occupied by members of the two races so near and yet so different from one another.

Great rolling seas of waving grass, broken by a few stony hills, are the chief features of the landscape of the frontiers in both republics. *Estancia* houses, dazzlingly white, buried in peach and fig groves, dot the plains, looking like islands in the sea of grass. Great herds of cattle roam about, and men on horseback, galloping like clockwork, sail across the plains like ships upon a sea. Along the river-banks grow strips of thorny trees, and as the frontier line trends northward palm-trees appear, and monkeys chatter in the woods. Herds of wild asses, shyer than antelopes, gaze at the passing horsemen, scour off when he approaches, and are lost into the haze. Stretches of purple borage, known as La Flor Morada, carpet the ground in spring and early summer, giving place later on to red verbena; and on the edges of the streams the tufts of the tall Pampa grass recall the feathers on a Pampa Indian's spear.

Bands of grave ostriches feed quietly upon the tops of hills, and stride away when frightened, down the wind, with wings stretched out to catch the breeze.

Clothes are identical, or almost so; the *poncho* and the loose trousers stuffed into high patent-leather boots, the hat kept in its place by a black ribbon with two tassels, are to be seen on both sides of the frontier. Only in Brazil a sword stuck through the girth replaces the long knife of Uruguay. Perhaps in that one item all the differences between the races manifests itself *[sic = manifest themselves]*, for the sword is, as it were, a symbol, for no one ever saw one drawn or used in any way but as an ornament. It is, in fact, but a survival of old customs, which are cherished both by the Portuguese and the Brazilians as the apple of the eye.

The vast extent of the territory of Brazil, its inaccessibility, and the enormous distances to be travelled from the interior to the coast, and the sense of remoteness from the outer world, have kept alive a type of man not to be found in any other country where the Christian faith prevails. Risings of fanatics still are frequent; one is going on to-day in Paraná, and that of the celebrated Antonio Concelheiro, *[sic=Conselheiro]* twenty years ago, shook the whole country to its core. Slavery existed in the memory of people still alive. Women in the remoter towns are still secluded almost as with the Moors. The men still retain something of the Middle Ages in their love of show. All in the province of Rio Grande are great horsemen, and all use silver trappings on a black horse, and all have horses bitted so as to turn round in the air, just as a hawk turns on the wing.

The sons of men who have been slaves abound in all the little frontier towns, and old grey-headed negroes, who have been slaves themselves, still hang about the great estates. Upon the other side, in Uruguay, the negro question was solved once and for all in the Independence Wars, for then the negroes were all formed into battalions by themselves and set in the forefront of the battle, to die for liberty in a country where they all were slaves the month before. War turned them into heroes, and sent them out to die.

When once their independence was assured, the Uruguayans fell into line like magic with the modern trend of thought. Liberty to them meant absolute equality, for throughout the land no snob is found to leave a slug's trail on the face of man by his subserviency.

Women were held free, that is, as free as it is possible for them to be in any Latin-peopled land. Across the line, even to-day, a man may stay a week in a Brazilian country house and never see a woman but a mulata girl or an old negro crone. Still he feels he is watched by eyes he never sees, listens to voices singing or laughing, and a sense of mystery prevails.

Spaniards and Portuguese in the New World have blended just as little as they have done at home. Upon the frontier all the wilder spirits of Brazil and Uruguay have congregated. There they pursue the life, but little altered, that their fathers led full fifty years ago. All carry arms, and use them on small provocation, for if an accident takes place the frontier shields the slayer, for to pursue him usually entails a national quarrel, and so the game goes on.

So Jango Chaves, feeling inclined for sport, or, as he might have said, to "brincar un bocadinho," saddled up his horse. He mounted, and, as his friends were looking on, ran it across the plaza of the town, and, turning like a seagull in its flight, came back to where his friends were standing, and stopped it with a jerk.

His silver harness jingled, and his heavy spurs, hanging loosely on his high-heeled boots, clanked like fetters, as his active little horse bounded into the air and threw the sand up in a shower.

The rider, sitting him like a statue, with the far-off look horsemen of every land assume when riding a good horse and when they know they are observed, slackened his hand and let him fall into a little measured trot, arching his neck and playing with the bit, under which hung a silver eagle on a hinge. Waving his hand towards his friends, Jango rode slowly through the town. He passed through sandy streets of flat-roofed, whitewashed houses, before whose doors stood hobbled horses nodding in the sun.

He rode past orange gardens, surrounded by brown walls of sun-baked bricks with the straw sticking in them, just as it had dried. In the waste the castor-oil bushes formed little jungles, out of which peered cats, exactly as a tiger peers out of a real jungle in the woods.

The sun poured down, and was reverberated back from the white houses, and on the great gaunt building, where the captain-general lived, floated the green-and-yellow flag of the republic, looking like a bandana handkerchief. He passed the negro rancheria, without which no such town as Santa Anna do Libramento is complete, and might have marked, had he not been too much used to see them, the naked negro children playing in the sand. Possibly, if he marked them, he referred to them as "cachorrinhos pretos," for the old leaven of the days of slavery is strongly rooted in Brazil. So he rode on, a slight and graceful figure, bending to each movement of his horse, his mobile, olive-coloured features looking like a bronze masque in the fierce downpour of the sun.

As he rode on, his whip, held by a thong and dangling from his fingers, swung against his horse's flanks, keeping time rhythmically to its pace. He crossed the rivulet that flows between the towns and came out on the little open plain that separates them. From habit, or because he felt himself amongst unfriendly or uncomprehended people, he touched his knife and his revolvers, hidden beneath his summer *poncho*, with his right hand, and with his bridle arm held high, ready for all eventualities, passed into just such another sandy street as he had left behind.

Save that all looked a little newer, and that the stores were better supplied with goods, and that there were no negro huts, the difference was slight between the towns. True that the green-and-yellow flag had given place to the barred blue-and-white of Uruguay. An armed policeman stood at the corners of the main thoroughfares, and water-carts went up and down at intervals. The garden in the plaza had a well-tended flower-garden.

A band was playing in the middle of it, and Jango could not fail to notice that Rivera was more prosperous than was his native town.

Whether that influenced him, or whether it was the glass of caña which he had at the first *pulperia*, is a moot point, or whether the old antipathy between the races brought by his ancestors from the peninsula; anyhow, he left his horse untied, and with the reins thrown down before it as he got off to have his drink. When he came out, a policeman called to him to hobble it or tie it up.

Without a word he gathered up his reins, sprang at a bound upon his horse, and, drawing his mother-of-pearl-handled pistol, fired at the policeman almost as he sprang. The shot threw up a shower of sand just in the policeman's face, and probably saved Jango's life. Drawing his pistol, the man fired back, but Jango, with a shout and pressure of his heels, was off like lightning, firing as he rode, and zigzagging across the street. The policeman's shot went wide, and Jango, turning in the saddle, fired again and missed.

By this time men with pistols in their hands stood at the doors of all the houses; but the Brazilian passed so rapidly, throwing himself alternately now on the near side, now on the off side of his horse, hanging by one foot across the croup and holding with the other to the mane, that he presented no mark for them to hit.

As he passed by the "jefatura" where the alcalde and his friends were sitting smoking just before the door, he fired with such good aim that a large piece of plaster just above their heads fell, covering them with dust.

Drawing his second pistol and still firing as he went, he dashed out of the town, in spite of shots from every side, his horse bounding like lightning as his great silver spurs ploughed deep into its sides. When he had crossed the little bit of neutral ground, and just as a patrol of cavalry appeared, ready to gallop after him, a band of men from his own town came out to meet him.

He stopped, and shouting out defiance to the Uruguayans, drew up his horse, and lit a cigarette. Then, safe beyond the frontier, trotted on gently to meet his friends, his horse shaking white foam from off its bit, and little rivulets of blood dripping down from its sides into the sand.

Brought Forward

El Tango Argentino

Motor-cars swept up to the covered passage of the front door of the hotel, one of those international caravansaries that pass their clients through a sort of vulgarising process that blots out every type. It makes the Argentine, the French, the Englishman, and the American all alike before the power of wealth.

The cars surged up as silently as snow falls from a fir-tree in a thaw, and with the same soft swishing noise. Tall, liveried porters opened the doors (although, of course, each car was duly furnished with a footman) so nobly that any one of them would have graced any situation in the State.

The ladies stepped down delicately, showing a fleeting vision of a leg in a transparent stocking, just for an instant, through the slashing of their skirts. They knew that every man, their footman, driver, the giant watchers at the gate, and all who at the time were going into the hotel, saw and were moved by what they saw just for a moment; but the fact did not trouble them at all. It rather pleased them, for the most virtuous feel a pleasurable emotion when they know that they excite. So it will be for ever, for thus and not by votes alone they show that they are to the full men's equals, let the law do its worst.

Inside the hotel, heated by steam, and with an atmosphere of scent and flesh that went straight to the head just as the fumes of whisky set a drinker's nerves agog, were seated all the finest flowers of the cosmopolitan society of the French capital.

Lesbos had sent its legions, and women looked at one another appreciatively, scanning each item of their neighbours' clothes, and with their colour heightening when by chance their eyes met those of another priestess of their sect.

Rich rastaquaoures, their hats too shiny, and their boots too tight, their coats fitting too closely, their sticks mounted with great gold knobs, walked about or sat at little tables, all talking strange varieties of French.

Americans, the men apparently all run out of the same mould, the women apt as monkeys to imitate all that they saw in dress, in fashion and in style, and more adaptable than any other women in the world from lack of all traditions, conversed in their high nasal tones. Spanish-Americans from every one of the Republics were well represented, all talking about money: of how Doña Fulana Perez had given fifteen hundred francs for her new hat, or Don Fulano had just scored a million on the Bourse.

Jews and more Jews, and Jewesses and still more Jewesses, were there, some of them married to Christians and turned Catholic, but betrayed by their Semitic type, although they talked of Lourdes and of the Holy Father with the best.

After the "five-o'clock," turned to a heavy meal of toast and buns, of Hugel loaf, of sandwiches, and of hot cake, the scented throng, restored by the refection after the day's hard work of shopping, of driving here and there like souls in purgatory to call on people that they detested, and other labours of a like nature, slowly adjourned to a great hall in which a band was playing. As they walked through the passages, men pressed close up to women and murmured in their ears, telling them anecdotes that made them flush and giggle as they protested in an unprotesting style. Those were the days of the first advent of the Tango Argentino, the dance that since has circled the whole world, as it were, in a movement of the hips. Ladies pronounced it charming as they half closed their eyes and let a little shiver run across their lips. Men said it was the only dance that was worth dancing. It was so Spanish, so unconventional, and combined all the æsthetic movements of the figures on an Etruscan vase with the strange grace of the Hungarian gipsies . . . it was so, as one may say, so . . . as you may say . . . you know.

When all were seated, the band, Hungarians, of course, — oh, those dear gipsies! — struck out into a rhythm, half rag-time, half habanera, canaille, but sensuous, and hands involuntarily, even the most aristocratic hands — of ladies whose immediate progenitors had been pork-packers in Chicago, or gambusinos who had struck it rich in Zacatecas, — tapped delicately, but usually a little out of time, upon the backs of chairs.

A tall young man, looking as if he had got a holiday from a tailor's fashion plate, his hair sleek, black, and stuck down to his head with a cosmetic, his trousers so immaculately creased they seemed cut out of cardboard, led out a girl dressed in a skirt so tight that she could not have moved in it had it not been cut open to the knee.

Standing so close that one well-creased trouser leg disappeared in the tight skirt, he clasped her round the waist, holding her hand almost before her face. They twirled about, now bending low, now throwing out a leg, and then again revolving, all with a movement of the hips that seemed to blend the well-creased trouser and the half-open skirt into one inharmonious whole. The music grew more furious and the steps multiplied, till with a bound the girl threw herself for an instant into the male dancer's arms, who put her back again upon the ground with as much care as if she had been a new-laid egg, and the pair bowed and disappeared.

Discreet applause broke forth, and exclamations such as "wonderful," "what grace," "Vivent les Espagnoles," for the discriminating audience took no heed of independence days, of mere political changes and the like, and seemed to think that Buenos Aires was a part of Spain, never having heard of San Martin, Bolivar, Paez, and their fellow-liberators.

Paris, London, and New York were to that fashionable crowd the world, and anything outside — except, of course, the Hungarian gipsies and the Tango dancers — barbarous and beyond the pale.

After the Tango came "La Maxixe Brésilienne," rather more languorous and more befitting to the dwellers in the tropics than was its cousin from the plains. Again the discreet applause broke out, the audience murmuring "charming," that universal adjective that gives an air of being in a perpetual pastrycook's when ladies signify delight. Smiles and sly glances at their friends showed that the dancers' efforts at indecency had been appreciated.

Slowly the hall and tea-rooms of the great hotel emptied themselves, and in the corridors and passages the smell of scent still lingered, just as stale incense lingers in a church.

Motor-cars took away the ladies and their friends, and drivers, who had shivered in the cold whilst the crowd inside sweated in the central heating, exchanged the time of day with the liveried doorkeepers, one of them asking anxiously, "Dis, Anatole, as-tu vu mes vaches?"

With the soft closing of a well-hung door the last car took its perfumed freight away, leaving upon the steps a group of men, who remained talking over, or, as they would say, undressing, all the ladies who had gone.

"Argentine Tango, eh?" I thought, after my friends had left me all alone. Well, well, it has changed devilishly upon its passage overseas, even discounting the difference of the setting of the place where first I saw it danced so many years ago. So, sauntering down, I took a chair far back upon the terrace of the Café de la Paix, so that the sellers of *La Patrie*, and the men who have some strange new toy, or views of Paris in a long album like a broken concertina, should not tread upon my toes.

Over a Porto Blanc and a Brazilian cigarette, lulled by the noise of Paris and the raucous cries of the street-vendors, I fell into a doze.

Gradually the smell of petrol and of horse-dung, the two most potent perfumes in our modern life, seemed to be blown away. Dyed heads and faces scraped till they looked blue as a baboon's; young men who looked like girls, with painted faces and with mincing airs; the raddled women, ragged men, and hags huddled in knitted shawls, lame horses, and taxi-cab drivers sitting nodding on their boxes — all faded into space, and from the nothing that is the past arose another scene.

I saw myself with Witham and his brother, whose name I have forgotten, Eduardo Peña, Congreve, and Eustaquio Medina, on a small rancho in an elbow of the great River Yi. The rancho stood upon a little hill. A quarter of a mile or so away the dense and thorny monté of hard-wood trees that fringed the river seemed to roll up towards it like a sea. The house was built of yellow pine sent from the United States. The roof was shingled, and the rancho stood planked down upon the plain, looking exactly like a box. Some fifty yards away stood a thatched hut that served as kitchen, and on its floor the cattle herders used to sleep upon their horse-gear with their feet towards the fire.

The corrals for horses and for sheep were just a little farther off, and underneath a shed a horse stood saddled day in, day out, and perhaps does so yet, if the old rancho still resists the winds.

Four or five horses, saddled and bridled, stood tied to a great post, for we were just about to mount to ride a league or two to a Baile, at the house of Frutos Barragán. Just after sunset we set out, as the sweet scent that the grasses of the plains send forth after a long day of heat perfumed the evening air.

The night was clear and starry, and above our heads was hung the Southern Cross. So bright the stars shone out that one could see almost a mile away; but yet all the perspective of the plains and woods was altered. Hillocks were sometimes undistinguishable, at other times loomed up like houses. Woods seemed to sway and heave, and by the sides of streams bunches of Pampa grass stood stark as sentinels, their feathery tufts looking like plumes upon an Indian's lance.

The horses shook their bridles with a clear, ringing sound as they stepped double, and their riders, swaying lightly in their seats, seemed to form part and parcel of the animals they rode.

Now and then little owls flew noiselessly beside us, circling above our heads, and then dropped noiselessly upon a bush. Eustaquio Medina, who knew the district as a sailor knows the seas where he was born, rode in the front of us. As his horse shied at a shadow on the grass or at the bones of some dead animal, he swung his whip round ceaselessly, until the moonlight playing on the silver-mounted stock seemed to transform it to an aureole that flickered about his head. Now and then somebody dismounted to tighten up his girth, his horse twisting and turning round uneasily the while, and, when he raised his foot towards the stirrup, starting off with a bound.

Time seemed to disappear and space be swallowed in the intoxicating gallop, so that when Eustaquio Medina paused for an instant to strike the crossing of a stream, we felt annoyed with him, although no hound that follows a hot scent could have gone truer on his line.

Dogs barking close at hand warned us our ride was almost over, and as we galloped up a rise Eustaquio Medina pulled up and turned to us.

"There is the house," he said, "just at the bottom of the hollow, only five squares away," and as we saw the flicker of the lights, he struck his palm upon his mouth after the Indian fashion, and raised a piercing cry. Easing his hand, he drove his spurs into his horse, who started with a bound into full speed, and as he galloped down the hill we followed him, all yelling furiously.

Just at the hitching-post we drew up with a jerk, our horses snorting as they edged off sideways from the black shadow that it cast upon the ground. Horses stood about everywhere, some tied and others hobbled, and from the house there came the strains of an accordion and the tinkling of guitars.

Asking permission to dismount, we hailed the owner of the house, a tall, old Gaucho, Frutos Barragán, as he stood waiting by the door, holding a *maté* in his hand. He bade us welcome, telling us to tie our horses up, not too far out of sight, for, as he said, "It is not good to give facilities to rogues, if they should chance to be about."

In the low, straw-thatched rancho, with its eaves blackened by the smoke, three or four iron bowls, filled with mare's fat, and with a cotton wick that needed constant trimming, stuck upon iron cattle-brands, were burning fitfully.

They cast deep shadows in the corners of the room, and when they flickered up occasionally the light fell on the dark and sun-tanned faces of the tall, wiry Gauchos and the light cotton dresses of the women as they sat with their chairs tilted up against the wall. Some thick-set Basques, an Englishman or two in riding breeches, and one or two Italians made up the company. The floor was earth, stamped hard till it shone like cement, and as the Gauchos walked upon it, their heavy spurs clinked with a noise like fetters as they trailed them on the ground.

An old, blind Paraguayan played on the guitar, and a huge negro accompanied him on an accordion. Their united efforts produced a music which certainly was vigorous enough, and now and then, one or the other of them broke into a song, high-pitched and melancholy, which, if you listened to it long enough, forced you to try to imitate its wailing melody and its strange intervals.

Fumes of tobacco and rum hung in the air, and of a strong and heady wine from Catalonia, much favoured by the ladies, which they drank from a tumbler, passing it to one another, after the fashion of a grace-cup at a City dinner, with great gravity. At last the singing ceased, and the orchestra struck up a Tango, slow, marked, and rhythmical.

Men rose, and, taking off their spurs, walked gravely to the corner of the room where sat the women huddled together as if they sought protection from each other, and with a compliment led them out upon the floor. The flowing *poncho* and the loose chiripá, which served as trousers, swung about just as the tartans of a Highlander swing as he dances, giving an air of ease to all the movements of the Gauchos as they revolved, their partners' heads peeping above their shoulders, and their hips moving to and fro.

At times they parted, and set to one another gravely, and then the man, advancing, clasped his partner round the waist and seemed to push her backwards, with her eyes half-closed and an expression of beatitude. Gravity was the keynote of the scene, and though the movements of the dance were as significant as it was possible for the dancers to achieve, the effect was graceful, and the soft, gliding motion and the waving of the parti-coloured clothes, wild and original, in the dim, flickering light.

Rum flowed during the intervals. The dancers wiped the perspiration from their brows, the men with the silk handkerchiefs they wore about their necks, the women with their sleeves. Tangos, cielitos, and pericones succeeded one another, and still the atmosphere grew thicker, and the lights seemed to flicker through a haze, as the dust rose from the mud floor. Still the old Paraguayan and the negro kept on playing with the sweat running down their faces, smoking and drinking rum in their brief intervals of rest, and when the music ceased for a moment, the wild neighing of a horse tied in the moonlight to a post, sounded as if he called his master to come out and gallop home again.

The night wore on, and still the negro and the Paraguayan stuck at their instruments. Skirts swung and *poncho*s waved, whilst *maté* circulated amongst the older men as they stood grouped about the door.

Then came a lull, and as men whispered in their partners' ears, telling them, after the fashion of the Gauchos, that they were lovely, their hair like jet, their eyes bright as "las tres Marias," and all the compliments which in their case were stereotyped and handed down for generations, loud voices rose, and in an instant two Gauchos bounded out upon the floor.

Long silver-handled knives were in their hands, their *poncho*s wrapped round their left arms served them as bucklers, and as they crouched, like cats about to spring, they poured out blasphemies.

"Stop this!" cried Frutos Barragán; but even as he spoke, a knife-thrust planted in the stomach stretched one upon the floor. Blood gushed out from his mouth, his belly fell like a pricked bladder, and a dark stream of blood trickled upon the ground as he lay writhing in his death agony.

The iron bowls were overturned, and in the dark girls screamed and the men crowded to the door. When they emerged into the moonlight, leaving the dying man upon the floor, the murderer was gone; and as they looked at one another there came a voice shouting out, "Adios, Barragán! Thus does Vicente Castro pay his debts when a man tries to steal his girl," and the faint footfalls of an unshod horse galloping far out upon the plain.

I started, and the waiter standing by my side said, "Eighty centimes"; and down the boulevard echoed the harsh cry, "*La Patrie, achetez La Patrie*," and the rolling of the cabs.

Brought Forward

In a Backwater

"This 'ere war, now," said the farmer, in the slow voice that tells of life passed amongst comfortable surroundings into which haste has never once intruded, "is a 'orrid business."

He leaned upon a half-opened gate, keeping it swaying to and fro a little with his foot. His waistcoat was unbuttoned, showing his greasy braces and his checked blue shirt. His box-cloth gaiters, falling low down upon his high-lows, left a gap between them and his baggy riding-breeches, just below the knee. His flat-topped bowler hat was pushed back over the fringe of straggling grey hair upon his neck. His face was burned a brick-dust colour with the August sun, and now and then he mopped his forehead with a red handkerchief.

His little holding, an oasis in the waste of modern scientific farming, was run in the old-fashioned way, often to be seen in the home counties, as if old methods linger longest where they are least expected, just as a hunted fox sometimes takes refuge in a rectory.

His ideas seemed to have become unsettled with constant reading of newspapers filled with accounts of horrors, and his speech, not fluent at the best of times, was slower and more halting than his wont.

He told how he had just lost his wife, and felt more than a little put about to get his dairy work done properly without her help.

"When a man's lost his wife it leaves him, somehow, as if he were like a 'orse hitched on one side of the wagon-pole, a-pullin' by hisself. Now this 'ere war, comin' as it does right on the top of my 'ome loss, sets me a-thinkin', especially when I'm alone in the 'ouse of night."

The park-like English landscape, with its hedgerow trees and its lush fields, that does not look like as if it really were the country, but seems a series of pleasure-grounds cut off into convenient squares, was at its time of greatest beauty and its greatest artificiality. Cows swollen with grass till they looked like balloons lay in the fields and chewed the cud. Geese cackled as they strayed upon the common, just as they appear to cackle in a thousand water-colours. The hum of bees was in the limes. Dragon-flies hawked swiftly over the oily waters of the two slow-flowing rivers that made the farm almost an island in a suburban Mesopotamia, scarce twenty miles away from Charing Cross. An air of peace and of contentment, of long well-being and security, was evident in everything. Trees flourished, though stag-headed, under which the Roundhead troopers may have camped, or at the least, veterans from Marlborough's wars might have sat underneath their shade, and smoked as they retold their fights.

A one-armed signboard, weathered, and with the lettering almost illegible, pointed out the bridle-path to Ditchley, now little used, except by lovers on a Sunday afternoon, but where the feet of horses for generations in the past had trampled it, still showing clearly as it wound through the fields.

In the standing corn the horses yoked to the reaping machine stood resting, now and again shaking the tassels on their little netted ear-covers. They, too, came of a breed long used to peace and plenty, good food and treatment, and short hours of work. The kindly landscape and the settled life of centuries had formed the kind of man of which the farmer was a prototype, — slow-footed and slow-tongued, and with his mind as bowed as were his shoulders with hard work, by the continual pressure of the hierarchy of wealth and station, that had left him as much adscript to them as any of his ancestors had been bound to their glebes. He held the *Daily Mail*, his gospel and his *vade mecum*, crumpled in his hand as if he feared to open it again to read more details of the War. A simple soul, most likely just as oppressive to his labourers as his superiors had always showed *[sic]* themselves to him, he could not bear to read of violence, as all the tyranny that he had bent under had been imposed so subtly that he could never see more than the shadow of the hand that had oppressed him.

It pained him, above all things, to read about the wounded and dead horses lying in the corn, especially as he had " 'eard the 'arvest over there in Belgium was going to be good." The whirr of the machines reaping the wheatfield sounded like the hum of some gigantic insect, and as the binder ranged the sheaves in rows it seemed as if the golden age had come upon the earth again, bringing with it peace and plenty, with perhaps slightly stouter nymphs than those who once followed the sickle-men in Arcady.

A man sat fishing in a punt just where the river broadened into a backwater edged with willow trees. At times he threw out ground-bait, and at times raised a stone bottle to his lips, keeping one eye the while watchfully turned upon his float. School children strayed along the road, as rosy and as flaxen-haired as those that Gregory the Great thought fitting to be angels, though they had never been baptized.

Now and again the farmer stepped into his field to watch the harvesting, and cast an eye of pride and of affection on his horses, and then, coming back to the gate, he drew the paper from his pocket and read its columns, much in the way an Arab reads a letter, murmuring the words aloud until their meaning penetrated to his brain.

Chewing a straw, and slowly rubbing off the grains of an ear of wheat into his hand, he gazed over his fields as if he feared to see in them some of the horrors that he read. Again he muttered, with a puzzled air, "'Orrible! 'undreds of men and 'orses lying in the corn. It seems a sad thing to believe, doesn't it now?" he said; and as he spoke soldiers on motor-cycles hurtled down the road, leaving a trail of dust that perhaps looked like smoke to him after his reading in the *Daily Mail*.

"They tell me," he remarked, after a vigorous application of his blue handkerchief to his streaming face, "that these 'ere motor-cycles 'ave a gun fastened to them, over there in Belgium, where they are a-goin' on at it in such a way. The paper says, 'Ranks upon ranks of 'em is just mowed down like wheat.' . . . 'Orrid, I call it, if it's true, for now and then I think those chaps only puts that kind of thing into their papers to 'ave a sale for them." He looked about him as if, like Pilate, he was looking for an elusive truth not to be found on earth, and then walked down the road till he came to the backwater where the man was fishing in his punt. They looked at one another over a yard or two of muddy water, and asked for news about the war, in the way that people do from others who they must know are quite as ignorant as they are themselves. The fisherman " 'ad given up readin' the war noos; it's all a pack of lies," and pointing to the water, said in a cautious voice, "Some people says they 'ears. I ain't so sure about it; but, anyhow, it's always best to be on the safe side." Then he addressed himself once more to the business of the day, and in the contemplation of his float no doubt became as much absorbed into the universal principle of nature as is an Indian sitting continually with his eyes turned on his diaphragm.

Men passing down the road, each with a paper in his hand, looked up and threw the farmer scraps of news, uncensored and spiced high with details which had never happened, so that in after years their children will most likely treasure as facts, which they have received from long-lost parents, the wildest fairy tales.

The slanting sun and lengthening shadows brought the farmer no relief of mind; and still men, coming home from work on shaky bicycles, plied him with horrors as they passed by the gate, their knee-joints stiff with the labours of the day, seeming in want of oil. A thin, white mist began to creep along the backwater. Unmooring his punt, the fisherman came unwillingly to shore, and as he threw the fragments of his lunch into the water and gathered up his tackle, looked back upon the scene of his unfruitful labours with an air as of a man who has been overthrown by circumstances, but has preserved his honour and his faith inviolate.

Slinging his basket on his back, he trudged off homewards, and instantly the fish began to rise. A line of cows was driven towards the farm, their udders all so full of milk that they swayed to and fro, just as a man sways wrapped in a Spanish cloak, and as majestically. The dragon-flies had gone, and in their place ghost-moths flew here and there across the meadows, and from the fields sounded the corncrake's harsh, metallic note.

The whirring of the reaper ceased, and when the horses were unyoked the driver led them slowly from the field. As they passed by the farmer he looked lovingly towards them, and muttered to himself, "Dead 'orses and dead soldiers lying by 'undreds in the standing corn. . . . I wonder 'ow the folks out there in Belgium will 'ave a relish for their bread next year. This 'ere war's a 'orrid business, coming as it does, too, on the top of my own loss . . . dead 'orses in the corn. . . ."

He took the straw out of his mouth, and walking up to one of his own sleek-sided cart-horses, patted it lovingly, as if he wanted to make sure that it was still alive.

Hippomorphous

On the 12th of October 1524, Cortes left Mexico on his celebrated expedition to Honduras. The start from Mexico was made to the sound of music, and all the population of the newly conquered city turned out to escort him for a few miles upon his way.

The cavalcade must have been a curious spectacle enough. Cortes himself and his chief officers rode partly dressed in armour, after the fashion of the time. Then came the Spanish soldiers, mostly on foot and armed with lances, swords, and bucklers, though there was a troop of crossbowmen and harquebusiers to whom "after God" we owed the Conquest, as an old chronicler has said when speaking of the Conquest of Peru. In Mexico they did good service also, although it was the horsemen that in that conquest played the greater part. Then came a force of three thousand friendly Indians from Tlascala, and last of all a herd of swine was driven slowly in the rear, for at that time neither sheep nor cattle were known in the New World.

Guatimozin, the captive King of Mexico, graced his conquerors' triumphal march, and with the army went two falconers, Garci Caro and Alvaro Montañes, together with a band of music, some acrobats, a juggler, and a man "who vaulted well and played the Moorish pipe."

Cortes rode the black horse which he had ridden at the siege of Mexico. Fortune appeared to smile upon him. He had just added an enormous empire to the Spanish crown, and proved himself one of the most consummate generals of his age. Yet he was on the verge of the great misfortune of his life, which at the same time was to prove him still a finer leader than he had been, even in Mexico.

His black horse also was about to play the most extraordinary *rôle* that ever horse has played in the whole history of the world.

With varying fortunes, now climbing mountains, now floundering in swamps, and again passing rivers over which they had to throw bridges, the expedition came to an open country, well watered, and the home of countless herds of deer. Villagutierre, in his *History of the Conquest of the Province of Itza* (Madrid, 1701), calls it the country of the

351

Maçotecas, which name Bernal Diaz del Castillo says means "deer" in the language of those infidels. Fresh meat was scarce, and all the Spanish horsemen of those days were experts with the lance. Instantly Cortes and all his mounted officers set out to chase the deer. The weather was extraordinarily hot, hotter, so Diaz says, than they had had it since they left Mexico. The deer were all so tame that the horsemen speared them as they chose *(los alancearon muy á su placer)*, and soon the plain was strewed with dying animals just as it used to be when the Indians hunted buffalo thirty or forty years ago.

Diaz says that the reason for the tameness of the deer was that the Maçotecas (here he applies the word to the Indians themselves) worshipped them as gods. It appears that their Chief God had once appeared in the image of a stag, and told the Indians not to hunt his fellow-gods, or even frighten them. Little enough the Spaniards cared for any gods not strong enough to defend themselves, for the deity that they adored was the same God of Battles whom we adore to-day.

So they continued spearing the god-like beasts, regardless of the heat and that their horses were in poor condition owing to their long march. The horse of one Palacios Rubio, a relation of Cortes, fell dead, overcome with the great heat; the grease inside him melted, Villagutierre says. The black horse that was ridden by Cortes also was very ill, although he did not die — though it perhaps had been better that he should have died, for Villagutierre thinks "far less harm would have been done than happened afterwards, as will be seen by those who read the tale." After the hunting all was over, the line of march led over stony hills, and through a pass that Villagutierre calls "el Paso del Alabastro," and Diaz "La Sierra de los Pedernales" (flints). Here the horse that had been ill, staked itself in a forefoot, and this, as Villagutierre says, was the real reason that Cortes left him behind. He adds, "It does not matter either way, whether he was left because his grease was melted with the sun, or that his foot was staked." This, of course, is true, and anyhow the horse was reserved for a greater destiny than ever fell to any of his race.

Cortes, in his fifth letter to the Emperor Charles V, says simply, "I was obliged to leave my black horse *(mi caballo morzillo)* with a splinter in his foot." He takes no notice of the melting of the grease. "The Chief promised to take care of him, but I do not know that he will succeed or what he will do with him."

He told the Chief that he would send to fetch the horse, for he was very fond of him, and prized him very much. The Chief, no doubt, received the strange and terrible animal with due respect, and Cortes went on upon his way. That is all that Cortes says about the matter, and the mist of history closed upon him and on his horse. Cortes died, worn-out and broken-hearted, at the white little town of Castilleja de la Cuesta, not far from Seville; but El Morzillo had a greater destiny in store. This happened in the year 1525, and nothing more was heard of either the Maçotecas or the horse, after that passage in the fifth letter of Cortes, till 1697. In that year the Franciscans set out upon the gospel trail to convert the Indians of Itza, attached to the expedition that Ursua led, for the interior of Yucatán had never been subdued. They reached Itza, having come down the River Tipu in canoes.

This river, Villagutierre informs us, is as large as any river in all Spain. Moreover, it is endowed with certain properties, its water being good and clear, so that in some respects it is superior to the water even of the Tagus. It is separated into one hundred and ninety channels (neither more nor less), and every one of these has its right Indian name, that every Indian knows. Upon its banks grows much sarsaparilla, and in its sand is gold.

Beyond all this it has a hidden virtue, which is that taken (fasting) it cures the dropsy, and makes both sick and sound people eat heartily. Besides this, after eating, when you have drunk its water you are inclined to eat again.

At midday it is cold, and warm at night, so warm that a steam rises from it, just as it does when a kettle boils on the fire. Other particularities it has, which though they are not so remarkable, yet are noteworthy.

Down this amazing river Ursua's expedition navigated for twelve days in their canoes till they came to a lake called Peten-Itza, in which there was an island known as Tayasal. All unknown to themselves, they had arrived close to the place where long ago Cortes had left his horse. Of this they were in ignorance; the circumstance had been long forgotten, and Cortes himself had become almost a hero of a bygone age even in Mexico.

Fathers Orbieta and Fuensalida, monks of the Franciscan order, chosen both for their zeal and for their knowledge of the Maya language, were all agog to mark new sheep. The Indians amongst whom they found themselves were "ignorant even of the knowledge of the true faith." Moreover, since the conquest they had had no dealings with Europeans, and were as primitive as they were at the time when Cortes had passed, more than a hundred years ago.

One of the Chiefs, a man known as Isquin, when he first saw a horse, "almost ran mad with joy and with astonishment. Especially the evolutions and the leaps it made into the air moved him to admiration, and going down upon all fours he leaped about and neighed." Then, tired with this practical manifestation of his joy and his astonishment, he asked the Spanish name of the mysterious animal. When he learned that it was caballo, he forthwith renounced his name, and from that day this silly infidel was known as Caballito. Then when the soul-cleansing water had been poured upon his head, he took the name of Pedro, and to his dying day all the world called him "Don Pedro Caballito, for he was born a Chief."

This curious and pathetic little circumstance, by means of which a brand was snatched red-hot from the eternal flames, lighted for those who have deserved hell-fire by never having heard of it, might, one would think, have shown the missionaries that the poor Indians were but children, easier to lead than drive.

It only fired their zeal, and yet all their solicitude to save the Indians' souls was unavailing, and the hard-hearted savages, dead to the advantages that baptism has ever brought with it, clave to their images.

The good Franciscans made several more attempts to move the people's hearts by preaching ceaselessly. All failed, and then they went to several islands in the lake, in one of which Father Orbieta hardly had begun to preach, when, as Lopez Cogulludo[1] tells us, an Indian seized him by the throat and nearly strangled him, leaving him senseless on the ground.

At times, seated in church listening to what the Elizabethans called "a painful preacher," even the elect have felt an impulse to seize him by the throat. Still, it is usually restrained; but these poor savages, undisciplined in body and in mind, were perhaps to be excused, for the full flavour of a sermon had never reached them in their Eden by the lake. Moreover, after he was thus rudely cast from the pulpit to the ground, Father Fuensalida, nothing daunted by his fate, stepped forward and took up his parable. He preached to them this time in their own language, in which he was expert, with fervid eloquence and great knowledge of the Scriptures,[2] explaining to them the holy mystery of the incarnation of the eternal Word.[3] The subject was well chosen for a first attempt upon their hearts; but it, too, proved unfruitful, and the two friars were forced to re-embark.

1 Lopez Cogulludo, *Historia de Yucatán.*
2 Era gran Escriturario.   3 El sagrado misterio de la encarnacion de el eterno Verbo.

As the canoe in which they sat moved from the island and launched out into the lake, the infidels who stood and watched them paddling were moved to fury, and, rushing to the edge, stoned them whole-heartedly till they were out of reach.

It is a wise precaution, and one that the "conquistadores" usually observed, to have the spiritual well supported by the secular arm when missionaries, instinct with zeal and not weighed down with too much common sense, preach for the first time to the infidel.

This first reverse was but an incident, and by degrees the friars, this time accompanied by soldiers, explored more of the islands in the lake. At last they came to one called Tayasal, which was so full of idols that they took twelve hours to burn and to destroy them all.

One island still remained to be explored, and in it was a temple with an idol much reverenced by the Indians. At last they entered it, and on a platform about the height of a tall man they saw the figure of a horse rudely carved out of stone.

The horse was seated on the ground resting upon his quarters, his hind legs bent and his front feet stretched out. The barbarous infidels[1] adored the abominable and monstrous beast under the name of Tziunchan, God of the Thunder and the Lightning, and paid it reverence. Even the Spaniards, who, as a rule, were not much given to inquiring into the history of idols, but broke them instantly, *ad majorem Dei gloriam*, were interested and amazed. Little by little they learned the history of the hippomorphous god, which had been carefully preserved. It appeared that when Cortes had left his horse, so many years ago, the Indians, seeing he was ill, took him into a temple to take care of him. Thinking he was a reasoning animal,[2] they placed before him fruit and chickens, with the result that the poor beast — who, of course, was reasonable enough in his own way — eventually died.

The Indians, terrified and fearful that Cortes would take revenge upon them for the death of the horse that he had left for them to care for and to minister to all his wants, before they buried him, carved a rude statue in his likeness and placed it in a temple in the lake.

The devil, who, as Villagutierre observes, is never slack to take advantage when he can, seeing the blindness and the superstition (which was great) of those abominable idolaters, induced them by degrees to

1 Los barbaros infieles.
2 Entendiendo que era animal de razon.

make a God of the graven image they had made. Their veneration grew with time, just as bad weeds grow up in corn, as Holy Writ sets forth for our example, and that abominable statue became the chiefest of their gods, though they had many others equally horrible.

As the first horses that they saw were ridden by the Spaniards in the chase of the tame deer, and many shots were fired, the Indians not unnaturally connected the explosions and the flames less with the rider than the horse. Thus in the course of years the evolution of the great god Tziunchan took place, and, as the missionaries said, these heathen steeped in ignorance adored the work of their own hands.

Father Orbieta, not stopping to reflect that all of us adore what we have made, but "filled with the spirit of the Lord and carried off with furious zeal for the honour of our God,"[1] seized a great stone and in an instant cast the idol down, then with a hammer he broke it into bits.

When Father Orbieta had finished his work and thus destroyed one of the most curious monuments of the New World, which ought to have been preserved as carefully as if it had been carved by Praxiteles, "with the ineffable and holy joy that filled him, his face shone with a light so spiritual that it was something to praise God for and to view with delight." Most foolish actions usually inspire their perpetrators with delight, although their faces do not shine with spiritual joy when they have done them; so when one reads the folly of this muddle-headed friar, it sets one hoping that several of the stones went home upon his back as he sat paddling the canoe.

The Indians broke into lamentations, exclaiming, "Death to him, he has killed our God"; but were prevented from avenging his demise by the Spanish soldiers who prudently had accompanied the friar.

Thus was the mystery of the eternal Word made manifest amongst the Maçotecas, and a deity destroyed who for a hundred years and more had done no harm to any one on earth . . . a thing unusual amongst Gods.

1 Arrebatado de un furioso zelo de la honra de Dios.

Mudejar

Brown, severe, and wall-girt, the stubborn city still held out.

Its proud traditions made it impossible for Zaragoza to capitulate without a siege. As in the days of Soult, when the heroic maid, the *artillera*, as her countrymen call her with pride, when Palafox held up the blood and orange banner in which float the lions and the castles of Castille, the city answered shot for shot.

Fire spurted from the Moorish walls, built by the Beni Hud, who reigned in Zaragoza, when still Sohail poured its protecting rays upon the land. The bluish wreaths of smoke curled on the Ebro, running along the water and enveloping the Coso as if in a mist.

A dropping rifle-fire crackled out from the ramparts, and above the castle the red flag of the Intransigent-Republic shivered and fluttered in the breeze.

The Torre-Nueva sprang from the middle of the town, just as a palm tree rises from the desert sands. It was built at the time when Moorish artisans, infidel dogs who yet preserved the secrets of the East amongst the Christians (may dogs defile their graves), had spent their science and their love upon it.

Octagonal, and looking as if blown into the air by the magician's art, it leaned a little to one side, and, as the admiring inhabitants averred, drawing their right hands open over their left arms, laughed at its rival of Bologna and at every other tower on earth.

No finer specimen of the art known as Mudéjar existed in all Spain. Galleries cut it here and there; and ajimeces, the little horseshoe windows divided by a marble pillar, loved of the Moors, which tradition says they took from the rude openings in their tents of camel's hair, gave light to the inside. Stages of inclined planes led to the top, so gradual in their ascent that once a Queen of Spain had ridden up them to admire the view over the Sierras upon her palfrey, or her donkey, for all is one when treating of a queen, who of a certainty ennobles the animal she deigns to ride upon. Bold ajaracas, the patterns proper to the style of architecture, stood up in high relief upon its sides, and near the balustrade upon the top a band of bluish tiles relieved the brownness of the brickwork and sparkled in the sun. Sieges and time and storms, rain, wind, and snow had spared it; even the neglect of centuries had left it unimpaired — erect and elegant as a young Arab maiden carrying water from the well. Architects said that it inclined a little more each year, and talked about subsidences; but they were foreigners, unused to the things of Spain, and no one marked them; and the tower continued to be loved and prized and to fall into disrepair. On this occasion riflemen lined the galleries, pouring a hot fire upon the attacking forces of the Government.

Encamped upon the heights above Torero, the Governmental army held the banks of the canal that gives an air of Holland to that part of the adust and calcined landscape of Aragon.

The General's quarters overlooked the town, and from them he could see Santa Engracia, in whose crypt repose the bodies of the martyrs in an atmosphere of ice, standing alone upon its little plaza, fringed by a belt of stunted and ill-grown acacia trees. The great cathedral, with its domes, in which the shrine of the tutelary Virgin of the Pilar, the Pilarica of the country folk, glittering with jewels and with silver plate, is venerated as befits the abiding place on earth of the miraculous figure sent direct from heaven, towered into the sky.

Churches and towers and convents, old castellated houses with their overhanging eaves and coats-of-arms upon the doors, jewels of architecture, memorials of the past, formed as it were a jungle wrought in a warm brown stone. Beyond the city towered the mountains that hang over Huesca of the Bell. Through them the Aragon has cut its roaring passages towards Sobrarbe to the south. Northwards they circle Jaca, the virgin little city that beat off the Moors a thousand years ago, and still once every year commemorates her prowess outside the walls, where Moors and Christians fight again the unequal contest, into which St. James, mounted upon his milk-white charger, had plunged and thrown the weight of his right arm. The light was so intense and African that on the mountain sides each rock was visible, outlined as in a camera-lucida, and as the artillery played upon the tower the effects of every salvo showed up distinctly on the crumbling walls. All round the Government's encampment stood groups of peasantry who had been impressed together with their animals to bring provisions. Wrapped in their brown and white checked blankets, dressed in tight knee-breeches, short jackets, and grey stockings, and shod with alpargatas — the canvas, hemp-soled sandals that are fastened round the ankles with blue cords — they stood and smoked, stolid as Moors, and as unfathomable as the deep mysterious corries of their hills.

When the artillery thundered and the breaches in the walls grew daily more apparent and more ominous, the country people merely smiled, for they were sure the Pilarica would preserve the city; and even if she did not, all Governments, republican or clerical, were the same to them.

All their ambition was to live quietly, each in his village, which to him was the hub round which the world revolved.

So one would say, as they stood watching the progress of the siege: "Chiquio, the sciences advance a bestiality, the Government in the Madrids can hear each cannon-shot. The sound goes on those wires that stretch upon the posts we tie our donkeys to when we come into town. . . ."

Little by little the forces of the Government advanced, crossing the Ebro at the bridge which spans it in the middle of the great double promenade called the Coso, and by degrees drew near the walls.

The stubborn guerrilleros in the town contested every point of vantage, fighting like wolves, throwing themselves with knives and scythes stuck upright on long poles upon the troops.

So fought their grandfathers against the French, and so Strabo describes their ancestors, adding, "The Spaniard is a taciturn, dark man, usually dressed in black; he fights with a short sword, and always tries to come to close grips with our legionaries."

As happens in all civil wars, when brother finds himself opposed to brother, the strife was mortal, and he who fell received no mercy from the conqueror.

The riflemen upon the Torre Nueva poured in their fire, especially upon the Regiment of Pavia, whose Colonel, Don Luis Montoro, on several occasions gave orders to the artillerymen at any cost to spare the tower.

Officer after officer fell by his side, and soldiers in the ranks cursed audibly, covering the saints with filth, as runs the phrase in Spanish, and wondering why their Colonel did not dislodge the riflemen who made such havoc in their files. Discipline told at last, and all the Intransigents were forced inside the walls, leaving the moat with but a single plank to cross it by which to reach the town. Upon the plank the fire was concentrated from the walls, and the besiegers stood for a space appalled, sheltering themselves as best they could behind the trees and inequalities of the ground.

Montoro called for volunteers, and one by one three grizzled soldiers, who had grown grey in wars against the Moors, stepped forward and fell pierced with a dozen wounds.

After a pause there was a movement in the ranks, and with a sword in his right hand, and in his left the colours of Castille, his brown stuff gown tucked up showing his hairy knees knotted and muscular, out stepped a friar, and strode towards the plank. Taking the sword between his teeth he crossed himself, and beckoning on the men, rushed forward in the thickest of the fire.

He crossed in safety, and then the regiment, with a hoarse shout of "Long live God," dashed on behind him, some carrying planks and others crossing upon bales of straw, which they had thrown into the moat. Under the walls they formed and rushed into the town, only to find each house a fortress and each street blocked by a barricade. From every window dark faces peered, and a continual fusillade was poured upon them, whilst from the house-tops the women showered down tiles.

Smoke filled the narrow streets, and from dark archways groups of desperate men came rushing, armed with knives, only to fall in heaps before the troops who, with fixed bayonets, steadily pushed on.

A shift of wind cleared off the smoke and showed the crimson flag still floating from the citadel, ragged and torn by shots. Beyond the town appeared the mountains peeping out shyly through the smoke, as if they looked down on the follies of mankind with a contemptuous air.

Dead bodies strewed the streets, in attitudes half tragical, half ludicrous, some looking like mere bundles of old clothes, and some distorted with a stiff arm still pointing to the sky.

Right in the middle of a little square the friar lay shot through the forehead, his sword beside him, and with the flag clasped tightly to his breast.

His great brown eyes stared upwards, and as the soldiers passed him some of them crossed themselves, and an old sergeant spoke his epitaph: "This friar," he said, "was not of those fit only for the Lord; he would have made a soldier, and a good one; may God have pardoned him."

Driven into the middle plaza of the town, the Intransigents fought till the last, selling their lives for more than they were worth, and dying silently.

The citadel was taken with a rush, and the red flag hauled down.

Bugles rang out from the other angle of the plaza; the General and his staff rode slowly forward to meet the Regiment of Pavia as it debouched into the square.

Colonel Montoro halted, and then, saluting, advanced towards his chief. His General, turning to him, angrily exclaimed, "Tell me, why did you let those fellows in the tower do so much damage, when a few shots from the field guns would have soon finished them?"

Montoro hesitated, and recovering his sword once more saluted as his horse fretted on the curb, snorting and sidling from the dead bodies that were strewed upon the ground.

"My General," he said, "not for all Spain and half the Indies would I have trained the cannon on the tower; it is Mudejar of the purest architecture."

His General smiled at him a little grimly, and saying, "Well, after all, this is no time to ask accounts from any man," touched his horse with the spur and, followed by his staff, he disappeared into the town.

Brought Forward

A Minor Prophet

The city sweltered in the August heat. No breath of air lifted the pall of haze that wrapped the streets, the houses, and the dark group of Græco-Roman buildings that stands up like a rock in the dull tide-way of the brick-built tenements that compose the town.

Bells pealed at intervals, summoning the fractioned faithful to their various centres of belief.

When they had ceased and all the congregations were assembled listening to the exhortations of their spiritual advisers, and were employed fumbling inside their purses, as they listened, for the destined "threepenny," that obolus which gives respectability to alms, the silence was complete. Whitey-brown paper bags, dropped overnight, just stirred occasionally as the air swelled their bellies, making them seem alive, or as alive as is a jelly-fish left stranded by the tide.

Just as the faithful were assembled in their conventicles adoring the same Deity, all filled with rancour against one another because their methods of interpretation of the Creator's will were different, so did the politicians and the cranks of every sort and sect turn out to push their methods of salvation for mankind. In groups they gathered round the various speakers who discoursed from chairs and carts and points of vantage on the streets.

Above the speakers' heads, banners, held up between two poles, called on the audiences to vote for Liberal or for Tory, for Poor Law Reform, for Social Purity, and for Temperance. Orators, varying from well-dressed and glibly-educated hacks from party centres, to red-faced working-men, held forth perspiring, and occasionally bedewing those who listened to them with saliva, after an emphatic burst.

It seemed so easy after listening to them to redress all wrongs, smooth out all wrinkles, and instate each citizen in his own shop where he could sell his sweated goods, with the best advantage to himself and with the greatest modicum of disadvantage to his neighbour, that one was left amazed at the dense apathy of those who did not fall in with the nostrums they had heard. Again, at other platforms, sleek men in broadcloth, who had never seen a plough except at Agricultural Exhibitions, nor had got on closer terms of friendship with a horse than to be bitten by him as they passed along a street, discoursed upon the land.

"My friends, I say, the land is a fixed quantity, you can't increase it, and without it, it's impossible to live. 'Ow is it, then, that all the land of England is in so few hands?" He paused and mopped his face, and looking round, began again: "Friends — you'll allow me to style you Friends, I know, Friends in the sycred cause of Liberty — the landed aristocracy is our enemy.

"I am not out for confiscation, why should I? I 'ave my 'ome purchased with the fruits of my own honest toil . . ."

Before he could conclude his sentence, a dock labourer, dressed in his Sunday suit of shoddy serge, check shirt, and black silk handkerchief knotted loosely round his neck, looked up, and interjected: " 'Ard work, too, mate, that 'ere talkin' in the sun is, that built your 'ome. Beats coal whippin'."

Just for an instant the orator was disconcerted as a laugh ran through the audience; but habit, joined to a natural gift of public speaking, came to his aid, and he rejoined: "Brother working-men, I say ditto to what has fallen from our friend 'ere upon my right. We all are working-men. Some of us, like our friend, work with their 'ands, and others with their 'eds. In either case, the Land is what we 'ave to get at as an article of prime necessity."

Rapidly he sketched a state of things in which a happy population, drawn from the slums, but all instinct with agricultural knowledge, would be settled on the land, each on his little farm, and all devoted to intensive culture in the most modern form. Trees would be all cut down, because they only " 'arbour" birds that eat the corn. Hedges would all be extirpated, for it is known to every one that mice and rats and animals of every kind live under them, and that they only serve to shelter game. Each man would own a gun and be at liberty to kill a "rabbut" or a " 'are" — "animals, as we say at college, *feery naturrey*, and placed by Providence upon the land."

These noble sentiments evoked applause, which was a little mitigated by an interjection from a man in gaiters, with a sunburnt face, of: "Mister, if every one is to have a gun and shoot, 'ow long will these 'ere 'ares and rabbuts last?"

A little farther on, as thinly covered by his indecently transparent veil of reciprocity as a bare-footed dancer in her Grecian clothes, or a tall ostrich under an inch of sand, and yet as confident as either of them that the essential is concealed, a staunch Protectionist discoursed. With copious notes, to which he turned at intervals, when he appealed to those statistics which can be made in any question to fit every side, he talked of loss of trade. "Friends, we must tax the foreigner. It is this way, you see, our working classes have to compete with other nations, all of which enjoy protective duties. I ask you, is it reasonable that we should let a foreign article come into England?"

Here a dour-looking Scotsman almost spat out the words: "Man, can ye no juist say Great Britain?" and received a bow and "Certainly, my friend, I am not here to wound the sentiments of any man . . . as I was saying, is it reasonable that goods should come to England . . . I mean Great Britain, duty free, and yet articles we manufacture have to pay heavy duties in any foreign port?" " 'Ow about bread?" came from a voice upon the outskirts of the crowd.

The speaker reddened, and resumed: "My friend, man doth not live by bread alone; still, I understand the point. A little dooty upon corn, say five shillings in the quarter, would not hurt any one. We've got to do it. The foreigner is the enemy. I am a Christian; but yet, readin' as I often do the Sermon on the Mount, I never saw we had to lie down in the dust and let ourselves be trampled on.

"Who are to be the inheritors of the earth? Our Lord says, 'Blessed are the meek; they shall inherit it.' "

He paused, and was about to clinch his argument, when a tall Irishman, after expectorating judiciously upon a vacant space between two listeners, shot in: "Shure, then, the English are the meekest of the lot, for they have got the greater part of it."

At other gatherings Socialists held forth under the red flag. "That banner, comrades, which 'as braved a 'undred fights, and the mere sight of which makes the Capitalistic blood-sucker tremble as he feels the time approach when Lybor shall come into its inheritance and the Proletariat shyke off its chains and join 'ands all the world over, despizin' ryce and creed and all the artificial obstructions that a designin' Priest-'ood and a blood-stained Plutocracy 'ave placed between them to distract their attention from the great cause of Socialism, the great cause that mykes us comrades . . . 'ere, keep off my 'oof, you blighter, with your ammunition wagons. . . ."

Religionists of various sects, all with long hair and dressed in shabby black, the Book either before them on a campaigning lectern or tucked beneath one arm, called upon Christian men to dip their hands into the precious blood and drink from the eternal fountain of pure water that is to be found in the Apocalypse. "Come to 'Im, come to 'Im, I say, my friends, come straight; oh, it is joyful to belong to Jesus. Don't stop for anything, come to 'Im now like little children. . . . Let us sing a 'ymn. You know it, most of you; but brother 'ere," and as he spoke he turned towards a pale-faced youth who held a bag to take the offertory, that sacrament that makes the whole world kin, "will lead it for you."

The acolyte cleared his throat raucously, and to a popular air struck up the refrain of "Let us jump joyful on the road." Flat-breasted girls and pale-faced boys took up the strain, and as it floated through the heavy air, reverberating from the pile of public buildings, gradually all the crowd joined in; shyly at first and then whole-heartedly, and by degrees the vulgar tune and doggerel verses took on an air of power and dignity, and when the hymn was finished, the tears stood in the eyes of grimy-looking women and of red-faced men. Then, with his bag, the pale-faced hymn-leader went through the crowd, reaping a plenteous harvest, all in copper, from those whose hearts had felt, but for a moment, the full force of sympathy.

Suffragist ladies discussed upon "the Question," shocking their hearers as they touched on prostitution and divorce, and making even stolid policemen, who stood sweating in their thick blue uniforms, turn their eyes upon the ground.

After them, Suffragette girls bounded upon the cart, consigning fathers, brothers, and the whole male section of mankind straight to perdition as they held forth upon the Vote, that all-heal of the female politician, who thinks by means of it to wipe out all those disabilities imposed upon her by an unreasonable Nature and a male Deity, who must have worked alone up in the Empyrean without the humanising influence of a wife.

Little by little the various groups dissolved, the speakers and their friends forcing their "literatoor" upon the passers-by, who generally appeared to look into the air a foot or two above their heads, as they went homewards through the streets.

The Anarchists were the last to leave, a faithful few still congregating around a youth in a red necktie who denounced the other speakers with impartiality, averring that they were "humbugs every one of them," and, for his part, he believed only in dynamite, by means of which he hoped some day to be able to devote "all the blood-suckers to destruction, and thus to bring about the reign of brotherhood."

The little knot of the elect applauded loudly, and the youth, catching the policeman's eye fixed on him, descended hurriedly from off the chair on which he had been perorating, remarking that "it was time to be going home to have a bit of dinner, as he was due to speak at Salford in the evening."

Slowly the square was emptied, the last group or two of people disappearing into the mouths of the incoming streets just as a Roman crowd must have been swallowed up in the vomitoria of an amphitheatre, after a show of gladiators.

Torn newspapers and ends of cigarettes were the sole result of all the rhetoric that had been poured out so liberally upon the assembled thousands in the square.

Two or three street boys in their shirt-sleeves, bare-footed and bare-headed, their trousers held up by a piece of string, played about listlessly, after the fashion of their kind on Sunday in a manufacturing town, when the life of the streets is dead, and when men's minds are fixed either upon the mysteries of the faith or upon beer, things in which children have but little share.

The usual Sabbath gloom was creeping on the town and dinner-time approaching, when from a corner of the square appeared a man advancing rapidly. He glanced about inquiringly, and for a moment a look of disappointment crossed his face. Mounting the steps that lead up to the smoke-coated Areopagus, he stopped just for an instant, as if to draw his breath and gather his ideas. Decently dressed in shabby black, his trousers frayed a little above the heels of his elastic-sided boots, his soft felt hat that covered long but scanty hair just touched with grey, he had an air as of a plaster figure set in the middle of a pond, as he stood silhouetted against the background of the buildings, forlorn yet resolute.

The urchins, who had gathered round him, had a look upon their faces as of experienced critics at a play; that look of expectation and subconscious irony which characterises all their kind at public spectacles.

Their appearance, although calculated to appal a speaker broken to the platform business, did not influence the man who stood upon the steps. Taking off his battered hat, he placed it and his umbrella carefully upon the ground. A light, as of the interior fire that burned in the frail tenement of flesh so fiercely that it illuminated his whole being, shone in his mild blue eyes. Clearing his throat, and after running his nervous hands through his thin hair, he pitched his voice well forward, as if the deserted square had been packed full of people prepared to hang upon his words. His voice, a little hoarse and broken during his first sentences, gradually grew clearer, developing a strength quite incommensurate with the source from which it came.

"My friends," he said, causing the boys to grin and waking up the dozing policeman, "I have a doctrine to proclaim. Love only rules the world. The Greek word *caritas* in the New Testament should have been rendered *love*. Love suffereth long. Love is not puffed up; love beareth all things. That is what the Apostle really meant to say. Often within this very square I have stood listening to the speeches, and have weighed them in my mind. It is not for me to criticise, only to advocate my own belief. Friends . . ."

As his voice had gathered strength, two or three working-men, attracted by the sight of a man speaking to the air, surrounded but by the street boys and the nodding policeman on his beat, had gathered round about. Dressed in their Sunday clothes; well washed, and with the look as of restraint that freedom from their accustomed toil often imparts to them on Sunday, they listened stolidly, with that toleration that accepts all doctrines, from that of highest Toryism down to Anarchy, and acts on none of them. The speaker, spurred on by the unwonted sight of listeners, for several draggled women had drawn near, and an ice-cream seller had brought his donkey-cart up to the nearest curb-stone, once more launched into his discourse.

"Friends, when I hear the acerbity of the address of some; when I hear doctrines setting forth the rights but leaving out the duties of the working class; when I hear men defend the sweater and run down the sweated, calling them thriftless, idle, and intemperate, when often they are but unfortunate, I ask myself, what has become of Love? Who sees more clearly than I do myself what the poor have to suffer? Do I not live amongst them and share their difficulties? Who can divine better than one who has imagination — and in that respect I thank my stars I have not been left quite unendowed — what are the difficulties of those high placed by fortune, who yet have got to strive to keep their place?

"Sweaters and sweated, the poor, the rich, men, women, children, all mankind, suffer from want of Love. I am not here to say that natural laws will ever cease to operate, or that there will not be great inequalities, if not of fortune, yet of endowments, to the end of Time. What the Great

Power who sent us here intended, only He can tell. One thing He placed within the grasp of every one, capacity to *love*. Think, friends, what England might become under the reign of universal love. The murky fumes that now defile the landscape, the manufactories in which our thousands toil for others, the rivers vile with refuse, the knotted bodies and the faces scarcely human in their abject struggle for their daily bread, would disappear. Bradford and Halifax and Leeds would once again be fair and clean. The ferns would grow once more in Shipley Glen, and in the valleys about Sheffield the scissor-grinders would ply their trade upon streams bright and sparkling, as they were of yore. In Halifax, the Roman road, now black with coal-dust and with mud, would shine as well-defined as it does where now and then it crops out from the ling upon the moors, just as the Romans left it polished by their caligulæ. Why, do you ask me? Because all sordid motives would be gone, and of their superfluity the rich would give to those less blessed by Providence. The poor would grudge no one the gifts of fortune, and thus the need for grinding toil would disappear, as the struggle and the strain for daily bread would fade into the past.

"Picture to yourselves, my friends, an England once more green and merry, with the air fresh and not polluted by the smoke of foetid towns.

" 'Tis pleasant, friends, on a spring morning to hear the village bells calling to church, even although they do not call you to attend. It heals the soul to see the honeysuckle and the eglantine and smell the new-mown hay. . . .

"Then comes a chill when on your vision rises the England of the manufacturing town, dark, dreary, and befouled with smoke. How different it might be in the perpetual May morning I have sketched for you.

"Love suffereth all things, endureth all things, createth all things. . . ."

He paused, and, looking round, saw he was all alone. The boys had stolen away, and the last workman's sturdy back could be just seen as it was vanishing towards the public-house.

The speaker sighed, and wiped the perspiration from his forehead with a soiled handkerchief.

Then, picking up his hat and his umbrella, a far-off look came into his blue eyes as he walked homewards almost jauntily, conscious that the inner fire had got the better of the fleshly tenement, and that his work was done.

Brought Forward

El Masgad

The camp was pitched upon the north bank of the Wad Nefis, not far from Tamoshlacht. Above it towered the Atlas, looking like a wall, with scarce a peak to break its grim monotony. A fringe of garden lands enclosed the sanctuary, in which the great Sherif lived in patriarchal style; half saint, half warrior, but wholly a merchant at the bottom, as are so many Arabs; all his surroundings enjoyed peculiar sanctity.

In the long avenue of cypresses the birds lived safely, for no one dared to frighten them, much less to fire a shot. His baraka, that is the grace abounding, that distils from out the clothes, the person and each action of men such as the Sherif, who claim descent in apostolic continuity from the Blessed One, Mohammed, Allah's own messenger, protected everything. Of a mean presence, like the man who stood upon the Areopagus and beckoned with his hand, before he cast the spell of his keen, humoristic speech upon the Greeks, the holy one was of a middle stature. His face was marked with smallpox. His clothes were dirty, and his haik he sometimes mended with a thorn, doubling it, and thrusting one end through a slit to form a safety-pin. His shoes were never new, his turban like an old bath towel; yet in his belt he wore a dagger with a gold hilt, for he was placed so far above the law, by virtue of his blood, that though the Koran especially enjoins the faithful not to wear gold, all that he did was good.

Though he drank nothing but pure water, or, for that matter, lapped it like a camel, clearing the scum off with his fingers if on a journey, he might have drank [sic] champagne or brandy, or mixed the two of them, for the Arabs are the most logical of men, and to them such a man as the Sherif is holy, not from anything he does, but because Allah has ordained it. An attitude of mind as good as any other, and one that, after all, makes a man tolerant of human frailties.

Allah gives courage, virtue, eloquence, or skill in horsemanship. He gives or he withholds them for his good pleasure; what he has written he has written, and therefore he who is without these gifts is not held blamable. If he should chance to be a saint, that is a true descendant, in the male line, from him who answered nobly when his foolish followers asked him if his young wife, Ayesha, should sit at his right hand in paradise, "By Allah, not she; but old Kadijah, she who when all men mocked me, cherished and loved, she shall sit at my right hand," that is enough for them.

So the Sherif was honoured, partly because he had great jars stuffed with gold coin, the produce of his olive yards, and also of the tribute that the faithful brought him; partly because of his descent; and perhaps, more than all, on account of his great store of Arab lore on every subject upon earth. His fame was great, extending right through the Sus, the Draa, and down to Tazaûelt, where it met the opposing current of the grace of Bashir-el-Biruk, Sherif of the Wad-Nun. He liked to talk to Europeans, partly to show his learning, and partly to hear about the devilries they had invented to complicate their lives.

So when the evening prayer was called, and all was silent in his house, the faithful duly prostrate on their faces before Allah, who seems to take as little heed of them as he does of the other warring sects, each with its doctrine of damnation for their brethren outside the pale, the Sherif, who seldom prayed, knowing that even if he did so he could neither make nor yet unmake himself in Allah's sight, called for his mule, and with two Arabs running by his side set out towards the unbeliever's camp.

Though the Sherif paid no attention to it, the scene he rode through was like fairyland. The moonbeams falling on the domes of house and mosque and sanctuary lit up the green and yellow tiles, making them sparkle like enamels. Long shadows of the cypresses cast great bands of darkness upon the red sand of the avenue. The croaking of the frogs sounded metallic, and by degrees resolved itself into a continuous tinkle, soothing and musical, in the Atlas night. Camels lay ruminating, their monstrous packs upon their backs. As the Sherif passed by them on his mule they snarled and bubbled, and a faint odour as of a menagerie, mingled with that of tar, with which the Arabs cure their girth and saddle galls, floated towards him, although no doubt custom had made it so familiar that he never heeded it.

From the Arab huts that gather around every sanctuary, their owners living on the baraka, a high-pitched voice to the accompaniment of a two-stringed guitar played with a piece of stiff palmetto leaf, and the monotonous Arab drum, that if you listen to it long enough invades the soul, blots from the mind the memory of towns, and makes the hearer long to cast his hat into the sea and join the dwellers in the tents, blended so inextricably with the shrill cricket's note and the vast orchestra of the insects that were praising Allah on that night, each after his own fashion, that it was difficult to say where the voice ended and the insects' hum began.

Still, in despite of all, the singing Arab, croaking of the frogs, and the shrill pæans of the insects, the night seemed calm and silent, for all the voices were attuned so well to the surroundings that the serenity of the whole scene was unimpaired.

The tents lay in the moonlight like gigantic mushrooms; the rows of bottles cut in blue cloth with which the Arabs ornament them stood out upon the canvas as if in high relief. The first light dew was falling, frosting the canvas as a piece of ice condenses air upon a glass. In a long line before the tents stood the pack animals munching their corn placed on a cloth upon the ground.

A dark-grey horse, still with his saddle on for fear of the night air, was tied near to the door of the chief tent, well in his owner's eye. Now and again he pawed the ground, looked up, and neighed, straining upon the hobbles that confined his feet fast to the picket line.

On a camp chair his owner sat and smoked, and now and then half got up from his seat when the horse plunged or any of the mules stepped on their shackles and nearly fell upon the ground.

As the Sherif approached he rose to welcome him, listening to all the reiterated compliments and inquiries that no self-respecting Arab ever omits when he may chance to meet a friend.

A good address, like mercy, is twice blest, both in the giver and in the recipient of it; but chiefly it is beneficial to the giver, for in addition to the pleasure that he gives, he earns his own respect. Well did both understand this aspect of the question, and so the compliments stretched out into perspectives quite unknown in Europe, until the host, taking his visitor by the hand, led him inside the tent. "Ambassador," said the Sherif, although he knew his friend was but a Consul, "my heart yearned towards thee, so I have come to talk with thee of many things, because I know that thou art wise, not only in the learning of thy people, but in that of our own."

The Consul, not knowing what the real import of the visit might portend, so to speak felt his adversary's blade, telling him he was welcome, and that at all times his tent and house were at the disposition of his friend. Clapping his hands he called for tea, and when it came, the little flowered and gold-rimmed glasses, set neatly in a row, the red tin box with two compartments, one for the tea and one for the blocks of sugar, the whole surrounding the small dome-shaped pewter teapot, all placed in order on the heavy copper tray, he waved the equipage towards the Sherif, tacitly recognising his superiority in the art of tea-making. Seated beside each other on a mattress they drank the sacramental three cups of tea, and then, after the Consul had lit his cigarette, the Sherif having refused one with a gesture of his hand and a half-murmured "Haram" — that is, "It is prohibited" — they then began to talk.

Much had they got to say about the price of barley and the drought; of tribal fights; of where our Lord the Sultan was, and if he had reduced the rebels in the hills, — matters that constitute the small talk of the tents, just as the weather and the fashionable divorce figure in drawing-rooms. Knowing what was expected of him, the Consul touched on European politics, upon inventions, the progress that the French had made upon the southern frontier of Algeria; and as he thus unpacked his news with due prolixity, the Sherif now and again interjected one or another of those pious phrases, such as "Allah is merciful," or "God's ways are wonderful," which at the same time show the interjector's piety, and give the man who is discoursing time to collect himself, and to prepare another phrase.

After a little conversation languished, and the two men who knew each other well sat listlessly, the Consul smoking and the Sherif passing the beads of a cheap wooden rosary between the fingers of his right hand, whilst with his left he waved a cotton pocket handkerchief to keep away the flies.

Looking up at his companion, "Consul," he said, for he had now dropped the Ambassador with which he first had greeted him, "you know us well, you speak our tongue; even you know Shillah, the language of the accursed Berbers, and have translated Sidi Hammo into the speech of Nazarenes — I beg your pardon — of the Rumi," for he had seen a flush rise on the Consul's cheek.

"You like our country, and have lived in it for more than twenty years. I do not speak to you about our law, for every man cleaves to his own, but of our daily life. Tell me now, which of the two makes a man happier, the law of Sidna Aissa, or that of our Prophet, God's own Messenger?"

He stopped and waited courteously, playing with his naked toes, just as a European plays with his fingers in the intervals of speech.

The Consul sent a veritable solfatara of tobacco smoke out of his mouth and nostrils, and laying down his cigarette returned no answer for a little while.

Perchance his thoughts were wandering towards the cities brilliant with light — the homes of science and of art. Cities of vain endeavour in which men pass their lives thinking of the condition of their poorer brethren, but never making any move to get down off their backs. He thought of London and of Paris and New York, the dwelling-places both of law and order, and the abodes of noise. He pondered on their material advancement: their tubes that burrow underneath the ground, in which run railways carrying their thousands all the day and far into the night; upon their hospitals, their charitable institutions, their legislative assemblies, and their museums, with their picture-galleries, their theatres — on the vast sums bestowed to forward arts and sciences, and on the poor who shiver in their streets and cower under railway arches in the dark winter nights.

As he sat with his cigarette smouldering beside him in a little brazen pan, the night breeze brought the heavy scent of orange blossoms, for it was spring, and all the gardens of the sanctuary each had its orange grove. Never had they smelt sweeter, and never had the croaking of the frogs seemed more melodious, or the cricket's chirp more soothing to the soul.

A death's-head moth whirred through the tent, poising itself, just as a humming-bird hangs stationary probing the petals of a flower. The gentle murmur of its wings brought back the Consul's mind from its excursus in the regions of reality, or unreality, for all is one according to the point of view.

"Sherif," he said, "what you have asked me I will answer to the best of my ability.

"Man's destiny is so precarious that neither your law nor our own appear to me to influence it, or at the best but slightly.

"One of your learned Talebs, or our men of science, as they call themselves, with the due modesty of conscious worth, is passing down a street, and from a house-top slips a tile and falls upon his head. There he lies huddled up, an ugly bundle of old clothes, inert and shapeless, whilst his immortal soul leaves his poor mortal body, without which all its divinity is incomplete; then perhaps after an hour comes back again, and the man staggering to his feet begins to talk about God's attributes, or about carrying a line of railroad along a precipice."

The Sherif, who had been listening with the respect that every well-bred Arab gives to the man who has possession of the word, said, "It was so written. The man could not have died or never could have come to life again had it not been Allah's will."

His friend smiled grimly and rejoined, "That is so; but as Allah never manifests his will, except in action, just as we act towards a swarm of ants, annihilating some and sparing others as we pass, it does not matter very much what Allah thinks about, as it regards ourselves."

"When I was young," slowly said the Sherif, "whilst in the slave trade far away beyond the desert, I met the pagan tribes.

"They had no God . . . like Christians. . . Pardon me, I know you know our phrase: nothing but images of wood.

"Those infidels, who, by the way, were just as apt at a good bargain as if their fathers all had bowed themselves in Christian temple or in mosque, when they received no answer to their prayers, would pull their accursed images down from their shrines, paint them jet black, and hang them from a nail.

"Heathens they were, ignorant even of the name of God, finding their heaven and their hell here upon earth, just like the animals, but . . . sometimes I have thought not quite bereft of reason, for they had not the difficulties you have about the will of Allah and the way in which he works.

"They made their gods themselves, just as we do," and as he spoke he lowered his voice and peered out of the tent door; "but wiser than ourselves they kept a tight hand on them, and made their will, as far as possible, coincide with their own.

"It is the hour of prayer. . . .

"How pleasantly the time passes away conversing with one's friends"; and as he spoke he stood erect, turning towards Mecca, as mechanically as the needle turns towards the pole.

His whole appearance altered and his mean presence suffered a subtle change. With eyes fixed upon space, and hands uplifted, he testified to the existence of the one God, the Compassionate, the Merciful, the Bounteous, the Generous One, who alone giveth victory.

Then, sinking down, he laid his forehead on the ground, bringing his palms together. Three times he bowed himself, and then rising again upon his feet recited the confession of his faith.

The instant he had done he sat him down again; but gravely and with the air of one who has performed an action, half courteous, half obligatory, but refreshing to the soul.

The Consul, who well knew his ways, and knew that probably he seldom prayed at home, and that the prayers he had just seen most likely were a sort of affirmation of his neutral attitude before a stranger, yet was interested.

Then, when the conversation was renewed, he said to him, "Prayer seems to me, Sherif, to be the one great difference between the animals and man.

"As to the rest, we live and die, drink, eat, and propagate our species, just as they do; but no one ever heard of any animal who had addressed himself to God."

A smile flitted across the pock-marked features of the descendant of the Prophet, and looking gravely at his friend, —

"Consul," he said, "Allah to you has given many things. He has endowed you with your fertile brains, that have searched into forces which had remained unknown in nature since the sons of Adam first trod the surface of the earth. All that you touch you turn to gold, and as our saying goes, 'Gold builds a bridge across the sea.'

"Ships, aeroplanes, cannons of monstrous size, and little instruments by which you see minutest specks as if they were great rocks; all these you have and yet you doubt His power.

"To us, the Arabs, we who came from the lands of fire in the Hejaz and Hadramut. We who for centuries have remained unchanged, driving our camels as our fathers drove them, eating and drinking as our fathers ate and drank, and living face to face with God. . . . Consul, you should not smile, for do we not live closer to Him than you do, under the stars at night, out in the sun by day, our lives almost as simple as the lives of animals? To us He has vouchsafed gifts that He either has withheld from you, or that you have neglected in your pride.

"Thus we still keep our faith. . . . Faith in the God who set the planets in their courses, bridled the tides, and caused the palm to grow beside the river so that the traveller may rest beneath its shade, and resting, praise His name.

"You ask me, who ever heard of any animal that addressed himself to God. He in His infinite power . . . be sure of it . . . is He not merciful and compassionate, wonderful in His ways, harder to follow than the track that a gazelle leaves in the desert sands; it cannot be that He could have denied them access to His ear?

"Did not the lizard, Consul . . ., Hamed el Angri, the runner, the man who never can rest long in any place, but must be ever tightening his belt and pulling up his slippers at the heel to make ready for the road . . ., did he not tell you of El Hokaitsallah, the little lizard who, being late upon the day when Allah took away speech from all the animals, ran on the beam in the great mosque at Mecca, and dumbly scratched his prayer?"

The Consul nodded. "Hamed el Angri," he said, "no doubt is still upon the road, by whose side he will die one day of hunger or of thirst. . . . Yes; he told me of it, and I wrote it in a book. . . ."

"Write this, then," the Sherif went on, "Allah in his compassion, and in case the animals, bereft of speech, that is in Arabic, for each has his own tongue, should not be certain of the direction of the Kiblah, has given the power to a poor insect which we call El Masgad to pray for all of them. With its head turned to Mecca, as certainly as if he had the needle of the mariners, he prays at El Magreb.

"All day he sits erect and watches for his prey. At eventide, just at the hour of El Magreb, when from the 'alminares' of the Mosques the muezzin calls upon the faithful for their prayers, he adds his testimony.

"Consul, Allah rejects no prayer, however humble, and that the little creature knows. He knows that Allah does not answer every prayer; but yet the prayer remains; it is not blotted out, and perhaps some day it may fructify, for it is written in the book.

"Therefore El Masgad prays each night for all the animals, yet being but a little thing and simple, it has not strength to testify at all the hours laid down in Mecca by our Lord Mohammed, he of the even teeth, the curling hair, and the grave smile, that never left his face after he had communed with Allah in the cave."

The Consul dropped his smoked-out cigarette, and, stretching over to his friend, held out his hand to him.

"Sherif," he said, "maybe El Masgad prays for you and me, as well as for its kind?"

The answer came: "Consul, doubt not; it is a little animal of God, ... we too are in His hand . . . ."

Feast Day in Santa Maria Mayor

The great Capilla, the largest in the Jesuit Reductions of Paraguay, was built round a huge square, almost a quarter of a mile across.

Upon three sides ran the low, continuous line of houses, like a "row" in a Scotch mining village or a phalanstery designed by Prudhon or St. Simon in their treatises; but by the grace of a kind providence never carried out, either in bricks or stone.

Each dwelling-place was of the same design and size as all the rest. Rough tiles made in the Jesuit times, but now weathered and broken, showing the rafters tied with raw hide in many places, formed the long roof, that looked a little like the pent-house of a tennis court.

A deep verandah ran in front, stretching from one end to the other of the square, supported on great balks of wood, which, after more than two hundred years and the assaults of weather and the all-devouring ants, still showed the adze marks where they had been dressed. The timber was so hard that you could scarcely drive a nail into it, despite the flight of time since it was first set up. Rings fixed about six feet from the ground were screwed into the pillars of the verandah, before every door, to fasten horses to, exactly as they are in an old Spanish town.

Against the wall of almost every house, just by the door, was set a chair or two of heavy wood, with the seat formed by strips of hide, on which the hair had formerly been left, but long ago rubbed off by use, or eaten by the ants.

The owner of the house sat with the back of the strong chair tilted against the wall, dressed in a loose and pleated shirt, with a high turned-down collar open at the throat, and spotless white duck trousers, that looked the whiter by their contrast with his brown, naked feet.

His home-made palm-tree hat was placed upon the ground beside him, and his cloak of coarse red baize was thrown back from his shoulders, as he sat smoking a cigarette rolled in a maize leaf, for in the Jesuit capillas only women smoked cigars.

At every angle of the square a sandy trail led out, either to the river or the woods, the little patches planted with mandioca, or to the maze of paths that, like the points outside a junction, eventually joined in one main trail, that ran from Itapua on the Paraná, up to Asuncion.

The church, built of wood cut in the neighbouring forest, had two tall towers, and followed in its plan the pattern of all the churches in the New World built by the Jesuits, from California down to the smallest mission in the south. It filled the fourth side of the square, and on each side of it there rose two feathery palms, known as the tallest in the Missions, which served as landmarks for travellers coming to the place, if they had missed their road. So large and well-proportioned was the church, it seemed impossible that it had been constructed solely by the Indians themselves, under the direction of the missionaries.

The overhanging porch and flight of steps that ran down to the grassy sward in the middle of the town gave it an air as of a cathedral reared to nature in the wilds, for the thick jungle flowed up behind it and almost touched its walls.

Bells of great size, either cast upon the spot or brought at vast expense from Spain, hung in the towers. On this, the feast day of the Blessed Virgin, the special patron of the settlement, they jangled ceaselessly, the Indians taking turns to haul upon the dried lianas that served instead of ropes. Though they pulled vigorously, the bells sounded a little muffled, as if they strove in vain against the vigorous nature that rendered any work of man puny and insignificant in the Paraguayan wilds.

Inside, the fane was dark, the images of saints were dusty, their paint was cracked, their gilding tarnished, making them look a little like the figures in a New Zealand pah, as they loomed through the darkness of the aisle. On the neglected altar, for at that time priests were a rarity in the Reductions, the Indians had placed great bunches of red flowers, and now and then a humming-bird flitted in through the glassless windows and hung poised above them; then darted out again, with a soft, whirring sound. Over the whole capilla, in which at one time several thousand Indians had lived, but now reduced to seventy or eighty at the most, there hung an air of desolation. It seemed as if man, in his long protracted struggle with the forces of the woods, had been defeated, and had accepted his defeat, content to vegetate, forgotten by the world, in the vast sea of green.

On this particular day, the annual festival of the Blessed Virgin, there was an air of animation, for from far and near, from Jesuit capilla, from straw-thatched huts lost in the clearings of the primeval forest, from the few cattle ranches that then existed, and from the little town of Itapua, fifty miles away, the scanty population had turned out to attend the festival.

Upon the forest tracks, from earliest dawn, long lines of white-clad women, barefooted, with their black hair cut square across the forehead and hanging down their backs, had marched as silently as ghosts. All of them smoked great, green cigars, and as they marched along, their leader carrying a torch, till the sun rose and jaguars went back to their lairs, they never talked; but if a woman in the rear of the long line wished to converse with any comrade in the front she trotted forward till she reached her friend and whispered in her ear. When they arrived at the crossing of the little river they bathed, or, at the least, washed carefully, and gathering a bunch of flowers, stuck them into their hair. They crossed the stream, and on arriving at the plaza they set the baskets, which they had carried on their heads, upon the ground, and sitting down beside them on the grass, spread out their merchandise. Oranges and bread, called "chipa," made from mandioca flour and cheese, with vegetables and various homely sweetmeats, ground nuts, rolls of sugar done up in plaintain leaves, and known as "rapadura," were the chief staples of their trade. Those who had asses let them loose to feed; and if upon the forest trails the women had been silent, once in the safety of the town no flight of parrots in a maize field could have chattered louder than they did as they sat waiting by their wares. Soon the square filled, and men arriving tied their horses in the shade, slackening their broad hide girths, and piling up before them heaps of the leaves of the palm called "Pindó" in Guarani, till they were cool enough to eat their corn. Bands of boys, for in those days most of the men had been killed off in the past war, came trooping in, accompanied by crowds of women and of girls, who carried all their belongings, for there were thirteen women to a man, and the youngest boy was at a premium amongst the Indian women, who in the villages, where hardly any men were left, fought for male stragglers like unchained tigresses. A few old men came riding in on some of the few native horses left, for almost all the active, little, undersized breed of Paraguay had been exhausted in the war. They, too, had bands of women trotting by their sides, all of them anxious to unsaddle, to take the horses down to bathe, or to perform any small office that the men required of them. All of them smoked continuously, and each of them was ready with a fresh cigarette as soon as the old man or boy whom they accompanied finished the stump he held between his lips. The women all were dressed in the long Indian shirt called a "tupoi," cut rather low upon the breast, and edged with coarse black cotton lace, which every Paraguayan woman wore. Their hair was as black as a crow's back, and quite as shiny, and their white teeth so strong that they could tear the ears of corn out of a maize cob like a horse munching at his corn.

Then a few Correntino gauchos next appeared, dressed in their national costume of loose black merino trousers, stuffed into long boots, whose fronts were all embroidered in red silk. Their silver spurs, whose rowels were as large as saucers, just dangled off their heels, only retained in place by a flat chain, that met upon the instep, clasped with a lion's head. Long hair and brown vicuña *ponchos*, soft black felt hats, and red silk handkerchiefs tied loosely round their necks marked them as strangers, though they spoke Guarani.

They sat upon their silver-mounted saddles, with their toes resting in their bell-shaped stirrups, swaying so easily with every movement that the word riding somehow or other seemed inapplicable to men who, like the centaurs, formed one body with the horse.

As they drew near the plaza they raised their hands and touched their horses with the spur, and, rushing like a whirlwind right to the middle of the square, drew up so suddenly that their horses seemed to have turned to statues for a moment, and then at a slow trot, that made their silver trappings jingle as they went, slowly rode off into the shade.

The plaza filled up imperceptibly, and the short grass was covered by a white-clad throng of Indians. The heat increased, and all the time the bells rang out, pulled vigorously by relays of Indians, and at a given signal the people turned and trooped towards the church, all carrying flowers in their hands.

As there was no one to sing Mass, and as the organ long had been neglected, the congregation listened to some prayers, read from a book of Hours by an old Indian, who pronounced the Latin, of which most likely he did not understand a word, as if it had been Guarani. They sang "Las Flores á Maria" all in unison, but keeping such good time that at a little distance from the church it sounded like waves breaking on a beach after a summer storm.

In the neglected church, where no priest ministered or clergy prayed, where all the stoops of holy water had for years been dry, and where the Mass had been well-nigh forgotten as a whole, the spirit lingered, and if it quickeneth upon that feast day in the Paraguayan missions, that simple congregation were as uplifted by it as if the sacrifice had duly been fulfilled with candles, incense, and the pomp and ceremony of Holy Mother Church upon the Seven Hills.

As every one except the Correntinos went barefooted, the exit of the congregation made no noise except the sound of naked feet, slapping a little on the wooden steps, and so the people silently once again filled the plaza, where a high wooden arch had been erected in the middle, for the sport of running at the ring.

The vegetable sellers had now removed from the middle of the square, taking all their wares under the long verandah, and several pedlars had set up their booths and retailed cheap European trifles such as no one in the world but a Paraguayan Indian could possibly require. Razors that would not cut, and little looking-glasses in pewter frames made in Thuringia, cheap clocks that human ingenuity was powerless to repair when they had run their course of six months' intermittent ticking, and gaudy pictures representing saints who had ascended to the empyrean, as it appeared, with the clothes that they had worn in life, and all bald-headed, as befits a saint, were set out side by side with handkerchiefs of the best China silk. Sales were concluded after long-continued chaffering — that higgling of the market dear to old-time economists, for no one would have bought the smallest article, even below cost price, had it been offered to him at the price the seller originally asked.

Enrique Clerici, from Itapua, had transported all his *pulperia* bodily for the occasion of the feast. It had not wanted more than a small wagon to contain his stock-in-trade. Two or three dozen bottles of square-faced gin of the Anchor brand, a dozen of heady red wine from Catalonia, a pile of sardine boxes, sweet biscuits, raisins from Malaga, esparto baskets full of figs, and sundry pecks of apricots dried in the sun and cut into the shape of ears, and hence called "orejones," completed all his store. He himself, tall and sunburnt, stood dressed in riding-boots and a broad hat, with his revolver in his belt, beside a pile of empty bottles, which he had always ready, to hurl at customers if there should be any attempt either at cheating or to rush his wares. He spoke the curious lingo, half-Spanish, half-Italian, that so many of his countrymen use in the River Plate; and all his conversation ran upon Garibaldi, with whom he had campaigned in youth, upon Italia Irredenta, and on the time when anarchy should sanctify mankind by blood, as he said, and bring about the reign of universal brotherhood.

He did a roaring trade, despite the competition of a native Paraguayan, who had brought three demi-johns of Caña, for men prefer the imported article the whole world over, though it is vile, to native manufactures, even when cheap and good.

Just about twelve o'clock, when the sun almost burned a hole into one's head, the band got ready in the church porch, playing upon old instruments, some of which may have survived from Jesuit times, or, at the least, been copied in the place, as the originals decayed.

Sackbuts and psalteries and shawms were there, with serpents, gigantic clarionets, and curiously twisted oboes, and drums, whose canvas all hung slack and gave a muffled sound when they were beaten, and little fifes, ear-piercing and devilish, were represented in that band. It banged and crashed "La Palomita," that tune of evil-sounding omen, for to its strains prisoners were always ushered out to execution in the times of Lopez, and as it played the players slowly walked down the steps.

Behind them followed the alcalde, an aged Indian, dressed in long cotton drawers, that at the knees were split into a fringe that hung down to his ankles, a spotless shirt much pleated, and a red cloak of fine merino cloth. In his right hand he carried a long cane with a silver head — his badge of office. Walking up to the door of his own house, by which was set a table covered with glasses and with home-made cakes, he gave the signal for the running at the ring.

The Correntino gauchos, two or three Paraguayans, and a German married to a Paraguayan wife, were all who entered for the sport. The band struck up, and a young Paraguayan started the first course. Gripping his stirrups tightly between his naked toes, and seated on an old "recao," surmounted by a sheepskin, he spurred his horse, a wall-eyed skewbald, with his great iron spurs, tied to his bare insteps with thin strips of hide. The skewbald, only half-tamed, reared once or twice and bounded off, switching its ragged tail, which had been half-eaten off by cows. The people yelled, a "mosqueador!" — that is, a "fly-flapper," a grave fault in a horse in the eyes of Spanish Americans — as the Paraguayan steered the skewbald with the reins held high in his left hand, carrying the other just above the level of his eyes, armed with a piece of cane about a foot in length.

As he approached the arch, in which the ring dangled from a string, his horse, either frightened by the shouting of the crowd or by the arch itself, swerved and plunged violently, carrying its rider through the thickest of the people, who separated like a flock of sheep when a dog runs through it, cursing him volubly. The German came the next, dressed in his Sunday clothes, a slop-made suit of shoddy cloth, riding a horse that all his spurring could not get into full speed. The rider's round, fair face was burned a brick-dust colour, and as he spurred and plied his whip, made out of solid tapir hide, the sweat ran down in streams upon his coat. So intent was he on flogging, that as he neared the ring he dropped his piece of cane, and his horse, stopping suddenly just underneath the arch, would have unseated him had he not clasped it round the neck. Shouts of delight greeted this feat of horsemanship, and one tall Correntino, taking his cigarette out of his mouth, said to his fellow sitting next to him upon his horse, "The very animals themselves despise the gringos. See how that little white-nosed brute that he was riding knew that he was a 'maturango,' and nearly had him off."

Next came Hijinio Rojas, a Paraguayan of the better classes, sallow and Indian looking, dressed in clothes bought in Asuncion, his trousers tucked into his riding-boots. His small black hat, with the brim flattened up against his head by the wind caused by the fury of the gallop of his active little roan with four white feet, was kept upon his head by a black ribbon knotted underneath his chin. As he neared the arch his horse stepped double several times and fly-jumped; but that did not disturb him in the least, and, aiming well he touched the ring, making it fly into the air. A shout went up, partly in Spanish, partly in Guarani, from the assembled people, and Rojas, reining in his horse, stopped him in a few bounds, so sharply, that his unshod feet cut up the turf of the green plaza as a skate cuts the ice. He turned and trotted gently to the arch, and then, putting his horse to its top speed, stopped it again beside the other riders, amid the "Vivas" of the crowd. Then came the turn of the four Correntinos, who rode good horses from their native province, had silver horse-gear and huge silver spurs, that dangled from their heels. They were all gauchos, born, as the saying goes, "amongst the animals." A dun with fiery eyes and a black stripe right down his back, and with black markings on both hocks, a chestnut skewbald, a "doradillo," and a horse of that strange mealy bay with a fern-coloured muzzle, that the gauchos call a "Pangaré," carried them just as if their will and that of those who rode them were identical. Without a signal, visible at least to any but themselves, their horses started at full speed, reaching occasionally at the bit, then dropping it again and bridling so easy that one could ride them with a thread drawn from a spider's web. Their riders sat up easily, not riding as a European rides, with his eyes fixed upon each movement of his horse, but, as it were, divining them as soon as they were made. Each of them took the ring, and all of them checked their horses, as it were, by their volition, rather than the bit, making the silver horse-gear rattle and their great silver spurs jingle upon their feet. Each waited for the other at the far side of the arch, and then turning in a line they started with a shout, and as they passed right through the middle of the square at a wild gallop, they swung down sideways from their saddles and dragged their hands upon the ground. Swinging up, apparently without an effort, back into their seats, when they arrived at the point from where they had first started, they reined up suddenly, making their horses plunge and rear, and then by a light signal on the reins stand quietly in line, tossing the foam into the air. Hijinio Rojas and the four centaurs all received a prize, and the alcalde, pouring out wineglasses full of gin, handed them to the riders, who, with a compliment or two as to the order of their drinking, emptied them solemnly.

No other runners having come forward to compete, for in those days horses were scarce throughout the Paraguayan Missions, the sports were over, and the perspiring crowd went off to breakfast at tables spread under the long verandahs, and silence fell upon the square.

The long, hot hours during the middle of the day were passed in sleeping. Some lay face downwards in the shade. Others swung in white cotton hammocks, keeping them in perpetual motion, till they fell asleep, by pushing with a naked toe upon the ground. At last the sun, the enemy, as the Arabs call him, slowly declined, and white-robed women, with their "tupois" slipping half off their necks, began to come out into the verandahs, slack and perspiring after the midday struggle with the heat.

Then bands of girls sauntered down to the river, from whence soon came the sound of merry laughter as they splashed about and bathed.

The Correntinos rode down to a pool and washed their horses, throwing the water on them with their two hands, as the animals stood nervously shrinking from each splash, until they were quite wet through and running down, when they stood quietly, with their tails tucked in between their legs.

Night came on, as it does in those latitudes, no twilight intervening, and from the rows of houses came the faint lights of wicks burning in bowls of grease, whilst from beneath the orange trees was heard the tinkling of guitars.

Enormous bats soared about noiselessly, and white-dressed couples lingered about the corners of the streets, and men stood talking, pressed closely up against the wooden gratings of the windows, to women hidden inside the room. The air was heavy with the languorous murmur of the tropic night, and gradually the lights one by one were extinguished, and the tinkling of the guitars was stilled. The moon came out, serene and glorious, showing each stone upon the sandy trails as clearly as at midday. Saddling their horses, the four Correntinos silently struck the trail to Itapua, and bands of women moved off along the forest tracks towards their homes, walking in Indian file. Hijinio Rojas, who had saddled up to put the Correntinos on the right road, emerged into the moonlit plaza, his shadow outlined so sharply on the grass it seemed it had been drawn, and then, entering a side street, disappeared into the night. The shrill neighing of his horse appeared as if it bade farewell to its companions, now far away upon the Itapua trail. Noises that rise at night from forests in the tropics sound mysteriously, deep in the woods. It seemed as if a population silent by day was active and on foot, and from the underwood a thick white mist arose, shrouding the sleeping town.

Little by little, just as a rising tide covers a reef of rocks, it submerged everything in its white, clinging folds. The houses disappeared, leaving the plaza seething like a lake, and then the church was swallowed up, the towers struggling, as it were, a little, just as a wreath of seaweed on a rock appears to fight against the tide. Then they too disappeared, and the conquering mist enveloped everything. All that was left above the sea of billowing white were the two topmost tufts of the tall, feathery palms.

Brought Forward

Bopicuá

The great corral at Bopicuá was full of horses. Greys, browns, bays, blacks, duns, chestnuts, roans (both blue and red), skewbalds and piebalds, with claybanks, calicos, buckskins, and a hundred shades and markings, unknown in Europe, but each with its proper name in Uruguay and Argentina, jostled each other, forming a kaleidoscopic mass.

A thick dust rose from the corral and hung above their heads. Sometimes the horses stood all huddled up, gazing with wide distended eyes and nostrils towards a group of men that lounged about the gate. At other times that panic fear that seizes upon horses when they are crushed together in large numbers, set them a-galloping. Through the dust-cloud their footfalls sounded muffled, and they themselves appeared like phantoms in a mist. When they had circled round a little they stopped, and those outside the throng, craning their heads down nearly to the ground, snorted, and then ran back, arching their necks and carrying their tails like flags. Outside the great corral was set Parodi's camp, below some China trees, and formed of corrugated iron and hides, stuck on short uprights, so that the hides and iron almost came down upon the ground, in gipsy fashion. Upon the branches of the trees were hung saddles, bridles, halters, hobbles, *lazos*, and boleadoras, and underneath were spread out saddle-cloths to dry. Pieces of meat swung from the low gables of the hut, and under the low eaves was placed a "catre," the canvas scissor-bedstead of Spain and of her colonies in the New World. Upon the catre was a heap of *poncho*s, airing in the sun, their bright and startling colours looking almost dingy in the fierce light of a March afternoon in Uruguay. Close to the camp stood several bullock-carts, their poles supported on a crutch, and their reed-covered tilts giving them an air of huts on wheels. Men sat about on bullocks' skulls, around a smouldering fire, whilst the "*maté*" circulated round from man to man, after the fashion of a loving-cup. Parodi, the stiff-jointed son of Italian parents, a gaucho as to clothes and speech, but still half-European in his lack of comprehension of the ways of a wild horse. Arena, the capataz from Entre-Rios, thin, slight, and nervous, a man who had, as he said, in his youth known how to read and even guide the pen; but now "things of this world had turned him quite unlettered, and made him more familiar with the *lazo* and the spurs." The mulatto Pablo Suarez, active and cat-like, a great race-rider and horse-tamer, short and deep-chested, with eyes like those of a black cat, and toes, prehensile as a monkey's, that clutched the stirrup when a wild colt began to buck, so that it could not touch its flanks. They and Miguel Paralelo, tall, dark, and handsome, the owner of some property, but drawn by the excitement of a cowboy's life to work for wages, so that he could enjoy the risk of venturing his neck each day on a "baguál,"[1] with other peons as El Correntino and Venancio Baez, were grouped around the fire. With them were seated Martin el Madrileño, a Spanish horse-coper, who had experienced the charm of gaucho life, together with Silvestre Ayres, a Brazilian, slight and olive-coloured, well-educated, but better known as a dead pistol-shot than as man of books. They waited for their turn at *maté*, or ate great chunks of meat from a roast cooked upon a spit, over a fire of bones. Most of the men were tall and sinewy, with that air of taciturnity and self-equilibrium that their isolated lives and Indian blood so often stamp upon the faces of those centaurs of the plains. The camp, set on a little hill, dominated the country for miles on every side. Just underneath it, horses and more horses grazed. Towards the west it stretched out to the woods that fringe the Uruguay, which, with its countless islands, flowed between great tracks of forest, and formed the frontier with the Argentine.

Between the camp and the corrals smouldered a fire of bones and ñandubay, and by it, leaning up against a rail, were set the branding-irons that had turned the horses in the corral into the property of the British Government. All round the herd enclosed, ran horses neighing, seeking their companions, who were to graze no more at Bopicuá, but be sent off by train and ship to the battlefields of Europe to die and suffer, for they knew not what, leaving their pastures and their innocent comradeship with one another till the judgment day. Then, I am sure, for God must have some human feeling after all, things will be explained to them, light come into their semi-darkness, and they will feed in prairies where the grass fades not, and springs are never dry, freed from the saddle, and with no cruel spur to urge them on they know not where or why.

1 Wild horse.

For weeks we had been choosing out the doomed five hundred. Riding, inspecting, and examining from dawn till evening, till it appeared that not a single equine imperfection could have escaped our eyes. The gauchos, who all think that they alone know anything about a horse, were all struck dumb with sheer amazement. It seemed to them astonishing to take such pains to select horses that for the most part would be killed in a few months. "These men," they said, "certainly all are doctors at the job. They know even the least defect, can tell what a horse thinks about and why. Still, none of them can ride a horse if he but shakes his ears. In their bag surely there is a cat shut up of some kind or another. If not, why do they bother so much in the matter, when all that is required is something that can carry one into the thickest of the fight?"

The sun began to slant a little, and we had still three leagues to drive the horses to the pasture where they had to pass the night for the last time in freedom, before they were entrained. Our horses stood outside of the corral, tied to the posts, some saddled with the "recado,"[1] its heads adorned with silver, some with the English saddle, that out of England has such a strange, unserviceable look, much like a saucepan on a horse's back. Just as we were about to mount, a man appeared, driving a point of horses, which, he said, "to leave would be a crime against the sacrament." "These are all pingos," he exclaimed, "fit for the saddle of the Lord on High, all of them are bitted in the Brazilian style, can turn upon a spread-out saddle-cloth, and all of them can gallop round a bullock's head upon the ground, so that the rider can keep his hand upon it all the time." The speaker by his accent was a Brazilian. His face was olive-coloured, his hair had the suspicion of a kink. His horse, a cream-colour, with black tail and mane, was evidently only half-tamed, and snorted loudly as it bounded here and there, making its silver harness jingle and the rider's *poncho* flutter in the air. Although time pressed, the man's address was so persuasive, his appearance so much in character with his great silver spurs just hanging from his heel, his jacket turned up underneath his elbow by the handle of his knife, and, to speak truth, the horses looked so good and in such high condition that we determined to examine them, and told their owner to drive them into a corral.

Once again we commenced the work that we had done so many times of mounting and examining. Once more we fought, trying to explain the mysteries of red tape to unsophisticated minds, and once

---

[1] Argentine saddle.

again our "domadores" sprang lightly, barebacked, upon the horses they had never seen before, with varying results. Some of the Brazilian's horses bucked like antelopes, El Correntino and the others of our men sitting them barebacked as easily as an ordinary man rides over a small fence. To all our queries why they did not saddle up we got one answer, "To ride with the recado is but a pastime only fit for boys." So they went on, pulling the horses up in three short bounds, nostrils aflame and tails and manes tossed wildly in the air, only a yard or two from the corral. Then, slipping off, gave their opinion that the particular "bayo," "zaino," or "gateao " was just the thing to mount a lancer on, and that the speaker thought he could account for a good tale of Boches if he were over there in the Great War. This same great war, which they called "barbarous," taking a secret pleasure in the fact that it showed Europeans not a whit more civilised than they themselves, appeared to them something in the way of a great pastime from which they were debarred.

Most of them, when they sold a horse, looked at him and remarked, "Pobrecito, you will go to the Great War," just as a man looks at his son who is about to go, with feelings of mixed admiration and regret.

After we had examined all the Brazilian's "Tropilla" so carefully that he said, "By Satan's death, your graces know far more about my horses than I myself, and all I wonder is that you do not ask me if all of them have not complied with all the duties of the Church," we found that about twenty of them were fit for the Great War.   Calling upon Parodi and the capataz of Bopicuá, who all the time had remained seated round the smouldering fire and drinking *maté*, to prepare the branding-irons, the peons led them off, our head man calling out "Artilleria" or "Caballeria," according to their size. After the branding, either on the hip for cavalry and on the neck for the artillery, a peon cut their manes off, making them as ugly as a mule, as their late owner said, and we were once more ready for the road, after the payment had been made. This took a little time, either because the Brazilian could not count, or perhaps because of his great caution, for he would not take payment except horse by horse. So, driving out the horses one by one, we placed a roll of dollars in his hand as each one passed the gate. Even then each roll of dollars had to be counted separately, for time is what men have the most at their disposal in places such as Bopicuá.

Two hours of sunset *[sic=sunlight]*still remained, with three long leagues to cover, for in those latitudes there is no twilight, night succeeding day, just as films follow one another in a cinematograph. At last it all was over, and we were free to mount. Such sort of drives are of the nature of a sport in South America, and so the Brazilian drove off the horses that we had rejected, half a mile away, leaving them with a negro boy to herd, remarking that the rejected were as good or better than those that we had bought, and after cinching up his horse, prepared to ride with us. Before we started, a young man rode up, dressed like an exaggerated gaucho, in loose black trousers, *poncho*, and a "golilla"[1] round his neck, a *lazo* hanging from the saddle, a pair of boleadoras peeping beneath his "cojinillo,"[2] and a long silver knife stuck in his belt. It seemed he was the son of an estanciero who was studying law in Buenos Aires, but had returned for his vacation, and hearing of our drive had come to ride with us and help us in our task. No one on such occasions is to be despised, so, thanking him for his good intentions, to which he answered that he was a "partizan of the Allies, lover of liberty and truth, and was well on in all his studies, especially in International Law," we mounted, the gauchos floating almost imperceptibly, without an effort, to their seats, the European with that air of escalading a ship's side that differentiates us from man less civilised.

During the operations with the Brazilian, the horses had been let out of the corral to feed, and now were being held back *en pastoreo*, as it is called in Uruguay, that is to say, watched at a little distance by mounted men. Nothing remained but to drive out of the corral the horses bought from the Brazilian, and let them join the larger herd. Out they came like a string of wild geese, neighing and looking round, and then instinctively made towards the others that were feeding, and were swallowed up amongst them. Slowly we rode towards the herd, sending on several well-mounted men upon its flanks, and with precaution — for of all living animals tame horses most easily take fright upon the march and separate — we got them into motion, on a well-marked trail that led towards the gate of Bopicuá.

At first they moved a little sullenly, and as if surprised. Then the contagion of emotion that spreads so rapidly amongst animals upon the march seemed to inspire them, and the whole herd broke into a light trot. That is the moment that a stampede may happen, and accordingly we

1 *Golilla,* which originally meant a ruff, is now used for a handkerchief round the
   neck.
2 *Cojinillo,* part of the recado.

pulled our horses to a walk, whilst the men riding on the flanks forged slowly to the front, ready for anything that might occur. Gradually the trot slowed down, and we saw as it were a sea of manes and tails in front of us, emerging from a cloud of dust, from which shrill neighings and loud snortings rose. They reached a hollow, in which were several pools, and stopped to drink, all crowding into the shallow water, where they stood pawing up the mud and drinking greedily. Time pressed, and as we knew that there was water in the pasture where they were to sleep, we drove them back upon the trail, the water dripping from their muzzles and their tails, and the black mud clinging to the hair upon their fetlocks, and in drops upon their backs. Again they broke into a trot, but this time, as they had got into control, we did not check them, for there was still a mile to reach the gate.

Passing some smaller mud-holes, the body of a horse lay near to one of them, horribly swollen, and with its stiff legs hoisted a little in the air by the distension of its flanks. The passing horses edged away from it in terror, and a young roan snorted and darted like an arrow from the herd. Quick as was the dart he made, quicker still El Correntino wheeled his horse on its hind legs and rushed to turn him back. With his whip whirling round his head he rode to head the truant, who, with tail floating in the air, had got a start of him of about fifty yards. We pressed instinctively upon the horses; but not so closely as to frighten them, though still enough to be able to stop another of them from cutting out. The Correntino on a half-tamed grey, which he rode with a raw-hide thong bound round its lower jaw, for it was still unbitted, swaying with every movement in his saddle, which he hardly seemed to grip, so perfect was his balance, rode at a slight angle to the runaway and gained at every stride. His hat blew back and kept in place by a black ribbon underneath his chin, framed his head like an aureole. The red silk handkerchief tied loosely round his neck fluttered beneath it, and as he dashed along, his *lazo* coiled upon his horse's croup, rising and falling with each bound, his eyes fixed on the flying roan, he might have served a sculptor as the model for a centaur, so much did he and the wild colt he rode seem indivisible.

In a few seconds, which to us seemed minutes, for we feared the infection might have spread to the whole "caballada," the Correntino headed and turned the roan, who came back at three-quarter speed, craning his neck out first to one side, then to the other, as if he still thought that a way lay open for escape.

By this time we had reached the gates of Bopicuá, and still seven miles lay between us and our camping-ground, with a fast-declining sun. As the horses passed the gate we counted them, an operation of some difficulty when time presses and the count is large. Nothing is easier than to miss animals, that is to say, for Europeans, however practised, but the lynx-eyed gauchos never are at fault. "Where is the little brown horse with a white face, and a bit broken out of his near forefoot?" they will say, and ten to one that horse is missing, for what they do not know about the appearance of a horse would not fill many books. Only a drove road lay between Bopicuá and the great pasture, at whose faraway extremity the horses were to sleep. When the last animal had passed and the great gates swung to, the young law student rode up to my side, and, looking at the "great tropilla," as he called it, said, "*Morituri te salutant.* This is the last time they will feed in Bopicuá." We turned a moment, and the falling sun lit up the undulating plain, gilding the cottony tufts of the long grasses, falling upon the dark-green leaves of the low trees around Parodi's camp, glinting across the belt of wood that fringed the Uruguay, and striking full upon a white *estancia* house in Entre-Rios, making it appear quite close at hand, although four leagues away.

Two or three hundred yards from the great gateway stood a little native hut, as unsophisticated, but for a telephone, as were the gauchos' huts in Uruguay, as I remember them full thirty years ago. A wooden barrel on a sledge for bringing water had been left close to the door, at which the occupant sat drinking *maté*, tapping with a long knife upon his boot. Under a straw-thatched shelter stood a saddled horse, and a small boy upon a pony slowly drove up a flock of sheep. A blue, fine smoke that rose from a few smouldering logs and bones, blended so completely with the air that one was not quite sure if it was really smoke or the reflection of the distant Uruguay against the atmosphere.

Not far off lay the bones of a dead horse, with bits of hide adhering to them, shrivelled into mere parchment by the sun. All this I saw as in a camera-lucida, seated a little sideways on my horse, and thinking sadly that I, too, had looked my last on Bopicuá. It is not given to all men after a break of years to come back to the scenes of youth, and still find in them the same zest as of old. To return again to all the cares of life called civilised, with all its littlenesses, its newspapers all full of nothing, its sordid aims disguised under high-sounding nicknames, its hideous riches and its sordid poverty, its want of human sympathy, and, above all, its barbarous war brought on it by the folly of its rulers, was not just at that moment an alluring thought, as I felt the little "malacara"[1] that I rode twitching his bridle, striving to be off. When I had touched him with the spur he bounded forward and soon overtook the caballada, and the place which for so many months had been part of my life sank out of sight, just as an island in the Tropics fades from view as the ship leaves it, as it were, hull down.

When we had passed into the great enclosure of La Pileta, and still four or five miles remained to go, we pressed the caballada into a long trot, certain that the danger of a stampede was past. Wonderful and sad it was to ride behind so many horses, trampling knee-high through the wild grasses of the Camp, snorting and biting at each other, and all unconscious that they would never more career across the plains. Strange and affecting, too, to see how those who had known each other all kept together in the midst of the great herd, resenting all attempts of their companions to separate them.

A "tropilla"[2] that we had bought from a Frenchman called Leon, composed of five brown horses, had ranged itself around its bell mare, a fine chestnut, like a bodyguard. They fought off any of the other horses who came near her, and seemed to look at her both with affection and with pride.

Two little bright bay horses, with white legs and noses, that were brothers, and what in Uruguay are known as "seguidores," that is, one followed the other wherever it might go, ran on the outskirts of the herd. When either of them stopped to eat, its companion turned its head and neighed to it, when it came galloping up. Arena, our head man, riding beside me on a skewbald, looked at them, and, after dashing forward to turn a runaway, wheeled round his horse almost in the air and stopped it in a bound, so suddenly that for an instant they stood poised like an equestrian statue, looked at the "seguidores," and remarked, "Patron, I hope one shell will kill them both in the Great War if they have got to die." I did not answer, except to curse the Boches with all the intensity the Spanish tongue commands. The young law-student added his testimony, and we rode on in silence.

---

[1] *Malacara*, literally Badface, is the name used for a white-faced horse. In old days in England such a horse was called Baldfaced.

[2] Little troop.

A passing sleeve of locusts almost obscured the declining sun. Some flew against our faces, reminding me of the fight Cortes had with the Indians not far from Vera Cruz, which, Bernal Diaz says, was obstructed for a moment by a flight of locusts that came so thickly that many lost their lives by the neglect to raise their bucklers against what they thought were locusts, and in reality were arrows that the Indians shot. The effect was curious as the insects flew against the horses, some clinging to their manes, and others making them bob up and down their heads, just as a man does in a driving shower of hail. We reached a narrow causeway that formed the passage through a marsh. On it the horses crowded, making us hold our breath for fear that they would push each other off into the mud, which had no bottom, upon either side. When we emerged and cantered up a little hill, a lake lay at the bottom of it, and beyond it was a wood, close to a railway siding. The evening now was closing in, but there was still a good half-hour of light. As often happens in South America just before sundown, the wind dropped to a dead calm, and passing little clouds of locusts, feeling the night approach, dropped into the long grass just as a flying-fish drops into the waves, with a harsh whirring of their gauzy wings.

The horses smelt the water at the bottom of the hill, and the whole five hundred broke into a gallop, manes flying, tails raised high, and we, feeling somehow the gallop was the last, raced madly by their side until within a hundred yards or so of the great lake. They rushed into the water and all drank greedily, the setting sun falling upon their many-coloured backs, and giving the whole herd the look of a vast tulip field. We kept away so as to let them drink their fill, and then, leading our horses to the margin of the lake, dismounted, and, taking out their bits, let them drink, with the air of one accomplishing a rite, no matter if they raised their heads a dozen times and then began again.

Slowly Arena, El Correntino, Paralelo, Suarez, and the rest drove out the herd to pasture in the deep lush grass. The rest of us rode up some rising ground towards the wood. There we drew up, and looking back towards the plain on which the horses seemed to have dwindled to the size of sheep in the half-light, some one, I think it was Arena, or perhaps Pablo Suarez, spoke their elegy: "Eat well," he said; "there is no grass like that of La Pileta, to where you go across the sea. The grass in Europe all must smell of blood."

Appendix 1

Cunninghame Graham's Treatment of American Landscapes

Graham can from the simplest forms of language create a memorable picture, as when describing a sunset he draws together a variety of sensory effects :

> "The sun set in a glare, the hot, north wind blowing as from a furnace, making the cattle droop their heads, and bringing troops of horses, with a noise like thunder, down to the water-holes."
>
> ("San Andrés", *Charity*)

The Argentine location then emerges as he uses Argentine Spanish terms for two birds and for the great plains :

> "The teru-teros, flying low, like gulls upon the sea, almost unseen in the fast-coming darkness, called uncannily. The tame chajá screamed harshly behind the cattle pens… and from the pampa rose the acrid smell that the first freshness of the evening draws from the heated ground."
>
> ("San Andrés", *Charity*)

Graham as a writer has to evoke for the reader a landscape that the reader has probably never seen. He has to deliver a piece of prose that allows the reader almost to touch, feel, taste, smell and hear that remote landscape. Again using a simple vocabulary flavoured with only one item of Argentine Spanish usage (and that item carefully given a context), Graham seeks to depict the effects of light at dawn on the pampa :

> "Morning broke fine and clear, with a slight film of frost upon the grass. In the *chiquero* the sheep were bleating to be let out, and cattle on the hills got up and stretched themselves, looking like camels as they stood with their heads high and their hind quarters drooping on the ground. A distant wood behind a little hill was hung suspended in the sky, with the trees growing towards the earth by an effect of mirage, and from the world there came a smell of freshness and a sensation of new birth."
>
> ("Anastasio Lucena", *A Hatchment*)

To be successful, a landscape presented through the medium of words cannot be a mere haphazard listing of physical details. The material needs to be shaped carefully into a harmonious whole. Graham, ever fond of Paraguay, describes the great stretch of forest between Caraguatá-Guazú and Caballero Punta, focusing in turn on the forest track, log obstacles, dense vegetation, lack of light, hugely varied animal life and the overall impact of such a place on a lone traveller :

"... For miles the track ran through the woods; the trail worn deep into the red and sandy soil looked like a ribbon, dropped underneath the dark metallic-foliaged trees.

At times a great fallen log, round which the parasitic vegetation had wrapped itself, turned the path off, just as a rock diverts the current of a stream. In places the road, opened long ago, most likely by the Jesuits, ran almost in the dark, under the intertwining ceibas and urandéys ...

Occasionally a crashing in the bushes near the trail told of the passage of a tapir, through the underwood, and once as I came to a little clearing a tiger lay stretched flat upon a log, watching the fish in some dark back-water, just as a cat lies on the garden wall to watch the birds. Butterflies floated lazily about, scarce moving their broad, velvet wings, reminding one somehow of owls, flitting across a grass ride in a wood, noiseless, but startling by their very quietness.

The snakes, the humming-birds, the alligators basking in the creeks, the whir of insects and the metallic croaking of the frogs, the air of being in the grip of an all-powerful vegetation, reduced a man, travelling alone through the green solitude, to nothingness."

("A Meeting", *Charity*)

Graham's writing now and again catches the sense of wonderment that the first European explorers felt and recorded when confronted with the often awesome landscapes of Mexico, Central and South America. In "Los Pingos" he describes a bay used as a landing-place by the steamers on the River Uruguay where some European-style commercial enterprise had come to grief :

"Above the bay the ruins of a great building stood...

A group of roofless workmen's cottages gave an air of desolation to the valley in which the factory and its dependencies had stood. They too had been invaded by the powerful sub-tropical plant life... It seemed that man for once had been subdued, and that victorious nature had resumed her sway over a region wherein he had endeavoured to intrude, and had been worsted in the fight.

Nature had so resumed her sway that buildings, planted trees, and paths long overgrown with grass, seemed to have been decayed for centuries, although scarce twenty years had passed since they had been deserted and had fallen into decay.

They seemed to show the power of the recuperative force of the primeval forest, and to call attention to the fact that man had suffered a defeat...

The triumph of the older forces of the world had been so final and complete that on the ruins there had grown no moss, but plants and bushes with great tufts of grass had sprung from them, leaving the stones still fresh as when the houses were first built. Nature in that part of the New World enters into no compact with mankind..."

("Los Pingos", *Brought Forward*)

Graham, while able to see the beauty of American landscapes, is not tempted to idealise.

The *pampero* wind from the south-west could cause havoc, even in the major city:

"A fierce pampero had sprung up in an hour, the sky had turned that vivid green that marks storms from the south in Buenos Aires. Whirlfire kept the sky lighted, till an arch had formed in the south-east, and then the storm broke, blinding and terrible, with a strange, seething noise. The wind, tearing along the narrow streets, forced everyone to fly for refuge.

People on foot darted into the nearest house, and horsemen, flying like birds before the storm, sought refuge anywhere they could, their horses, slipping and sliding on the rough, paved streets, sending out showers of sparks as they stopped suddenly, just as a skater sends out a spray of ice. The deep-cut streets, with their raised pavements, soon turned to water-courses, from three to four feet deep, through which the current ran so fiercely that it was quite impossible to pass on foot. The horsemen, galloping for shelter, passed through them with the water banking up against their horses on the stream side, though they plied whip and spur.

After the first hour of the tempest, when a little light began to dawn towards the south, and the peals of thunder slacken a little in intensity, men's nerves became relaxed from the over-tension that a pampero brings with it, just as if nature had been overwound, and by degrees was paying out the chain."

("Christie Christison", *Charity*)

Graham's accumulated life experience and his wide travels allow him to make comparisons that can be both apposite and striking, as when he contemplates a cemetery on the pampa for the descendants of Scots settlers :

> "… railed off their little cemetery with a high fence of ñandubay. The untrimmed posts stuck up knotty and gnarled just as they do in a corral, but all the graves had head- and foot-stones, mostly of hard and undecaying wood, giving an air as of a graveyard in Lochaber by some deserted strath.
>
> There, "Anastasio McIntyré, killed by the Indians," rested in peace. "May God have mercy on him."
>
> A little further on, "Cruz Camerón, assassinated by his friends," expected glory from the intermediation of the saints. "Passers-by, pray for him." "

("San Andrés", Charity)

Graham deals confidently with river-based scenarios. In the plains of central Uruguay he presents a major river, its crossing-place and its 'flying bridge' (the flat-bottomed raft operated by pulleys) thus:

> "Day in, day out, horses and cattle waited at the Pass, their owners hailing the *balsa*, which was safe *[from Sp. 'seguro', sure]* to be on the other side, and sitting, with one leg crossed on the pommel of the saddle, smoking their cigarettes.
>
> A fine green dust, composed of every kind of animal manure, filled all the air upon fine days, and as there were no trees within a quarter of a mile, the heat was tropical, and the few sheds which stood about for shelter from the sun, sure to be occupied.
>
> The cattle hung their heads as if they had been on *rodeo*, and the peons, placed on the bank for fear of a stampede, slumbered upon their saddles, though with one eye always half open for the first sign of movement in the herd."

("The Pass of the River", A Hatchment)

There are hints in the selections above of Graham's urge to fill the landscape with moving animals and men. A good example of a landscape charged with action is when Graham describes a group of riders making their way at night across the pampa to attend a dance :

"The night was clear and starry, and above our heads was hung the Southern Cross. So bright the stars shone out that one could see almost a mile away; but yet all the perspective of the plains and woods was altered. Hillocks were sometimes undistinguishable, at other times loomed up like houses. Woods seemed to sway and heave, and by the sides of streams bunches of Pampa grass stood stark as sentinels, their feathery tufts looking like plumes upon an Indian's lance. . .

Now and then little owls flew noiselessly beside us, circling above our heads, and then dropped noiselessly upon a bush. Eustaquio Medina, who knew the district as a sailor knows the seas where he was born, rode in the front of us. As his horse shied at a shadow on the grass or at the bones of some dead animal, he swung his whip round ceaselessly, until the moonlight playing on the silver-mounted stock seemed to transform it to an aureole that flickered about his head."

("El Tango Argentino", *Brought Forward*)

A similar example occurs when Graham describes a group of Paraguayan women walking through the forest towards a market due to be held in an old Jesuit Mission station :

"Upon the forest tracks, from earliest dawn, long lines of white-clad women, barefooted, with their black hair cut square across the forehead and hanging down their backs, had marched as silently as ghosts. All of them smoked great, green cigars, and as they marched along, their leader carrying a torch, till the sun rose and jaguars went back to their lairs, they never talked; but if a woman in the rear of the long line wished to converse with any comrade in the front she trotted forward till she reached her friend and whispered in her ear. When they arrived at the crossing of the little river they bathed, or, at the least, washed carefully, and gathering a bunch of flowers, stuck them into their hair. They crossed the stream, and on arriving at the plaza they set the baskets, which they had carried on their heads, upon the ground, and sitting down beside them on the grass, spread out their merchandise... and if upon the forest trails the women had been silent, once in the safety of the town no flight of parrots in a maize field could have chattered louder than they did as they sat waiting by their wares."

("Feast Day in Santa Maria Mayor", *Brought Forward*)

The great plains of Argentina and Uruguay were especially meaningful to Graham, an expert horseman and horse-lover, because they were home to seemingly countless millions of wild or semi-wild horses. He built up considerable experience herding these wild horses :

"At first they moved a little sullenly, and as if surprised. Then the contagion of emotion that spreads so rapidly amongst animals upon the march seemed to inspire them, and the whole herd broke into a light trot. That is the moment that a stampede may happen, and accordingly we pulled our horses to a walk, whilst the men riding on the flanks forged slowly to the front, ready for anything that might occur. Gradually the trot slowed down, and we saw as it were a sea of manes and tails in front of us, emerging from a cloud of dust, from which shrill neighings and loud snortings rose. They reached a hollow, in which were several pools, and stopped to drink, all crowding into the shallow water, where they stood pawing up the mud and drinking greedily. Time pressed, and as we knew that there was water in the pasture where they were to sleep, we drove them back upon the trail, the water dripping from their muzzles and their tails, and the black mud clinging to the hair upon their fetlocks, and in drops upon their backs. Again they broke into a trot, but this time, as they had got into control, we did not check them, for there was still a mile to reach the gate.

("Bopicuá", *Brought Forward*)

Graham often seeks to look beyond the surface landscape or scene to tease out a deeper meaning or significance. Once, in the south-west of the United States, he and a group of riders discovered a Mescalero Apache Indian dead in his tent. He tells the reader of local Indian rock carvings, particularly a scene where a chief sets free his favourite horse, either before his death or in reward of its faithful service. A description that would have been perfectly serviceable at the surface level moves towards the reflective:

"Once in the Sierra Madre ... we came upon a little shelter made of withies, and covered with one of those striped blankets woven by the Návajos ...

The little wigwam, shaped like a gipsy tent, stood close to a thicket of huisaché trees in flower. Their round and ball-like blossoms filled the air with a sweet scent. A stream ran gently tinkling over its pebbly bed, and the tall prairie grasses flowed up to the lost little hut as if they would engulf it like a sea...

Somehow it had an eerie look about it, standing so desolate, out in those flowery wilds.

Inside it lay the body of a man, with the skin dry as parchment, and his arms beside him, a Winchester, a bow and arrows, and a lance. Eustaquio, taking up an arrow, after looking at it, said that the dead man was an Apache of the Mescalero band, and then, looking upon the ground and pointing out some marks, said, "He had let loose his horse before he died, just as the chief did in the picture-writing."

That was his epitaph, for how death overtook him none of us could conjecture; but I liked the manner of his going off the stage."

(Preface, *Brought Forward*)

In 1916 Graham was sent by the British Government to South America to buy horses to be shipped back to Britain for service in the Great War. This experience gave him the material for the final scene in the last sketch of the collection *Brought Forward* of 1916, one of his most disturbing images of the world of the pampa :

"The evening now was closing in, but there was still a good half-hour of light. As often happens in South America just before sundown, the wind dropped to a dead calm, and passing little clouds of locusts, feeling the night approach, dropped into the long grass just as a flying-fish drops into the waves, with a harsh whirring of their gauzy wings.

The horses smelt the water at the bottom of the hill, and the whole five hundred broke into a gallop, manes flying, tails raised high, and we, feeling somehow the gallop was the last, raced madly by their side until within a hundred yards or so of the great lake. They rushed into the water and all drank greedily, the setting sun falling upon their many-coloured backs, and giving the whole herd the look of a vast tulip field. We kept away so as to let them drink their fill, and then, leading our horses to the margin of the lake, dismounted, and, taking out their bits, let them drink, with the air of one accomplishing a rite, no matter if they raised their heads a dozen times and then began again.

Slowly Arena, El Correntino, Paralelo, Suarez, and the rest drove out the herd to pasture in the deep lush grass. The rest of us rode up some rising ground towards the wood. There we drew up, and looking back towards the plain on which the horses seemed to have dwindled to the size of sheep in the half-light, some one, I think it was Arena, or perhaps Pablo Suarez, spoke their elegy: "Eat well," he said; "there is no grass like that of La Pileta, to where you go across the sea. The grass in Europe all must smell of blood."

("Bopicuá", *Brought Forward*)

The clue to Graham's fascination with South America, particularly with the pampa landscape and its old way of life, is given in the sketch entitled "La Pampa". In the opening lines Graham revels in its immensity and its ability to sustain millions of grazing animals :

"All grass and sky, and sky and grass, and still more sky and grass, the Pampa stretched from the *pajonales* on the western bank of the Paraná right to the stony plain of Uspallata, a thousand miles away.

It stretched from San Luis de la Punta down to Bahia Blanca, and again crossing the Uruguay, comprised the whole republic of that name and a good half of Rio Grande, then with a loop took in the *misiones* both of the Paraná and Paraguay.

Through all this ocean of tall grass, green in the spring, then yellow, and in the autumn brown as an old boot, the general characteristics were the same.

A ceaseless wind ruffled it all and stirred its waves of grass. Innumerable flocks and herds enamelled it, and bands of ostriches (Mirth of the Desert, as the Gauchos called them) and herds of palish-yellow deer stood on the tops of the *cuchillas* and watched you as you galloped past..."

("La Pampa", *Charity*)

In the sketch's closing lines he goes deeper, revealing the meaning of the pampa for the old-style gaucho - and for himself when in the 1870s he first saw the to him still unspoilt pampa :

"Silence and solitude were equally the note of north and south, with a horizon bounded by what a man could see when sitting on his horse.

... Well did the ancient Quichuas name the plains, with the word signifying "space," for all was spacious - earth, sky, the waving continent of grass; the enormous herds of cattle and of horses; the strange effects of light; the fierce and blinding storms and, above all, the feeling in men's minds of freedom, and of being face to face with nature, under those southern skies."

("La Pampa", *Charity*)

Graham was blessed with a very sharp eye for natural landscapes, a phenomenal memory and a very considerable literary talent. These gifts made him a fine landscape artist in words.

(JMcI)

Appendix 2

Cunninghame Graham's Treatment of Scottish Landscapes

In the five volumes of the present comprehensive collection of Robert Cunninghame Graham's stories and sketches there are some fifty which have a Scottish background. Eleven of the fifty-one items in Volume Four are set in Scotland and these constitute a good selection of his sometimes brief representations of landscape. The sketches concerned are: "The Craw Road", "Caisteal-Na-Sithean", "A Braw Day", "A Princess", "Mist in Menteith", "The Beggar Earl", "Falkirk Tryst", "Loose and Broken Men", "Brought Forward", "With the North-East Wind" and "Fidelity". Eight of these pieces are located in or near his own ancestral fiefdoms in Menteith and the Lennox, in the territories around Gartmore, the Lake of Menteith and the Flanders mosses on the upper reaches of the River Forth. Two are set in the townscapes of industrial Glasgow and one on the coast of Fife.

The term *landscape* carries with it the notion of a location, natural or man-made, which is viewed as an aesthetic experience. For his part, Graham tends to interpret and construct his landscapes from the varied perspectives of an estate owner, a horseman, a member of an family of old aristocratic lineage, a historian, an experienced traveller and a political activist. In a key essay, "Fate", in Volume Three, he delicately probes the symbiosis between landscape as a created artefact and the territory which it purports to represent. He parallels the gentle decay of an old needlework portrait of a mansion house and its surroundings, and the actual deterioration of the estate, which is clearly Gartmore:

> "So it hung on, getting a little yellower, more fly-blown, and with the varnish scaling from the rosewood frame and the gold falling off in particles from the interior rim as winter damp and summer sun succeeded year by year in the long corrridor of the old Georgian house."

Some of Graham's sketches strive to convey fully the inscape of a particular landscape. Others use a location as context for the development of a character sketch or narrative episode. In a few we find only lightly suggested touches of landscape. To use one of his own phrases, he often sees in his chosen settings "the charm of desolation".

In 1930 Graham and the landscape artist D.Y. Cameron collaborated in the publication of an illustrated version of the 1906 edition of *Notes on the District of Menteith*. Re-titled the *District of Menteith*, this folio volume, which was designed as a *de luxe* collector's item, contained one original etching and ten wash drawings by Cameron. Only 250 copies were produced, individually signed by both men. Cameron's contributions, some drawn from his favourite vista above Kippen, feature the familiar beauty spots of the area, including Flanders Moss, Ben Ledi, Ben Lomond, Loch Ard, the Lake of Menteith, Doune Castle and Stirling Castle. Mostly these are elegantly structured, austere drawings with a few tumultuous skyscapes and sunsets but no living creatures. They show traces of Cameron's restrained melancholy and offer a striking contrast to Graham's highly personal and intense visions of the region.

Mist

Among the ingredients available on Graham's palette as a writer of landscape sketches, the misty climate exhaled by the boggy levels around the lake of Menteith is prominent. In the Preface to the third edition of his *Notes on the District of Menteith* (1906) he inserted a few vigorous sentences on the topic of mist, concluding, "Then [. . .] I said the District of Menteith seemed to me 'shadowy' ; now, after long reflection, all that I can say is that I find it full of mist".

The sketch "Mist on Menteith" is his most detailed attempt to distil the essential mood of this terrain. He observes that when "the mantle of the damp" descends, all is mysteriously transmuted, and apparently ordinary certainties dissolve. The mist floods back in waves like the sea which once covered the district. It is an agent which conceals and offers refuge, as it did in the turbulent history of the region. It can amplify some sounds and muffle others. In nicely detailed imagery he directs the creative power of its lens on to mountains, woods and trees; wild fowl, cattle and human beings:

"Boats on the Loch o' the Port, with oars muffled by the cloud of vapour that broods upon the lake, glide in and out of the thick curtain spread between earth and sky, the figure of the standing fisher in the stern looming gigantic as he wields his rod in vain, for in the calm even the water-spiders leave a ripple as they run."

Despite acknowledging the peculiar charm of these transformations Graham conjures up a thoroughly gloomy, decaying landscape which he sees as a metaphor for human transience:

"What, then, shall we, who have seen mists rising up all our lives, feared them as children, loved them in riper years, cling to but mist."

Graham touches more briefy on the influence of mist in other sketches in Volume Four, viz. "The Craw Road", "Caisteal-na-Sithean", "A Braw Day", "The Beggar Earl" and "Loose and Broken Men".

Old Houses

As a failed landowner himself, and with family connections to other estates in the area, Graham was drawn to contemplate the deterioration of once grand houses and their ambitiously planned landscapes. "A Braw Day", "The Craw Road" and "Caisteal-na-Sithean" are all sketches in which for differing purposes he explores "the enthralling beauty of decay" in these contexts.

"A Braw Day" is a deeply felt autobiographical reflection on Graham's final leave-taking after he had sold off his beloved house and lands of Gartmore. On his last days the laird wistfully surveys the state of his neglected property:

"To bid good-bye to buildings and familiar scenes seemed natural, as life is but a long farewell: but to look for the last time on the trees — trees that his ancestors had planted [. . .] that seemed a treason to them, for they had always seemed so faithful, putting out their leaves in spring, standing out stark and rigid in the winter and murmuring in the breeze."

From the reader's first entry by its deserted lodge, "Caisteal-na-Sithean" cleverly develops as a Gothic horror story of a recluse shut off from the world in a dilapidated castle set in nightmarish woodland. It culminates in a grim discovery in a frozen local pond — "The laird is oot". To an almost comical extent the natural environment is charged with ill omens:

"Beyond it stretched a gloomy road, winding between dark trees. At night when you rode through it, your horse snorting occasionally when rabbits ran across the path or birds stirred in the trees, it felt as if you were a thousand miles from help. In front, the dark road wound as it seemed, interminably, through overhanging trees. Between you and the world was the half-mile or so of the mysterious woods and the dark sullen ponds."

"The Craw Road" is a remote byway that leads us to a fiercely irascible old laird who has loved trees and lives out his final days doggedly in his ancient tower house and neglected parklands in a glen near Fintry:

"Time had been impotent to bow or mellow him: so he stood still defiant, like an old ash grown on stony ground that stretches out its bows to meet the elements."

This cantankerous colonel in his lonely tower is revisited more fully in the "The Colonel" in Volume 3.

In all of these sketches Graham reveals an expert eye for telltale images of decay: dying stagheaded trees, neglected driveways, sour pasture, broken doors and fences, and crumbling masonry. He has a countryman's grasp of the characteristics of trees and plants, and he is also sensitive to the ways in which nature reasserts itself in these situations: deer, rabbits, bats and owls come and go at will, and dank mosses spread everywhere.

There seems, in these pieces, to be an assumption that particular landscapes and their owners may grow in time to match each other. In one other sketch, "Fidelity", Graham's cultivated elderly host is presented as someone who survives contentedly in his well furnished Georgian country house with its surrounding moorlands, even if the experience he is recalling is one of murderous cruelty to animals.

Old Roads

In several sketches in Volume Four — "The Craw Road", "Mist in Menteith", "The Beggar Earl", "Falkirk Tryst" and "Loose and Broken Men" — the sentimental historian in Graham enlists his intimate knowledge of the old networks of tracks and trails that run throughout his region. He celebrates them, sometimes in nostalgic detail, for their connections with its history and legends, and with his own youthful experiences on foot and horseback. Here in "Loose and Broken Men" he is recalling with obvious affection a local stretch of an old cattle raiding trail:

"[. . .] the 'mad herdsmen', as the phrase went then, drove the 'creagh' towards Aberfoyle. The path by which they carried it was probably one I knew well.

"It runs from Gartmore village, behind the Drum, out over a wild valley set with junipers and whins, till after crossing a little tinkling, brown burn, it enters a thick copse. Emerging from it, it leaves two cottages on the right hand, near which grow several rowans and an old holly, and once again comes out upon a valley, but flatter than the last. In the middle of it runs a larger burn, its waters dark and mossy, with little linns in which occasionally a pike lies basking in the sun."

In "The Craw Road" the trail which Graham traces from Kippen to Fintry affords a romantic resumé of the different kinds of travellers who might have passed along that hilly route from pre-Roman times:

"Camseyan chiefs, and then Fingalians, have passed along it in their light deerskin brogues."

Further north "Mist in Menteith" gives us a vividly imagined glimpse of Highland marauders coming down through the Glen of Glenny:

"When the wind blew aside the sheltering wreaths of snow and the rare gleams of sun fell on the shaggy band, striking upon the heads of their Lochaber axes, and again shifted and covered them from sight,"

The historical account of "The Beggar Earl", with whom Graham clearly felt some Graham family comradeship in misfortune, represents another type of traveller, the wretched vagrant who might possibly meet his end like the Earl smoored in the snow somewhere on "the wild track that leads down to the vale of Leven."

And finally he recalls the cattle drovers who used to traverse all the old trails leading to the sales at the great "Falkirk Tryst":

"With their targets at their back, girt with their claymores, their feet shod in the hairy brogues by which they gained the name of the Rough-Footed Scots, they drove down their kyloes and their ponies through the very *bealach [pass]* that I remember in my youth."

It was old half-forgotten trackways such as these that gave Graham access to the secret lochans and corries, and the deserted shielings which he evokes in loving detail in other volumes of this collection, in, for example, "Lochan Falloch" in *Faith,* (Volume 3), "The Laroch' in *Progress,* (Volume 2) and "Tobar Na Reil" in *His People,* (Volume 3).

Old Names

A certain poetic zest in Graham's writing is generated by his relish for the intriguing place-names to be found around Gartmore, a border territory where the cultures of the Gaelic Highlands and Lowland Scotland had for centuries interacted. In "Loose and Broken Men", for example, when he is scanning estate papers, he rejoices that:

> "All the place-names remain unchanged, although a certain number of them have been forgotten, except by me, and various old semi-Highlanders interested in such things, or accustomed to their sound. Ballanton, Craiguchty, Cullochgairtane (now Cooligarten), Offerance of Garrachel, Gouston of Cashlie, Bochaistail, Gartfarran, Craigieneult, Boquhapple, Corriegreenan, and others which I have not set down, as Milltown of Aberfoyle, though they occur in one or other of the documents, are household words to me."

Beyond Menteith

Taken as whole, Graham's Scottish stories and sketches are by no means confined to his cherished   district of Menteith: locations as diverse as Skye, Douglas, Fife and Beattock also feature in his work. In the present volume two pieces are set in Glasgow. Dealing with aspects of the lives of working class urban Scots, these bleak sketches emphasize briefly but strongly the dreariness of their environment. In "Brought Forward" we are taken through "the dingy smoke-grimed streets and mean houses" to the giant Parkhead Forge where Jimmy and Geordie labour. "With the North-East Wind" is set in the vicinity of Maryhill Crematoriam on the occasion of the funeral of the miners' leader Keir Hardie:

> "A north-east haar had hung the city with a pall of grey. it gave an air of hardness to the stone- built houses blending them with the stone-paved streets, till you could scarce see where the houses ended and the street began.[. . .] The wind, boisterous and gusty, whisked the soot-grimed city leaves about in the high suburb at the foot of a long range of hills,

making one think that it would be easy to have done with life on such an uncongenial day."

In both sketches the grimness of the townscapes is contrasted with the vitality, "the dry vivacity", of the Scots working classes, and in "With the North-East Wind" we are consoled by a glimpse of the friendly shoulder of Ben Lomond, "peeping out shyly over the Kilpatrick hills".

Finally another *memento mori*. "A Princess" is an imaginative speculation based loosely on a strange gravestone inscription which still survives in the kirkyard of St Adrian's Church, Anstruther, in Fife. Here Graham explores the interaction between environment and human character. How could a young woman from the Cook Islands, a Princess of Raratonga[1], possibly adjust to married life in the steely hardness of an East Neuk coastal village?:

"As any district, country or race of men must have its prototype, its spot or person that sums up and typifies the whole, so does this hard gray land find its quintessence in the town of Buckiehaven, a windswept fisher village, built on a spit of sand."

The sketch starts with a powerful accumulation of images conveying the forbidding nature of the landcape, and ends sadly with her husband standing by Sinakalula's early grave:

"When he was gone the island princess would be left alone with the wind sweeping across the sea, sounding around the Bass and whistling wearily above Inch Keith to sing her threnody."

This appendix has sought to identify some of the main preoccupations and processes at work in Graham's landscape writings. These are features which are likely to be found in the other Scottish sketches in this collection. It seems reasonable to claim that his persisting fascination, over many years, with a region such as Menteith is rare, if not unique, in modern Scottish literature.

[1] A factual account of the real 'Princess' is to be found in Fiona J Mackintosh, *From the South Seas to the North Sea: The Story of Princess Titaua of Tahiti* (Scotland, the Kilrenny and Anstruther Burgh Collection, 2011). (www. Anstrutherburghcollection.org)

(JNA)

Brought Forward

Index of Stories in Volume 4

Lightning Source UK Ltd.
Milton Keynes UK
UKOW050502211211

184158UK00001B/8/P